GRASPING AT ETERNITY

"It takes a special kind of book to make me cry in the first chapter. *Grasping at Eternity* took hold of my heart and carried me away in a story both haunting and heart-breaking."

~AMBER ARGYLE,
author of *Witch Song*

"This novel is an outstanding sojourn into what it means to truly love and the depths of sacrifice one will go to for that love. Once *Grasping at Eternity* had me in its grip, it never let me go. The stars will always seem brighter to me now."

~HEATHER McCORKLE,
author of the Channeler series and *To Ride a Puca*

"Brilliantly written! This epic love story had me turning pages late into the night. Truly one of the best books I've read in a very very long time."

~SARRA CANNON,
author of the Peachville High Demons series

GRASPING
AT
ETERNITY

GRASPING AT ETERNITY

Copyright © 2012 Karen Amanda Hooper

First Edition

ISBN 978-0-9855899-8-1

Published by Starry Sky Publishing

Cover design by Alexandra Shostak
www.coversbyalexandra.com

Edited by Marie Jaskulka
http://mariejaskulka.wordpress.com

Visit author Karen Amanda Hooper on the web at
www.karenamandahooper.com

Dedicated to anyone who has loved and lost,
but found the courage to love again.

GRASPING AT ETERNITY

karen amanda hooper

Starry Sky Publishing

"If you love someone, put their name in a circle;
because hearts can be broken, but circles never end."

~Anonymous

THE BEGINNING
OF THE ALMOST-END

Maryah

I wanted to punch a hole in the sky, rip it open, and fly out of this world and into a magical one. Except I'd never punched anything in all my seventeen years of life, I didn't believe in magic, and I sure as heck couldn't fly.

As my dad pointed out at dinner, "Some people are destined to be average."

He was referring to me, of course.

Whenever Dad made wisecracks about me, I'd escape to the boat docked behind our house. It was the perfect hideout since it had a mini kitchen, bathroom, and bedroom. Unfortunately, our old Bayliner hadn't run since summer break started, so in a tragic reversal of the old cliché, I could hide, but I couldn't run.

I smacked my pillow then flopped down on the bed. My back knew every lump in the mildewed mattress by heart. Beyond the dirty film on the boat hatch window, high above the occasional blinking firefly, one star shined brighter than the others. It winked at me from light-years away. "Star light, star bright, first star I see tonight...I wish my family would leave me the crap alone."

The boat dipped, and I knew my twin brother, Mikey, had climbed aboard. He peeked into the cabin and tossed me a pack of Oreos. "Figured you might be hungry since you left most of your food on your plate. You okay, Ry?"

"You mean besides being destined for averageness?"

He ducked through the narrow doorway and sat on the bed. "Dad knows he messed up. He's setting up another Forgive and Forget soirée."

I rolled my eyes, but not at Mikey. "Is he using the temporary insanity plea again?"

"Hope not. He forgets you have a stellar memory."

My memory was the closest I'd ever get to having magic powers. Except my talent only worked for useless stuff like filing away every harsh word my dad ever said, memorizing song lyrics after hearing them only once, or remembering the bra size of every customer who came into my mother's lingerie shop. Anytime she measured ladies and had me write down a size bigger than my pathetic 30A, I'd silently beg the boob fairy to let me trade with them. Lame, for sure, but that pretty much summed up my existence.

Mikey got the good looks, brains, athletic abilities, and every other trait that secured his spot as the favorite child. Mom and Dad pulled double doting duty when it came to him. Most sisters would hate their twin brother in a situation like ours, but how could I hate him? He was my own personal superherbro.

"Mom's already got cookies baking." He pulled off my flip-flop and hid it behind his back. "I'm holding this hostage until you come inside."

I laughed and shoved him with my foot. "Fine. Just give me a few more minutes."

"Hurry up—before I eat all the snickerdoodles." He cracked my big toe—which I hate—then escaped just as my other flip-flop went sailing past his head and hit the wall. I listened to his footsteps stride up our dock then fade away.

Crickets chirped and waves lapped against the side of the boat. I cherished my last few moments of solitude before I went back inside for the I'm Sorry Party.

Dad would play my favorite records—Ella Fitzgerald or Frank Sinatra—and twirl me around the living room while telling me I'm his favorite girl. Mikey would show off by doing a flawless waltz with Mom. A couple dances, a few heartfelt apologies, and several snickerdoodles later, all would be forgiven. That's how it worked in our family—like something straight out of a '50s sitcom. I could say I hated it, but that would make me borderline cool. Like most do-gooders, I loved my family: dancing, cookies, Donna Reed flashbacks, and all.

A faraway shriek interrupted my thoughts. I assumed it was a bird until I heard another sound. Glass breaking? My ears pushed everything else into the background.

No more waves or crickets. No more breathing. I think I even silenced my heart from beating.

The bird wailed again. Except the bird was my mother, and the wailing was filled with terror.

I leapt off the bed and sprung from the cabin. Above deck, I froze, staring at our house. Shadows moved behind the backlit curtains of the living room windows. They must be dancing.

So why did my mother scream? The rocking boat nudged my wobbly legs forward. I stepped onto the dock and took a deep breath, hoping the noise couldn't be as frightening as the rigid hairs on my arms indicated. No matter what scary scenario my overactive imagination created, I had to make sure Mom was okay.

As I neared the back patio, Frank Sinatra sang about fairytales and young hearts. Our screen door creaked when I opened it. The music grew louder as I entered the kitchen. The smell of cookies baking should have calmed me, but the house was too quiet. No laughing or talking meant something was very wrong.

Mikey staggered into the doorway. "Run."

One hand clenched his chest, the other slid down the doorframe, holding a butcher knife. Then I saw the blood seeping through his fingers. A deep red blot on his t-shirt grew bigger.

"Mikey, what—?" My trembling voice couldn't finish the question.

A huge man dressed in black appeared behind him. Mikey turned and lunged at him with the knife. The man flung Mikey against the wall like a rag doll, choking him, and lifting him off his feet. I wanted to yell, hit the stranger, and pull him away from Mikey, but I couldn't. I stood there paralyzed, not comprehending.

My brother's flailing legs and arms blurred through my tears.

"Ry, run." Mikey gasped.

And like a coward, I did.

I ran away.

I stumbled through the kitchen, out the back door, and across the backyard. The music from the house faded as I got closer to the dock. What now? Hide in the boat? No, jump in the water. Swim away. Just get to the water.

Heartbeat-heartbeat-heartbeat breath. Heartbeat-heartbeat-heartbeat breath. Both involuntary actions came at unrealistic speed, but my legs wouldn't run fast enough. Get to the water. Focus. Almost there.

I tripped over my own feet, hitting the dock with full force. Pain shot through my ankle, and splinters stung my cheek and palms as they skidded against the wooden planks. I tried to push myself up, but my foot buckled and I fell back down.

Laughter echoed behind me. "Ah lass, aren't you going to fight back?"

Panicking, I glanced around. One of the dock planks had come loose. I crawled onto my knees, yanked the board free, and spun around, waving it like a bat. Except now there were two men. "T-t-take whatever you want. Just please, d-d-don't kill us."

The second man kept laughing while the younger one squatted beside me. "They're already dead."

No. He had to be lying. Please let him be lying.

My breathing became more rapid. The planks under me were vibrating. No, the dock wasn't shaking—I was.

A female voice whispered in my ear. *Concentrate on the eyes.* I looked around, not seeing anyone else, but the voice spoke again. *Concentrate on the eyes.*

Shuddering, I made eye contact with the monster from the kitchen. His pupils were like a snake's—golden with black slits.

The older man walked closer, eating a snickerdoodle. He bent down so close I could see crumbs in his black beard. "Why didn't you stay and fight for—" He paused, his forehead wrinkling as he tilted his head. "It's not her," he said. "We've got the wrong house!"

"They swore she lived here. What a waste of time." He snatched the plank from my hand and cracked it over his knee, splitting it in two. He handed Snake Eyes half of the broken plank and clapped his hands. "Finish her."

Snake Eyes didn't hesitate. He stabbed the jagged edge into my stomach so fast I didn't even try to protect myself. Fire ripped through the middle of me, tunneling upward through my chest. I gagged on my failed attempt to scream.

He pulled a metal pipe from a holster behind his shoulder. "Wrong place, wrong time."

"Please, no!" I tried to block the first hit with my arm. The stake gouged my insides when I lifted my leg to absorb the second swing. Every hit felt like dynamite exploding through my limbs. I couldn't even be sure my leg and arm were still attached to my body. With all I had left, I tried rolling over to crawl away, but the flames in my stomach burned hotter. I got so dizzy I saw spots.

Just shoot me, I mentally begged. The last world-shattering swing came at my head in slow motion. The loud crack swallowed every other sound. Then he was gone.

And so was I.

∞

I'd always heard that when people die, there is a bright light. Nothing but pitch black surrounded me. Where was the light I was supposed to follow? As if answering my question, one star appeared, shining dimly but hovering close enough to touch.

Concentrate on the eyes. Those words rumbled through me like an earthquake.

The star split into two, morphing into light-filled eyes. A face formed around them, turning into a full bodied angel equipped with heavenly good looks. His emerald green eyes sparkled with an inhuman intensity. They had to be the eyes my intuition whispered about. They had to be the light I was meant to follow. Death had found me, and he was mesmerizing.

"My family, help them," I whispered.

God-awful pain blasted through me, forcing me back into consciousness. Tons of real stars filled the sky. I had imagined the angel. I was alone. Alone, but alive.

Water still lapped calmly under the dock. Crickets continued chirping. A spider spun its web on a nearby railing. The world hadn't stopped, and neither could I.

Mikey fought back. I would too.

Reaching down, I touched the wood jutting out from the bottom of my shirt, not believing it could be lodged through the middle of me. I grabbed it with my left hand and pulled hard.

A rush of warmth flowed over my skin, but my teeth were chattering so hard they should've shattered. How could it be so cold in the middle of June? Green specks of light flashed in front of me. My heartbeat and breathing slowed. The rumbling in my head stilled. Even the pain eased.

The star-angel appeared again. He leaned over me, looking so real.

Howling sirens grew louder, but help would be too late. My angel had come to take me home. He peeled off his red and black motorcycle jacket and covered me with it. His tan face almost shimmered against the dark sky above us. He stared at me with enough love to fill eternity.

Then his face blurred. Colors faded. He slipped further away until I saw only pure white. Lost in eternity, I was content never to be found.

Quiet.

Stillness.

Peace…

"Clear!" Someone shouted.

Agonizing pain snapped me awake. The earthquake in my head increased to a 9.5 on the Richter scale. My chest blazed, and a metallic taste soaked my tongue.

"I've got a heartbeat! Honey, can you hear me? What's your name?"

At least I think that's what the paramedic said. His words were muffled by the throbbing in my head.

I choked and spit out blood. "It hur-urts."

"We're giving you something to help the pain. Hang in there, okay?"

I stared at the black sky and blurry stars, yearning to see the angel's face again. The sensation of floating up into the sky felt nostalgic—like I belonged there. I had an aerial view of the paramedics working on me.

My arms and legs looked like pale twigs, bent and snapped into pieces—just like the wood lodged into my stomach. I could've sworn I pulled that out. Blood matted my strawberry blond hair. I floated away, unable to look at myself anymore.

One of the paramedics said to the other, "She's out, poor thing. Only survivor."

No. My family can't be dead. This can't be real.

A force kept tugging me toward the sky. Part of me wanted to drift away. If my family were gone, I had no reason to stay. Fire trucks and police cars swarmed our street. Flashing red and blue lights reflected off every window of our house.

I kept floating higher. Stars pulsated around me. I reached out, trying to grasp onto them, but I couldn't. The stars slipped through my fingers.

Please remember, the brightest star whispered.

Then a hole ripped open in the sky, sucking me out of this world and into blackness.

REMEMBERING EVERYTHING

NATHANIEL

*P*lease, no.

   Please don't let this happen.

                                    Not now, not like this.

"Open your eyes," I begged. "Fight for this. Fight for us."

She had always been a fighter.

Every life.

She was the bravest soul I'd ever known.

I looked up at the hospital room ceiling as if I could see through it to the stars and midnight sky. Rage pulsed through me, singeing my veins and scorching my heart. "Give her memories back! I don't care what she chose! This isn't how it's supposed to be."

I didn't care if the nurses heard me. I'd be gone by the time they came to investigate.

Her face was like porcelain, beautiful but motionless. I imagined her eyelids opening, seeing the endless light I loved so much. I took for granted it would always be there.

I pressed my lips to the back of her hand. "You and me for eternity, remember? Don't break your promise. It's not your style."

Her heart monitor continued beeping slow but steady.

"Fight," I demanded. "Live. Open your eyes." I leaned forward and kissed her forehead. "And *please*, remember."

COMING UP FOR AIR

Maryah

Being in a coma for two weeks was nothing. Literally, I remembered nothing. Those two weeks just disappeared from my existence.

But waking up in the hospital and remembering my parents and Mikey were gone—that I ran away while intruders robbed them of their lives—was the worst pain I'd ever experienced. Doctors pumped me with enough pain meds to ease the physical hurt of my broken arm and leg, but no one and nothing could fix my broken heart.

I blocked out reality by sleeping as much as possible. Two weeks hadn't been long enough. I wanted to hide from the waking world forever.

Krista, my cousin, my best friend, born one day after me, refused to let that happen. For over a month, since the moment I woke up at the hospital, she'd been at my side. She held me while I cried, drew hearts and flowers on my casts, promised me we'd get through it, and tried brainwashing me with her feel-good philosophies.

Fortunately, or maybe unfortunately, my blow to the head required me to have brain surgery, so her brainwashing didn't work. Too bad my head trauma didn't wipe out my bionic memory. I'd never forget *that night*.

Dreary clouds passed by my airplane window. Krista sat beside me, trying to fix the wobbly latch of her tray table. We'd only been on the plane for twenty minutes, but my emotional claustrophobia was as strong as ever. Sadness and guilt had been suffocating me all day every day until I wanted to permanently stop breathing. So when my aunt and uncle offered me a chance to escape for the weekend and meet my godmother, I took it.

I never even knew I had a godmother. My parents used to live in Arizona, but they moved to Maryland after Mikey and I turned one. My uncle said Louise Luna was my mother's childhood best friend, but they hadn't spoken in over a decade. My aunt and uncle didn't want me moving away, but this Louise lady insisted that she was my legally appointed guardian and convinced them that my mother would want me to consider my options.

I just wanted to get away. I didn't know what awaited me in Sedona, but it wouldn't be pieces of my past. No guilt or reminders of my old life.

"I never said goodbye."

Krista blinked her big brown eyes like she was surprised to hear me speak. I hadn't said much the last few weeks. "To my parents? You said goodbye."

"No. Last time I saw Mom and Dad I gave them dirty looks and stormed out of the house. How could angry silence be the last thing I said to them?"

"What about at the cemetery? You stood there a long time. I'm sure they heard everything you said."

Imagining my parents and Mikey stretched out in coffins freaked me out, so I was relieved that the funerals took place while I was in a coma. Aunt Sandy had stood over a plot of newly laid grass and told me it was Mikey's. A bunch of sunflowers sat in a metal vase by her feet. No way would Mikey want a bunch of flowers. A bouquet of Tootsie Roll Pops or a case of Orange Gatorade? Sure. Sunflowers? No way.

My brother and parents couldn't be covered in dirt, sentenced to darkness and living with bugs. I kept picturing them alive: smiling, laughing, dancing, and talking about when we would adopt a dog or what we needed from the grocery store. None of those things could happen if they were buried in the earth.

I fought back tears. "Talking to their tombstones doesn't count."

"Sure it does. Spirits hang around awhile before they cross over. They know how much you miss them."

I shook my head, unable to look at Krista. I had to tell her. We didn't keep secrets from each other, and I'd already bottled up the truth too long. "That night, I wished on a star that they'd leave me alone. Seconds later those men broke into our house and—"

"Whoa, Pudding, don't be ridiculous." She turned my chin so I faced her. "You didn't wish for them to die."

"But I ran away. Mikey was still alive. I should've helped him, but I ran out of the house. Mom and Dad might've been alive too." I searched Krista's gaze for blame. Even though I couldn't find any, she probably wondered if I would've left her to die too. "I should've grabbed a knife, or…done something. Being alive is my punishment."

"You aren't being punished. Sometimes terrible things happen." She pushed a stray hair behind my ear. "The universe works in mysterious and heartbreaking ways."

I faced the window again.

Outside, gray clouds stretched to infinity. Were my parents and Mikey out there somewhere? I imagined them soaring like birds through the heavens, and wondered how, in a sky so endless, could there be no room for me?

I lowered the plastic window shade and let the roar of engines lull me to sleep.

∞

Unexpectedly, in all of his breathtaking gorgeousness, my angel of death was back.

In my dream, he strutted through a parking lot, looking less like an angel and more like a movie star. He was six feet tall with a confident swagger. I appreciate those who stand out in a crowd, but he surpassed that. Crowds would part and roll out a red carpet just so this guy could have a VIP path to heaven. I'd be the invisible wallflower who got trampled by paparazzi and his fans.

He'd been at my side when I first woke up from my coma, standing next to Krista like he was there to take me. But then he vanished and I hadn't seen him since. Why would he take my family but leave me behind?

He pulled out a cell phone and looked at the sky. "Maryah's flight took off safely. I'm coming home."

It was only a dream, but I smiled when he said my name correctly. In real life most people butchered the pronunciation. Mariah is the common spelling, but my mother wanted me to be "special."

He tucked his phone into his jacket and climbed onto a motorcycle, pulling a helmet over his short, dark chocolate hair. When he started the engine, I jumped in front of the bike and grabbed his handle bars, not wanting him to disappear again. Through the shield of his helmet, his spellbinding green eyes blindly stared past me.

"I could get lost in your eyes for centuries," I confessed.

His engine rumbled to life, and he drove through me. I followed him, hovering above him as he turned down a deserted road.

Up ahead, a barrier with a large sign warned that the road was closed. Movie-star angel man swerved around it, accelerating to a speed not possible in real life. Another sign read *Bridge Closed*. The road ended where a dilapidated bridge dropped off into a dried-up river.

"Slow down!" I yelled, as if he could hear me over the roaring motorcycle—or like anything in dreams ever mattered.

He gunned the gas one last time. The bike launched off the bridge and flew through the air. Right before he would have crashed into the ground below, he and the motorcycle instantly disappeared.

I floated there, staring at the barren valley. "When you get back to heaven, tell my family I'm waiting for them."

I don't know why I said it. He was gone.

And so was my family.

A NOT-SO-NEW BEGINNING

Maryah

We walked off the jetway and I paused at a row of chairs to set my bag down. "This was a stupid idea. I can't meet a bunch of strangers. Look at me. I'm a train wreck."

"You do look a little derailed," Krista teased. "But they don't care how you look. It's your soul they love."

"They don't even know me. Besides, I feel like I lost my soul."

"It's there. It's just going to take us a while to get it to shine again." She smoothed my disheveled hair. "Your hair on the other hand..."

My long hair was the only pretty thing about me, but even that had been taken away. A section had to be shaved off before my surgery. My aunt cut the rest in layers until it was shoulder length because she claimed my short patch wasn't as noticeable. I swatted Krista's hands away and put on Mikey's favorite Ravens hat.

"Good idea." She tugged on the rim. "It'll hide the grease."

"And the short patch," I grumbled.

"It's grown out enough that no one will notice."

"Easy for you to say." Her Pocahontas hair looked flawless. Krista had Egyptian ancestors on her mother's side and she was exotically beautiful. What I wouldn't give to trade my tissue paper complexion for her smooth, olive skin.

I eyed the check-in desk a couple feet away. "Let's buy a ticket back to Baltimore. I can't do this."

"Your instincts told you to come to Sedona, and your instincts are never wrong." She handed me my duffel bag. "Come on, something tells me we'll like these people."

I took a deep breath and forced my feet to carry me forward.

We spotted Louise Luna at the end of the terminal.

My aunt had showed me old pictures of her, and Louise hadn't changed much. She held tulips and a heart-shaped balloon. I could see why my mother loved her, but I still wanted to run in the opposite direction.

"You okay?" Krista asked.

I nodded, but my legs felt like they had anchors tied to them.

Louise waved as we got closer. Circular sunglasses covered her eyes, but I suspected she was giving me the poor-orphan look. She had a definite hippie vibe going on. A medium bob of silky brown hair framed her makeup-free face, and a wooden necklace hung low against her gauzy—probably earth-friendly fiber—shirt. Her flowing skirt grazed the tops of her open-toed sandals.

A tall bronze-skinned man towered behind her with his hands in the pockets of his jeans. His dark hair draped like a curtain on either side of his navy blue sunglasses.

Before I could say hello, Krista steamrolled Louise with a hug. What the? Why would Krista hug a total stranger like that?

Louise squeezed Krista tight. "We're so happy to have you girls here."

When they let go of each other, Louise removed her glasses, placed her hands on either side of my face, and looked into my eyes.

"Ah, Maryah, how I have waited for this day."

Double what the? I flinched, trying to silence the annoying buzzing in my ears. Spasms of pain pulsed behind my temples. Worst time ever for one of my famous headaches to start.

Louise hugged me, and the balloon thumped against the rim of my hat. "I'm so sad about what happened to your parents."

My heart cracked. "And Mikey."

"Yes, of course, and Michael. Such a terrible tragedy."

She handed me the embarrassingly large bouquet of tulips attached to an annoying balloon that kept floating at my head. "These are for you."

"Um, thank you."

She leaned against the dark-haired man and patted his cheek. "This is my better half, Anthony."

"Nice to meet you, Mr. Anthony."

"Just Anthony." He spoke gruffly. "Great to see you, girls. How was your flight?"

Krista groaned. "Long."

"I see your casts are off." Louise practically petted my arm.

Why was everyone so touchy feely? I tucked my hand behind my duffel bag. "My arm and leg are fine, so my aunt convinced the doctors to remove them yesterday."

"Her doctors were drama queens," Krista said. "They exaggerated about how severe her injuries were then acted all surprised and proud of themselves when she bounced back so fast."

"Glad you healed so quickly." Louise grinned at Krista then put her arm around me. "Let's get your bags and take you home."

We waited by the luggage carousel for our suitcases while Anthony left to pull the car around. Much to my relief, Louise and Krista made small talk so I didn't have to. We found Anthony in the loading zone, leaning against an old but exquisite convertible.

"Nice car," I said with sincerity.

"Thank you. She's a 1964 ½ Mustang, original Guardsman Blue color." He shoved my balloon and our suitcases into the trunk.

"My parents had a '57 Desoto. We rode in it every weekend."

"What happened to it?"

"My uncle sold it. Apparently medical bills and college funds are more important than beloved, *priceless* cars." I didn't hide my sarcasm.

"That's a shame." Anthony shook his head and opened the passenger side door.

Krista and I climbed in the back then he assisted Louise into the passenger seat. It reminded me of the way my father treated my mother—with old-fashioned manners.

We pulled out of the airport and I sighed. Arizona—right back where I started. How ironic if I returned to my birthplace only to die of heartbreak.

At first Phoenix was like any other city, except for the brown mountains in the distance and an occasional palm tree. Further out of the city, a sign said "Carefree Highway." I snickered at its nauseatingly cheerful name.

Cacti popped up everywhere. I didn't want to be interested in what Arizona looked like but I couldn't resist. The longer we drove, the more unique the scenery became.

"It's so beautiful," Krista cooed.

The car's engine was loud, and with the top down, it would've been difficult to carry a conversation. Instead, we enjoyed the warm Arizona sun and the wind in our hair while shades of orange, brown, and green surrounded us.

The mountains kept growing larger and at times it felt like we were driving *through* them. A little over an hour into the drive, my ears popped. I pictured Arizona as a flat desert, so I felt like an idiot when a sign revealed we were at an elevation of 4,000 feet. I swallowed a few times, trying to release the pressure in my ears. The air tasted crisp and clean.

We exited the main highway and huge red rock formations came into view. I'd seen a lot of the East Coast, and had visited my father's hometown in England, but never experienced any place like Sedona. The contrast of the bright red rocks against the cerulean sky was mesmerizing.

After turning onto a narrow road, we climbed a long winding driveway. My eyes bugged when I saw the huge house.

Anthony parked in front of a large garage. The drive had taken almost two hours, but Louise and Anthony held hands the whole time—just like my parents used to do.

Krista and I followed Louise to a gated archway, flanked on either side by a chest-high wall of stones. Above the gate hung a carved sign, *Peace to All Who Enter Here.*

"This is your house?" I asked with disbelief.

"Well," Louise hesitated, "think of it as your home."

I peered through the iron bars of the gate, staring at the terracotta-colored house behind it. Shades of green accented the roof, doors, and windows.

Anthony pushed the gate open, and we crossed the threshold of a private oasis. A main path led to the entrance of the house, but smaller paths snaked off in random directions. Yards in Maryland were mostly grass, but in Sedona, they were red dirt or gravel and pebbles. Boulders sat amongst pots of colorful flowers.

I spotted a fountain, made of large dark stones with a Buddha statue sitting on top.

Wind chimes tinkled above us as we stepped onto the front porch, covered by a wooden pergola. The second I passed through the double doors I knew I'd been here before. My parents must've brought me when I was a baby. My bionic memory skills were at their finest.

"It's lovely," Krista said.

"Thank you. We like it." Louise glanced over the spacious area in front of us.

A double-sided fireplace divided the space into two rooms. Floor to ceiling windows overlooked breathtaking red rock formations and cliff sides. Colors were everywhere: bright area rugs covering tile floors, sculptures of lizards and birds on the walls, paintings, masks, tiled mirrors. Flowers and plants blossomed in every corner and on every table.

An unusual scent wafted through the air—floral yet earthy. Just like how Louise smelled when she hugged me. Music played softly: flutes, drums, and other instruments I didn't recognize, but the song fit the feel of the house. The front door thudded shut behind us.

Louise stood at my side but Anthony had disappeared. "Would you like a tour?"

"Sure." Krista and I answered in surround sound.

Louise guided us through an archway into a colossal kitchen. Beyond the kitchen, fourteen chairs circled the biggest table I'd ever seen.

Krista nudged my shoulder and pointed at the ceiling. "Look how gorgeous."

I knew about the skylight before I looked up. A giant star made from colored glass produced beams of light that shone on the table. I hid my smile, knowing no one would believe me if I claimed to remember that far back. I would've been a year old at most. Even I had trouble believing it.

"This is where we gather for special meals and meetings." Louise rested her hands proudly on the wooden surface. "We have a large family."

I hoped I'd never have to sit at a table with so many strangers, but it was impressive.

"Louise." Krista fidgeted. "May I use your bathroom?"

"Down that hall and to the right."

Krista left and I momentarily panicked at the thought of being left alone with Louise, but she just smiled and waved me down another hall.

Abstract paintings decorated most of the walls. Many looked old, while others looked newer. They were full of vivid streaks and swirls of colors. Some shined like metal, others shimmered and sparkled.

"These paintings are amazing."

"Thank you very much." Louise placed her hands over her chest. "Each one holds a special place in my heart."

"Are they all by the same artist?"

"Yes, I painted all of them."

"*You* painted them?"

She laughed. "Is it so surprising that I can paint?"

"No, I'm sorry. I didn't mean—it's just—I've never seen paintings like that. You should sell them. You'd make a fortune."

"Oh, I could never sell these." She touched one with admiration. "Each one is an extension of my soul. I add details as needed, but they're never finished. They are *all* works in progress."

"You're very talented."

"Thank you. What about you? What's your talent?"

"Ha!" I snickered. "I have no talent whatsoever. My dad tried coaxing some creativity out of me, but I'm hopeless."

"Oh, I don't believe that. Everyone has a gift. It's a matter of figuring out what yours is and using it for good—and to the best of your ability."

"Don't hold your breath. I'm pretty useless."

Louise made a discerning humming noise but didn't say anything else. I noticed there were no photographs anywhere. Louise seemed like such a family-oriented person, I expected to see pictures plastered all over the place.

"Mine and Anthony's room," she announced, pausing at a set of open doors.

Suns, moons, and stars decorated the large room. Their midnight blue king-sized bed was centered on the far wall with a plaque above it that said, *Love knows no limits.*

A lump formed in my throat. My parents had the same saying in their room. I didn't plan on so many reminders of home. I'd be fighting back tears no matter where I lived.

We continued down the wide hallway and I stopped at a closed door. I had an overwhelming desire to look inside, but I knew that would be rude.

"That's Nathaniel's room, but he left for Colorado yesterday," Louise said. "My oldest son, Dylan, and his wife live there, and Nathaniel is starting school there this fall, so he moved in with them."

"Right." Embarrassed that I'd stared at his door so long, I forced myself to step away.

"And this is your room." Louise pushed open a large wooden door.

It took my breath away.

The room was much bigger than anything I'd had in Maryland. It might have been bigger than Louise's room. The wood beam ceilings looked twelve-feet high. Forest green curtains draped the towering windows. A crystal hung in each one, reflecting rainbows in numerous directions. Glass doors led to a private balcony.

"It's so…enchanting." I couldn't believe I used that word, but wow.

Louise stood in the doorway. "I'm glad you like it."

I felt like I'd entered a woodland fantasy. The bed frame was made from thick tree branches that extended to the ceiling. White flowing material canopied the bed and draped down each side onto the floor, enclosing whoever slept there. Me. I'd be sleeping there. In the fanciest bed I'd ever seen. I should've felt weird about sleeping in a strange new bed, but something about the room comforted me.

A round thing made of twigs, strings, and peacock feathers swung gently above the bed. "What's that?" I nodded upward.

"A dream catcher. It's a Native American talisman. Bad dreams are caught in the web while good dreams travel along the feathers and into the mind of the person sleeping beneath it. As the sun rises, the light dissolves any negativity it captured during the night."

"Hmph. Nice idea." Not that I believed it, but it would be great if a circle of wood and feathers could keep my nightmares away.

"Ooooh," Krista sailed into the room, running her fingers over a bowl of pink and white stones on the nightstand. "Himalayan Salt Rocks. They enhance your wellbeing." Krista loved natural hippie stuff, so of course she knew what they were. "I am so jealous of this room. Can I move in here too?"

I wanted to smack her. I hadn't decided to move anywhere yet. "You didn't do all this for me, did you?"

"It was a joint effort by the family," Louise replied. "However, Nathaniel did most of the decorating. He wanted to make sure you had a special place to escape."

I gazed around again. "He outdid himself."

Louise tapped softly on the door knob. "Carson's room is down the hall. He'll be home later. And Edgar and Helen live in the in-law cottage next door, but they're out of town."

Krista kicked off her sandals. "Do you have anything to snack on? I'm starving."

"Certainly," Louise replied.

Krista bolted across the room, but I wanted some alone time. "I'm really tired. Mind if take a nap?"

"Do whatever you like. This is your home, Maryah. Make yourself comfortable." Krista gave me a thumbs-up just before Louise shut my bedroom door.

I rifled through my suitcase until I found what I needed. Krista had been making scented candles for years and they always made me feel better. I lit one for each of my parents and Mikey. My favorite three scents: Green Clover, Nag Champa, and Ocean.

I climbed into the big fluffy bed and closed my eyes. It was the first sense of peace I had since the night of the attack. Sedona seemed like the perfect place to hide from my memories.

FANNING AN OLD FLAME

NATHANIEL

Before my motorcycle fully skidded to a stop in the garage, I ripped off my helmet. I put the kickstand down and paced the driveway. None of my daredevil distractions kept Maryah out of my mind.

I'd been so insistent about moving away. Dylan and Amber refused to let me go alone, so they packed up their life and also moved to Colorado. I'd never live it down if they knew how badly I wanted to go back.

Both of their cars were gone. They'd never know if I made one quick trip to Sedona.

Over the last several lifetimes, I'd mastered my ability to traverse, so the process took merely the length of one breath. I opened every cell in my body so the ions could flow through me. Borrowing a surge of energy from the ionosphere, I prepared to let the flux of a stellar flare form a bridge to my destination.

I resurfaced atop Cathedral Rock, staring across the desert at the house—our house.

She chose to return to our home.

Maryah and her choices: they'd be the death of me.

Waves of adrenaline shot across my chest. I pictured her walking down our hallways, standing in our kitchen, entering our bedroom, gazing out the windows at a land she used to be so in love with.

Could she be looking out a window right now? Looking in my direction? From the far distance, I'd only be a silhouette of a hiker—a stranger—standing on the cliffs. God, how I ached to see her again. I squinted, trying to detect any movement in the house, but the sun hung too low in the sky, creating a blinding glare against the windows.

Throughout this lifetime I had occasionally checked in on her, but only from afar. Once, I sat behind her on the bleachers at a football game. My knees rested inches from her back. Even then, she felt miles away. Now, she and Krista were in our home, surrounded by people Maryah assumed were strangers. Almost a mile of desert separated us, but this was the closest I'd felt to her in nearly two decades.

The strong urge to traverse inside the house made my skin prickle. I wanted to see her, talk to her, and make sure she was okay. But seeing her would only reopen my wounds. She had demoted me to a stranger, and I couldn't bear seeing that truth every time she looked at me. Not after hundreds of years together.

I'd follow my original plan and stay away from her. I had to for my own sanity.

My cell phone rang and Dylan's name appeared on the screen. I sent it to voicemail. He and Amber placed bets on how long it would take me to visit Maryah. Technically, the bet was still on, but I didn't want to admit I had come to Sedona.

My phone rang again. Louise. Perhaps she had an update on Maryah.

"Hello, Louise."

"Plan on stopping by to say hello to your mother?"

"Come again?"

"Nathan, don't play dumb. I see you over at Cathedral Rock."

I glanced at the house then turned my back. It's not like Louise had preternatural sight. "It must be someone who looks like me. I'm in Colorado."

"Have you forgotten who you're talking to? I'd know your aura anywhere."

Bollocks. She did have super-powered vision when it came to seeing a soul's energy. My unique color pattern of light would be like a blinking beacon on top of the cliffs. That should have occurred to me before coming here. Acting like a stalker, ignoring Dylan, and caught lying to Louise: not the most righteous day of my existence.

"Forgive me, Louise. This situation has me acting crazy. I'm not myself lately."

She sighed. "Lately? You haven't been yourself this whole cycle of life. But no one can fault you for that."

Silence ensued. We'd had this conversation so many times that I stopped responding long ago. Numerous times I wished I could trade this life for the one I lived two lifetimes ago. Granted, I had been deaf, but in hindsight it had been one of my best go-rounds. I had lived a long, comfortable life in England, technology hadn't taken over the world, and my soul mate was still by my side.

"Nathan, come visit. Having you here might trigger something."

I shut my eyes so tightly that I saw stars. "The only thing it will trigger is more anguish for me."

"But what if—"

"No. Please understand. I can't—not yet. I'm still trying to recover from her attack. If she would have died ..." The thought made my heart implode.

"I know, but she's still with us."

If Maryah had died, she would've been severed from me and our kindrily for eternity. Between every life, we made our choice: erase or retain. As Elements, my kindrily and I were allotted a different set of rules than average humans. We chose when we'd return to our next life, and to whom we'd be born, allowing us to continuously retain our memories and ensure we stayed connected forever.

No member had *ever* erased—until this lifetime.

If Maryah died not knowing about us, she would have most likely erased her memory again. This time we'd have no way of knowing when or where she'd be reborn. Last go-round she had a plan and she stuck with it—all except the erasure. We had agreed that nothing could ever be so terrible that we would erase, so how and why did it happen? The burden of that unanswered question was mine to carry for at least another lifetime.

"Nathan, Edgar confirmed our suspicions. The Nefariouns were the ones that attacked Maryah and her family. They've been aggressively targeting Elements and building an army."

"An army for what? What upstanding Element would ever join their cause?"

"Edgar hasn't figured that out yet, but Dedrick is acting as leader."

Elements who didn't follow universal laws and exploited their gifts were outcasted and had their abilities taken away from them. A few continued to perpetually reincarnate, and their desire to regain supernatural abilities strengthened over time. Most of them resorted to sorcery or witchcraft to obtain power, and they had harmed and killed people along the way. Dedrick's ruthlessness had escalated over the last couple decades.

"So Dedrick doesn't know Maryah erased. If he assumes she has her gift, he may still be hunting her."

"It's a possibility. And he might come after more of us. Abilities such as Anthony's, Edgar's, or Dylan's would be extremely valuable to him."

My stomach seethed. "Mark my words, if he hurts anyone in our kindrily I will—"

"Hush." Louise's tone changed drastically. Through the phone I heard bamboo wind chimes clanging together. She was in the backyard.

"Help!" Krista's faraway scream sent chills through me. My exceptional hearing wasn't a gift in situations such as this.

The trickling pond grew louder at an alarming rate. Louise was running through the backyard. My pulse beat double time. "What's wrong?"

Her bracelets jingled as her footsteps thudded faster.

I whipped around and scanned the house. It looked peaceful, but Louise's panic radiated through the phone. "What's wrong?"

In a labored breath, she answered, "Something's burning."

In that instant, I knew Maryah was in danger.

And I reacted on instinct.

FIGHTING FIRE

Maryah

I was dreaming about Mikey in a Technicolor forest. He was happy and laughing and waving me over to him, but then my mind yelled at itself to wake up.

I felt torn: the warmth, the colors, the peace of watching Mikey exist in such a beautiful world. I wanted to stay there forever, but then a deep voice screamed my name.

Everything happened so fast.

I opened my eyes, and for a split second I saw my angel of death standing beside my bed. In the instant he vanished, my waking mind processed what was happening.

Fire.

Next to me, above me, crawling all around me. Hissing, whooshing, feeding on the canopy, the bedspread, and soon, me—if I didn't react. A loud pop exploded above me. I scrambled to the foot of the bed.

I couldn't get out. The flames surrounded me.

I tried to yell for help but choked on the smoke. Sweat dripped down my face and arms. I grabbed the blanket I was kneeling on and tossed it over the bonfire that used to be my pillows, but the flames kept crawling closer and growing hotter.

Every panicked breath I took singed my nose and throat. My eyes stung, but through the wall of fire I saw my bedroom door was open. A guy rushed in with a fire extinguisher, spraying a burst of snow at the bed. I leapt through the clearing in the flames and fell onto the floor. At the same time, Anthony and Krista appeared in the doorway.

I tried blinking away the stinging in my eyes. In that single blink, the guy with the extinguisher moved across the room, Krista was kneeling by my side, and Anthony blasted water from a garden hose.

When I blinked again, the heat and flames had diminished. I couldn't see through the thick smoke, but someone lifted me off the floor.

Through my coughing fit, I glanced up to see Anthony looking much too calm. He carried me down the hallway, out the front door, and set me down. "Easy. You're all right."

My whole body trembled. "I'm sorry. I'm so sorry."

Louise rubbed my back. "Take deep breaths, sweetheart. You need fresh air."

I collapsed onto the front step, hiding my face in my shaking hands. "I'm so sorry. What did I do? I could've—oh God, I'm so sorry."

Krista squatted in front of me. "Shh, it's okay. Accidents happen."

I almost killed another family. Was I cursed? "I almost burned down the house. I could've killed someone!"

Louise sat beside me and wrapped her arm around my shoulder. "But you didn't. No one got hurt."

"Actually," Krista examined my elbow and the back of my arm. "You did get burned, but that will heal."

I was borderline hyperventilating, whether from shock or guilt I wasn't sure. "I lit candles then fell asleep and...it.... I'm so stupid. I don't blame you if—"

"Maryah, breathe." Louise whispered. "You didn't do it intentionally."

"Wait," Krista half-laughed. "Please tell me it wasn't one of my candles."

I nodded.

"Oh, how perfect! So *we* almost burned down the house together!"

Most times I could predict Krista's reactions, but her laughing caught me off guard. "Kris, this is serious." My heart hadn't stopped pounding since I woke up. The sun had begun to set, but I couldn't look at it. The blending shades of yellow and orange looked like flames erupting in the sky. "I'll pay for the damage. I'll get a job and—"

"You'll do nothing of the sort," Anthony said. "Money's no concern. Your wellbeing is what matters."

A dull buzzing rang through my ears. Something didn't feel right.

Time felt off, like pieces were missing. It all happened too fast. How did Anthony get a hose in the house that quickly?

I stuck my hands between my knees, trying to stop them from shaking. "How did you put out the fire so fast?"

Just then, the guy with the fire extinguisher stepped onto the porch. He tucked his dark hair behind his ears then folded his arms across his chest. "No need to send up smoke signals. I knew you arrived."

"Carson, put the jokes on hold," Louise said.

Of course. Louise's son. He looked calm too. Why wasn't anyone but me rattled by this? I set a bed on fire while I slept in it and people were cracking jokes? "Thanks for rushing in and putting out the fire. You probably saved my life."

"I was saving our house. Plus, it was a team effort." He raked his hands through his wet hair. "You sure do know how to spark up drama. Pun intended."

"Carson," Anthony grunted.

"I'll go clean up Maryah's mess." Carson glared at me before he went inside. "Talk about a housewarming." Mikey was probably watching from heaven, laughing, and saying, *way to make a first impression, Ry.*

"I should help." I tried to stand, but Louise kept her arm around me.

"No. You relax while Carson and Anthony take care of it."

"But I—"

"No buts."

Anthony went inside while Louise, Krista, and I sat in silence, staring out at the garden.

A million questions gushed through my mind as I replayed the details. How could so many flames be put out in what felt like two seconds? How did Carson move across the room in an actual blink of an eye? Where did Anthony get the hose from so fast?

"Something is wrong with me."

Krista placed two fingers on my neck, checking my pulse, and surveyed me for visual damage. Always playing nurse. "Are you feeling light-headed? Nauseated? Having trouble breathing?"

"I don't mean because of the fire. I think my brain is messed up."

Louise took off her glasses and looked at me with a strangled smile. "Why do you think that?"

I paused, trying to think of how to explain it without sounding crazy. "Maybe from when I got hit in the head, or my surgery, but my brain short-circuited during the fire. Like it stopped working for a few minutes."

Louise's expression softened. "Fight-or-flight syndrome causes the mind to react strangely in dangerous situations."

"Yeah, but..." It didn't feel anything like that. My mind shut off. But, then again, I'd never been near a raging fire before so maybe she was right. "Maybe I'm just paranoid about doctors fiddling with my brain."

She patted my hand. "Understandably so, but let's assume they did their job correctly."

Krista flashed me a hesitant look, but I agreed with Louise. "Okay."

"Let's go inside so you can calm down and eat something." Louise stood and offered to help me up. When I reached up, her wooden necklace brushed against my fingers.

"I meant to ask, what's the symbol on your necklace mean?"

Looking down, she rubbed her thumb over the carving. "It's an ancient symbol from Antiquity. The modern interpretation means 'lunar halo' but interestingly enough its original meaning is," she paused then smiled, "fire."

∞

My angel of death came for me twice. Maybe the third time would be a charm.

Why did I fight so hard to get out of the fire? I should've inhaled every last bit of smoke. I should've grabbed onto my angel of death and demanded he take me to my family.

Louise set a steaming cup of tea on the kitchen counter in front of me. "It's called Calming Wind. It will help with the shock."

"Thank you."

I swiveled back and forth in my stool, watching Louise flit around and make dinner as if nothing had happened.

Carson came in, scooped some pasta into a bowl and sat beside Krista. He was cleaner—and drier—and his hooded sweatshirt looked blaringly white against his tan skin. "So, Maryah, you hated your room so much you had to burn it down?"

"Carson, enough," Louise warned.

Krista tried making light of my humiliation. "She wanted a flaming hot debut."

No, I wanted to run away and hide. "I feel awful for ruining your brother's decorating job. Should I email him and apologize or something?"

"Email him?" Carson stopped chewing his food. "Nathan isn't a fan of email, and don't even think about texting him."

"Ohh-kay." Why wouldn't someone be a fan of text and e-mail? "Should I call him? I'd feel rude not thanking him and explaining what happened."

Louise and Carson looked at each other. Krista shrugged.

"You should apologize in person," Carson said curtly.

"He'll stop by one of these days," Louise said. "Everyone returns home at some point."

My clothes and hair still smelled like smoke, and every swallow of tea hurt my irritated throat. Plus, being around Carson wasn't exactly comfortable. "I'd like to shower and go to bed early if that's okay."

Carson's fork bounced across the countertop. "You're going to trust her with another bed?"

Krista swatted the back of his head. His chin-length hair fell over his eyes as he swiveled out of his stool and left the room. I couldn't tell if he meant to be rude, or if he just had an obnoxious sense of humor, but I loved Krista for smacking him, and I loved Louise for saying nothing about it.

"Come on, Maryah," Louise urged. "Anthony moved your bags to the guest room."

"I'll be in later," Krista said.

I followed Louise to a bedroom I hadn't seen during our tour.

"You should be comfortable in here." Louise reached into her pocket. "And I want you to have this." She examined my fingers then slid a silver ring onto my thumb. The round face had shimmering shades of blue, green, and amber. It was the eye of a peacock feather.

I almost burned down her house and she was giving me a gift? "It's beautiful, but I can't accept it."

She squeezed my hand shut and pressed it against my chest. "It's been passed down in your family for generations. It belongs to you."

"Was it my mother's?"

"Not exactly. It's a long story—a very long story. But trust me, it's a cherished possession, and it looks perfect on you."

She fluffed pillows as I held up my hand, admiring how the colors sparkled in the light. Then I did a double take. I could've sworn something squirmed under the curved glass, just behind the feather. Squinting, I turned the ring from side to side and opened my mouth to ask Louise to look at it, but she silenced me by saying, "Don't light any candles."

My eyes were still playing tricks on me because of the shock and adrenaline rush from the fire. "No candles. I promise."

Louise left and I grabbed my pajamas then headed down the hallway to shower. I paused at Carson's room when I heard him shouting.

"Her first day here and she torched the place! How much more is everyone going to tolerate? It's like you said, her being here is—"

The sudden silence should have been my warning. Three long strides and I could've made it to the bathroom. Carson wouldn't have known I'd been listening. But I was too stupefied to react. He cracked his door open and stuck his head out.

So busted. "I was, um, on my way to...to the bathroom."

"Need a map? Or should I install a peephole in my door so you can watch while you listen?"

I wanted the floor to open up and swallow me. Carson hated me. Not only that, he was talking to someone else who didn't like me. Was Anthony in his room? Was he on the phone? To top it off, he caught me eavesdropping on him. I was used to people ignoring me, but this was way worse. This made me want to cry, or puke, or run away, or all three. "I wasn't listening. I didn't hear anything. I—"

"Go away, Sparky."

I pried my feet off the ground, forcing one to step in front of the other, until I was inside the bathroom with the door shut. I climbed in the shower and turned it as hot as it would go. My skin squeaked against the porcelain as I sat down and let the water beat down on me. The burn on my arm stung, but the emotional sting of humiliation was way worse. I hugged my knees to my chest and let the pain wash over me.

No way could I ever move here. I wanted to go home.

Except I didn't know where home was anymore.

BLURRING THE LINE BETWEEN
LOVE & HATE

NATHANIEL

After he slammed the door, Carson pulled his sweatshirt off and threw it at the bed. "See, she's a snoop!"

I chuckled at the irony. At least she didn't lose her sleuth abilities when she erased—well, not all of them.

Carson moved so fast he was a blur. His hypersonic speed intensified when he was emotional. Barely a second passed, but he'd already pulled a suitcase from his closet and stuffed it with clothes. "I'm out. I'm coming to live with you guys in Colorado."

I leaned against his desk. "You're needed here. Imagine what might have happened if you hadn't been here during the fire."

"You and Anthony would have handled it." He whirled by me so fast that papers flew into the air. "Was she this accident-prone in her other lives?"

I grinned, restacking the papers and setting his laptop on top of them. "More so. That's why I need you to look out for her."

"What's the word you always use? Abolished? She abolished our family. Why should we go out of our way to help her?" He finally stood still to zip his suitcase. "Tell Dylan to come pick me up. I'm not living with her. I can't stand her."

"You have experienced only this lifetime of knowing her."

"Whatever. I met her last lifetime."

"You were four years old—hardly enough time, or memories, to judge someone." I sat on his bed, resting my head in my hands. "She has no memory of abandoning us. You can't hold that against her."

"Ha." He huffed. "For years I've watched you mope around and shut yourself off from the world because she broke your heart. She deprived me of a normal relationship with you. Both of my brothers moved away because of her. I hold *that* against her."

For the first time I realized how deeply my depression had hurt Carson. This was his only experience of having brothers, and I had been a terrible one. "I'm sorry for that. Dylan didn't want to leave, but Amber felt being around Maryah would cause her too much guilt."

"Right. The bitch drove everyone away."

"Carson, watch your mouth. She's still my soul mate."

"What? I don't get you, man! You moved away because she *might* come live with us. Then you go out of your way to create your old frou-frou bedroom and—"

"She needed a safe haven when she arrived. She lost her family. Our bed and the elements in our room might give her serenity." It devastated me that my arms no longer provided her that.

"Serenity? Peacock stuff and a dream catcher? She doesn't remember that crap!"

I nodded at his Howlite necklace. "That doesn't negate their powerful energy."

The white stone helped calm tempers, and Carson had anger issues. It also helped souls remember past lives, and Carson wanted to remember more of his last one. It was his initiation life as an Element, but he died as a toddler, so he'd mostly only remember from this life forward.

"How can you pretend she didn't screw this family over in every way possible?" He threw his hands up in the air. "Harmony suffers every day because of what she did!"

"Carson, enough!" I tried pushing his flailing arms to his side, but his strength was no match for me. He tossed me across the room like a feather. Just before I hit the wall, I traversed in midair and reappeared in front of him. "You aren't the only fast one in this kindrily."

We were face to face, blood bonding us physically, supernal selection uniting us eternally. Anger still flashed in his eyes, but I remained calm. I possessed volumes of life lessons he hadn't begun to learn. "I won't tolerate you scathing her."

His jaw tightened. "Why'd you even move out? You made a huge deal about how her being around would push you over the edge, but here you are, saving her from fires and watching over her anyway. You're totally contradicting yourself."

"Until you find yours, you can't understand how impossible it is to be separated from your soul mate—or how difficult it is to be around them when they have no idea who you are."

Carson held up his index finger. "One, I will never get roped into the soul mate BS. I've seen how it turns out. Two," he extended his middle finger as well then poked my chest. "Just tell her the truth."

I flinched, resisting the urge to rub my chest. I could already feel it bruising. I envied his strength. "I wish it were that simple. The past has taught us that no one believes in our way of existence unless they've experienced it firsthand—and *remember* it. If we tried explaining who and what we are, Maryah would be terrified and probably cut us off completely."

"Good. Let her." He must have seen the pain register on my face. "I'm sorry, Nate. I didn't mean that."

"Apology accepted." Carson was more upset by the situation—and by the absence of me and Dylan—than I ever would have guessed. I promised myself I'd be a better brother to him. "Thank you again for your help during the fire. You never fail to impress me in dire situations."

A proud grin replaced his irritation. "It was nothing."

I couldn't shake the image of Maryah surrounded by flames. "Do you think she saw me?"

"She didn't mention anything. She questioned Anthony freezing time, but Louise fed her some brain instinct theory."

"It's like I'm invisible to her." The words escaped my mouth by accident and sounded as insecure as I felt. Carson had already seen enough of my pain and weakness.

"I thought you weren't ready to see her again. So *why* do you keep stalking her?"

I needed to tell him about the Nefariouns, but it wasn't the proper time. Edgar could explain the situation better than I could. "Because she keeps ending up in danger."

He grabbed his phone and began texting, knowing it drove me insane when he did that during conversations. "You said when Maryah woke up, there were flames between the two of you. Maybe she couldn't see past the fire. Or if she did catch a glimpse of you, your disappearing into thin air probably made her think she was hallucinating."

"What about the night she was attacked? She hasn't mentioned me being there either, or at the hospital." For fourteen nights I sat by her side, making sure her heart monitor continued beeping, and willing her to fight for her life.

Carson looked up from his phone. "Dude, she was practically dead. You've died a bunch of times. Can you remember all the details?"

"Most of them, yes."

He rolled his eyes just as his phone chirped then he flicked the screen. "What a dickhead."

"Who?"

"Dylan. He says I can't move in with you guys."

I sat beside him. "You have friends here, and Harmony and Louise would be crushed if you left them. Besides, I'm counting on you to look after Maryah. We all need to be on high alert right now."

"Those pathetic outcasts thought they had the wrong girl. They wouldn't follow her out here."

"You already know it was the Nefariouns who attacked her?"

"Yeah. Louise and Anthony told me."

"Then you know they might come after someone else in our kindrily. If they have any common sense they may figure out it was Maryah, and that she erased. If they find out she's here, it could lead them right to us."

"Good. This time we'll be ready." Carson punched the palm of his hand. "Those lowlifes kidnapped Gregory and murdered nine of us in the process. It's time for paybacks."

"We won't stand a chance unless we stick together."

"Exactly my point. You, Dylan, and Amber should move back home."

I considered his logic. "If I promise to work on convincing Dylan and Amber to return, will you help look after Maryah?"

He looked down, tossing his phone back and forth. After several seconds of silent juggling, he countered. "That *and* you promise to answer all my phone calls and texts. And traverse here whenever I need you."

He was too smart for his own good. "Within reason. At times it may be impossible."

He squinted as if trying to assess how much more he could demand of me. "I'm only doing it because I miss you guys."

"Thank you, Carson."

Before I finished standing, he had stripped down to his boxers and blurred into bed. "It doesn't mean I give a crap about her." He threw a pillow at me much too fast for me to catch or dodge. "I still don't understand what you see in that girl."

That was the soul-shattering issue. I saw nothing inside of her. No flicker of the depthless light in her eyes, no trace of the soul I had loved for centuries. She had let go of our eternity, and I couldn't stop grasping onto the memory of who she used to be.

TIME HEALS ALL WOUNDS

Maryah

Krista crawled into bed with me and rubbed aloe on my arm. "They don't hate you."

"I almost burned down their house, and Carson definitely hates me."

"He's just a kid. He probably hates everyone."

"He's only a year younger than us."

She set the aloe bottle on the nightstand. "Yeah, but we're old souls. He has a lot of growing up to do."

"What if they all end up hating me? Or what if death came for me that night, but something went wrong? Now it's going to keep coming for me. Like the fire, maybe that was death's second attempt. What if I'm putting people in danger by being here?"

She laughed. "You watch too many scary movies. Death isn't some black-robed figure hunting you down and staging freak accidents to kill you."

No, death is a gorgeous movie-star angel man that rides a motorcycle and sat beside you at the hospital. I wanted to say that, but I chose something less loony. "What's up with you being all buddy-buddy with everyone?"

"What do you mean?"

"Hugging everyone, and smacking Carson. You're making yourself right at home."

"They're very hospitable—and loveable."

"Loveable? You hardly know them."

"Shhh." Her fingers glided over my burn in her trademark figure eight pattern. "Think healing thoughts."

Krista had an obsession with wanting to make people feel better. She'd done the healing thoughts thing since as far back as I could remember.

I faked a smile. "Seriously, my arm is okay. Stop stressing."

"How's your head?"

"Fine." Since the age of two I'd gotten chronic headaches that doctors couldn't prevent or cure. My brain surgery didn't help matters. My ears had been buzzing so loud it made me dizzy, like a dozen bumblebees drag racing around my head. Thankfully, the bees had gone to bed. "What about you? You've got those dark circles under your eyes that always show up right before you get sick."

"I'm just tired." She wrapped her pinky around mine. "Let's get some sleep. We've been through a lot today."

"That's an understatement."

Krista recited the same line she'd used every night since we were little. "Sweet dreams, Pudding. The stars are waiting for you."

Freakin' stars. She had no idea how much guilt the mention of them caused me.

I fell asleep within minutes, but woke up several times, tossing and turning. Each time I felt disoriented because of the unfamiliar room. Blame it on the dream catcher, or the mental overload of being in Sedona, but when I did reach deep sleep, my dreams were intense.

I stood in the guestroom, watching Krista and me sleep. The dreaming version of me crawled into my side of bed, melding like a vaporous cloud with my sleeping body. Even in my dreams Krista smelled like a yummy candle store.

Her dark wavy hair cascaded across her pillow. I rested my forehead against hers and she stirred, pulling the comforter up around her shoulder. Her hand was glowing.

"Wake up," I said. "Your hand looks like the moon."

I placed my ghost-like fingers on her eyelids, and gently pushed them open. They were a kaleidoscope of light and colors: lavender, lime, and silver. A million flecks of shimmery dust swirled through her eyeballs like a glittery snowstorm. I snapped my fingers, but she wouldn't wake up.

My new but very old ring looked similar to Krista's eyes. The peacock feather floated in the tiny glass bubble. Speckles of shimmery light churned around it like the inside of a miniature snow globe. The feather floated up and out of my ring, quadrupling in size, and drifted toward the bedroom door. I followed it into the hallway.

Louise's paintings were glowing just like Krista's eyes. The peacock feather looped through the air, landing on a canvas covered with an extraordinary mixture of green and yellow. I tried grabbing the feather, but it sunk deep into the painting. The colors crawled off the canvas and up my arm, wrapping around me. I giggled at the tingly sensation. Emerald and gold swirled around my phantom body then expanded and filled the hallway. The river of colors flowed forward, carrying me down the hall until I reached the door that Louise said was Nathan's room.

I heard rustling inside so I tried going in. The doorknob rattled, but I couldn't open it.

"Hello?" said a deep voice from the other side.

I panicked, feeling like a trespasser. The river of colors turned ice cold. I gasped as the door opened and I glimpsed my movie-star angel man. Luminous beams of emerald, gold, and sapphire poured out of his room, mixing with the river and filling the hallway up to the ceiling.

I was pulled under until I drowned in an endless ocean of multicolored light.

∞

My eyes were still swollen and itchy from crying the night before, so when I woke up and saw green and blue glitter swirling around our bed, I had to question it.

"Kris, is there sparkly dust floating above you?"

When she didn't answer, I rolled over to nudge her awake, but her side of the bed was empty. I looked up, but the shimmery cloud had disappeared. The swaying peacock feathers of the dream catcher combined with the sunlight pouring through the windows must have created an optical illusion. I threw on Mikey's hat before making my way to the kitchen.

Louise and Krista sat at the counter looking at a book together.

"Good morning, Maryah," Louise said. "How'd you sleep?"

"Fine."

"How's your arm?"

I twisted my elbow around to look at my burn, but it looked almost normal. "All good."

"That aloe must have done wonders," Louise said to Krista.

"Nah, Maryah's always been a fast healer." Krista shimmied her eyebrows at me then pointed toward the floor-to-ceiling windows. "See that huge red rock formation in the distance? It's Cathedral Rock, one of the major vortexes."

"Vortexes?"

"Yes," Louise answered. "Sedona is home to four major sacrosanct funnels."

"Sacro what?"

Krista stuck her nose back in the book, but Louise smiled. "Sacred centers of omnipotent energy."

No clue what she was talking about, but the view was epic. Like the Lunas carved their house into the side of a cliff so they could gaze down at the colorful earth. Why in the world did my parents ever leave Sedona? "It's some view."

"The original owner thought so too," Louise said. "That's why she built the house here." She gazed out the window and thumbed her necklace. "Would you like some breakfast?"

"I'll make myself some cereal if that's okay."

"You don't have to ask permission. Help yourself to whatever you like. Cereal is in the pantry."

I grabbed two boxes and poured milk onto my sweet and healthy combo. Louise eyed my bowl. "I see you like to mix your flavors."

"One flavor is too boring."

"Interesting, Nathaniel does the same thing."

This guy sure did come up a lot. Maybe he was Louise's favorite. Mothers aren't supposed to have a favorite child, but regardless of the unwritten rule, they usually did. (Mine definitely did.) Or maybe it was because Nathaniel left for college a couple days ago and Louise missed having him around.

The side door to the kitchen flew open and a blur of white and pink barreled into me. I almost fell over, but the girl held me in place with a bear hug.

"It's so good to see you again!" she squealed.

Louise closed her book. "Maryah, Krista, meet Faith."

The girl pulled back to look at me, but kept her grip on my arms. "We've missed you so much! Tell me everything! What adventures have you had? What was Maryland like? I'm loving your straight hair!"

I stared at her in shock. She was a little shorter than me, but her energy made her seem ten feet tall. Her hair was white as snow with random pieces dyed bright pink. Silver sunglasses with rhinestones sparkled on her head like a tiara. Iridescent shades of pink shadowed her aquamarine eyes, accented by a diamond brow ring. Her tan skin even shimmered because her face powder had glitter in it.

"What do you mean it's good to see me again?"

"Technically the last time I saw you was—"

"Faith," Louise interrupted. "Let's keep the explanations to *recent* interactions."

"Sorry, Louise, ancient habits die hard." Faith looked me up and down with a big grin. "For now, let's stick to the basics. We met when we were younger and got along famously, but you wouldn't remember that." She squeezed my arms. "I'm so glad you're back!"

She turned to Krista and let out an ear-piercing shriek then hugged her too. Krista played along, rocking her side to side like they'd known each other forever.

Faith looked the same age as us, so how could she remember meeting me as a baby? I couldn't remember anyone from my childhood before like, age five, four at the most. Either this girl had a remarkable brain as a baby or she had mental issues.

Heavy footsteps out on the deck got progressively louder. Then, a girl with the exact same face as Faith's—in a much darker package—stepped through the kitchen door.

Louise spooned cookie dough onto a baking sheet. "And this is Faith's twin sister, Harmony."

"Did she return mentally challenged and you have to explain we're twins?" Harmony snarled.

"I won't dignify your childish question with an answer." Louise casually slid a pan of cookies into the oven and winked at me. "I'm sure you've guessed which one is the evil twin."

Harmony was the complete opposite of her sister, with the exception of the identical facial structure and similar hairstyle. Where Faith's hair was white, Harmony's was jet black, and her colored sections were deep purple. Nothing sparkled on this girl. She had the same facial piercing as Faith, but instead of a diamond, her stone looked like obsidian and was located above the opposite eye. She wore head to toe black, including combat boots.

She removed her sleek sunglasses and wrapped them around her neck like a choker. Her charcoal eyes glanced to the left and right of me—back and forth, never making contact with mine. After a minute of optical ping-pong, she plopped down on a kitchen stool. "I don't see what all the fuss is about."

The good twin's chipper voice eased my discomfort. "Harmony's in a bad mood. Don't take anything she says personally, Maryah."

Faith stood in perfect posture, her feet turned out like a ballerina, her shoulders pulled back elegantly. It caused me to involuntarily stand up straight. "Louise, is it okay if I take Maryah and Krista to Tlaquepaque with me? I want to show them around town."

I answered Faith's question before Louise could. "No thanks. I need to talk to Louise and Anthony about my guardianship thing today."

Faith scrunched her face up like she smelled something bad. "Before or after they repair the fire damage in your room?"

My eyes opened so wide a pain shot through my head. How did she know about the fire?

"She has a point," Krista said. "Louise, would you rather us get lost for a while?"

"Heavens, no. I love having both of you around. However, Maryah, I do think you should see more than just our house before you decide whether or not to live here."

"Krista, how long are you here?" Faith asked.

"Our flight home is booked for tomorrow night."

"Then we're definitely spending the day together. No debating."

Krista shoved Evil Twin's shoulder and I worried she was about to get punched. "Are you going?"

Much to my relief, Harmony didn't shove her back. She didn't even look up from her purple fingernails. "No, I'm meeting Carson here. We need to talk to Louise and Anthony about Carson's birthday present."

"I thought his birthday wasn't for another couple months?" Krista asked.

How the heck did she know that?

"Right," Harmony agreed. "But he can't wait that long. He needs his Mustang now."

I must've made my What-the-Fudge face because Louise glanced at me and elaborated. "All of the men in this family have Mustangs. Dylan and Nathaniel both received theirs on their sixteenth birthday. It's tradition."

I couldn't imagine anyone giving me a car. I couldn't even imagine owning a car. As bratty as Carson was, it hardly seemed fair. But nothing about life seemed fair anymore.

Faith grabbed a handful of cookies before heading for the foyer. "I'll wait for you two out front!"

The front door slammed shut. Louise and Harmony's tense silence was my and Krista's cue to exit, and we happily took it.

As we got ready in the guest room, I kept thinking about the ominous vibe Harmony gave off. I'd seen and met Goth kids that put effort into looking scary, but Harmony didn't wear pale powder or dark lipstick, or draw dramatic lines around her eyes. She didn't need to. "Something about Harmony is genuinely shuddersome."

Krista tied her hair into a loose bun. "You think so? I like her."

"Like her? She barely said two sentences, and she looked like she wanted to kill someone."

"Maybe she's had a rough life."

"How rough could it be? Her sister is like a real-life Tinkerbell—a vividly colorful version. How'd she end up so happy, and Harmony end up so...not?"

Krista waited by the door. "People walk different paths, even when they're family."

I pulled on Mikey's Ravens hat. "Can you believe she has the audacity to think she can talk Louise and Anthony into giving Carson his car early?"

"Who are we to judge?"

"You act like everyone here is perfect, even when they act weird or mean. Seriously, what's going on with you?"

She looked away and dug through her purse. After several seconds I realized she wasn't going to answer me.

My breath caught in my throat.

How could I have been so blind? Krista *wanted* me to move to Sedona. That's why she kept acting like these people could do no wrong.

I clenched my jaw and forced my eyes to stay dry. I'd been so caught up in my own misery that I didn't think about what others were going through. I was an uninvited dark presence in Krista's previously happy home. I'd be a constant reminder to my uncle that his only sister was gone forever. I probably brought everyone down. No one deserved that.

"You ready?" Krista asked.

I didn't want to ruin Krista's perfect life. Or be a burden to my aunt and uncle. If I really loved my family, I'd move to Sedona so they could get on with their lives.

"Sorry I took so long, but yes, I'm ready."

SEEING ISN'T ALWAYS BELIEVING

Maryah

Faith sat behind the wheel of a white Toyota Prius. Krista climbed in the back, so I sat in the passenger seat.

Faith said goodbye to someone then snapped her phone shut. "Where are your sunglasses?"

"Um, my hat will block the sun."

"No way. No friend of mine is traveling around town without sunglasses. An outfit is never complete without a pair of great shades. They are essential to your wellbeing." She reached into her bag and pulled out what appeared to be a Japanese fan, but then pulled a pair of glasses out of the fan— carrying case—and handed them to me.

"Thanks," I muttered, sliding them on.

"Wow, those are fabulous," Krista said.

We all sat in silence until I noticed Faith still staring at me. "What?"

"I hand you a pair of newly released, spun silk, jade-embellished, handcrafted sunglasses by one of the most elite fashion designers in the world, eyewear that according to Chinese tradition will bring you love and prosperity, and you flop them onto your face like they're a pair of dollar store knockoffs!" She didn't take a breath throughout her entire speech. "You're not the least bit excited. Frankly, I'm insulted."

Of course Faith would be passionate about sunglasses. She seemed like she'd be passionate about everything. I took the glasses off, examining them closely. She had a point; they were beautifully detailed. I felt guilty for being unappreciative.

"Sorry. They're exquisite, but Jinx is my middle name these days. You should take them back so nothing bad happens."

After a few seconds of staring at me, she giggled. "Harmony's right, you *are* mentally challenged. Nothing bad will happen *because* you're wearing them. They're yours now." She waved her hand dismissively. "You can thank me someday when you appreciate how fabulous they are."

I glanced behind me to confirm Krista also thought Faith was crazy, but Krista's attention was locked on the scenery outside of her window. Good thing she was wearing sunglasses, or she would have probably got lectured, too.

∞

Talakee-wherever-we-were wasn't a mall like I'd pictured. It was an outdoor Spanish-style shopping area. Apparently there were no large malls in Sedona, so we strolled along the cobblestone streets while Faith told us facts about every fountain, sculpture, and piece of artwork we passed.

"You should be a tour guide," I said. "Are you a history buff or something?"

"I had this friend who taught me that the best parts of a story are the history and secrets buried inside." She sipped her smoothie while kicking a stone along our path.

"You said 'had'. What happened to her?"

"She just sort of disappeared. No one really knows why."
Faith sat by a fountain and patted the concrete beside her. Krista and I sat on either side of her.

"Losing someone like that takes its toll," Krista said.

"It's been extremely hard on all of us." Faith ran her hand through the fountain. Water dripped from her sparkly painted fingernails. "But I have faith she'll be back one day."

"Faith has faith," I joked.

"I do." She raised her sunglasses and leaned close to me. "But ultimately *she* has to make the decision to come back. And when she does, I'll do everything I can to help her."

Tires squealing caused all of us to look at the parking lot. A dark gray Jaguar screeched to a halt diagonally, taking up two parking spots. A guy our age climbed out of it. His forearms were covered with black tattoos, and more peeked out from the collar of his t-shirt. His jet-black fauxhawk and leather wristbands matched the interior of his Jaguar. I'd never seen anyone resemble their car, but he definitely did. What kind of jobs did his parents have that made him privileged enough to drive a new Jaguar?

"Must be nice," I said to Faith.

"Ugh." She lowered her sunglasses and sucked on her straw. By her flaring nostrils, I could tell she wasn't impressed.

When I looked up, he was slinking toward us. The guy even moved as sleek as a jaguar.

"What's going on, shorty?" he asked Faith.

"You're looking at it," Faith answered in a monotone voice.

He said hi to Krista then he looked me up and down. "Sorry, didn't catch your name during Faith's non-existent intro."

"Uh, Maryah," I muttered pathetically.

"Okay, Uh Maryah, I'm River." He smiled, revealing perfect, straight teeth. "You girls coming to my show?"

I glanced at Faith, but she was ignoring him.

"Show?" Krista asked.

"My band, The Rebel Junkies, we're playing here tonight."

"No," Faith chimed in. "We have other plans."

"Too bad. I'm singing a rad new song. Shame you'll miss it."

"Cataclysmic shame." Faith's straw made a gurgling sound as she sucked the last bit of smoothie out of her cup. "You should probably go practice."

"I don't practice. Don't need to."

He did have a nice voice, raspy and confident.

Faith snickered before standing and grabbing my hand. "We were just leaving."

"See ya, Krista." He flashed me another perfect smile. "Bye, Melissa."

I didn't bother correcting him. "Bye."

Once we were in the car and out of earshot, I asked Faith about her apparent dislike of River. "What'd he do to get on your bad side?"

"He's just full of himself. He's as shallow as a kiddie pool."

With the push of a button, Faith lowered the top of her convertible. She lifted her face to the sky and inhaled. "I love how August sunshine smells!"

I laughed. "Because July sunshine smells so different?"

"July is okay. January snow, however, yuck! Smells and tastes like licorice."

I looked back at Krista to make sure she didn't miss the moment of weirdness, but she had her head back and eyes closed like she was enjoying the sunshine just as much as Faith.

"Months have a smell," I grumbled. "Interesting."

"And taste. So many fantastic details exist in this world that most people never notice." Faith squeezed my knee. "You should pay more attention."

Krista leaned between the seats to turn up the radio. "Ooooh! This is my favorite song."

"Yes!" Faith bounced in her seat. "I adore this band."

They both sang *Déjà vu of You* at the top of their lungs while my phone chimed with a text message from my aunt. *Hope ur okay. Call if u need us. Love you.*

My heart sank. I missed her and my uncle. I missed all of my family. Part of me felt guilty for not being sad all day. Did that make me a horrible daughter and sister because I hadn't thought about my parents or Mikey for the past few hours?

I missed my old life, but there was something peaceful about Sedona. I wasn't constantly looking over my shoulder for two men the police couldn't find. For the first time in months, I felt safe, or hopeful, or something besides sad and scared. It was refreshing to be in a town where I wasn't constantly reminded of everything I had loved and lost.

NOTHING SHINES FOREVER

NATHANIEL

Being that it was only eight o'clock, I didn't want to risk traversing without proper clearance.

Carson answered his phone on the second ring. "I'm at the house, and no, Maryah isn't here."

"Right. See you in a second."

I didn't focus on a specific room. I focused on reappearing eye to eye with Carson. I traversed and resurfaced standing on the kitchen island—in the dark. Carson's hands were stretched above his head fiddling with a light fixture.

"This is a first," I said.

Louise stood below us with a flashlight aimed at Carson's hands. "One of Harmony's ghosts got angry and blew out all the lights."

Carson finished spinning a bulb into place. "Hit the switch, Dakota."

Light flooded the room and Carson and I hopped down off the counter.

I peered down the dark hallway. "It blew out all the lights?"

"Yes indeedy," Dakota answered. "I could only find one flashlight, so Shiloh's running around fixing the rest."

"Must have been one powerful spirit."

Louise cringed. "His aura was brown and thick as mud—so much hostility and unresolved anger. He also broke a couple dishes. Harmony has her hands full with that one."

"Is she still here?"

"No." Dakota pushed his haphazard waves of blond hair from his eyes. "She didn't want him doing any more damage to the house."

Dakota wasn't a member of our kindrily, but he was a member of our family. To Harmony and Faith, he was related by blood. The rest of us became connected to him by heart, which in many cases is as strong as blood or soul ties.

He grabbed a rag and scrubbed at wet spots on the Element logo of his t-shirt. "I tried a Repelling Evil spell on him, but the poltergeist prick exploded a can of soda on me."

I grinned. Dakota had never successfully cast a spell. "Trying to protect your sister again?"

"Some spirits just don't know when to let up," he spat. "In my next life I'm going to be a Ghostbuster."

Louise and I laughed. Carson rolled his eyes.

At age thirteen, Dakota's harness malfunctioned during a rock-climbing adventure and he nearly fell to his death. Carson and I reacted instinctively. Dakota witnessed me safely anchored to the rocks above him one second, and below him on the ground the next. In actuality, Carson saved his life. My intention was only to break his fall, but Carson grabbed him mid-plummet, and Dakota halted within inches of my arms. He refused to believe the explanations we constructed, so the kindrily entrusted Dakota with our basic secret of abilities. Over the years he attained further knowledge about us, and it strengthened his desire to be an Element.

"Anyway," Carson said, as the hallway light flickered on. "Shiloh had me text you."

Shiloh spun out of the hallway into the kitchen, singing a chimerical song about lights and ghosts. A head full of braids had replaced the thick unkempt hair I'd seen him with a few days earlier. "Natty bro!"

"Carson said you had him text me. Why didn't you just call me?"

"Left my phone at the dance studio." He dumped an armful of bulbs into the trashcan. "All the lights are fixed, Louise."

Louise patted his back. "What would I do without you, Shiloh?"

"You'd use a flashlight."

She playfully shoved him, and in true Shiloh style he dramatically fell against the refrigerator. "Maybe so, but none of us have the ability to know what you told us earlier. Hurry up and tell Nathan."

"Tell me what?"

"Let's go outside," Shiloh said. "I'd rather show you."

∞

We walked to the far end of the deck where the spiral staircase led to the rooftop. I traversed to the top and waited for him.

When he reached the top stair, I asked, "Why are we up here?"

"The closer the better."

"Closer to what?"

He pointed upward.

I glanced at the sky. "Beg your pardon."

"This might sound crazy, but keep in mind I see differently than the rest of you. Just like you see colors and I can't, I can see things that you can't." He rubbed his hands together. "Promise you won't push me off the roof when I tell you this."

"I'll do my best to refrain."

He sucked air through his teeth and blew out a long breath. "Okay, last night, I thought I saw something in the sky, but I dismissed it due to Faith's contagious optimism. Tonight though, it's a tad brighter. I can't deny it's there."

"Deny what's there?"

He stepped past me so he wasn't near the roof's edge. "Maryah's star."

My eyes darted upward, searching for the celestial light that used to shine beside mine. I saw only darkness. The empty grave in the sky matched the black hole inside me. I lowered my chin and glared at Shiloh.

"Dang. You don't see it either. I'm telling you, where her star used to be is a pulsing spec of mist that's halfway between gray and silver of my color spectrum."

"Her star burned out almost two decades ago. Once a star falls it doesn't rise again."

"I discussed that with Faith and Louise. Maybe it never fell. What if it just faded like her memory, and now it's slowly being rekindled?"

"The star that represented her has burned out. The heavens are through weeping for her, and so am I."

"Do you really expect me to believe you're not going to fight to bring her memory back?" I stared at him, unblinking. "You aren't yourself anymore, bro. We miss the old Nathaniel, the believer of love and miracles. I swear, Nate, there is a trace of light up there."

I shook my head. "Impossible."

"We'll see about that." Shiloh sat down, dangling his legs over the side of the roof. "Carson thinks I can see it because of my ability to see in the dark. He's hoping to reproduce my gift by designing special hi-tech glasses. If he pulls it off, I'll prove you wrong."

"I'll believe that when I see it."

He reclined back with his hands behind his head and smiled. "We know. That's why Carson is making the glasses."

JUMPING TO CONCLUSIONS

Maryah

After an all day tour of Sedona, and lots of Faith singing, we pulled into the Lunas' driveway. That's when I saw it: a white Mustang.

She did it. Faith's scary sister convinced the Lunas to give Carson his car months before his birthday. He wasn't even sixteen yet! It's not like he'd be able to drive it. How could Harmony talk Anthony and Louise into breaking their family tradition?

Maybe they feared Evil Twin as much as I did.

As we entered the house, Carson's voice echoed through the foyer. He was discussing nitrous and racing stripes, but the conversation halted when we entered the kitchen. I tried to stay behind Krista, using her as a shield from Carson's dirty looks.

"See my new ride?" Carson asked, grinning smugly.

Faith fist bumped him. "Very swank. Congrats." She punched a blonde boy's shoulder when he was in mid-sip of his drink. Soda spilled down the front of him and onto the kitchen counter. "This is my little brother, Dakota."

"Seriously? I just cleaned this shirt!" Dakota rubbed his arm where Faith hit him. "Hi, Maryah. Hi, Krista."

Krista spoke for both of us. "Nice to meet you."

Dakota was shorter and smaller than Carson. His scabbed elbows and wrist brace made him look breakable and corruptible. Carson would probably turn him against me—if he hadn't already.

"Shiloh will be in in a sec," Faith said after glancing at her phone. As if Krista and I knew who Shiloh was. She poured herself a drink. "We're going to hang out here and watch a movie. You boys want to join us?"

Carson flipped through the pages of a car magazine. "Sure. What are you guys watching?"

Wow. Carson agreed to an activity that involved my company? Guess the excitement of getting a car curbed his bad attitude toward me. I didn't want to hang out with Carson, but I also didn't want to look like an anti-social brat by hiding out in my room all night.

"No chick flicks," Dakota moaned.

"I second that!" A guy with braids and caramel skin came through the kitchen door. "Hey, Maryah, I'm Shiloh. Faith's other half. It's awesome to see you."

"Thanks. You, too." I'd learned from meeting so many people in the last twenty-four hours that people in Arizona didn't say it was nice to *meet* you, they said it was nice to see you. No use fighting their system.

His smile gleamed. "Hello, Krista."

"Love your bandana," she said.

"Much thanks. One of my dance students gave it to me as a gift." He wasn't much taller than Faith, but he looked pretty buff under his baggy black t-shirt and white basketball shorts. His day-glo sneakers coordinated with Faith's hair and bright outfit.

"You're a dancer?" I asked.

"Shiloh's parents own a studio," Faith explained. "His mom is from Jamaica and his dad is from Asia. They do everything from

Salsa to African. It's where my Jamasian gets his talent from. They're the coolest people in the world—well, besides us." She playfully elbowed me. She obviously had no idea how *uncool* I was.

Shiloh demonstrated a fancy foot-work spin, then dipped Faith and kissed her.

I smiled at how cute and in-sync they were. "How long have you two been together?"

Faith giggled. "A looong time."

"What flick are we watching?" Shiloh asked.

Carson glared at me through his parted curtain of bangs and stepped way too close to me—way too quickly. "Have you seen *Jumper?*"

I stumbled backward but the kitchen wall stopped me. "*Jumper?*"

"About the guy who can teleport."

"Never heard of it." I made tentative eye contact with him. His words sounded neutral, but his expression was intense.

"*Jumper* it is!" Faith announced. "I'll start the popcorn." She danced over to the kitchen pantry.

"Should we see if Harmony wants to join us?" Krista asked.

Great. Let's invite all the members of my lynch mob.

Dakota answered before unease fully washed over me. "Nah. She's hanging out with Nathan tonight."

Faith whipped her head around, and Carson threw a bottle cap at Dakota. Why were they acting so weird?

"Oh, it's Nathan from Oak Creek." Dakota peeled the corner of his bottle label. "Not Nathan-Nathan,"

Carson faced me again. "*Our* Nathan has *Jumper* on DVD. You should help me find it."

"Sure," slipped out of my mouth before I could stop it.

I followed Carson down the hallway, staring at the back of his white hoodie, certain he'd turn around any second and say something mean. Maybe he was trying to get me alone so there'd be no witnesses.

He opened the door to Nathan's room and my worry turned to confusion. *This* was Nathan's room? The same Nathan who designed my gorgeous bedroom? His room was so small and plain. The bed had a boring green comforter and no headboard. His dresser, bookshelves, and desk looked like they came from a thrift store.

Carson searched through DVDs while I studied the pictures on the walls. Several sketches hung around one of Louise's paintings. They were all the same—a pair of female eyes drawn in intricate detail. Their shape reminded me of my own, but they were prettier than mine and the brows were darker.

I spotted a framed photo on the nightstand of a tall curvy girl with long curly hair. She had dazzling green eyes—definitely the ones in the drawings—and a warm smile. She looked like a supermodel.

Carson walked over and stood beside me. "That's Mary."

"Your brother's girlfriend?"

He tugged on the strings of his sweatshirt. "You could call her that."

I thought about how Dylan was already married at twenty. "Are they married?"

"Let's just say they've been together forever."

I held the frame close to my face, examining the dull coloring. "Looks like an old photo."

"Nathan is old-fashioned. That was taken with real film. Eighties-style camera."

"She's beautiful."

Carson's mad-at-the-world look resurfaced. "She's not my favorite person."

I was beginning to think he didn't like anyone. "Why don't you like her?"

"She's selfish. She's caused Nathan a lot of pain."

In a way it was sweet, him being protective of his big brother. I looked at the picture again, wondering if Carson judged Mary as harshly as he did me. My mother always said there are many sides to every story.

"Did she go off to school with Nathan?"

Carson's laugh bordered on sinister. "Nope, she's here in Sedona."

"Must be tough for them to be so far apart."

"You have no idea." Carson took the frame from me and laid it face down on the nightstand. "Movie time."

∞

As the closing credits rolled up the screen, Faith grabbed my hand. "What'd you think?"

"Pretty good. Krista used to make up stories about a boy with the same kind of power when we were little."

Faith's sparkly grin gushed free when she looked at Krista. "You did?"

"I told her about all kinds of supernatural stuff," Krista said.

Dakota brushed potato chip crumbs off of his seat. "If I had powers, I'd want to fly."

Throughout the movie Dakota commented on teleporting like it was real. Faith mentioned he was only fifteen, but did he really believe people had supernatural powers?

Faith squeezed my hand. "What's wrong? You're irritated. Do you not like discussing this stuff?"

"I'm not irritated."

"Yes, you are. I can sense these things. What ability would you want if you were a superhero?"

It wouldn't be much different from reality. "I'm sure I'd have the power of invisibility."

Faith scrunched up her nose. "Well, it's been a long day, and I have to take Shiloh home."

"Ready when you are." Shiloh yawned and stretched his arms above his head. The sleeve of his t-shirt crinkled up, exposing a tattoo on his shoulder—the number twelve surrounded by linking circles.

"What's your tattoo mean?" I asked.

"Oh, uhh." He looked over his shoulder then at Faith. "My soccer number is twelve."

"And the rings?"

He smiled. "They represent an unbreakable bond."

Kind of odd someone would love their soccer team that much, but who was I to judge?

Faith wrapped her arms around Shiloh's waist and said something in a foreign language. He answered in the same sort of incomprehensible words.

"What language is that?" I asked.

"Duh," Carson said. "Japanese."

"You *both* know how to speak Japanese?"

"Just a little," Shiloh replied, holding his thumb and index finger close together.

"We should get going." Faith giggled. "Dakota, you want a ride?"

"Nah," he replied. "I'm spending the night here so I can beat Carson at his new video game."

Krista and I said goodbye to Faith and Shiloh, then ended up following Carson and Dakota toward the game room.

Carson stopped short and I ran into his back. "Where do you think you're going?"

Yet another awkward hallway encounter with Carson. "To the guest room."

He pointed down the hall. "No, we fixed yours today. No more guest room for you two."

No way could they repair that much fire and water damage in one day. After he and Dakota walked away, Krista and I headed for our original room.

I took a few weary steps toward the door. "He's messing with us, right?"

Krista shrugged.

I squinted, like that would make the scene easier to look at, and pushed the door open. "What the—?"

MOVING AWAY
BUT GETTING CLOSER

Maryah

Everything looked *exactly* like it did before the fire. The same tree branch bed posts, same linens, even the dream catcher looked identical to the one that hung there before. No scorched floors or ceiling. No water damage or smoke smell.

"How?" I asked Krista.

"They work fast."

"It doesn't make sense."

"It's a big family. They must have pulled together and worked all day. They're trying hard to make you feel comfortable and happy here. It's sweet."

Another hint that she wanted me to live with the Lunas. I'd always believed that Krista and I were inseparable, but ever since we arrived in Sedona, it felt like she was pushing me away. Only one way to be sure.

"I've decided I'm staying."

And there it was. A gleam in her eye. "You are? You're sure?"

I hesitated, not sure whatsoever. "It'll be a fresh start."

She actually smiled—a huge, blinding, so-relieved-to-be-ditching-my-zombie-cousin smile. "I am so jealous. I mean, I'm sad we'll be so far apart, but I know you'll feel much better here."

Sad? She was so far from sad she'd need a GPS to find it. I'd never seen her look happier. I didn't know whether to cry or yell at her for being so heartless.

"Oh, Pudding, this is going to be your healing place. I just know it. I'll explain everything to my mom and dad so they understand. And I'll make sure all your stuff gets packed and shipped to you."

She didn't even want me flying home with her to pack my stuff! I couldn't open my mouth or I was certain I'd cry or scream, so I just nodded.

"You should go tell Louise. She'll be thrilled."

Go tell Louise. What if Louise didn't want me either? What if she was being nice and hospitable out of respect for my mother, but never expected me to actually move into her home?

A headache unfurled at the base of my neck. I sucked in air, realizing I hadn't taken a breath in at least fifty sprinting heartbeats. What if no one wanted me?

∞

I found Louise in the library, working on her laptop. I knocked on the doorframe before entering. "Hi."

"Hello." She stopped typing and folded her screen down. Her silver bracelets clinked together initiating a long moment of us silently staring at each other until finally, "Carson told me you watched one of Nathaniel's favorite movies tonight."

Poor Louise. She had a severe case of Nathan withdrawal. "You miss him, don't you?"

"Do *I* miss him?"

"You talk about him a lot. I figured it's because you miss him."

"Oh." She paused. "You're right. Maybe I miss him more than I realized."

I sat in the chair across the desk from her, and glanced around at the towering shelves of books. "Such a big house for only a few people."

"Well, it used to be much more crowded, but things change."

Sweat dripped down my back. Two of her own kids had just moved out. Why would she want a runt like me hanging around?

She took off her glasses and cleaned them with her sleeve. "You'd have a lot of privacy if you lived here."

My heart pounded so hard I thought the desk between us was shaking. "I wouldn't want to disrupt your life."

"You are the furthest thing from a disruption. You are eternally welcome in this home and in our hearts."

Louise was probably trying to be polite. She didn't want to make me feel unwanted, so she gave politically correct responses. She folded her hands on top of the desk. "However, I won't force you to live with us. *You* must decide which path is right for you."

I nodded and pressed my fingers into the arms of my chair. They were clammy and squeaked across the polished wood.

Louise leaned closer. "I spoke to the local high school and classes start next week. If you stay, you could start the year on time."

My head spun trying to process it all. She'd made preparations for my arrival? Maybe she really did want me to live with her.

"Maryah, I understand the emotional torment you're going through, but please know that I love you more than you can imagine. We want nothing more than for you to stay with us."

That settled it. Krista was pushing me away, and Louise was inviting me in. Decision made. I choked on my words. "If you're sure you want me...I'd like to live with you."

She squealed, springing up and running around the desk to hug me. "You have no idea how happy this makes me—how happy this will make everyone!"

Not everyone. My happiness died on our boat dock that night when a monster told me my family was gone.

I fake-smiled at Louise and motioned toward the living room. "Mind if I watch TV?"

"Go right ahead. I'll be in here working if you need anything."

I wasn't ready to talk to Krista yet, so I watched reruns of old sitcoms by myself for a while. Around midnight, Louise passed through the living room.

"Still up?" she asked.

"I'm not tired yet." I also wasn't in the mood to share a bed with Krista.

"Well, I'm turning in for the night. Herbal teas are in the pantry if you need help relaxing."

"Thanks. Goodnight, Louise."

"Sweet dreams, dear. I'm so glad you decided to stay with us."

Even as I watched TV, I stressed about telling my aunt and uncle that I wasn't going back to Maryland. Relaxation sounded good, so I raided the pantry and found a glass jar of tea with "Tranquil Sleep" written on the label. I brewed myself a cup and curled up on the couch. The tea worked better than expected.

In my dream I was still on the Lunas' sofa. My movie-star angel of death was walking away from me. I'd know his strong, broad back anywhere. Could he take me to wherever my parents and Mikey were?

I called out to him, but my voice came out weak. "Take me" *with you.* Only the first half of my groggy thought surfaced.

He turned, his lean muscles bulging underneath of his t-shirt. They looked effortless, which made sense because angels didn't seem like the gym-obsessed type. His eyes were cold and guarded, but he stepped closer then handed me my tea. Would an angel of death poison my tea? Brutal attack, raging fire, tea: one of these didn't belong.

I took a few sips while we stared at each other. I wanted to ask him what death was like, and if he knew where my parents and brother were, but talking required so much effort that I couldn't seem to muster.

"Does it hurt?" I whispered. That one question took every ounce of energy I had.

He winced then glanced around the room. "Does what hurt?"

Dying. I thought, but I couldn't say it out loud.

"Do you know who I am?" he asked.

I tried nodding, but my head only nestled further into my pillow. My eyelids were heavy and my muscles had melted away. He got up and walked down the bedroom hallway. I wanted to follow him, but I couldn't. So much for talking to angels.

I woke up, startled by a bang. The television flashed like a strobe light as a late night infomercial played.

"Maryah." Carson poked my shoulder. "Wake up."

I rubbed my eyes. "What time is it?"

"Two a.m."

"What are you doing up?"

"Apparently, I couldn't sleep, so I came out to get a drink and the TV was on." His words sounded forced like he was reciting a speech.

I stood, but had to steady myself on the end table while a wicked headrush flowed through me.

"Any weird dreams?"

My jaw almost dropped, stunned that he was concerned if I was okay, *and* that he asked about my dreams. *Yes Carson, I had a tea party with my angel of death.* He'd believe that—if we lived in the Twilight Zone.

"None that I remember," I lied.

Carson hit the off button on the remote.

"Thanks for checking on me," I whispered, walking close behind him down the hallway.

He raised his hand in an almost-wave as he closed his bedroom door.

Krista was still awake and reading when I went to our room. On the nightstand, she had set out a framed photo of my parents, Mikey, and me. I slumped onto the floor, hugging their picture to my chest.

"You okay, Pudding?"

I looked at the ceiling, fighting back tears, but something new hung beside the dream catcher.

"What's that?" I asked her.

She slid down onto the floor and leaned against me. "It's a little narcissistic, but I hung up a photo of me. I figure that way, I'll still be here watching over you."

And then I did cry. How could I be mad at her after doing something so sweet? More importantly, how was I going to survive living so far away from her?

She hugged me and I sobbed into her shoulder. "What will happen to us, Kris?"

"Nothing," she whispered. "Miles can't separate hearts and souls. We'll be apart less than a year. Then we'll graduate and I'll move here too."

I pulled back, shocked. "You will?"

She smiled and wiped my cheeks. "Absolutely. I love this place, and all these people. I know staying here is what's best for you, but you're my best friend. I'll miss you more than chocolate."

Our private saying should've made me smile, but my lips—and heart—felt like quicksand. I hugged her with all the strength I had, which wasn't much due to the tea. "Saying goodbye to you tomorrow is going to shatter my heart to pieces."

"Mine too. But I've got enough miracle glue to put us back together again."

CHASING THE TRUTH

NATHANIEL

B loody hell, I had become a stalker.

I paced my room, debating whether or not to traverse back to Colorado. Anthony and Louise wouldn't let anything happen to Maryah. I didn't need to stand guard over her like an overprotective Neanderthal.

Or did I?

Dedrick had gone to great lengths to find Maryah and kill anyone who got in his way. I wouldn't let history repeat itself. I'd be damned if I'd let those fiends get to Maryah—or any member of our kindrily.

My door opened and Carson stepped inside.

"She's in her room. She didn't remember dreaming anything. I'm going to bed."

"Wait," I grabbed his arm. "She didn't mention seeing me at all? Maybe she knew I was real."

He sighed heavily. "Look, the girl doesn't seem too bright, but don't you think she would've said something if she saw a stranger in our house—especially in the middle of the night?"

"But she spoke to me. She's never been one to talk in her sleep. Travel, yes. Talk, no."

He pressed his palm against his forehead. "Nate, you're driving me insane. Either stop stalking her and introduce yourself so we can end these secret rendezvous, or stay away from her. Two options. Pick one. I'm tired of being your undercover wingman."

He made introducing myself sound so simple.

"Pick one," he demanded, "right now, or I'm telling Mom what's going on."

That made me chuckle. Members of our kindrily had changed roles many times. The first time a member was born as a relative was hard to accept, but after many lifetimes of switching from brother, cousin, uncle, son, neighbor, etcetera, label or age stopped carrying any significance. Being born to family or friends made it easier for us to stay connected.

Three lifetimes ago Louise had been my youngest sister, so Carson's "Mom" references reminded me just how inexperienced he was.

"Get some sleep, Carson. I promise not to wake you again tonight."

He cocked his jaw and murmured, "mm-hmm," before leaving.

I sat on my bed, replaying my interaction with Maryah. She had said *take me*. What did that mean? The testosterone-filled teenage side of me hoped she meant in a physical sense. As in, *I can't resist my intense attraction to you, so take me and have your way with me.* Blood rushed to a certain body part just thinking about it, but the wise, logical side of me reasoned that she probably wanted me to take her somewhere. Where? And who did she think I was? Why would she ask a supposed stranger to take her anywhere?

She also asked if it hurt. Did what hurt? Losing her? No, she couldn't know we had a past together. And her ring. Seeing her wearing it made me feel like a small shard of my shattered universe had been put back into place.

The distinctive soft slapping of Louise's bare feet neared my door. I'd heard her walk the floors of this house many nights for over a decade.

Carson, the little git, had actually told on me.

She tapped on the door just before I opened it. Her reading glasses sat atop her head, and her pajamas didn't look wrinkled or slept-in. "I'm glad you're here. I planned to call you in the morning, but when Carson told me you were visiting I figured best to talk now.

"Louise, I don't want to discuss—"

"No." She waved her hand and closed the door quietly behind her. "My old friend Marcus spotted Dedrick in Liverpool."

The hairs on the back of my neck rose. Maryah and I had lived in Liverpool for quite some time. Dedrick was still trying to track her down.

"Marcus tailed him around town for hours and ended up at Empire Theater. He waited outside awhile, but Dedrick didn't come out. Marcus tried to go in and look for him, but the place was locked. It's not much, but it's a start."

In my mind, I was already standing on the cobblestone street outside of the theater, searching, hunting with unstoppable determination. "When? What time did Marcus last see him?"

"That's the strange part. He followed him out of a pub at closing. By the time he tried to get into the theater it was almost five a.m. No theater is open at that time of day."

I calculated the time difference and wanted to punch something. "That was two hours ago! Why didn't he ring you right away?"

"He did as soon as he could. He despises cell phones and doesn't carry one."

That I could understand, but we had lost two hours of precious time. Dedrick could be anywhere.

"Edgar and Helen are still in Venice?"

Louise nodded.

"I'm going to Liverpool." I stiffened, preparing to traverse, but Louise grabbed my arm.

"Wait. Marcus said you could traverse to his flat."

"I've never met him, or been to his flat."

"I know." She reached into her book and pulled out a photograph. "Here."

I studied his stern face, focusing on the history and unique identifying markers in his eyes. "He's ancient."

"Even older than Edgar. Dylan and Amber are flying out any minute. They'll pick up Edgar and Helen then contact you as soon as they land."

I nodded then streamlined my body. The electrifying tingle of traversing grew more intense. Picturing Marcus's eyes, I dissolved from my room.

Louise's last words faded away. "Don't do anything rash."

I heard the crackling fireplace before the smell of tobacco flooded my nose. I opened my eyes to see Marcus in a plaid smoking jacket, sitting in a Wingback chair, looking much older—physically—than his photo had suggested.

He lowered his pipe. "An entrance such as that requires no introduction." His thick accent made me miss my jolly old England days.

"Hello, Marcus." I shook his hand. "Thank you for calling us about Dedrick, and for allowing me to traverse here."

He looked me up and down then squinted at his photo still clutched in my hand. "By George, you're wearing clothes, and you've even brought a photograph."

"Yes."

"I've met one other Traverser in my lives and when she traveled, she'd come out the other side without a stitch of clothing. She certainly couldn't carry additional items with her. How do you do it?"

Before I mastered the ability to take objects with me, I had ended up in many dreadful predicaments. Traveling without a wallet or clothes isn't for the faint of heart.

"Evolution," I answered.

"Evolution—my, how I know about that. Can you take people with you?"

"No, only inanimate objects, and even those have limits. I still haven't been able to keep a car attached to me."

"A car?" He poured himself a Scotch. "What happened when you tried?" He tilted an empty glass, offering to make me a drink.

I raised a declining hand. "I'd be honored to exchange stories, but first we must find Dedrick."

"We? Nathaniel, this body is too old and knackered for me to play Sherlock Holmes with you. I'll tell you what I know, but then you're on your own."

"That's fine. I've grown accustomed to being alone."

He puffed on his pipe. "I've heard your story. My condolences." Rain pelted the windows. The flames of the hearth dimly lit Marcus's face. "Louise believes your lady will recover. She says she's too powerful to perish."

My voice was flat. "She used to be powerful."

He leaned forward, looking like he sensed that I had no hope left. "Perhaps you should plan an extended stay with me. I could teach you a thing or two about love and life."

I almost declined, anxious to stop chatting and start hunting, but then I remembered Marcus's true age. I had the utmost respect for elderly wisdom and couldn't turn away such a gift. Besides, it would take some time to track down Dedrick.

I bowed with respect. "I'll stay however long it takes."

MAKING AN IMPRESSION

Maryah

Within a matter of days my whole world had changed—again.

Dragonflies—way worse than butterflies—flitted in my stomach as I stared out of the living room windows, dreading my first day of school.

The front door opened and Faith yelled a cheerful hello as she sashayed around the corner. Talk about making yourself at home. We'd hung out every day since Krista left, but still, I couldn't ever remember any of Mikey's friends walking into our house without knocking.

She skipped over and pinched me. She was like a sparkler that never fizzled out. "First day at your new school! Who's excited?"

"I give up, who?"

"Aw, you'll love it. Let's go. We're late."

I grabbed my book bag and headed for the car.

The ride was a blur of stoplights, other cars, and Faith singing. I was so nervous that it took everything I had to keep my cereal from coming back up.

When we pulled into the school parking lot, I gawked at all the nice cars. Jaguar Boy's was among them. He pounded on the roof of a Lexus and laughed while talking to the flawless girl inside. I didn't stand a chance of fitting in.

Faith and Harmony were in my first and last period classes, but I didn't have any with Shiloh. Carson and Dakota were Juniors, so no surprise that we didn't have classes together. The majority of my days would be spent alone, and I was good with that.

After a non-eventful homeroom with a bunch of strangers, I followed my map to English. Nametags were on each desk. Really? Nametags? Were we in kindergarten?

"Looks like she alphabetized us." Faith pouted. "You're in the back row and I'm way up there."

"I'm grateful to be a Woodsen. A seat in the back makes it easy to hide."

"Oh, stop. Maybe she'll let us move seats once she gets to know everyone."

I sat down in a wobbly legged chair. If I could go unnoticed everything would be fine. The bell rang and students scurried to their seats. A tall woman with auburn hair stood at the front of the room.

"Good morning, and welcome to the first day of your senior year! Isn't this exciting?"

Why did everyone think today was so exciting? It was the beginning of another school year—long and painful like the others.

"What a monumental time in your lives!" The teacher made exaggerated hand gestures as she spoke. "My name is Ms. Barby, and I just moved here from Ohio." Her smile never floundered. I'd have to drink six cups of coffee to have her energy.

Faith had a big grin on her face as she watched the teacher walk the aisles and continue with her perky introduction. Faith obviously liked Ms. Barby and I could understand why. Happy hyper people always like other happy hyper people.

Ms. Barby proceeded to ask each of us to stand and introduce ourselves, throwing a huge wrench in my "go unnoticed" plan.

Most kids stated their name and how they'd lived here forever, if they played a sport, and what college they were hoping to attend. I hadn't noticed Jaguar Boy sitting beside me until he gave his introduction. He stood up and leaned against my desk before talking. I scooted back, trying to get some distance from his uncomfortable closeness, but my chair almost toppled over. Luckily, he had the full attention of the class.

"You all know me. I'm River Malone, lead singer of the Rebel Junkies—future professional rock star." He held up his hands. "No autographs, please."

Most of the class laughed or clapped. One guy high-fived him.

Faith jumped to her feet, temporarily silencing the room with an animated introduction of herself. Again, people whistled or clapped for her as she graciously curtsied. They made it look easy, so why was I terrified for my turn?

I was last to introduce myself. I took a deep breath, stood up, and began. "I'm Maryah Woodsen from Maryland. I've been living in Sedona for a few days and I don't play sports." I sat down before the last word came out of my mouth.

"You're from Maryland? How nice!" Ms. Barby exclaimed with a cheesy grin. "What brought you and your family to Sedona?"

Was she really asking for more information, worse yet, about my family?

Faith tried to save me. "You forgot to mention your plans after graduation. Any certain college in mind?"

"Excuse me," Ms. Barby said, "but I asked her a question."

"Sorry," Faith mumbled.

I clenched my teeth together. "I moved here to live with my godmother. My parents and brother died." I glanced at Faith. "And no, no college plans yet."

The room was so quiet the class probably heard me struggling to breathe. River turned to look at me. His eyebrows furrowed together in what looked like sympathy. I pulled the brim of my hat over my eyes, focusing on the book in front of me, and fighting the urge to cry.

Ms. Barby walked down the aisle and touched my desk. "Maria, I'm so sorry."

"Her name is Ma-ry-ah." Faith's sympathetic stare penetrated me from the front of the room, but I couldn't look at her. If I cried, I'd be guaranteed to make the headlines of the school rumor mill.

"Maryah. Right. What a beautiful name. Okay, let's dive into our first lesson." Ms. Barby handed out textbooks while River slid a note onto my desk.

Welcome to Sedona. I'm sorry about your family. I know how you feel. Let me know if you need a tour guide.

Peace, River

Faith and I might have to agree to disagree about being a fan of River's. I looked at him and mouthed the words "thank you."

∞

I got lost only once while trying to find history. The rest of the day had gone pretty well, with no more drama, tearing up, or awkwardness—until last period music class.

River dragged a chair in front of my desk then straddled it to face me. My pulse pounded between my ears.

Our teacher hadn't announced his name yet, but he didn't look pleased. "River Malone, eyes to the front of the room please."

"In a sec, Mr. Milton!" River kept his focus on me and lowered his voice. "Something about you left an imprint on my soul. You've been stuck in my head all day."

I didn't know whether to be creeped out or flattered. I clicked my pen repeatedly as if the noise would make up for my stunned silence.

"Mr. Malone!" our teacher yelled. The rest of the class stared at us.

"I said in a second," River retorted calmly—the epitome of cool.

Mr. Milton held up a pad of pink paper, shaking it in the air as he spoke. "Your second is up. Turn around right now or you will be taking a trip to the principal's office."

River rose from his seat in one jaguar-smooth movement then strutted to the front of the class. He took the pad from Mr. Milton's hand, tore off the top sheet, and scribbled on it. "I do love a good trip. I'll sign my own ticket."

He made a kissing noise at the teacher, and some of the class laughed while he strutted down the aisle to my desk. He whispered, "I'm gonna write a song about you."

After he left the room, I looked up to see every member of my class, including Faith and Harmony, staring at me. A redhead one desk over had her phone aimed at me.

"What are you doing?" I asked her.

"Taking a video so April can see this."

"April? Who is April?" I swatted at her phone. "Stop recording me."

"April," she said, typing frantically, "is River's girlfriend."

Girlfriend. Oh my god. Had he been flirting with me? I'd never been flirted with before. I wasn't sure how I reacted, but would I look guilty on video? I tried to plead innocence. "I didn't—it's not like—I had no idea that—"

"Save it, new girl. Video has been sent."

Mr. Milton started class and everyone but me seemed to be paying attention. I stared at a water stain on the floor, wishing it would turn into a pool I could jump in and drown myself. Somewhere River's girlfriend was watching a video of her boyfriend causing a scene because of me, the new girl. Nothing good could come of that.

My plan to go unnoticed had failed miserably.

SWAPPING STORIES

Maryah

My movie-star angel appeared in my dreams again. He didn't say a word. He just sat on the roof of a building, staring down at a city of cobblestone streets. I could almost see him mentally mapping out his next move. He would find a way to lead me home—to be with my family again.

Until then, I had to endure another day at school. I asked Louise if I could take a sick day (they really should implement a number of coward days), but she denied me.

River didn't show up for school, and I had no idea what his girlfriend looked like. She could have been anyone. All day I caught myself scanning the halls between classes, worrying that every rocker girl I saw was going to bash me in the face with a binder. I didn't want to ask Faith—or anyone else—about her because I worried it might trigger more drama.

Even the last period bell ringing didn't make me feel better. What if she was waiting for me in the parking lot? Maybe she hadn't been in school all day because she was arming herself to attack me.

If Mikey were here, he'd tell me I was being a paranoid nut job.

After making it safely to Faith's car, I finally relaxed. My muscles ached from being so tense. When Faith suggested stopping by Tlaquepaque to get smoothies, I agreed, hoping they had one with a shot of something that could calm me down.

We were walking through the shopping village, minding our own business, just feet away from the smoothie place, when a raspy voice shouted my name. I turned around and saw River, but then I noticed the girl holding his hand, and I almost puked. They were coming toward us. I turned to Faith to tell her I was about to get my butt kicked, but she hadn't stopped. She stood in the open doorway of the store. "I really have to pee. I'll meet you inside."

"Hey, Maryah." River stopped in front of me. "This is April. Ape, this is the new girl."

Ape. She looked nothing like an ape. She was tall and thin with hair that flowed like honey over her shoulders. Her clothes were pastel-colored and feminine with ruffles and all. And she was smiling. At me. A sweet smile, like she was the type who volunteered to feed the homeless and read to lonely old people in nursing homes. *This* was the girl I had feared for the past twenty-four hours?

"Hi, Maryah. It's so nice to meet you." Her smile drooped when I didn't respond, but I was so shell shocked. I hadn't slept all night in fear of having to fight this girl, and here she was all pretty and sweet and being nice to me. She glanced at River then tried again. "How do you like Sedona so far?"

It took me a few seconds to get my mouth moist enough to speak. "It's rocky."

It's rocky? Why was I so lame?

Her laugh sounded like rainbow Skittles spilling onto a glass table, all colorful and sugary. "We do have plenty of rocks, especially red ones."

River looked at us like we were ridiculous, and we kind of were. "Maryah's shy. We might have to bust her out of her shell."

"We will have you out of your shell in no time," April said. "I remember what it's like being the new girl, constantly slaying the dragonflies in your belly."

"Yes!" I practically shouted. "That's exactly how I feel. Way worse than butterflies."

"Way worse," April agreed. "Hey, you should hang out here with me tonight. River's band is playing, and I can introduce you to some cool people."

April seemed like someone Krista would've been good friends with, or Mikey would've dated. I could almost hear Mikey encouraging me to make more friends. "Maybe. I'll have to see, but it sounds like fun."

"Cool. Save my number and call me if you can make it. River goes on at nine."

After exchanging numbers and saying goodbye, I strolled into the smoothie shop feeling like a new person.

∞

Faith didn't want to go to River's show, but she offered to give me a ride. She couldn't understand why April was with River, but agreed that she was great. When I confessed my earlier suspicion that she wanted to beat me up, Faith laughed hysterically.

"After what you've been through, punches from her would feel like butterfly kisses."

I nodded in agreement like I was all tough and confident, but why hadn't I thought of that? I'd been beaten and left on death's doorstep by an evil man three times the size of April. I survived *that*, yet I was worried about getting into a fight in the cafeteria?

"Here we are." Faith pulled up outside of Tlaquepaque. "Have fun."

"You sure you don't want to come?"

"And listen to River scream into a microphone all night? No, thank you. I cherish my eardrums. Plus, I have plans with Shiloh. But if April can't bring you home, call me. We'll come back and get you."

"Thanks." I climbed out of the car and waved to Faith as she drove away.

The sky had darkened, but the street lights of the shopping village were glowing. Strings of large white bulbs hung from balconies and archways, making it feel more like Christmas than the end of August.

April waved me over to the garden wall where she was sitting.

"Thanks again for inviting me."

"Have a seat. The show's not starting for a few minutes."

More people trickled into the courtyard. A guy in front of us dropped popcorn all over the ground while aiming for his mouth. The buttery smell made my stomach growl. I looked around at the store windows, trying to think of something to talk about. "We didn't have any place like this in Maryland."

She almost fell off the wall she whipped around so fast. "You're from Maryland? Me too! What part?"

"Baltimore."

"We lived near the Eastern Shore!"

"How'd you end up in Sedona?"

She looked around like she didn't want anyone to overhear. "My mom is sick, and there's a clinic out here that's supposedly amazing. She thinks this is some kind of magical healing town."

"Oh." I almost asked what kind of sickness, but figured it might be too personal. "I heard the healing town theory too. Hopefully this place will help her."

April nodded. I thought I saw tears, but then a breeze blew her hair over her face, "So, what's your story? River said you lost your parents. I'm sorry."

I ran my finger over the curves of a flower pot beside me, trying to get my voice to work.

"Was it a car accident?"

I shook my head. "They were murdered."

"Oh my gosh! That's horrible."

I swallowed the boulder in my throat and focused on the flower pot again.

"I'm so sorry. I don't even know what to say. I...Okay, let's talk about something else." April spun a strand of her hair around her finger. "What about a boyfriend? No lucky guy missing you back in Maryland?"

I choked on the cool air. "Me? Are you kidding? In case you haven't noticed, I'm no guy magnet."

"What do you mean? You're pretty and seem cool."

"I'm sorry, have we met? I'm Maryah, member of the socially challenged."

"You don't give yourself enough credit. I've seen you with Faith and Shiloh. Everyone loves them. You're part of their in-crowd."

In-crowd. It seemed like an untouchable exclusive club when I lived in Maryland. Mikey would be so proud that I had evolved from my wallflower status.

"Trust me," April watched River fiddle with speakers on stage. "Their club is hard to get into."

"Their club? What do you mean?"

She kicked her long legs against the wall under us. "I don't mean this in a bad way, so please don't think I'm talking trash, but Shiloh and Faith, her twin sister, their little brother Carson and his brothers, they've always been this tight clique that no one else can join. I mean, Faith is really nice and she makes lots of surface friends, but forget trying to hang out with her or go any deeper. They don't welcome outsiders. They're all like that. It's surprising to see Faith buddy up with you so fast."

I was dumbfounded. "Carson seems like that, and Harmony definitely, but Shiloh and Faith? Dakota? They're so far from snobby."

April shrugged. "You'll see what I mean as time goes by. I hope you don't get roped into being that way. You seem really genuine."

"I could never be a snob. I have nothing to be snobby about."

The band tested their instruments, playing a few notes on the guitars and drums. A couple people waved hello to April, but they stayed gathered close to the stage.

She twirled her hair around her finger again. "I know we just met, and this may seem really weird, but could I ask you for a favor?"

"Sure."

"I'm not going to be in school for the rest of the week. My mom is having a rough time and I have to help her, so it might even be a couple weeks, we aren't sure yet. But—gosh, I feel so insecure for even asking this."

"No, go ahead."

She took a deep breath. "River is really popular. And, well, we've been having some issues lately, so... I'd just like to know how he acts when I'm not around." She covered her face with her hands. "Gosh, I'm such a horrible person."

"That's not horrible. It's natural. I think." What did I know? I'd never had a boyfriend.

"I feel so sneaky asking you to spy on him. It's just so many girls throw themselves at him, even my friends. I'm scared to leave him alone for so long, but I have no choice."

Why was she with him if she didn't trust him? She'd probably already asked herself that, and spying was a way to determine if she could. "We're only in two classes together, so I don't really see him that much."

She leaned in, bumping her shoulder against mine. "Something about you left an impression on his soul."

My heartbeat sped up. "You know about that?"

"Tiffany showed me the video, and River played me the song he's working on about you. If you inspire him musically, which you did, he won't leave you alone."

I couldn't believe she was being so nonchalant about her boyfriend writing a song for another girl. I had a lot to learn about the dating world. "What was the song about?"

"It was haunting and sad. About death and how it brings strangers together. He feels a real connection with you. He gets all artsy and deep like that. He's written dozens of songs for me."

I realized—feeling stupid—that April wasn't threatened by me because I could never be a threat. Hot, popular guys would never be romantically interested in someone like me.

River's voice came through the microphone. "Thanks for coming out tonight. We're the Rebel Junkies. I'm River Malone, and I'd like to dedicate this set to two captivating chicks in the audience. You know who you are." He looked back at his drummer, and after three clicks of the drumsticks, the band burst into its first song.

April yelled into my ear. "I'm glad you came! We're going to be lifelong friends. I just know it." She jumped up and started dancing—if you could call it that.

I smiled, watching her thrash around to the screechy music. I'd never expect someone like her to love such loud, awful noise. She obviously loved River very much.

People gathered in front of me, blocking my view of the stage, so I looked up at the stars. One shot across the sky then dissolved into darkness. For the first time since my nightmare night, I closed my eyes and made a wish.

I wish to find my true love, and for us to last forever.

WHEN SOULS COLLIDE

Maryah

Over the next month, April's prediction came true. River and I became friends—or the closest thing I could be with the most popular guy in school. He even walked me to classes sometimes. He'd slip me notes asking me what I thought about his new song lyrics. No matter how many times he acknowledged me, it continued to astonish me.

River shot me an irritated glance during music class. He thought our teacher hated him because he was doing what Mr. Milton could only dream about—sing in a band. River made lots of snide remarks like that, but I never took him seriously. No one could be as full of himself as River pretended to be.

Mr. Milton had been giving lessons on the "musical greats." He started a few weeks ago with music from the 1890s and early 1900s. My favorite week of lessons was the 1920s to the 1950s. Each song Mr. Milton played for the class made me think of my parents dancing around our living room.

Music during that time had so much dignity and soul. There wasn't a bunch of obscene language, or lyrics about murder, sex, or how cool it was to be a criminal. It wasn't that I'd been dropped off on the wrong planet—which is how I felt most of the time. I'd been born in the wrong era. If I had my way, I'd have been born in the 1920s. That way I could see the greats like Louie Armstrong and Ella Fitzgerald.

It was Friday, and our last lesson on the '90s. We'd studied many genres, but Mr. Milton seemed to actually get excited about the grunge scene: Pearl Jam, Stone Temple Pilots, and Nirvana.

Kurt Cobain was the main topic of discussion and people gave their opinions about his suicide. Since the attack, I'd considered ending my own life a few times, but I was too much of a coward to shoot myself or take a bunch of pills.

The bell rang. River approached my desk as I packed up my books. "Dope lesson, huh?"

"I guess so."

"Do you like Nirvana?"

"I like a few of their songs." I wasn't going to admit I was a geek and preferred music before the rock era.

"You seemed to be zoning out during class."

"Guess my mind was somewhere else." In my peripheral vision I saw Faith and Harmony looking in our direction.

"And where was that?" He sat on my desk.

"With April. I'm worried about her. Promise you'll tell her to call me next time you talk to her?"

"I told you. She barely returns *my* phone calls. But she's fine. Just busy playing nurse to her mom."

Faith interrupted us. "Maryah, let's go! Louise and Anthony want to leave right away."

"Right." I stood up and rolled my eyes. "I have to go."

He straightened, looking more alert. "Do you want to hang out this weekend? There's a big party Saturday night."

River was asking *me* to go to a party with him? Talking to me at school was one thing, but being seen with me in public? "I, um—I would, but we're going to this thing in New Mexico."

"You're skipping town." He smiled his Cheshire cat grin. "I'm jealous."

Faith whined from the doorway. "Come on, Maryah!"

I shrugged my backpack over my shoulder. "Please tell April to call me."

"Enjoy New Mexico. Don't miss me too much."

I followed Faith as she prattled on about how much fun this weekend would be. We were taking a road trip to Albuquerque for a Balloon Fiesta to celebrate Nathan's birthday. I'd never seen a hot air balloon in real life, so I was kind of looking forward to it.

Not to mention, I'd finally meet the renowned Nathan.

∞

Everyone was ready to go when we arrived at the house.

Anthony had already loaded my bag into the trunk. Carson had changed clothes and packed his car. It felt like River and I had only talked for a few minutes, but Carson grumbled something about me taking forever as I passed him on the porch.

"Let's get this train out of the station!" Anthony shouted from the driveway.

Louise explained that Helen's company sponsored a balloon in the event, and she and Edgar were supposed to be home in time to go with us, but they got delayed in England. Anthony's Mustang led the parade of cars, followed by Shiloh's boxy FJ Cruiser, containing him, Faith, Harmony, and Dakota.

Carson insisted on illegally driving his new car. How Louise and Anthony were okay with it baffled me. Everyone else refused to ride with him, so I had to choose between riding with Mr. McSnotty, getting windburn from riding in the convertible, or being smashed in a backseat for hours with Dakota and Harmony. Reluctantly, I chose physical comfort over mental ease.

The first hour of the ride, Carson and I didn't talk. Then, during the best part of a great song, he turned down the radio and pushed his white mirrored sunglasses to the top of his head. "Can I ask you something?"

Oh boy. "Sure."

"Do you like River Malone?"

I peered at him under my hat. What an out-of-nowhere question. "Why does it matter?"

"He's cocky, and an attention whore." Yet another wrongly accused victim on Carson's growing list. "I've seen you two walking around school together. He's obviously interested in you. I didn't think you'd go for that type of guy, but lately you look kind of...happy, when I see you with him."

No way was River interested in me. Not only was he way out of my league, but he loved April and had been pretty good about not flirting with other girls. "We're just friends. We relate to each other."

"Relate how?"

"Music. Friends. He lost his father at a young age and I...lost everyone."

"You didn't lose everyone. Lots of people here love you."

I couldn't believe it. Carson said something nice to me. "Thanks for saying that, but don't worry. River's not interested in me. Plus, I'm friends with his girlfriend."

"How come you never had a boyfriend in Maryland?"

"I don't know, guess I never—wait, how do you know I didn't have a boyfriend?"

He fiddled with his rearview mirror. "Lucky guess."

I refused to let Carson make me feel inferior again. "I made the choice not to date. Why waste my time with the wrong person? I like the idea of waiting for that one person meant for only me—no matter how long it takes to find him."

The car slowed. Carson gaped at me as the engine grew quieter, then he fixed his eyes on the road and accelerated again. The shock of me sticking up for myself must have temporarily incapacitated him.

He reclined in his seat. "I guess we're opposites. I don't date because I know there's no *one* person meant for me."

"You don't know that. My mother says everyone has a soul mate."

"If she believed that then why—" He paused. "Never mind."

Sadness body slammed me against my seat. I realized something for the first time. My mother would never see me fall in love, never attend my wedding, and never know her grandchildren. "Say it. If my mom believed that, then what?"

I thought I saw warmth flicker in his eyes before he covered them with his sunglasses. "Then she'd agree that River isn't right for you, and to be on the lookout for your soul mate. I've heard they're never far away."

My stomach felt queasy. My mother used to tell me the mean boys on the playground only teased me or said cruel things because they liked me. Was Carson's crappy attitude his twisted way of flirting? I didn't know what to say, so I grunted and watched the desert zip past us for the rest of the ride.

∞

By the time we arrived at our hotel, the sun had disappeared and the temperature dropped. I put on my sweater before climbing out of the car. Shiloh had already parked his truck and Faith was bouncing around the parking lot.

"How exciting is this?" She clapped her hands together like a toy monkey with cymbals.

Carson, Shiloh, and Dakota grabbed bags from the truck. Harmony didn't bother waiting for anyone. The back of her black-and-purple head disappeared through the hotel entrance.

Louise and Anthony looked even happier than usual. I felt so out of place. This was an important family event, and I didn't want to be a party pooper. I faked a smile. "Woo-hoo, my first trip to Albuquerque. I'm stoked."

Faith's smile fizzled, and she reached for my hand. "Come on, ya big liar, let's go see if Nathan's here yet. Shiloh, you guys can handle our bags, right?" She didn't wait for an answer.

We entered the lobby and found Harmony sitting in a chair shuffling several keycards. "Sorry to kill your buzz, but he hasn't checked in yet."

Faith stomped her foot. "Dang it!"

"Don't worry. He'll be here soon." Louise patted Faith's back. "Let's get settled into our rooms. My head is vibrating from listening to that engine for the past five hours."

I knew how she felt. Mustangs were loud, and my head was rattling with a headache too. Then again, I always had headaches, but complaining never helped.

Faith, Harmony, and I were sharing a room. Louise and Anthony took the one next door to us. Carson, Shiloh, and Dakota claimed the room across the hall. The illustrious Nathan would be staying in the guys' room. I had to admit I wanted to see what all the fuss was about. I'd heard about Nathan every day since I arrived in Sedona. It was time to put a face with the name.

Faith and Louise wanted to wait for Nathan before going to dinner, but it was getting late and Anthony and the guys were starving, so we made our way to the hotel restaurant. Faith checked her phone about a hundred times during the meal, hoping to get an update from Nathan about his arrival time. But no calls or messages ever came, and he didn't reply to the ones she sent him.

"Where is he?" Faith whined.

"Give the guy a break," Carson chimed in from the end of the table. "It's hard for him."

"I wouldn't blame him if he didn't show at all," Harmony snorted beside me. I was majorly disappointed when she chose the seat next to mine. "He might take a rain check given the circumstances."

Trying to keep up with everyone's encrypted conversations was draining. We had to get up early in the morning, and I had tried to decipher enough for one night. The waiter brought the bill, and I asked where the restrooms were then excused myself.

I splashed water on my face, unsuccessfully trying to wash away my headache and tiredness. I headed back to the restaurant, determined to get our room key so I could go to bed, but everyone had gathered in the hotel lobby. They all turned to look at me at the exact same moment—all except one.

I froze dead in my tracks. Everybody else disappeared into the background.

All I saw was *him*.

He was looking down at his phone. Black sporty sunglasses covered his eyes, but I knew without question, it was him. His short dark hair, the sharp angle of his jaw, his flawless skin, even the way he dressed. My movie-star angel man. Was I asleep? Or was I so obsessed with him that I didn't need to be asleep to see him? Maybe he really was the angel of death and he had come to finish his job.

Faith stepped out of the fuzzy cloud of figures surrounding him. She came into focus and took my hand into hers. "Maryah, it's time you met Nathan."

My feet wouldn't move. They were cemented to the floor. There couldn't have been more than six feet between us, but he felt so far away. He raised his head and stepped toward me.

I couldn't say anything. I just stood there, paralyzed, as he made his way over to me. The dinging of the elevators, the murmurs of hotel guests, they all faded away until only he and I existed.

He slid his phone into the pocket of his jeans then stopped in front of me.

His chest rose, expanding wider, then his warm breath grazed my forehead and I fought the urge to touch him. I slowly raised my chin. He seemed so tall now that he was close to me, close enough that I could see my ghostly reflection in the lenses of his sunglasses. He took them off and locked his emerald green eyes with mine. The same perfect, breathtaking, jewel-like eyes that had been haunting my dreams were now very real. My knees weakened. My heart stopped beating.

"Hello, Maryah. I am Nathaniel."

They were the only five words he uttered, but that's all it took. My ears buzzed louder than ever. Pain radiated from the back of my head into my eyes. Faith gasped beside me, and then I passed out.

PIECING IT TOGETHER

NATHANIEL

"Nathan!" Harmony bellowed, clenching the dashboard. "How about demonstrating some self-control?"

It was a childish thing to do, but I squealed my tires as I drove out of the hotel parking lot. "Please put on your seatbelt."

Harmony was used to my adrenaline-fueled actions. She joined me in almost every extreme sport I participated in regardless of the danger, so the speed of my Mustang Cobra hardly alarmed her.

"Well, *that* was unexpected." She relaxed into her seat.

"You find it comical that she fainted?" My engine roared as I merged onto the highway at a speed well above the legal limit.

"Come on, Nate. The girl has been walking around like a shattered shell of a human. The first real spark of light she showed was when she saw you. You revealed your eyes to her and she collapsed from the overwhelming love she felt. Comical—no, entertaining—yes, and it takes a lot to entertain me these days."

"We don't know for certain what caused her to faint."

"Faith said she felt *love*, Nate—love *and* recognition. What if she does remember?"

"She doesn't. You've seen her eyes. They are devoid of all imprints and indicators. Not one shred of who she used to be shines through."

"We've been wrong before. What if there's an exception to this rule too?"

With great care and empathy I chose my next words. "Harmony, you and I share a similar pain, but Gregory did not erase. I know how desperately you want to find him, but," I placed my hand on top of hers, "Maryah does not, nor will she ever, have the ability to help you. It's impossible."

For a moment Harmony fell silent then she turned to face me. "For once in your lives, stop clinging to the old. Most ancient rules have been broken, or at least bent. Besides, I thought you were coming here to push the envelope. What happened to that plan?"

My stomach lurched like it had when Marcus first told me the story. Marcus knew of an Element who erased in the eighteenth century, but was reunited with his kindrily. "The circumstances were different, and his memories and ability never returned."

"But he chose to retain after every lifetime since his erasure. And he's still with his soul mate, right?"

I nodded.

"Can you imagine? Existing without your ability? Knowing what you once had, and watching everyone around you have exceptional gifts? How miserable."

I shot her a sideways glare, waiting for her to realize that type of existence is precisely the only kind Maryah would ever live, but Harmony was focused on the star-filled sky.

"Still," she said. "If we could ease Maryah into understanding our way of life then you two might have a fresh start."

I didn't want to start over, but it seemed the only way we could be together again.

"Of all people," Harmony grunted. "I can't believe someone outside of our kindrily convinced you to face Maryah. I also can't believe you've found no trace of Dedrick." Her pierced brow rose as she leaned across my armrest. "You *are* telling me the truth about not finding out anything, right?"

My thoughts sped by as fast as the yellow lines of the road. No trace of Dedrick existed anywhere in Liverpool, but I had discovered something about the Nefariouns. Something I didn't want to accept as truth. Something so disheartening that I couldn't tell anyone until it was confirmed. And even then, I'd need time to sort out a complicated plan.

"Nate?" Harmony snapped her fingers. "Earth to Nathan."

"Sorry. I can't get the look on Maryah's face out of my mind." It wasn't a lie, and it served its purpose of changing the subject. "Even though it's impossible, it did seem like she knew me."

"If Faith is right, if she did recognize you, then maybe—and if you say it's impossible again, I swear, I'll punch you—she might have retained some things. Even a broken clock shows the correct time twice a day."

Did Faith assess the situation correctly? Had Maryah felt love and recognition? Faith was rarely wrong in her analysis, yet how could she be correct? Maryah had been staying at the house for over a month and hadn't uttered a word about any memories.

"There has to be a realistic explanation. Even Marcus agreed, retaining any memories would be imposs—"

Harmony clobbered me in the shoulder. "You of all people should know that anything is possible!" She folded her arms over her chest. "Gregory should've been there. He'd tell us whether or not she remembered."

My soul ached at her words. We were approaching the two-decade mark since her soul mate had been taken by the Nefariouns. If I could trade places with Gregory so he and Harmony could be together again, I'd do so without hesitation. I'd give my own life if it spared Harmony from the pain she suffered.

She gazed out the passenger window again. Her eyes fixed upon Gregory's star. "Do you think he's okay?"

"Gregory's star still burns. He *is* out there and we *will* find him."

"Yes, but wherever he is, do you think he's safe?"

"Neither you nor I know the answer to that, but as always, time will tell."

"And time will heal," she vowed firmly.

I pulled to the side of the road. "As you can imagine, the incident at the hotel was difficult for me. I'm asking you to grant me time to myself."

"Louise will be upset if she finds out I left you alone."

"I'll speak with Louise and explain that I made a reasonable request, and you sympathetically respected it."

"Are you sure you want to be alone?"

"Place yourself in my situation. What if it had been Gregory standing in that hotel lobby? Wouldn't you want—wouldn't you *need* time to yourself?"

"No. I would've never left his side—passed out or awake, memories or no memories. I would've stayed just as you should've stayed." Harmony was the only soul I knew who could relate to my feelings.

"Forgive me. It's insensitive of me to keep mentioning Gregory, but you and I are different."

"Different, but so similar."

I nodded. Perhaps I should have stayed at the hotel and waited for Maryah to wake up, but running away had become my defense mechanism. "You're welcome to take my car back to the hotel. I'll be gone for a while."

She held out her hand.

I placed my keys in her open palm then grabbed my boots and snowboard from the trunk. "Thank you for understanding. I'll find you in the morning before the ascension. Please make sure Maryah gets sleep and eats something before seeing me tomorrow. I didn't enjoy watching her crumble to the floor, and I don't wish to see a repeat performance."

Harmony chuckled. "Every entertainer deserves an encore."

"Good night, Harmony." I closed my eyes, imagining the summit marker at the top of the peak and recalled the exact magnetic frequency of my desired location. Opening every cell in my body, I attached my energy to a lunar flare and prepared to dissolve into the wave.

"Night, Nate. You know where I am if—"

I was standing atop the mountain before she finished her sentence.

At just over fourteen-thousand feet, Mount Massive lived up to its name. I threw my board down and prepared to ride the slopes until the shock of interacting with Maryah wore off. Which meant I was in for a long night.

∞

Our hotel bathroom served as an inconspicuous place for my return. Much to my relief, it was empty when I traversed, so I stripped out of my snow-covered clothes and took a quick shower.

I glanced at my phone: twelve unread text messages, three missed calls from Faith, and one from Louise. I tossed my phone into my knapsack, refusing to address the situation until later— much later.

I pushed open the bathroom door and discovered Shiloh still awake, sitting in the side chair of our room, working on choreography notes.

"Shiloh." I nodded, greeting him quietly.

"Hey, Nate."

I gathered a dry shirt and jeans while Dakota and Carson slept. A conversation about the incident with Maryah was inevitable, but I didn't want to involve them. I finished getting dressed and turned to Shiloh.

"Shall we step outside?"

He pulled a wool cap over his braids and stood. "As you wish."

Our first-floor room allowed us to exit through the patio door. We walked through the dark with no path to follow, but Shiloh's gift of inherent night vision allowed him to guide us. I paused at a bench on the outskirts of the parking lot.

Shiloh looked back at me. "Nah, no way, just because *you* enjoy exposing yourself to extreme activities and temperatures doesn't mean I have to suffer with you. We're sitting in the truck where I can crank up the heat."

I followed him, and for several minutes we sat in silence while the engine ran. He rubbed his hands together in front of the heating vents like they were a fireplace. I shot him an amused grin.

He shrugged. "Call it evolution, or call it being spoiled. I like my creature comforts."

"Yes, you have always embraced the latest human advancements."

"Dang skippy!" Shiloh danced in his seat then moments later his energy and smile dimmed. "So what's up, Natty Bro?"

I glanced at the sky. "Stars, the moon, a few planets—"

"Don't be cheeky. The quicker you give me info, the quicker we can be done with this and catch some Zs. If you would've answered your phone when Faith called, I could be chillin' with the bed bugs right now." Shiloh always embodied each of his personas with ease. I enjoyed having him and Faith so close this go-round.

"Don't let me keep you." I gestured at the heat vents which were making Shiloh's truck feel like an oven. "You are free to chill, or roast, with the bed bugs whenever you desire." He set the control to a lower flow. "I'm sorry you've had to wait up for me. What would you like to know?"

"What would *you* like to know?"

I paused, considering my answer. "Is she okay?"

"Do you mean did she wake up from her fainting spell? No, she's in a magically induced sleep." He added a dramatic flair to each word. "Only a kiss from her true love can break the spell."

I played along. "No one warned her not to eat the apple?"

Shiloh erupted with laughter. "Nah, we assumed she *remembered* it was poisonous."

"You know what they say about assuming."

"Yes, I do, and yes, you are an ass. Seriously man, why'd you run off like that?"

My grin waned. "I couldn't bear it. She's so different. So empty."

"But it's still her. She's just missing most of what made her the shining light we remember."

I sighed at the memory of Maryah's hollow eyes. "I hope you're spared from ever enduring such torture."

"I couldn't do it. I don't know how you've made it this long. I give you props." He extended his fist to meet mine—one of his latest interpretations of a handshake. "But don't you want to know what happened?"

"I figured it highly probable someone would tell me."

"She woke up a few minutes after you left, all disoriented. Faith said she felt confusion at first, then embarrassment, and rightfully so." Shiloh snickered. "Then it got weird. Louise asked her if she was okay and Maryah looked around the lobby. Faith felt panic. Maryah asked where Harmony went, and Louise told her she left with you. Maryah mumbled something under her breath. Faith thought it sounded like 'he was real.' Then Maryah's excitement turned into confusion again. Is any of this making sense to you?"

"No."

"Cool. Me neither. On we go. Faith and I helped Maryah to her room. Throughout the walk, Faith said she felt waves of excitement, confusion, and joy—in no particular order. When we got her to the room, we asked her why she fainted. Louise and Anthony were there too. Maryah kept looking at us all nervously. She concocted some excuse about eating bad food at dinner."

"Perhaps that's the truth."

"Nah, Prince Charming, nobody had poisoned apples for dinner." He shook his head. "That's the kicker. As soon as Maryah said it was food, Faith felt *guilt*—guilt, Nathan!" Shiloh bounced up and down like he made the game-winning play of an important football match.

"Guilt," I repeated flatly. "I don't follow."

"I know, neither did I until Faith broke it down for me. Maryah felt guilt when she blamed it on food. She felt guilty because she was lying. She's hiding something."

"What would she possibly be hiding?"

"That part we don't know. Faith thinks Maryah has seen you before. She swears by her original assessment of love and recognition right before Sleeping Beauty passed out. Wait, or was it Snow White who did the apple thing? Not important. Wherever she saw you, she felt uncomfortable discussing it with anyone. She blamed her passing out episode on food. And what a terrible excuse. At least say lack of sleep or something more believable."

Shiloh kept referencing it, yet he didn't know his jokes could be the answer. My eyes gave my revelation away.

"What?" Shiloh asked. "One of those cartoon light bulbs just appeared above your head."

"It's impossible."

"What's impossible?"

"Sleeping Beauty, lack of sleep." I looked at Shiloh with wide eyes. At first he showed no signs of understanding, then his jaw dropped, and his forehead lifted.

"She couldn't possibly."

"I know, but what if?" I could hardly think the words, much less believe them. "What if, by some obscure miracle, she still has her gift?"

"You think she's still able to astral travel?"

"It would explain why she hasn't said anything about seeing me the night of the attack, or during the fire." I thought back to our first few lives, when we were learning how to use our abilities. For decades she believed she had to be asleep to travel. "She may have seen me, but assumed she was dreaming or hallucinating. There have been several occasions since she arrived in Sedona—always at night—when I felt someone watching me."

Shiloh tugged at his braids. "Why haven't you said anything?"

"It never occurred to me. As we've both stated, it's impossible, or so we thought. What if she retained her ability; or it's resurfacing?" The play by play of the evening led me to wonder if it could—by some miracle—be true.

"For the love of peanut butter!" Shiloh exclaimed. I squinted at him with bewilderment. "It's a new Faithism—long story— some other time."

I nodded. "It would explain the recognition."

Shiloh inhaled through his teeth. "I feel like we're jumping the gun. It doesn't seem likely. What are the other explanations?"

"Surely you and Faith, along with the others, have been pondering that question all evening. You tell me, what other explanations have you come up with?"

Shiloh pursed his lips. "None." He glanced around the truck. "Hey, do you think…?"

"She's not here now. I would have sensed it."

"Nate, this is crazy. What if it's true? What if—" Shiloh's eyes locked on the sky. "Harmony."

"I've already thought what it could mean." Only I didn't want to think of where we might find Gregory even if Maryah could track him.

Shiloh crossed his hands in front of himself like an umpire calling a player safe. "Nah, that's where it doesn't add up. Maryah would have to *know* you to watch you. She'd have to *remember* you to track you. That's not possible. Is it?"

I stared at him, processing his words. He was right. She'd need to picture me clearly in her mind, not my face—that was of no importance—but she'd have to envision my eyes in great detail—the way only Elements can see each other. I raised my defeated glance to meet Shiloh's. "You're right. She wouldn't be able to see the intricacies of our eyes anymore. Not after an erasure."

"Damn, I didn't want to be right." We both sat in silence, watching the beautiful possibility vanish. Maryah's reaction to me would remain a mystery.

"Come, Shiloh." I reached for my door handle. "You're late for your engagement with the bed bugs."

"Wait! What about Maryah? You're going to see her in a few hours. What do we do now?"

I tried to sound confident. "We assume it really was bad food, and we carry on as planned."

"I liked the miracle scenario better."

I sighed. "Me, too."

∞

I left the hotel before five a.m. and made my way to the Dawn Patrol ceremony.

Only a few hot air balloons participated in Dawn Patrol, and we were honored that ours was one of them. The balloons' lighting systems allowed us to fly through the dark, illuminating the sky until sunrise. Our crew consisted of six members, but only three would ride in the basket during the choreographed show flight.

Everything went perfectly and we landed just before seven. I tried to stay distracted by assisting the other crew members with preparations for the Mass Ascension launch. The total number of participating balloons neared seven hundred—a remarkable sight to behold. It wouldn't be long before the kindrily made their way to our landing site to watch the event.

Surely, Maryah would be with them.

SILVER LININGS

Maryah

I finished almost-calling Krista for the fifth time and put away my phone with a sigh. If I would have told her about my dreams *before* I met Nathan, she might believe all this madness. But what could I possibly say now? *Hey Kris, check this out. I saw this gorgeous guy I thought was my angel of death the night I almost died, and again during the fire. He keeps popping up in my dreams, and this weekend I found out he's Louise's son, Nathan.*

How do you spell mentally unstable? M-A-R-Y-A-H.

How could the person I'd been dreaming about be real? Much less, be the famous Nathan, whom everyone put on a pedestal? Did my head injury make me psychic?

We were leaving for the Balloon Fiesta any minute. Would Nathan make fun of me for passing out? Or would he think I was a spaz and never talk to me again? For weeks I believed he was a gorgeous angel with divine powers watching over me, or trying to reunite me with my family. It was absurd, but I'd developed a glorified crush on him. How could I go from *that* to trying to make normal conversation? His first impression of me was my embarrassing fainting spell.

Faith bounded through the hotel doors. "You ready?"

I gripped the bench I was sitting on. "I think I'll hang out here."

"Noooo! Watching hundreds of hot air balloons launch into the sky is spectacular. You can't miss it."

"I'm still not feeling well."

"Is this because you passed out? Are you embarrassed to see Nathan?"

"It was humiliating."

She sat beside me. "Look at it this way, nothing you do today could be more embarrassing than falling on top of him."

I bolted upright. "Falling on top of him? I fell on him?"

She gave a sympathetic giggle. "More like you fell forward, and he caught you."

"Oh my god. Even more humiliating."

"It was cute. He'll never forget you, that's for sure. So there's a silver lining you can cling to."

My fingers were bleeding from grasping onto life's silver linings. They felt more like silver bullets aimed directly at me.

Anthony, Louise, and the rest of the gang walked out of the hotel toward the parking lot. Faith yanked me up off the bench. "Time to go witness some magic."

∞

I could barely see Nathan when we approached. I stayed behind Carson, and his oversized sweatshirt blocked my view.

"Our balloon looked beautiful, Nathan!" Louise exclaimed.

"Helen will be proud," Anthony complimented.

"Nice flight," Carson added before walking away to talk to one of the crew members.

Nathan's eyes locked with mine. I'd never felt so exposed, yet I couldn't look away from him. Mikey's cap had gone missing last night so it quadrupled how vulnerable I felt. I prayed Nathan didn't notice the shorter section of my hair.

"Good morning, Maryah. How are you?" he asked.

"Fine, thanks." I wasn't fine. I was still in shock that my movie-star angel man was a real live human being. To top it off, he was the son of my godmother. He was talking to me, and looking more amazing than ever. I wasn't even close to fine. I was freaking out. "Sorry about last night. I think I caught a bug or something."

"No apology necessary. I hope you're feeling better."

I wrapped my sweater around me. I wanted to thank him for catching me when I fainted, but I didn't want to remind him what a mess I was.

Faith broke the tension by punching his shoulder. She danced around, modeling her bright attire. "Notice I match the balloon?"

"Yes, so you do." He returned her look of amusement.

Her clothes coordinated with the balloon's shades of red, yellow, and orange. "We watched the Dawn Patrol from the hotel. Your balloon looked extra majestic against the sunrise."

Nathan put on his sunglasses. "All compliments should be addressed to Jesse and Gina. They did all the work."

A pretty brunette strutted up behind Nathan and squeezed his shoulders. "It's not work when your crew chief makes it so fun."

She wasn't the girl I'd seen in the picture on his nightstand, but she sure was touchy feely with him.

"Did you enjoy the show?" Nathan asked me.

Dakota and Harmony had been standing on either side of me, but as if on cue they both stepped away. My cheeks warmed as I stammered a reply. "Yes—um—it was amazing."

"This is Maryah's first time seeing hot air balloons," Faith said.

"Is that so?" Nathan stepped closer to me.

"I've seen them on TV before, but never in person."

"Colorful, isn't it?"

"Yes, it is." My voice trailed off as I looked around at all the balloons. "I like the two kissing bumble bees."

"Joey and Lilly Little Bee. They hold hands and dance through the skies." Being so close to him was electrifying. My fingers and toes tingled.

"What's the name of your balloon?"

"That depends who you ask. I fancied the name Aftermath, but Helen wouldn't allow it. So its official title is Eternal Flame." He didn't have an accent, but I had to ask.

"Have you ever lived in England?"

For a second he looked shocked, but then he kind of laughed. "Not in this lifetime, no. Why do you ask?"

"You said you 'fancied the name.' My father was from England, and he said that a lot. You don't talk like a normal American teenager."

He seemed at a loss for words. I nervously back pedaled. "Aftermath sounds kind of dreary. Eternal Flame is much better."

"Yes, the Aftermath leaves a qualm of distaste for most people I know." His words had angry bite. Great, I probably insulted him. First, I criticize the way he speaks then I tell him his taste in names sucks. Would I ever stop alienating this guy?

Everyone else was chatting with each other. Their sunglasses hid their gazes, but I sensed them all watching us. Most likely they were waiting to see if I'd pass out again.

I jumped when Nathan pushed my hair away from my face.

"I'm sorry," he said. "I didn't mean to startle you."

Fire burned in my cheeks. I mumbled something resembling "it's okay."

Gina glared at me like we were kids on a playground and I had just stolen her swing. "Nathan, everything is taken care of. You ready to eat?"

He didn't take his eyes off of me. "Where are my manners? Gina, this is Maryah. Maryah, allow me to introduce Gina, my *friend*, and fellow crew member."

"Nice to meet you." I offered a handshake.

She stuck her hands in her back pockets. "Hi."

What a snob. Nathan glared at her then returned his attention to me. "Have you had breakfast?"

Gina let out a frustrated sigh. Part of me wanted to say no just to annoy her, but I chickened out. "We ate before the balloon launch."

She gloated. "Looks like it's just the two of us! We better get going."

"I am famished, and we have a full schedule today." Nathan leaned in close enough to make me tremble. He smelled like a mixture of mountain air, honey, and pears. The gods must have bottled up nectar from heaven and sent it to Earth for Nathan to wear. "I look forward to seeing you at dinner."

"Sure." I nodded skittishly, but didn't back away from him. The tingling had spread to every inch of my skin. I'd never felt anything like it, and I didn't want it to end.

"Enjoy the rest of your day." He bowed, grinning one last time. His smile put the glow of the sun to shame. As he walked off with Gina, he glanced at me over his shoulder then stopped. "Jesse! Will you be joining us for breakfast?"

"Yeah! I'm starving!" Jesse jogged over to them. Gina's body language oozed disappointment.

Good, I thought. What kind of girl throws herself at someone who has a girlfriend? But a pang of guilt filled my chest. Just standing close to Nathan left me all warmer than toast. If he made every girl feel that way then I couldn't blame Gina for flirting with him.

WISHING ENDLESSLY

NATHANIEL

When everyone finished singing Happy Birthday, I glanced to my right where Maryah sat. She had participated, but seemed distracted.

"Thank you." I closed my eyes, making a wish as I blew out the candles.

Faith knowingly smiled at me from a few seats down. I'd been wishing for the same miracle since I found out I had lost Maryah.

"It's so great to be spending time with you, Nathan! We miss you." Faith's sweet sentiments always brought a smile to my face.

Louise sliced and handed out cake as the table stirred with conversation, but the only voice I longed to hear was—

"Will Mary be here this weekend?" Maryah asked. The others didn't hear her question. If they had, shock would have silenced them.

"*Mary?*" I drew out the name, feeling its recent foreignness on my tongue.

"Your girlfriend."

Her conversation with Carson flooded back to me. "Right. Carson mentioned you saw her photograph."

Her eyes widened. "I wasn't snooping through your room or anything. Carson asked me to help him find a DVD."

"No one suspects you of being a snoop." Little did she know that I—and everything I possessed—was hers for the taking.

She probed her cake with her fork. "You must miss her."

"More than words can say." I looked at my own plate, trying to make sense of the fact that we were having this conversation. "Yet as much as I loved her, she chose to leave me."

"What?" Maryah gasped. "She broke up with you?"

I tilted my head, raising my eyes to meet hers. "That's one way to summarize what transpired between us."

"Are you okay?"

The genuineness of her concern allayed my pain. "Let's just say I am enduring the pain, in hopes that someday...I may find love again."

She nodded like she understood, but she couldn't begin to grasp the gravity of my words.

"Nathan, what time do you have to leave us?" Louise asked.

I cleared my throat. "I planned on attending this evening's events with you."

Maryah sat up straight.

"Yay!" Faith cheered, throwing her arms over her head. "*Now* it's a party!"

Almost everyone seemed pleased, except Maryah. She continued to absentmindedly push her cake around her plate. She was where she belonged, by my side, but not in the way I wanted and needed.

Sitting at the head of a table made me uncomfortable. I looked at Anthony who sat quiet but confident at the opposite end. He disfavored rectangular tables as well. We all did. Regardless of the order we were initiated into our kindrily, no ruler or chief sat in higher regard than the rest of us. Even Carson, young and inexperienced as he was, we considered an equal.

As painful as this life had been without my soul mate, it had also been an amazing bonding experience for our kindrily. Our union was never stronger throughout our existence. In the past, small groups of us lived near each other and we'd gather for special events. Our get-togethers became more frequent as technology and transportation evolved, but this life was exceptional. Never before had every member of our kindrily lived in America.

It had been Mary's plan. In our last life, she had an overwhelming worry that something tragic would happen. She made everyone agree that if it did, we would all gather in Sedona. She referred to it as her Hail Mary play. And here we all were, hailing Maryah.

"The Night Glow will be starting soon," Louise said. "Should we freshen up and head over to the park?"

"Sounds good." Anthony rose from his seat. "Everyone ready?"

We designated a time to gather before driving to the park then we dispersed to our rooms. Maryah's hair bounced against her shoulders as she walked down the hallway. I relished watching her every move, until she disappeared into her room.

"Big step for you my man!" Shiloh sang, closing our door behind him.

"Hardly a big step. I only want to see her reaction to the lights in the sky." I tried to sound nonchalant, but Shiloh continued grinning.

He pushed Carson toward me. "That's your cue."

"I told you they don't work," Carson mumbled to Shiloh.

"Maybe not for you," Shiloh argued. "You're a newbie, but they might work for Nate."

I knew they were referring to the stargazing glasses Carson had been creating, but I let the two of them squabble.

"I may be a newbie," Carson said, "but I'm the only Scion in this kindrily."

Dakota rolled his eyes. "Don't get cocky, Car."

"Stay out of it, epic-wannabe. You're just jealous that I have three abilities and you have none." He shoved Dakota.

Dakota stumbled backward onto the bed, but recovered quickly and didn't back down. "I can't argue with your speed and strength, but you couldn't even make those glasses work. Maybe you aren't as smart as you think."

Shiloh intervened. "Cool it, you two. Just give Nathan the glasses so he can try them."

Carson rifled through his suitcase and reluctantly handed me a heavy contraption that looked like a blend of glasses and binoculars. The lime green lenses glinted as if a light shone behind them.

"Let's go outside and give them a test run," Shiloh insisted.

Carson's face spoke volumes. He didn't believe they would work. I wanted to tell him I never expected him to successfully create miracle glasses. I never believed in Shiloh's impossible theory.

I set the apparatus on the desk. "We'll test it later. Right now, we have to meet the others."

Shiloh's eager grin disappeared, but Carson nodded, looking relieved.

I was relieved too. I wanted one more night of staring at the sky and believing—no matter how ridiculous—that somewhere,

Maryah's star might exist, and that it, and our love, was waiting to be rekindled.

∞

We all gathered on the launch field, watching balloons light up the sky.

Maryah used to have the most expressive face. One of my favorite pastimes was watching her delicate features twist and dance as thoughts ran through her mind. Tonight, her expressions gave nothing away, so I focused on her eyes. They were devoid of all light—like gazing upon the Black Hole. They used to sparkle like emeralds. My emeralds, my treasure, *then, now and eternally.*

What I wouldn't give to hear her speak those words again.

The crowd whooped and whistled as more balloons took to the sky. Faith excitedly pinched Maryah's hip. The "All Burns" tradition began. Every burner ignited as orbs of color floated across the sky.

Finally, Maryah's eyes twinkled.

For a few sacred moments, joy flooded through her. I couldn't look away. Even as an almost empty shell of a being, she was stunning. She lowered her chin and turned toward me. Alas, she smiled. Not a false or uncomfortable smile like she exhibited throughout the day, but a genuine smile. I took my place by her side.

"It's breathtaking," she whispered.

The breeze blew strands of hair across her face. I resisted the urge to push them away. "Indeed, it is."

"You get to see this every year?"

"Almost every year since the festival began." I felt safe saying it. She had no knowledge of the length of the festival's history, or that she'd been here before.

We stood together, watching hundreds of glowing balloons. It felt as if Maryah and I were the only two souls on Earth. At last, I admired the sky with the one soul whose beauty easily surpassed the heavens we looked upon.

I wanted to stay with her in that moment forever, but the first loud booms of fireworks erupted. It startled her, but she smiled when the explosion of color burst through the darkness.

"All this fuss for you and your birthday?" Maryah teased through chattering teeth.

I removed my jacket and wrapped it around her. "I assure you, all of this is about much more than me."

WAKE-UP CALL

Maryah

"Maryah, wake up," he whispered. "Maryah." I slowly opened my eyes. My body jerked, startled by the sight of Nathan in my hotel room leaning over me in the dark. "Nathan?"

"Shh, I'm trying not to wake Faith and Harmony." Glancing at the clock, I saw it wasn't even 5am yet. "I'd like to request your company on a clandestine journey before the others awaken."

"Could you speak more mainstream? I have no idea what you said."

"Would you like a behind-the-scenes tour of the festival?"

I had to be dreaming again. Why in the world would Nathan want me to go anywhere with him? Especially at five in the morning. I pinched my wrist, and Nathan lifted his eyebrows. I shrugged. "Thought I might still be asleep."

"Do you always talk in your sleep?" he asked with that dizzying angelic smile.

"Sometimes." Faith and Harmony were still sleeping—or pretending to be. We weren't exactly quiet, and Faith wore a close-lipped grin.

"Take a few moments to collect yourself. I'll wait for you in the hallway. Bring a coat. It's chilly out." He got up and left while I lay there dumfounded. I hadn't agreed to go anywhere with him. Up at five a.m. on vacation—with Nathan: pure insanity.

After changing, and finding my coat, I quietly left our room. Nathan was leaning against the wall in the hallway.

"It's five in the morning!" I said in a hushed voice.

"Sorry. I don't sleep much, and this is my favorite time of the day. Tranquility and stillness hasn't been lost due to the busyness of the world yet. Shall we go?"

How could I argue with tranquility? How could I argue about anything when he looked at me so tenderly with his heart-stopping green eyes? "Fine."

Neither of us said another word until Nathan paused at the lobby doors. "May I assist you with your coat?"

"I'm okay, but thanks."

He held open the door, and I stepped outside. The cold hit me like a bucket of ice water. I gasped and zipped up my jacket to my chin.

"It's freezing out here!"

"I'm sorry, but such is the desert at night. It will get warmer when the sun rises."

He put his hand on the small of my back. Even through my coat his touch sent a delicious shiver through me. I subtly leaned backward, wanting to feel more of him against me—even if it was just his arm. The shoulder of his jacket brushed my ear and I had to force myself to keep from whipping around and throwing my arms around him. How did I become so boy crazy?

A red Mustang with black racing stripes was parked nearby. The engine was running, and when Nathan opened the door for me, a wave of heat poured out. I practically dove into the passenger seat.

"There's cocoa, tea, cider, or coffee for you." He nodded to four steaming cups on the dashboard then shut my door.

I stared at them, amazed someone could be so thoughtful. Thoughtful of me.

He climbed into his seat, leaned over, and held the drink holder in front of me.

"Which one is the hot chocolate?" I asked.

He handed me the largest cup. "Some things never change."

"What?"

"Nothing." He threw away the remaining drinks in a nearby trash can.

He got back in, and his heavenly scent filled the car. Between him and my hot chocolate, I was almost drooling. "You didn't want any?"

"No, but now I know which you prefer, so I won't bother with the other choices in the future."

The future. Did he plan on hanging out with me again? "That was really nice. Thank you."

"It was my pleasure."

As he drove, I glanced around his trashless, spotless interior. "Where are we going?"

"It's a surprise." He pushed a button and Ella Fitzgerald started singing, *Someone to Watch Over Me*.

"Oh my god, I love Ella!"

His expression bordered on smugness. "You seem like the type who appreciates great music."

"Most people our age have never heard of her."

"Yes well, maybe you and I are old souls."

I stared at him with astonishment. "My cousin says the same thing."

"She must be perceptive."

"She is. I miss her." I mouthed the words to Ella's song in between sips of my drink. *Looking everywhere, haven't found him yet. He's a big affair I cannot forget.* "Do you prefer Nate, Nathan, or Nathaniel?"

He cocked his head, like he was giving it serious thought. "I answer to any of them."

"You introduced yourself as Nathaniel, and I've heard Louise call you that a few times, but Nathan seems to be the popular consensus."

He silently stared ahead while Ella sang my favorite line: *Tell me where's the shepherd for this lost lamb.*

He cleared his throat. "No one has addressed me as Nathaniel in quite some time."

"Okay, I'll be different. Nathaniel it is." He seemed more like a Nathaniel. Something about him was so sophisticated and charming, like he belonged in an earlier era when people were more well-mannered. My parents would have loved him.

We pulled into Balloon Fiesta Park. Shiloh, Carson, and Dakota waved through the glare of the car's headlights.

"The boys are here!"

Nathaniel cut off the engine. "They're assisting with our launch."

"I thought that wasn't for another couple hours?"

He opened his door. "Not *the* launch, *our* launch."

I went rigid. The numbing revelation allowed him time to reach my side of the car. He opened my door, but I didn't move. "You want *me* to go up in that balloon?"

"You'll enjoy it."

"But it's dangerous."

"It's far from dangerous. The correct word is enchanting." He extended his hand, but I didn't budge.

"But it's so dark out."

"You know the old saying, 'when it's dark enough, you can see the stars.'"

I peeked out of the car at the sky. "I can see the stars fine from here."

He burst out laughing, and that erased my fear. He reminded me of an old Jazz song I never got tired of, no matter how many times I'd heard it. The song began all sad and gruff with a saxophone and bass, but then exploded into upbeat trumpeting that made me want to dance like a madwoman.

"You have my word," he said. "There is no danger involved. You're in the safe hands of the most gifted crew I've ever had the privilege of trusting."

I placed my hand in his. Happy trumpets kept blaring, and his touch sent surges of electricity through me again. Worrying he felt my reaction, I pulled away and stuck my hands in my coat. He leaned in toward me, and his lips parted. A white cloud from his breath filled the inches of space between us. His lips looked so kissable that my mouth watered.

"Maryah, are you all right?"

I swallowed then licked my lips, hoping to erase the magnetic pull that wanted his mouth against mine. "Yes. Just nervous."

As I stepped away from the car, he did that thing again where he put his hand on my back. Even through my layers of clothing, warmth spread over me so intensely I thought I'd melt.

"First hot air balloon ride!" Shiloh yelled as we joined them.

Dakota elbowed me. "I'm jealous. I'd love to go up in this thing."

Carson was already filling the balloon with air. Dakota clumsily stumbled over to help him.

Nathaniel stepped toward the basket. He stared at me while urging me forward with his hands that had barely touched me, yet made me feel ecstatic. "It's time."

Carson and Shiloh held onto each side of the basket acting as anchors.

I took an exaggerated breath. "Right."

Heaven help me.

FALLING STARS

NATHANIEL

I hopped into the basket and reached out to assist Maryah with her entry. She looked unsure of how to perform the maneuver.

"Lean forward and place your arms around my neck." The balloon fought to lift off the ground, and my body pined for her touch again.

She looked at me hesitantly then let out a shaky sigh. A puff of white mist appeared where her breath met the air. I envied the air in that moment. How I longed to feel her breath against my skin again.

She placed her hands on my shoulders and I lifted her into the basket, surprised by how light she was. In recent lives, her bodies were taller and heavier. I gently placed her down. "Hang onto the side of the basket."

I released a steady flame from the burner and it roared like a dragon breathing fire. I nodded to Shiloh and Carson. We lifted off and floated into the air. Maryah looked even paler than usual.

"Maryah, breathe." Her chest rose and fell as she took controlled breaths. Her tension relaxed a bit. We continued to rise higher as I guided the balloon into the heavens. "Are you cold?"

"A little," she replied. I opened my knapsack, pulled out a fleece blanket and wrapped it around her. She looked up and our eyes met. "Thank you, Nathaniel."

"You're welcome." I thought of the way she used to say my name, 'Nathaniel,' with eternal love, and at times, unbridled lust. I was spellbound by being near her again. She still smelled the same, like vanilla and autumn moonlight.

Please remember me, I mentally pleaded. *I need you to remember.*

Her attention flitted away and she stared at the sky behind me. "Look how pretty the stars are."

"Stargazing used to be a treasured pastime. With the evolution of technology and fast-paced lives, humans have lost their connection to the cosmos. People are too busy and distracted to contemplate the universe or admire the stars."

"Do you believe in the whole wishing on stars thing?"

I guided us higher. "People have to make their wishes come true. Stars have other purposes."

"It almost feels like I can touch them." She stretched her hand out over the basket. "My cousin says a person's destiny is written in the stars. That the sky is a storybook, and the stars are characters in its pages."

"That's true. Each member of our family has a star that represents them. Well, almost every member," I added. Then I realized how strange that might sound to her.

She kept studying the sky. "I've heard about that. You register someone's name and they send you a certificate telling you which star is theirs, right?"

I wanted to laugh, but her interpretation provided me a way out of the corner I'd painted myself into. "Our family members were registered before it became a popular fad."

She tugged the blanket tighter around her. "So which star is yours?"

I moved to stand behind her, pointing over her shoulder. "Do you see Orion's Belt? The three stars directly in front of us?" She nodded and the breeze caught her hair, causing it to brush against my chin. My body ached lecherously. Regardless of the age of my soul, my body was reacting like an eighteen-year-old. She unknowingly seduced me with every motion she made.

"Count four stars east of the last star in the belt, then three stars back, and one star diagonally south. That's me." I wanted to add, *the empty place beside me is where you belong.*

"Nathaniel, can I be honest with you?"

The desire to kiss her overwhelmed me. It felt like ten lifetimes had passed since we exchanged breath and linked souls. "I hope you'll always be honest with me."

"I don't see it."

With the sunrise moments away the sky had lightened a bit, but even in the violet dawn the stars should have been visible to her. "Did my directions confuse you?"

"They didn't make sense. I don't get the back and diagonal stuff."

Simply asking my next question saddened me. I already knew the answer. "If you had to estimate, how many stars can you see surrounding us?"

She slowly spun in a circle. Her lips moved as she silently tried to count her way to a tragic answer. "I don't know—maybe a hundred?"

Of course. She had reset her soul. She digressed back to experiencing the world through basic senses—blind to the billions of lights twinkling around us. I tried to remember my first couple lives before my senses evolved. Back when I could see only the brightest and oldest of stars, when so much of life's beauty remained hidden from me.

"Right. Perhaps my vision is better than yours," I replied.

She craned her head back to look at me. "Next time bring magical binoculars so I can find you."

Carson's glasses came to mind. She had no idea how badly I wanted to believe in magical binoculars. I stepped sideways to resist wrapping my arms around her and kissing her exposed neck.

I nodded at her hand. "That's a beautiful ring."

"Oh." She looked down, spinning it around her thumb. "Louise gave it to me. She said it's been in my family for generations."

"Yes, it's obviously an antique."

Her lips twitched like she wanted to smile. "That's my favorite thing about it. If this ring could talk, I bet it would have some amazing stories to tell."

"I bet it would too." If she only knew the truth behind that statement.

The last time I took her on a balloon ride—when I proposed—was one of the highlights of my prior life. True, I had asked her to marry me each and every one of our lifetimes, many with the very ring she currently wore. I enjoyed making a big to-do about it because it always made her so happy. How could things have changed so drastically?

Waves of orange and pink weaved their way through the sky. She couldn't hear the sun's invigorating hum or taste the salty sweet air as the first beams bid farewell to the moon. A million strands of tingling sunlight spun and weaved throughout my skin. Magic is the details, and Maryah no longer knew such details existed.

"It's gorgeous," she remarked, watching the sun rise over the mountains.

And it sounds, tastes, and feels incredible. How could you give it all up? "I hoped you would like it."

"This sounds weird, but—" She squinted and looked at me. "I think I've been here before."

My pulse raced but I remained quiet. The more you discussed the phenomenon as it was occurring, the more you weakened the recollection.

"Sorry, that sounded ridiculous." She returned her barren eyes to the sunrise. "Promnesia," I said under my breath.

"What?"

"Commonly referred to as déjà vu, it's the soul trying to recall a place, person, or event from another life." For years I believed reviving her memory couldn't be done, but now, as she stood before me, her mind trying to revive itself, I begged for it to be possible.

I watched closely for her reaction. Her gaze darted across the sky then up into the blazing envelope of the balloon above us. For another brief moment, hope took over. I said a silent prayer for a spark of memory to ignite.

Light up, my love. Please remember.

She returned her focus to me, but I was gazing at a stranger.

"It's silly, right?"

"Not silly at all," I said.

"Have you ever had déjà vu?"

What a complicated question. I'd never experienced it because I'd never erased. Promnesia wasn't possible for me, so I avoided answering.

"Is this your first time experiencing it?" I acted as if I expected déjà vu to be a common occurrence, which was the truth.

Most souls who didn't retain experienced it many times throughout their lives.

"I've had déjà vu before, but it wasn't as strong as this." She sounded somber as she peered over the edge of the basket. "My mother was always fascinated by déjà vu."

Sarah—the mention of her stirred anger deep within me. She'd forsaken us when Louise and I went to her and disclosed our secret. I was only three at the time, but I comprehended more than a normal toddler. Some bits were blurry, but the emotional impact deeply infused the memory into my developing brain. Louise filled in the details when I was older.

Louise told Sarah about our kindrily and the concept of supernal soul mates. Louise entrusted her with the knowledge that we were Elements. She divulged the length of our history together and how the unthinkable occurred with Maryah. Louise even explained erasure and retainment. She begged her to move back to Sedona so Maryah and I could be raised together. The look of consternation in Sarah's eyes as she stared at me was one thing I did remember.

She accused Louise of being insane. Then she spoke the words that robbed me of my reason for living. *Don't ever come near me or my daughter again.*

Louise tried to fight for me—for us—in a peaceful and loving manner. She tried to make Sarah understand, but she lost the battle. Sarah erupted into fuming threats and we left—warned never to speak to her or to Maryah again or she would report Louise to the police for child endangerment.

Louise should have known Sarah wouldn't be able to comprehend such an omniscient way of life, but she believed in her. Sarah wasn't to be judged for her reaction, yet over the years I hadn't been able to eradicate the animosity I felt.

"I'm sorry for your loss," I said softly.

"Have you ever lost anyone you loved?"

"Yes." I leaned closer, feeling her aura penetrate my own, like two magnets trying to connect.

Her thoughts seemed a million miles away. "Do you wonder if there was something you could've done to stop it? Like you should've been able to change how it turned out?"

Every day, I thought. *Every day I wish I could go back and convince you not to erase me.* I nodded.

"Does the pain ever go away?"

"No, it does not," I replied honestly.

She sighed. "That's what I was afraid of."

My heart hurt for her. We'd lost so many loved ones throughout our lives together. I had built up somewhat of an emotional tolerance regarding death, but I could still remember the pain of permanently losing my first few dozen family members.

"Maryah, we can't replace the ones you lost, but I hope you know our family loves you dearly."

"It's not the same."

"No, surely it's not." We loved her more than she could imagine, but in her mind, her only parents and brother had died. She needed a sympathetic friend, not a heartbroken soul mate.

"If the heartache never goes away then what's the point?"

I moved closer, dying to hold her, but my fingers grasped her blanket instead. "The point to what?"

"Life."

"Life is a learning process. It's an unpredictable journey of—"

"What if I want my journey to be over?"

"You don't mean that." A tear ran down her cheek. I reached into my bag, removing a napkin from the supplies I packed for our picnic and dabbed her face. "I know it's difficult for you, but—"

"You have no idea what it's like. To lose the only people who truly loved you. To think of them constantly and wish they were here to talk to, or hug, or share an experience with. It's gut-wrenching. Every day I'm reminded they're never coming back. They're gone. Forever."

Her words burned me over and over. She was describing how I felt about her.

"I wish I would've died that night," she sobbed. "I miss them so much."

Disbelief tugged at my soul. We battled death's incessant grip for two straight weeks so she could survive her brutal attack. All the sleepless nights, sneaking into the hospital, and the hours upon hours of draining energy from her healer, yet here Maryah was, wishing she would have died?

I reminded myself that she didn't remember anything about how our system of life worked. The world was new to her. Life and death were new to her. "You're only seventeen. The pain you're feeling will diminish over time but you—"

"What? How dare you! You don't know how I feel! You have your whole family! A mother, a father, two brothers, even your grandparents!" She had never spoken to me—yelled at me—with such cruelty. "Who have you ever lost? Do you even know what love is?"

I strained to raise my voice over the deafening sound of my heart shattering. "Of all people, how can *you* ask me that?"

"Ask you what?" An angry glare had replaced her tears.

"*I* know more about love and loss than you can comprehend."

"Look, it sucks that your girlfriend dumped you, but don't take it out on me. You don't know me and I'm starting to think I don't want to know you. Take me back to Faith!" She folded her arms across her chest and turned her back like a child throwing a tantrum.

"Take you back? To your new friends? I thought you wanted to die?"

"I do!" She stomped her foot, shaking the basket. "But no matter how hard I pray, it hasn't happened!"

Pray? She had been praying for death? "Is your grief for your parents and your brother so overwhelming that you want to end this life? To say a final goodbye to Louise, Anthony, Faith, and all your family? Are they worth nothing to you?"

"I hardly know them! They'll never mean more to me than my parents and brother."

I saw red. We had known Louise and Anthony for centuries. Anthony had saved her life on numerous occasions. Louise and Faith had been there for her through so many traumas and losses. How could they mean so little to her? "So you'd choose to end it all? To say goodbye forever?"

"I would if I could," she hissed.

People pleaded for death all the time without meaning it. We would see if that's what she truly wanted. "So be it."

I reached up, shutting off the burner and releasing the lever that let out a constant release of air. We rapidly descended.

She fell backward but caught herself on the edge of the basket. "What are you doing?"

I continued letting air out. The balloon fell at increasing speed. "You said you wanted to die. Far be it from me to deprive you of your wish."

"Not like this!" she shrieked.

I stared at the Rio Grande River as we hurled closer to it, assessing how many more seconds of safe altitude we had left.

"Nathaniel, please! Don't do this!"

My eyes met hers and I knew I had made my point. I reached up to reignite the balloon's flame, but nothing happened. The burner wouldn't light.

I tried again, but we continued to plummet. My heart pounded as the Rio Grande grew closer. If we hit at such high velocity we'd die on impact. I could traverse to safety, but I couldn't take her with me.

What had I done? I would never put her in harm's way. How could I have been so careless?

There wasn't enough time to radio Carson and Shiloh for help. They'd be halfway to our landing site by now. I steered us away from the river as we swept over it much too closely. Maryah's screaming was muffled by the rushing wind and the whipping balloon fabric, but I could still hear the fear in her voice, and it tore a hole through my racing heart.

I threw my arms around her and tucked her head against my chest, bracing us for impact. If I could hold onto her, keep her from being thrown from the basket, her injuries would be minimal.

Her body tensed and she tried pushing me away. "Get off me!"

"Relax as much as you can. It will hurt less."

The wind howled louder. I held her tighter. We crashed into the ground.

Except it wasn't so much a crash, but an abrupt halt. We hadn't even bounced like we did on a normal landing. Maryah's heart pounded against my chest as a waterfall of red, orange, and yellow fabric rustled to the ground and covered us.

She let out a delayed squeal as the basket tipped onto its side. The balloon fabric was peeled off us and I looked up to see Carson's panicked eyes. That explained it. Thank the heavens for Carson and his stellar speed and strength.

Shiloh pulled up beside us in Carson's Mustang.

"You're a maniac!" Maryah screamed, kicking me as she crawled out of the basket. "He tried to kill us!"

Carson and Shiloh didn't say a word.

"Get me away from him!" Maryah's voice cracked and she was visibly shaking.

"Nate?" Shiloh asked, searching for an explanation.

"Take her away from me," I insisted.

Shiloh and Carson stared blankly. Maryah hid behind them in fear, paler than a ghost. How could I have been so heedless? How could I have put her in danger? As if she hadn't already been through enough. "I said take her away from me!"

Faith and Harmony drove up in Shiloh's truck, sending clouds of dust swirling through the air. Carson took Maryah by the arm and dragged her to his car.

"What happened?" Faith shouted.

Maryah's voice quivered. "That lunatic tried to kill me!"

"What?" Faith gasped.

"Nate, what the hell happened?" Shiloh whispered.

I stood up, my head hanging in shame, and headed for a nearby rock formation. The soft thud of heavy boots gained ground behind me.

"Nate!" Harmony shouted. I maintained a brisk pace, but her steps grew quicker. "Nathan! What was that?"

"I don't know."

"The balloon looked like it intentionally crashed."

"It did."

She clutched my arm, forcing me to stand still. "Why?"

I ran my hand through my hair. The desert was blurry and spinning. "She was shouting at me, saying we meant nothing to her, that she wanted to die so she could be with her *real* family. I thought scaring her would make her realize she didn't want to die. Then the burner wouldn't reignite and—I shouldn't have done it." I fell to my knees, holding my head in my hands. "Good gods, I could have killed her!"

"It's okay. You didn't."

"Our lives were only spared because of Carson." I stared at my filthy shaking hands. "I only meant to scare her, not hurt her." My excuse sounded horrid and pathetic, even to me. "What has happened to me?"

She knelt down beside me and closed her hands over mine. "You're broken, and it's understandable why."

Her words tugged at what was left of my heart. I'd felt broken and lost for nearly two decades, yet my kindrily clung to me, refusing to let me fall to pieces. Now, because of my stupidity and recklessness, I'd be forced down a lonely path. "It's unsafe for her to be around me."

Harmony opened her mouth but no words surfaced. Her silence said it all.

"So what now?" Harmony finally uttered.

My soul ached at the thought of what I had to do. The answer was simple but devastating. Until this life ended, Maryah and I couldn't be near each other. Someday, hopefully, my kindrily would find a way to forgive me.

The time had come for me to bid them farewell.

∞

Tiny stones shifted beneath my shoes as I stepped to the edge of Mera Peak. I would have preferred jumping from Everest, but the daunting leap to Nepal had already left me winded. Trying to breath at twenty-one thousand feet was excruciating. The icy Himalayan air would help numb my body and mind, but no degree of cold could numb my soul.

In the grand scheme of things, one lifetime is so short—so insignificant when compared to the centuries Mary and I experienced together. I was determined to erase Maryah from my thoughts so the aching in my heart would cease—as if that were possible.

I stood in the darkness, trying to clear my mind and stop my teeth from chattering before I jumped. All my weight rested on my heels, and my toes hung over the edge of the cliff. The moon glowed behind a web of rain clouds, illuminating the peaks and valleys below. Arcane symbols twinkled above me, the most beautiful star still missing from its place beside mine.

A frigid breeze blew over me. I begged the wind to carry me, to take me to a place where I'd no longer feel heartache. I lifted my face to the supreme element, Aether—the least known and talked about of the elements, but by far the strongest.

Aether exists in every speck of light, every star, every soul, and in parts of existence many minds cannot comprehend. It's the element that eternally bonds soul mates. Aether is everywhere and in everything at all times, leaving me in a perpetual state of incompleteness without her.

Drops of rain fell as memories of Maryah's frightened face plagued me. I recalled the night of her attack.

She had appeared from nowhere. Her face floated in front of me as if projected into midair on an ethereal screen. At one point her mouth moved, but no words materialized. I blinked and she dissolved into the moonlight.

She reappeared minutes later looking worse than the prior vision. I immediately traversed to her, disregarding the consequences.

Maryah was barely breathing and covered in blood. I checked her fading pulse and saw she'd been impaled. The wood stake had penetrated her celiac artery. Medical training from a previous life had taught me to contain the bleeding, but applying topical pressure wouldn't be enough. To an untrained eye, it would have looked like I was killing her. I carefully reinserted the wood into her wound, locating the pierced artery, and pressed hard.

The sirens were upon us. I kissed her eyes, vowing to do whatever it took to save her, praying the paramedics wouldn't be too late. I hid in her parents' boat and watched, ready to assist if needed, not caring if anyone questioned where I came from. But they stabilized her.

If Maryah had died, we'd have lost her forever. Forever is a long time when your existence is never-ending. The thought of Maryah returning to the Higher Realm with no knowledge of me or our kindrily made me shudder.

How could I have put her life in jeopardy again?

I prepared to jump. Silence and my steady heartbeat became my only soundtrack.

"Aether, Air, Earth, Fire, Water, I am you and you are I. Guide my soul so I may fly."

I leaned forward, and became one with the sky.

Wind ripped through me as my body tumbled over itself. Ground. Sky. Ground. Sky. My vision blurred into a streaky canvas of which I was one drop of paint.

I wanted to fall forever.

I completed four full flips before extending my arms. The wings of my flight suit caught the air beneath me. The comforting smell of dirt and moist air blasted through my nose.

Flying: it is the second greatest feeling in the world. I didn't want to think about the first. Tonight, love was my weakness. I wanted adrenaline to conquer all.

I kept my arms pressed against my side, gaining more speed. The mountains jagged walls whistled as I soared past them. BASE jumping in the dark meant I couldn't see my shadow floating beside me. However, I could see the earth, trees, and mountains. I needed more exhilaration, so I closed my eyes, relying on my other senses to know when and where to turn or swoop. One wrong move and my ride would be over.

My move. My choice. Up here, I had control. No one could take it away from me.

Raindrops stung my skin as I descended upon a twisting trail along the edge of the mountain. The strip of ground grew wider. Earth and I were in the midst of a deadly game of chicken. I smiled, and the hundred-mile-per-hour wind sucked all the moisture from my mouth. Soon, the ground would be close enough for me to reach out and touch. If I did, the slight change in aerodynamics would seal my fate.

At the last moment, I whisked myself upward, leveling my body so it glided parallel with the trail only inches above the snaking path. My precious seconds of flight time were running out. I drifted away from the mountain, choosing an open valley for my drop zone.

I didn't need an altimeter to tell me how close the ground was. If I had a parachute, I should've already released it.

Three thousand feet. As fast as the ground approached, my life should have flashed before my eyes.

Two thousand feet. Lightning pierced the sky.

One thousand feet. A punch of thunder shook the heavens.

Five hundred feet. My last breath.

One second before I would have splattered into the ground. I thought of Maryah.

Then I traversed.

I reappeared standing on the mountain I had just jumped from. My feet were back on the ground, planted in harsh reality.

Sheets of water poured down around me. I surveyed my body and emotions: no adrenaline rush, no excitement, not even a shiver from the cold rain. My flight barely served as a distraction. Without the love of my soul mate, I was dead inside.

I closed my eyes and jumped again.

A NAGGING PAIN

Maryah

Carson stomped past my room and slammed his bedroom door.

Convincing him to take me home early wasn't easy, but I refused to stay anywhere near Nathan, the Jekyll and Hyde monster. Carson could defend Nathan all he wanted, but his schizophrenic brother tried to kill me. *And* insulted my family.

Forget my theory about me possibly being psychic. If that were the case wouldn't I have known Nathan was a raging lunatic? And to think I wanted to call him Nathaniel because it sounded so sophisticated. No way. He nosedived off his pedestal and demoted himself back to Nathan, or better yet, Nut Job.

The others would be coming home tonight, but I wasn't ready to discuss the incident again. I tried to block Nathan's face out of my mind, to erase his voice and the memories of him—good and bad. That's when my head started throbbing.

My migraines usually hit twice a year like clockwork. It wasn't my birthday or Christmas, but the pain felt like the start of a migraine so I took my prescription meds to be safe.

It went from bad to worse. I woke up running for the bathroom, knowing I was moments from vomiting. As I ran, little specks of light flashed in front of my eyes. Definitely one of my torturous migraines. I wouldn't even wish one on Nathan, my new worst enemy.

I came out of the bathroom, steadying myself against the walls as I made my way to the kitchen for a drink.

"Hello, Mary," an older woman with black and silver hair said pleasantly.

Carson laughed. "Helen, her name is Maryah."

"Oh, that's right. My apologies, dear." She smiled at me through cherry-painted lips. A faded Italian accent lingered behind some of her words. "It's so nice to see you."

I had no idea she and Edgar were coming home tonight. I prayed Carson hadn't told them what happened. What would Helen think if she heard Nathan intentionally crashed her company balloon with me in it?

I tried to sound normal. "Hello, Mrs. Helen. Nice to meet you."

"Call me Helen. The missus makes me sound old."

She did look snazzy for a grandmother. Her pinned up curly hair looked like something from a photo shoot, and under her apron she wore a tailored pantsuit. She looked like someone I'd seen before. Maybe on television? She was definitely pretty enough to be a model or actress.

A surge of pain shot through my temples followed by a wave of nausea. I buckled over, holding my head and begging the universe to please not make me puke in front of Carson and Helen.

Helen rushed to my side. "Maryah dear, what's the matter?"

"I get migraines, and one's coming on fast."

"Let's get you into bed," Helen insisted.

I rubbed the back of my neck. My head was starting to spin.

Helen guided me out of the kitchen. I kept my eyes shut to help block out some of the light and movement.

"Hang on," I groaned. I tried steadying myself but my muscles went limp.

Helen held me up by my elbows. "Good heavens, it's that bad?"

I tried nodding in response, but it hurt too much.

"I've got her," Carson said beside me. He lifted me off my feet and cradled me in his arms.

"Careful," Helen warned. "Try not to move her too much. Motion makes it worse."

Carson carried me down the hallway like we were gliding on ice. I kept my eyes closed in fear of the pain that would follow if I opened them. As much as I didn't want to, I rested my thousand-pound head on his shoulder.

Seconds later, I felt cool sheets against my skin. I barely felt a bounce as Carson placed me on my bed.

"Would you like the covers on you?" Helen whispered.

"Yes," I murmured.

"Carson, draw all the curtains so there is no sunlight."

"Sure thing."

I heard Carson whooshing around the room, but my brain and body were shutting down. With the little bit of strength I had left I muttered, "Thank you."

Helen hushed me and then my bedroom door clicked shut.

I reached out my arm and grabbed the nightstand. The room was spinning and holding onto a solid object helped alleviate some of the dizziness. I prayed for sleep, but it never came. I floated in and out of consciousness, but the pain wouldn't allow me to fully rest.

I stayed that way for what felt like days until someone propped me up so I was almost sitting upright.

Helen's voice whispered through the darkness. "I need to you to sip and swallow."

I felt a plastic straw make its way between my lips. "No," I groaned, turning my head away.

"Please, angel. I really do believe it will help."

I knew I'd soon be throwing up whatever she was forcing me to drink, but she placed the straw between my lips again, and I took a sip.

The tea had a spicy yet tangy citrus flavor and the earthy aroma of the steam made my nose tingle. I waited for my gag reflex to kick in.

"Please, try to drink a little more," she whispered.

I don't know how many sips I took. I don't remember anything beyond the sipping because I finally fell asleep.

∞

Nut Job returned to my dreams. My curtains were pulled shut like in real life, and I saw myself asleep in bed. Nathan sat by my side in the rattan chair watching me. What a stupid dream. Why would anyone watch someone sleep? I hated the real Nathan, but in my dreams he was still gorgeous, protective, and sweet.

I moved closer to him. His chest rose and fell underneath his green t-shirt. He had worry creases around his eyes, so I tried to smooth them away with my thumbs like Krista always did to me. He snapped his head upward, startling me. I backed away and banged my hand into the corner of my dresser.

I looked down and noticed the peacock feather in my ring was shimmering and swirling again. When I looked up, Nathan's eyes met mine.

He squinted and stood up then walked toward me. I held my breath, half expecting him to reach out and touch me, but he froze as if someone had pressed the pause button on a remote control. A white fog rose all around us. He stood motionless in mid-stride, not even breathing. His green eyes stared ahead, but he didn't blink.

My bedroom door opened and Anthony came in. He looked around, shaking his head. With one swoop, he picked up Nathan and carried him out of the room. The door shut soundlessly behind him.

Beyond strange. Anthony had never been in my dreams before. And why would I dream that he took Nathan away? A therapist would have a field day trying to interpret the crap my mind created.

My dream flashed to Edgar and Helen's cottage. The fog lingered in this scene too. Anthony set Nathan down on the floor, and instantly the haze lifted. Nathan stepped forward—almost blindly—but he stopped right before knocking over Helen's floor vase.

"I hate it when you do that," Nathan grunted.

Anthony blew his dark bangs off his forehead and tightened the drawstring of his pajama pants. "Hate is a strong word. Now, what are you doing here?"

"I wanted to make sure she was okay, and to say my final goodbye."

"While she's sleeping? What good does that do? Besides, you know as well as I do that you'll never be able to permanently say goodbye to her."

Nathan paced the floor. "When she's asleep, I can still sense the amorous soul who loved me, *because* I don't have to look into her eyes. Seeing her as a stranger kills me. She was my home, my sanctuary, and my best friend. All that we had has been erased." Nathan ran his hands over his head and sat down. "Her eyes prove she's an empty vessel—a ghost ship—passing through this life with no idea that I'm her harbor."

Where did my subconscious get this romantic garbage?

Anthony pulled a chair over and placed it in front of Nathan, sitting to face him. "I can't imagine the anguish you're in. I couldn't endure it for an hour, much less eighteen years, but there is a reason for this. There is always a reason for everything. You have to take comfort in that."

"Take comfort in what? I have nothing left to take comfort in. Every touch, every conversation, everything we'd been through together, it's all gone—forever."

"Not forever." Anthony argued. "We both know how prodigious the term forever is. You thought at one point that she was physically gone forever—that you'd never see her again. Yet here she is, lusterless eyes and all, reconnecting with our kindrily."

Lusterless? Who was he calling lusterless? My eyes weren't beautiful or anything, but lusterless seemed harsh. And what did kindredlee mean? Now I was creating make-believe words in my dreams? I needed my head examined—again.

"She's not the same. She's so...empty, so hollow."

I flinched at Nathan's hurtful words.

Anthony sighed. "Every vessel is empty until someone takes the time to fill it. How is a ship expected to find her harbor if no lighthouse guides her through the darkness?" Anthony laid his hand on Nathan's shoulder. "There's still time. She was born a stranger, but not yet buried as one. This sojourn isn't finished for either one of you."

I'd seen the word sojourn in one of my Shakespeare assignments, but how could I dream about it if I didn't know its definition?

Nathan shook his head. "I did what all of you asked, what Marcus suggested. I attempted to reconnect with her. It made matters much worse. I put her life in danger. I can't forgive myself for that. For the sake of everyone involved, I can't be around Maryah. No more grand schemes and foolish hope that her memories will resurface. It's destroying me." He slumped forward. "I can't live another cycle of life without her."

Anthony's eyes widened. "You don't mean...?"

"Yes, I'm going to erase."

"Nathan, you're stronger than this."

I could barely hear Nathan's next words. "Sometimes the strong become the weak."

Cycle of life? Erase what? This dream was too much for me to handle. I wanted it to be over, so I imagined being back in my bed and pinched my wrist.

I woke up scanning my dark room. My headache was almost completely gone. At first, I thought maybe I'd imagined Helen and her miracle tea, but then I saw a half-empty mug sitting on my nightstand.

I stared at the chair where I dreamt Nathan had sat. He had been so full of sorrow it made my heart hurt. Wait. Why was I getting so emotional? Nathan Luna was probably sound asleep in New Mexico or Colorado and not the least bit sad.

I needed a drink, but it was three in the morning so I tiptoed to the kitchen. I'd just finished placing the mango-guava juice back into the refrigerator when the back door squeaked open.

Anthony came around the corner and I almost dropped my glass. He looked exactly like he had in my dream.

We'd never crossed paths during the night. I had no idea what he wore to bed. Even in the mornings, he never came out of his bedroom until he was dressed and ready for the day. So how did I dream up his exact plaid pajama pants and wrinkled yellow t-shirt? The colors didn't even go together. His wool slippers were identical to the ones in my dream. His dark hair was even sticking up in the same places.

"Maryah, you okay?"

"Oh—yeah. Sorry, Anthony. You startled me. I didn't know you and Louise were home." I fumbled over my words, trying to make sense of this latest psychic freak-out. What had he been doing outside in the middle of the night in his pajamas? "Where were you?"

"Where was I?" he repeated. "I couldn't sleep, so I worked on my car."

"In the dark?"

"There are lights in the garage," he countered.

"Oh. Okay." Anthony designed cars and planes for a living, so why wouldn't he work on them at night? An uncomfortable silence built up as we stood there in the dark.

"I'm sorry about the incident with Nathan." He stuck his hands in the pockets of his pajama pants while I stood there not knowing what to say. "Helen said you had a bad headache. You sure you're all right?"

"Yeah, she gave me tea that helped it."

"Ah, yes. Helen and her recipes. Universal Flavorings can't sell most of them in stores because they're too potent."

"Helen makes teas for Universal Flavorings?" My family drank that brand for years, not to mention it lined the shelves of every grocery store I'd ever been in.

"She founded the company."

"That's like, the biggest tea company in the world!"

"Mm, hmm. She's done well for herself."

No wonder the Lunas lived in such a big house. Helen must be a millionaire.

"Well, I'm going back to bed." He reached the hallway and called out, "Sweet dreams, Maryah."

I paused, shaken up by his choice of words. He couldn't possibly know that I'd been dreaming about him. Paranoia was getting the best of me again.

I went to my room and climbed into bed. My eyes were only closed for a few seconds when I heard a rustling behind my headboard. I sat up, and could've sworn I saw Nathan reflected in my dresser mirror, but when I turned around no one was there.

Just dandy. Nathan was my real life nightmare who wouldn't stay out of my dreams, and now I was hallucinating about him when I was awake. My brain was officially on the fritz.

SPILLING SECRETS

Maryah

Faith and Harmony picked me up for school as usual. Faith seemed to have more energy than normal if that's humanly possible.

"Good Morning, Ma-Ma!"

"Mama?" I asked, not amused.

"Ma-Ma. It's short for Maryah, but twice, so it's double the fun!"

"How can you be so energetic this early in the morning?"

If a drug existed that made people excessively happy and overly optimistic, Faith overdosed on it daily. I crawled into the back seat and mumbled hello to Harmony.

"Hola, Maryah," Harmony said.

I almost gasped. She never greeted me with more than a head nod if she greeted me at all. I expected her to join the dark side with Nathan and Carson and never speak to me again. If Harmony were in that balloon she probably would have cheered on Nathan in his mission to kill me.

Faith backed down the driveway. "How are you doing after the, you know, balloon escapade?"

"Fine. I'm just exhausted." My dream about Nathan left me tossing and turning all night. Why would I imagine him to be so sweet after he tried to kill me? And since when did my mental dictionary include words like sojourn? Faith loved Shakespeare, so maybe she'd know what it meant. "Faith, do you know what sojourn means?"

"Sure!" she answered, keeping her eyes on the road. Harmony on the other hand, whipped her head around to look at me. I was grateful for my sunglasses. With both of our eyes covered, it wasn't as uncomfortable as it could've been.

"It means a short visit," Faith explained. "A temporary stay."

"Got it." I pretended to examine my fingernails while Harmony continued glaring at me.

Faith elaborated. "There are theories that a soul completes many sojourns throughout its existence. That we come back life after life to learn and experience things."

"Like reincarnation?" I asked.

We had just stopped at a red light. Faith put the car in park and unfastened her seatbelt. She turned in her seat, crawled up onto her knees, and stared at me over her headrest. "Do you believe in reincarnation?"

Faith's craziness rarely fazed me, but this was weird even for her. "Faith, focus on the road."

"It's a yes or no question."

"I don't know."

"You don't know like it's a ridiculous concept and it's impossible, or like it's a humongous world and anything is possible?"

"I mean I don't know what is or isn't possible." The light turned green and people honked behind us. "The light is green!"

Harmony snapped her head back around and mumbled something, but it wasn't loud enough for me to hear.

Faith fastened her seatbelt while horns blasted behind us. "That's a good answer. You're only seventeen. How could you know the answer to such a mystical question? It's a sign of wisdom that you admit you don't know. It's your heartfelt answer, and as long as you follow your heart, you can never be wrong."

"You're only seventeen, do *you* believe in reincarnation?" I asked mockingly.

"Yes." Faith and Harmony's answer echoed through the car.

I stared at the back of Harmony's black and purple head. I expected this kind of belief in an improbable theory from Faith, but Harmony's certainty surprised me.

Faith looked at me in her rear-view mirror again. "Want to learn about it? I'd be happy to share what I know!"

"Sure," I answered, not caring if we ever discussed the topic again.

"It's a virtuous trait to be open to new things. There is always more to learn." Faith could go from childlike to savant in the blink of an eye. Sometimes it was hard to believe she was seventeen.

After we parked and got out of the car, Faith locked arms with me. "After school, I'll come over and we can do a research and retain session!"

"I don't think it's vital that I decide if I believe in reincarnation today."

"No better time than the present. But we do have school to get through, so in this case, there's no better time than three o'clock."

"Great, can't wait," I groaned. Once Faith had her mind set on something, nothing could stop her.

∞

River smiled as I approached English class. "How was your weekend?" he asked.

"Painful."

He flexed his calf muscle. "Mine too."

I glanced down at the new addition to his tattoos—a black guitar with purple and orange flames surrounding it. "Your mom must be so proud."

He squinted at me while visibly biting his tongue. For the first time ever he didn't have a comeback.

I laughed and walked into our classroom, plopping into my seat and dreading another week of school. River yanked on my ponytail before stealthily sliding a note into my binder. When Ms. Barby turned to write on the blackboard, I opened it.

M,

Today is really tough for me. Let's hang out after school. I'll give you a ride home later.

Peace, River

Why would today be tough for River? He didn't care about his classes. His hair and clothes looked perfect as usual, and looks and music seemed to be his only major concerns in life. Still, River wanted to talk to *me* about his problems? At least I'd be hanging out with someone outside of Nathan's family circle— someone who wouldn't want to discuss the balloon incident.

The bell rang and I met Faith at the door to tell her about hanging out with River after school.

"We had plans," she moaned.

"What plans?"

She pulled out a book from her bag that was by someone named Edgar Cayce. "Reincarnation education, remember?"

She thought *that* constituted an official plan?

"This is important," I whispered. "I think River's upset about something."

Faith glanced over my shoulder to River's desk. "Hmph. I didn't know Shady McShaderton had emotions."

"Don't be mean."

She shoved the book on top of my binder. "I'm teasing—sort of. Okay, do what you have to do, but I'm coming over at eight. You aren't ditching me that easily." She poked my chin before turning and bopping down the hall.

"Do you have permission to come out and play?" River snarled from behind me.

I turned and glared at him. "Be nice."

"She started it," he bantered in a childish voice then merged into the hallway full of traffic. "Come on. I couldn't be more done with this place."

"You want to leave right now?"

"I wanted to leave an hour ago."

"You mean play hooky?"

He stopped and leaned against a locker. "You sound so retro when you say it like that, but yes, play hooky."

I had never skipped a class before, not without a note or a legitimate excuse. I looked around, spotting a couple of teachers monitoring the hallway. "What if we get caught?"

"We won't. Come on, I'm really stressed about April and being here isn't helping."

April. I hadn't called her all weekend. She was going through so much and like a crappy friend, I hadn't thought about her one time because of all the drama in Albuquerque. "Is she okay?"

"I'll tell you when we get out of here. We've got to act right now." River grabbed my hand and positioned us directly behind the biggest—and widest—kid in school. He kept us blocked from the view of any teachers until we ducked out a side door. We ran for the parking lot.

I climbed into River's Jaguar, my heart pounding and my nerves frazzled. All I could think about was how many ways we could get busted.

"Badass car, huh?" River shut his door and the engine purred to life.

A King of Hearts air freshener swung from the rear view mirror making the car reek of lemons. The leather seats hugged my body, and the windows were tinted so dark no one would be able to see us inside. "It's gorgeous."

He flashed his standard cocky grin and squealed his tires as we pulled out of the lot. Way to be inconspicuous.

"Why is today so tough? Is everything all right with April?"

"It's the anniversary of my mother's death."

The shock prevented me from saying anything appropriate. I knew River's father died, but I assumed his mom was still alive.

"See, told you I knew how you felt," he snickered.

"I thought you meant because of your dad."

"Yeah, him too. I know how hard it is to lose your parents."

"River, I'm so sorry."

"Did you kill them?"

"No, but—"

"So why are you apologizing?"

We were quiet for a while then I remembered River was an only child. "Who do you live with?"

"My Uncle Eric plays backup dad."

"That's good," I muttered, not knowing what else to say. I didn't want to ask how either of his parents died. I hated discussing my family's death.

"It's nice to have someone who knows how I feel." River connected his iPod and hard rock songs blasted through the speakers.

We turned onto Dry Creek Road—a part of town I'd never been to—and I shouted over the music. "Isn't one of the vortexes out here?"

He lowered the volume and groaned. "Boynton Canyon is nearby. Locals claim it's a vortex, but I don't believe in that mumbo jumbo."

"Nice neighborhood," I said as we turned into a gated community.

"Would you expect any less from me?" Sometimes River's cockiness annoyed me, but most of the time I found it amusing.

We parked beside a huge pick-up truck covered in dirt. "Who owns Bigfoot?"

"That's my play vehicle."

"You have *two* cars?"

"Why have one when you can have two?"

"Of course, what was I thinking?" I rolled my eyes and climbed out of the car.

River's house had black leather couches and tables made of glass and marble, but very few decorations or artwork. The smell of bleach and cleaning products reminded me of my awful stay in the hospital.

"Where's your uncle?"

"He doesn't actually live here. He travels a lot, mainly Europe, and doesn't stay here much."

"You live here by yourself?" River had to be the luckiest kid I knew.

"Sort of, I have a housekeeper and chef that live here—my uncle's way of keeping tabs on me."

Lucky and spoiled. "So the Jag? Is that your Uncle's?"

"No, it's mine. I traded my old one in last winter."

"Your old one? You're seventeen. How old could it have been?"

"Uncle Eric bought me my first car when I was fourteen."

"*Fourteen?*"

"He isn't big on laws and rules. Besides, that's when my dad died. He didn't want me depending on my servants to drive me around."

"Servant sounds so demeaning."

"If the shoe fits," he shrugged. What a pompous thing to say. Sometimes I wondered how April and him ever ended up together. She seemed too sweet to go for his type.

"So, where are they?"

"They stay in their wing of the house, unless I ask them for something. Eightball is around here somewhere."

"Eightball?"

"My bulldog." He pulled a beer out of the refrigerator. "Want one?"

"What? No," I replied, stunned that he casually drank at home. But since he didn't have adults telling him what to do, it was probably normal for him. "Why'd you name him Eightball?"

River smiled, popping the cap off his bottle. "Eight ball of cocaine."

My face must have twisted with disgust because he almost spit out his beer, trying not to laugh. "I'm kidding. Hang on, you'll see why. Eightball!"

Paws tapped along the tile floors in another room and a wrinkled round body waddled around the corner. His head was mostly all black except for a white circle around one of his eyes.

"Ah, I get it. He does look like an eight ball." I squatted down and clapped my hands but Eightball just snorted and lay on the floor. "He's so cute." I tried petting him, but he jumped up and trotted away.

"He's scared of people. I think he might've been abused as a pup."

"Aw, poor thing."

River plopped down on a leather sofa and turned on the television. I sat on the other couch and focused on the huge flat screen, but River paused the show.

"Tell me something I don't know about you." He moved to the end of his sofa and snatched my hat off of my head.

I stood up and grabbed for it, but he put it between his legs, so I sat back down. "Like what?"

"Like a secret nobody else knows."

"My life isn't interesting enough to have secrets."

"Everyone has secrets," he argued.

No way was I telling him about my psychic visions of Nathan or what happened in New Mexico. And Krista was the only person who knew I blamed myself for my family being killed, but I wanted to keep it that way. River sensed my hesitation.

"Ha! There is something. I can tell."

I thought of another secret and looked away. "You'll think I'm mental."

"I doubt it. I've got some twisted thoughts of my own."

My focus darted between him and the television. Would he freak out like Nathan did, or would he understand because he lost his parents too? April told me he's the easiest person to talk to, that he never judges and always knows the right thing to say. She knew him better than I did, so I took a chance. "Sometimes," I confessed quietly, "I think about killing myself, so I can be with my family again."

"Seriously?" He looked more impressed than surprised.

"I could never go through with it, but I think about it a lot."

"Hmm," he mused, nodding his head. "Now it makes sense."

"What makes sense?"

"Why your eyes look like that."

"Like what?" I protectively blinked, thinking about my dream when Anthony called my eyes lusterless.

"Like they're, I don't know...haunted. Makes you seem mysterious." He took another swig of beer. "What do you want to know about me?"

Mysterious. I hoped that was a good thing. At least he didn't tell me I was crazy or try to grant my death wish like Nut Job Nathan. "What do you want to tell me?"

He stared at the ceiling like he was choosing from a long list of possibilities. "Some girl at school has a crush on me."

"All the girls have a crush on you."

He laughed louder than normal. "You think?"

"Oh please, they swoon over you."

"You don't."

"I'm friends with your girlfriend. Plus, you're not my type."

His eyes narrowed. "Who's your type?"

"I'm not sure." I smoothed down the ends of my hair. "But not you."

We both laughed. Sometimes I enjoyed putting River in his place.

"Whatever," he said. "You'd so date me." His conceit never ceased to amaze me. He finished his beer and let out an obnoxious burp. "Can I trust you with a secret?"

"Sure."

"I don't think I'm into April anymore, but with her mom being so sick I'd feel like a douche breaking up with her."

I did *not* want to know that secret. April would be heartbroken if she knew, and I certainly didn't want to be the one to tell her. Would that make me a horrible friend for knowing and keeping my mouth shut? "You're right. You can't break up with her. I'm sure things will get better once she's not so busy helping her mom."

"I don't know. Her mom could be this way for months, maybe longer." He leaned back, sinking into the couch. "We never have fun together anymore."

Guilt kicked in. Was this his idea of fun? Playing hooky and drinking beer while we were supposed to be in class? I couldn't picture April doing that stuff, but then again I couldn't picture me doing it either. "I'm sure it's hard for her to have fun when she's so worried about her mom."

He nodded but didn't look convinced. "Just don't say anything. It'll be our secret."

"Only if you swear not to tell anyone we skipped class today." Faith would never let me hear the end of it.

"Deal."

And just that easily, we became the keepers of each other's secrets.

HELPING THE HELPLESS

NATHANIEL

"**N**athaaannnn!" Amber's high-pitched scream rattled the house. "Help!"

I instantly envisioned her hazel eyes and traversed to her. She was standing alone on the back deck, nervously bouncing the ends of her scarf against her curly hair.

"What's wrong?" I scanned the dark backyard. "Is someone here?"

"I'm sorry," she said. "He made me do it."

She'd barely spoken the last word when I heard Dylan's voice. "Nathan, please—"

I threw my hands over my ears and traversed to the garage. Snickering, I pulled my phone from my pocket and texted Dylan. *Forget it. I'm not trying the glasses.*

It had become a game between us. Dylan trying to catch me so he could persuade me into testing Carson's glasses, and me traversing out of hearing range before he could use his ability to make me try them. Mainly, I enjoyed the friendly competition of outsmarting each other, but I also didn't want to look through Carson's glasses and see the dark place where Maryah's star used to be. Some delusional part of me figured if I didn't confirm it wasn't there, then Shiloh's theory might stand a chance of being true.

"You will not traverse," Dylan said.

Bollocks.

The garage light came on and Dylan strutted out from behind Amber's car. "Ha. Got you."

I couldn't traverse—no matter how badly I wanted to. That's the thing about Dylan's ability. If he gives an order, there's no choice but to follow it. "You were just out back."

"No," he grinned smugly. "My tape recorded voice was out back. I took a lucky guess that you'd flee to the garage."

I walked toward the door that led inside the house.

Dylan stepped in front of me. "You will—"

"Dylan, enough. Carson already said they don't work."

"He designed a new pair and made some adjustments." He reached up on a shelf and handed me glasses similar to the other ones, except they felt lighter. The automatic garage door opened. "Put them on and look at the sky."

Of all the things he could use his ability for, he chose trivial nonsense like this. I didn't want to follow his order, but my hands were already sliding the glasses over my eyes. I walked out of the garage and looked up.

Through the glasses, the black sky appeared almost white. Every visible star was sepia toned with a halo of gold surrounding it, like specks of glowing dirt thrown onto a white screen. The real sky put the altered version to shame. That couldn't be how Shiloh viewed the world, colorblind or not.

I located my star and squinted, searching the space beside mine. I stared for over a minute then removed the glasses from my head.

"Well?" Dylan asked, stroking his goatee. Amber stood on the front porch watching us.

I shook my head. "Nothing."

Amber sighed.

Dylan bowed his head. "I'm sorry. Carson thought—"

"It's done. Please don't mention her star or those shoddy glasses to me ever again. What's done is done, and I don't need to keep being reminded that she's gone."

"We were only trying to help," Dylan said.

"Imagine how horrible we feel." Amber plugged in the Happy Halloween sign attached to her scarecrow's hands. "She was killed at our wedding."

We had avoided this conversation for years, but apparently Amber was finally ready to discuss it.

"We all were," I said.

"Nathan!" She threw a tiny pumpkin at me. "Thanks for making me feel worse."

Dylan clarified. "What he meant was, nine of us were killed on that beach. Maryah is the only one who chose to erase."

"Nine," Amber repeated. "So then you don't think they killed Gregory?"

I hesitated, hiding the shiver that ran through me, but not from the cold. "No, I believe they wanted him for his ability."

Dylan lit a candle and set it inside a jack o' lantern. "He'd never help them."

"No, he wouldn't," I agreed. "Not willingly."

Amber sat on the porch swing beside the scarecrow, fiddling with fake spider webs. "I can't help wondering what if we all hadn't been gathered in one place. What if Dylan and I hadn't had our wedding on that island? We were trapped and unarmed. We didn't stand a chance."

I remembered the scene like it was yesterday. Amber looked exquisite in her wedding gown. It had been only months since we last gathered, but Amber was disappointed when Anthony and Louise's flight got cancelled. Edgar had a severe ear infection which prevented him from flying, so he and Helen were also unable to attend. In hindsight, it was a blessing the elders weren't present. Anthony tortured himself with the scenarios that might have played out had he been there to use his ability. But "what if" is an awful game to play with oneself.

"We had no idea they wanted any of us," I said.

Amber's cheeks were sucked in, possibly from fighting back tears, or biting back the memories. "Dylan shakes me awake sometimes. He says I punch and scream in my sleep. Every time it's been nightmares about the Nefariouns. The gunshots, the blood, the cracking of bones: like it's happening all over again. Sometimes, I only hear screaming. You're all screaming, fighting for your lives, but I can't get to anyone."

Dylan wrapped his arms around her. I remained silent, not knowing how to ease the heaviness of her grief or guilt.

"And Gregory," she choked on his name. "I keep seeing him there, chained to that tree, having to hear it all—even the horrible things none of us could."

"I'm sure he blocked it all out," Dylan said.

"No." Amber shook her head. "Not with all of us in danger. Especially Harmony and Carson. He probably kept his mind open to hear everything. Every fear, plea, and terrified thought running through our heads."

I sat down on the porch steps with my back to them. I couldn't tell them what I'd seen, what I knew. I couldn't tell anyone. As guilty as I felt for keeping such a grave secret, I had to. Our kindrily couldn't handle additional devastation.

"Speaking of Carson," I said. "What have you two decided about spending more time with him?"

The swing creaked then Amber moved into my peripheral vision and leaned against the porch railing. "Of course we will. It's easy to forget how hard the first few rounds of life were. And Carson, with no soul mate. I can't imagine how hard that must be."

Her hand darted to her mouth when she finished her sentence. "I'm sorry, Nathan. I can't believe I just said that."

I waved it off. "It's fine. I know what you meant."

She sat down beside me. "Dylan has been talking to Carson on the phone every night. We're going to spend Thanksgiving and Christmas with him. And I'm going to face my guilt and spend time with Maryah as if we've never met."

"You haven't met. She's not the soul we knew. She's a stranger."

Amber sighed and rested her head on my shoulder. "Are you still determined to stay away from her?"

"Maryah has forever forsaken us. I can't keep tormenting myself with impossible hopes of a miracle."

"You can't give up on her," Dylan said. "It's only been a few months. You have to believe. If you of all people don't believe in her, she doesn't stand a chance."

"Tell me, Dylan, are you the one laden with heavy, burdensome chains every day and night? Do you curse the sun every time it sets from the sky because if you sleep you'll dream of love only to have it vanish when you wake? Are you scared to blink your eyes because the image of your twin flame floods you with insufferable pain?"

He bowed his head and looked away from me.

"No," I continued. "You can't comprehend that anguish such as mine never receives a reprieve. Your soul mate stands beside you. Imagine looking into Amber's eyes and seeing that she erased every memory of you. You can't even imagine the torture."

Amber squeezed my hand and allowed a few moments of silence to pass before continuing the debate. "She's shown hints of remembering. What if there's an exception to the rule?"

"Glitches in her brain? Fleeting moments of déjà vu? Hypnosis-induced remnants of our former lives together? Those are the only exceptions. Is that what I'm supposed to be hoping for? Is that what all of you are fighting for?"

"It's better than nothing at all."

Dylan squatted down in front of us. "Maybe the soul is like a computer's hard drive. If files or information exist long enough, and are embedded deeply enough, traces of supposedly deleted information still remains. The imprint is too strong to disappear. Maryah's history and memories run extremely long and deep. She may still have memories imbedded in her soul."

"You're comparing her to a machine?"

Dylan smirked. "Edgar is always saying how the Akashic Records are now referred to as a universal supercomputer. It's a sign of the times. Maybe the soul can advance like technology."

I didn't want to admit to the tug-of-war between hope and hopelessness going on inside of me. "I'm determined to keep Maryah safe. Part of that is keeping my distance from her. The other part is finding Dedrick and making sure his hunt is over. Marcus and some members of another kindrily have agreed to help me."

"Dylan and I could help."

My patience had worn thin. "No. I want everyone from our kindrily to stay together in case the Nefariouns figure out who and where Maryah is. I'll be here within seconds if you need me."

"You being away so much makes me nervous," Amber said. "Promise me you're not on a mission to die and erase, and that you'll be careful over there."

"I'm not on a mission to die, and I promise I'll be careful."

I glanced at the sky where Maryah's star used to be—wishing harder than ever that Carson's glasses had revealed a miracle. I made a promise to myself that I'd do whatever it took to keep Dedrick away from Maryah, and that promise trumped the one I had made to Amber.

THANKING THE HEAVENS

Maryah

April sniffed again and cleared her throat. "Thanksgiving doesn't even feel like a holiday this year. How can I be thankful for anything when my mom is fighting for her life?"

I pressed my cheek against my phone, wishing I could reach through the line and hug her and tell her to be thankful she still had her mom, that even if—God forbid—her mom did die, she still had time to tell her how much she loved her. She'd have a chance to say goodbye. I'd give anything to have had that. But instead, all I said was, "I'm so sorry."

"Let's talk about something else. How are you? Any updates on Nut Job?"

"Yesterday, Louise dropped a bomb that Dylan and his wife were coming to stay for Thanksgiving. I figured Nathan would come too, but thankfully he's spending the weekend with friends."

"There." April chuckled. "Something to be thankful for."

Louise came into the kitchen.

"I should get going," I said. "Try to enjoy your holiday."

"Yeah." April seemed to perk up a little. "River's coming over later, so there's one bright spot in my life."

My stomach tightened. River had been getting more frustrated with their relationship, but I swore not to tell April. It would only hurt her, and that's the last thing she needed. "Good. You two have fun and try to forget about reality for a while."

As soon as we hung up, I heard the front door open. A gray lab galloped into the kitchen with its tail wagging and sniffed my feet and legs.

"Hello!" a female voice called out.

"We're in the kitchen!" Louise replied.

A fairly tall girl came around the corner smiling. A flower tucked behind her ear complimented the red highlights in her curly brown hair.

"I brought you homegrown Plumeria!" She set down a basket of colorful flowers and hugged Louise.

"Maryah," Louise said. "This is Dylan's wife, Amber."

Amber turned to face me, but I couldn't gauge her impression because of her dark tortoise shell sunglasses.

"Aloha, Maryah," she sighed.

"Hi."

The gray dog sat proudly by Amber's side looking up at her. "Oh right. This is Molokai."

Carson bounded into the kitchen. "Hey Amby! Where's Dylan?"

"He's out front showing off his new car."

"Another one?" Louise asked.

Carson headed for the foyer. "You coming, Maryah?"

I thought for sure Carson would never speak to me again over the Nathan thing, but lately he'd been somewhat nice to me. "Sure," I replied, hopping down from my stool. Any chance I got to make peace with Carson I took.

Anthony was laughing as we approached the gate.

The guy who had to be Dylan turned to Carson, beaming at the tropical blue Mustang convertible parked beside him. His goatee matched his short brown wavy hair. "Brand new GT Premium, not available to the public yet," he bragged. "And it's in Kona Blue, baby!"

"I can't believe you got them to name it that," Carson laughed.

"What do you think, Maryah?" Dylan threw his arm around my shoulder.

No hello. No nice to meet you. Just bam, I was part of the family. I liked him already. "It's awesome. You really named the color?"

"Anthony has friends at Ford. I could have suggested Smurf Blue and they'd approve it. Want to take her for a spin?"

"Me?" He'd known me all of ten seconds.

"She drives like a dream," Dylan insisted.

"I probably shouldn't."

"Come on, live a little!" Veins protruded out of his muscular forearms when he opened the driver's door. A wave of dark orange seemed to crest across his hazel eyes. "You drive. Carson will ride shotgun as a safety precaution."

Excitement took over and I hopped into the driver's seat. I inhaled the new car smell and Carson flashed me a reassuring smile. After carefully backing out of the driveway, I drove under five miles per hour on the narrow street that led out to 179. Once we were on the main road I loosened my grip on the steering wheel and glanced at Carson. "Your family has some serious connections, huh?"

"First of all, they're your family too. Secondly, it's not so much our connections but our gifts that help us out."

"Gifts?"

"Finally, she starts asking questions." Carson lowered his sunglasses. "If a giant meteoroid fell from the sky and landed on our house, would you notice?"

I stared ahead at the road. How the heck did we end up talking about meteoroids? "Um, yeah. I'd notice."

He laughed. "Are you sure?"

"What do meteors have to do with anything?"

"Forget it." He pointed out the window. "That turtle is passing us. Let's see what this car can do!"

In my confusion I hesitated, but then shook off Carson's random weirdness and pushed the gas pedal to the floor.

∞

Helen, Louise, and Anthony made Thanksgiving dinner while everyone watched football. Amber yelled at the television even more frequently than the guys. Edgar put on an apron at halftime, and in-between prepping food he'd tickle Helen or dip her like they were ballroom dancing. She'd tell him to stop, but always said it with a giddy grin on her face.

Even with his white hair, Edgar looked younger than I had pictured. He had been so quiet since our first meeting. The only words he'd actually spoken to me were, "Welcome home, Maryah." And that had been weeks ago. On the rare occasions I did see him, he was either napping or had his nose buried in a book. I was shocked when he asked me to set the table.

"Sure," I said, jumping up from my seat.

Carson and Dylan cleared away the extra dining room chairs, but left one extra. Were they hoping Nathan would show up? What if he wasn't coming home because of me? Was I keeping a mother from spending Thanksgiving with her son? I knew the holidays would be hard for me, but this Nathan issue added a new degree of difficulty.

I placed the last fork and knife on the table. When I looked up, Edgar was almost standing on top of me. He stared at me for an uncomfortably long time. My attention darted between his bifocals and leather loafers until he said, "It's been too long since we have all gathered at this table."

I swallowed hard, trying to think of something to say, but all I came up with was, "Yup."

He grinned, mussed up my hair, and then called everyone into the dining room for dinner.

Halfway through the meal, just when I had finally recovered from the awkward encounter with Edgar, Dylan stood up and tapped his fork against his glass.

"Amber and I have an announcement." Amber held his hand and blushed. "Amber is four months pregnant."

Happy cheers erupted around the table, but Louise looked like she already knew.

Carson smiled through a mouthful of potatoes. "I'm gonna be an uncle!"

They all looked so happy, so bonded. The way a family should be. The way my family had been, when I still had them.

Everyone chatted about names and whether they hoped for a boy or girl, but I excused myself. I needed to call my aunt and uncle to arrange going home for Christmas break. Louise would never skip two major holidays with her son, and I didn't want to be hanging around when Nathan—the maniac—came home to see his family.

∞

"Happy Thanksgiving, Pudding," Krista said sadly. She understood how rough the holidays would be for me.

"Happy Thanksgiving." I replied, trying not to sound gloomy. "How was your day with the family?"

"Good. I met Dylan and his wife. He let me drive his Mustang."

"Awesome."

That was it? She had nothing else to say? "How are things in your world?"

"Mom's side of the family came over, so we've had a house full of people all day. Oh, and I have the most exciting news!" Her voice sprang up several octaves.

I smiled at her contagious enthusiasm. "So, tell me already."

"Mom and Dad are taking me to Egypt for Christmas next month! Can you believe it? I'm going to visit the pyramids!"

My smile fizzled. Krista had always been fascinated with Egypt. This was a dream come true for her, but the greedy part of me was devastated. They were leaving the country for my first Christmas without my parents and Mikey? Had they not even considered that I'd want to spend the holidays with them? Talk about out of sight out of mind! How could they do this to me?

"I'm looking through my Egypt books and planning all the places I need to see."

I couldn't ruin Krista's moment, so I faked excitement. "That's amazing. Make sure to take pictures."

"Definitely!"

It wasn't Krista's fault that my aunt and uncle didn't consider I might want to come home for Christmas. I felt bad making up a lie, but if I kept talking she'd know I was upset. "Louise needs me for something so I have to go, but tell everyone I said Happy Thanksgiving."

"Okay. I will. Love you and miss you."

"You too." I hung up the phone, stood on my bed, and ripped down Krista's photo.

∞

A dark-haired stranger slid my peacock ring on my finger then kissed me. His warm breath against my ear, ocean waves, and ukulele music faded away as my dream of being on a tropical island dissolved into the sunlight pouring through my bedroom windows.

My dream catcher swayed above me. It looked lonely without Krista's photo hanging next to it, but whatever. She was obviously doing just fine without me. I'd do the same.

A delicious, sweet smell made my mouth water, so I climbed out of bed and made my way to the kitchen.

"Just in time!" Amber stood over the stove, wearing a flowered apron and a luminous smile.

Dylan swallowed his food. "Morning, Maryah."

"It smells amazing in here," I said.

"It's our Black Friday tradition, macadamia nut pancakes and fresh pineapple." Amber handed me a plate. "Homemade macadamia butter is on the table."

Molokai barked as the front door opened.

"Amberrrrr!" Faith sang, barreling through the kitchen until she had her locked in a hug. "I've missed you so much."

Amber scuffed up Faith's hair. "Missed you too, Pinkerbell."

Shiloh kissed Amber on the cheek as I chuckled at Faith's perfect nickname.

Harmony lurked behind them and I decided Harmony's nickname would be Stinkerbell. Although I'd never actually call her that, unless I had the urge to get knocked out. Faith stepped aside and Harmony hugged Amber, leaving me stunned by Harmony showing someone affection.

"Congrats on the bambino." Harmony brushed Amber's stomach with one finger.

"Thank you, Harmony."

"I've been jonesing for these pancakes!" Faith squealed, plopping one on her plate.

"Where's Dakota?" Dylan asked.

"He'll be here soon. He and Na—Nicholas were having breakfast." Faith glanced at me before continuing. "Carson is meeting them then he's picking up Dakota and coming back here."

"Ah, okay," Dylan replied, stuffing pineapple in his mouth.

Na-Nicholas? Did they think I was that clueless? I knew Nathan was in town! He probably had to stay at Shiloh or Dakota's house because of me. My guilt made me lose my appetite.

"What's new with you pixies?" Amber asked Faith and Harmony.

"Nada," Harmony replied bleakly.

Faith danced around the kitchen while eating. "You know what's new with me. I call you with all my updates."

"Yes, *you* do, but telephone skills don't run in the family." Amber jabbed Harmony with the spatula.

"If I had news I'd call you," Harmony said.

"What about school? I noticed college brochures lying around here, are you girls applying anywhere?"

They were my college brochures, but Faith shuffled through a stack sitting on the counter. "I'm weighing my options."

"I'm not going to college," Harmony grumbled.

"You're not?" I said without thinking. "What are you going to do?"

Harmony looked amped up, like one flick of a switch and sparks would fly out of her scary head. "The day I graduate, I'm taking off and searching every corner of the world."

"For what?"

The determination in her eyes nearly electrocuted me. "My soul mate."

Soul mate? Dark and dreary Harmony wanted to search the world for love? Was she serious? Nobody else seemed surprised by her answer, or her announcement about not going to college. The last thing I wanted was to pick a fight with her, so I shut up, but I still couldn't believe it.

"Shiloh, would you mind if we borrowed your truck next month?" Anthony asked. "We're going to Colorado for Christmas."

I almost choked on my milk. Shiloh had a puzzled look on his face then he said something in Japanese. Faith replied with more Japanese gibberish. When she finished, Shiloh looked up and said, "Ahhh" like he solved a mystery. "Sure, Chief, you're always welcome to borrow my ride."

"Thanks. I'll leave you the keys to my Mustang."

Realizing I would most definitely see Nathan, my stomach somersaulted. "We're going to Colorado?"

Dylan passed me a napkin and pointed at the corner of his mouth. "We'd like you to see our house and show you Colorado Springs."

Embarrassed, I wiped away milk, or butter, or whatever Dylan noticed on my face. I asked Faith, "You aren't coming with us?"

"Maryah, we have family of our own that we spend Christmas with."

"Right." I had to admit, there were times when I forgot Faith, Shiloh, Harmony, and Dakota weren't part of the Luna family. "Edgar and Helen are coming, right?" The more people the better—safety in numbers.

"No, Edgar doesn't like long car rides. It's a ten-hour drive," Louise explained.

The total count was in. It would be only the four of us: Anthony, Louise, Carson, and me. My stomach twisted in knots. I glanced up from my plate. Everyone was staring at me.

Faith reached over and held my hand. "Are you okay, Ma-Ma?"

"I'm fine," I lied.

"You're worried...about seeing Nathan?"

I wanted to kick her under the counter. Louise and Anthony were sitting right across from us! I couldn't admit their son terrified me, but I couldn't ask them to spend another holiday away from him.

"Nathan won't be home for Christmas," Amber interjected. "He's spending winter break in India."

I dropped my fork, and it clanged loudly against my plate. The recent dream I'd had about Nathan with an Indian princess had to be a random coincidence. Maybe I overheard Louise mention he'd gone to India and forgot about it. But it didn't explain why my dreams were getting more peculiar, or why some of them felt so real.

I told April about my dreams, and she always researched interpretations on some online dream dictionary, but none of the explanations ever made sense. Krista and I were growing apart so fast it was giving me whiplash, so I couldn't talk to her about it, and if I told Faith she'd go off on one of her philosophical tangents and make it into a headache-inducing research project.

I glanced around the table filled with people eating, talking, and laughing. I imagined April and River cuddled up on a couch together watching a movie. I thought about Krista planning her trip to Egypt, and Nathan traveling halfway across the world to India.

I had never felt more alone.

LIGHTING THE WAY

Maryah

Christmas had inched closer and closer until I was gagging on all the yuletide cheer. Winter break should have been a welcome relief, and yes, I was grateful for time away from school, but it meant I'd have to survive the dreaded Colorado Christmas.

River wanted to go to a real mall to go shopping, so we headed up to Flagstaff. I wasn't thrilled about the idea of cranky holiday shoppers, but after days of listening to him plead and whine, I caved just to shut him up.

We passed yet another store as River tried to decide what to get April.

"She might be getting a bulldog under her tree," he said.

"Aw, she'd love a puppy!"

"No, my bulldog. Eightball is an expensive, needy flea bag."

"Don't be mean. I love that dog."

"Good. I know what I'm giving you."

Passing by a music store window gave me an idea. "Why don't you make her a CD?"

"A CD?"

"You're a singer. Sing a bunch of sappy songs and burn it onto a CD."

"Who listens to CD's anymore? Besides, that's the kind of stuff poor people do because they can't afford a real gift."

"I think it's sweet."

"You would."

"What's that supposed to mean?"

River shot me a sideways glare. "Never mind. What do you want for Christmas, besides a CD of me singing?"

I'd become a pro at keeping up with River's asinine comments. "I asked Santa for a tattoo with your name on it, but they're on back order."

"You'd really get a tattoo?"

"No, I was kidding, Sir Inks-a lot."

"I'd buy you a tattoo. I'd even go with you to get it done, so I could watch while you writhe in pain."

"You're so sweet," I cooed sarcastically. "But I'll pass. I'm not the tattoo type."

"Everybody has them."

"Exactly, and I like being different."

"You've succeeded at that goal," he said with an arrogant head nod.

He ignored the dirty look I gave him and pulled me into a jewelry store. I'd never been a fan of expensive jewelry. The sentiment behind a gift meant more to me than the dollar amount on its price tag.

"That's badass" He pointed to a heart shaped necklace made of black and white diamonds. "What do you think?"

"It's pretty."

"How much?" River asked the stuffy sales lady. She looked irritated that we were even in the store.

"It's on sale for six-hundred and ninety nine dollars."

I laughed at the absurdly high price.

"I'll take it." River winked at her and she dropped her attitude, smiling and falling all over herself to find a box.

"Are you crazy?" I whispered. "It costs seven-hundred dollars."

"It's only money." He brushed it off like he was buying a five-dollar happy meal.

Arguing with him was pointless. River enjoyed flaunting his money—correction, his uncle's money. Making a big deal out of the situation would just feed his ego. If his ego grew any bigger the ozone layer would burst. The important thing was that he decided on a gift. I wanted to get out of the crowded mall and go home.

Anthony wanted to leave for Colorado first thing in the morning, and I still needed to pack.

∞

On our drive back to Sedona, River asked, "What am I supposed to do while you're out of town for a week?"

"I'm sure you'll survive." I channel-surfed the radio, trying to find anything *but* Christmas carols. "Trust me, I'd rather stay here."

"Why? I hear Colorado is dope."

"I guess I'm worried Louise's other son will show up. We don't get along."

"Nathan?"

"You know him?" I asked.

"Of course. We've been going to school together since we were little."

"I figured you might not know him since he's a year ahead of us."

"He's not a year ahead of us. He's a senior."

"No, he started college in Colorado this past fall."

"Well, he was a junior last year. Did he go to college without graduating?" River stomped on the gas pedal.

I stared ahead, replaying conversations about Nathan and him studying abroad. Louise wouldn't lie about Nathan going to college. Would she?

"Did you know his girlfriend too?" I asked.

"What girlfriend?"

"Mary. Tall with black curly hair—looks like a model."

"In all the years I've known him, I've never seen that guy even look at a girl. He was the loner type. The only girls he talked to were his brother's girlfriend and your freaky Cain and Abel twins."

I was too confused to smack River for the Cain and Abel reference. Besides, the names were appropriate for Faith and Harmony. We passed by houses decorated and lit up for the holiday. "Did he seem a little...*off* to you? Like a few bulbs were burnt out on his Christmas tree?" I tried making a joke so River wouldn't question why I cared. *I* wasn't ever sure why I cared.

"A few bulbs? I'm not sure his tree lit up at all."

Maybe Nathan really was crazy. Maybe Louise and Anthony had to send him away to a mental hospital in Colorado. Carson did act strange when I asked about Nathan's girlfriend. Maybe she was part of Nathan's issues. I knew she looked too much like a supermodel. Plus, the photo looked old. He probably cut her out of an old magazine.

River's snide comment caught my attention. "I have no idea why girls swooned over him."

"Huh?"

"He's a weirdo, but lots of girls crushed on him. He's not even that good-looking."

River was wrong about the last part. Nathan was by far the best-looking guy I'd ever seen. However, his mental issues disqualified him from ever being the total package.

"I'm glad to hear you didn't fall for his Mr. Mysterious crap," River snarled. "I knew you had good taste."

We arrived at my house and I hugged River, telling him to try to enjoy the holiday with April. It made me sad to know he didn't have family to celebrate Christmas with, and that April's mom was still so sick. It wouldn't be a happy holiday for any of us.

The Nathan thing ate away at me, but I didn't know how to approach the subject, so I left it alone. We were leaving for Colorado first thing in the morning and I didn't want the long drive to be awkward.

ANIMAL INSTINCTS

Maryah

We pulled into Amber and Dylan's driveway and I saw Nathan's Mustang sitting in the garage: red with black stripes, so appropriate for Satan's spawn. Then, another red and silver vehicle caught my attention.

Holy freaking crap. The motorcycle.

The *exact* motorcycle he rode in my hospital dream. The verdict was in: because of the blow to my head, or my brain surgery, I had acquired some kind of useless psychic power. Get some tape and stick the "freak" sign on my back. I couldn't even tell April about this one. Absolutely no one would understand—or believe it. Even I had trouble believing it.

"Maryah," Louise called from the front door. "Are you coming?"

I continued up the walkway, trying to shake away yet another stranger-than-fiction piece of a puzzle that made no sense to me. And honestly, it was a puzzle that scared me.

The moment I stepped inside, Dylan popped his head around a wall and smiled. "Hey, you made it!"

Amber and Dylan's house looked like a colorful island resort. They decorated the main room like a summery Christmas wonderland. Blue and white lights illuminated a fake palm tree, and a couple of large tiki statues wore Santa hats. It was absolutely nothing like I pictured for a Colorado Christmas.

"Aloha!" Amber called from the top of the stairway. She wore a super cute red and orange outfit, and dark-rimmed glasses that made her look studious. She made it halfway down the steps then suddenly slipped and fell onto her butt.

I lunged forward to help her. "Are you okay?"

Dylan waved his hand. "She's fine. That happens at least once a day."

"I've heard being pregnant messes up your balance." I tried defending Amber so she wouldn't be embarrassed, but she didn't seem fazed at all.

"It's not because I'm pregnant. I begged Dylan to get a ranch style house, but my clumsiness keeps him entertained."

The more I got to know Amber, the more I liked her. She gave me a tour of the house and when she opened the French doors to the backyard, I gasped. Not at the acres of land, or the view of snow-capped mountains, but at the small white horse sleeping on the deck.

"You have a pony?" I asked in disbelief.

"He's a class A miniature horse. His name is Baby Hilo."

"Can I pet him?" He looked like a big white cotton ball. His eyes opened and he sat up.

"Perfect, he's awake! Sure you can pet him, he loves people."

His pearly coat felt like satin, and he licked my hand while I petted him. "I love him."

"Good because he's fond of you too."

From the corner of my eye I saw another blur of fur. I almost screamed when an animal the size of a raccoon scurried up to Amber.

"This is Big Kahuna." She squatted down and gathered him in her arms.

"What is he?"

"A meerkat. A big, fat one," she teased. He reclined back in her arms and stared at me. "Coco and Nutty are normal-sized." She nodded at the end of the deck. Two little beige faces peered over the top step.

"Do they bite?"

"No, they're harmless. Unless you're a bug," Amber chuckled. "They aren't meant to be pets, but I have a permit for these guys because I participate in animal behavior programs. Do you want to hold him? He wants to check you out."

She passed him to me and he nuzzled into my neck. The two smaller meerkats scurried over and sniffed my shoes. I giggled as Big Kahuna tickled me with his nose. "They're so cute!"

"They're spoiled rotten."

The patio door opened and Carson came outside with a black cat in his arms, Molokai followed behind him.

"There's Hilo!" Carson set the cat down and petted the miniature horse.

"Our cat's name is Lulu," Amber told me.

Big Kahuna and I were still busy rubbing noses. His cuteness outweighed his musty smell. "Do all of the animals get along?"

"Yes, because if they step out of line, they'll have me to deal with." Amber acted all tough, but she bent down and lovingly petted Lulu.

"Amber has a gift with animals," Carson said.

I nodded. "No kidding. I've never met anyone with pets like these."

Amber snorted a laugh. "Compared to the rest of this family, my gift is nothing to brag about."

Carson pointed at the sky. "Look a meteoroid!"

Amber and I looked up, but the sky was a blank blue canvas. Carson laughed and shook his head. I assumed it was a reference to our meteor conversation from the day I drove Dylan's Mustang, but I was still clueless about what he meant.

Amber slugged his shoulder then put her arm around me. "Come on, Maryah, let's get you settled in."

I followed her through the house and up the stairs. When we reached the top, Amber turned to face me. "I know you don't like Nathan, and I'm sorry we have to do this to you, but you'll be staying in his room."

"Oh." My own personal nightmare before Christmas. Perfect.

"Just pretend it's a guest room. It's pretty generic, so it shouldn't be difficult," she said before opening a door.

She was right. Nathan's room in Sedona looked like the Taj Mahal compared to this one. There was a basic dresser, a nightstand, and a twin bed with a plain green comforter. No pictures or decorations anywhere.

I felt comfortable with Amber, maybe because she was like me, not related to the Lunas by blood. There must have been a point in time when she had to figure out a family different from her own. "Hey, Amber?"

"Yes."

"Can I ask you something and keep it just between you and me?"

"As long as keeping the secret doesn't violate any family oaths."

I had no idea what she meant, but I took it as a yes. "Is Nathan in college?"

"No, he's a senior."

Did I misunderstand? I tried to recall if Louise ever actually used the word *college*, but I couldn't think of a specific time. "How come he transferred schools right before senior year?"

"He wanted to get away from Sedona. We were happy to have him here, so it seemed like a good choice for everyone." Amber sat on the bed. "Now, can I ask you something?"

"Sure."

"Do you think you'll ever forgive him?"

I leaned against the wall. "Um..." Sure, if he was the great guy from my dreams, but he wasn't—far from it actually.

"Let me say this," she began, fiddling with the hair-tie on her wrist. "You are part of this family. Every member loves you and looks out for you—including Nathan. He had a funny way of showing it in Albuquerque, but there's a lot you don't understand about him yet." She looked around his room then pulled her curls back into a ponytail. "I would never ask you to do something you don't want to do, but please, consider forgiving him. You wouldn't believe how hard his life has been."

I didn't know what to say, so I just stared at her like a mute. Could I really ever forgive him?

She pushed her glasses up the bridge of her nose and stood up. "I'll let you get settled in. There are snacks downstairs to tide you over until dinner. Come down whenever you're ready."

I stared at Nathan's closed closet doors until curiosity got the best of me. Nothing exciting was inside: neatly hung clothes, shoes lined along the floor, and snowboards leaning against the wall. I shut the door and felt guilty for snooping.

Fighting back tears, it hit me that I was about to spend Christmas Eve with a family other than my own. I missed Mikey more than ever. He loved the holidays, and he would've loved Amber's animals. I wondered if he'd be friends with Carson or if—no. It didn't matter. Mikey was gone. I took a few calming breaths and headed downstairs to join the others.

Dylan had invited the guys downstairs so he could show off his new home theater system. I sat by the fireplace, admiring the ornaments on the tree and drinking hot chocolate. Amber updated Louise on her latest project—whale communications. It reminded me of Christmas Eves I'd spent with my real family, except Krista, Aunt Sandy, and Uncle Dave were missing. I wondered how they were doing in Egypt. I had no idea what time it was there, and I couldn't call Krista, but I did miss her.

Louise pointed at the glass doors. "Look, it's snowing!"

"Carson will be excited about having a white Christmas," Amber said, refilling my hot chocolate.

Baby Hilo peered at us through the flurries. Amber turned to let him in as if she sensed him standing there then he trotted in then curled up by the fireplace. Molokai snuggled up beside him.

"Where are the meerkats?" I asked.

"They came in while you were upstairs. They're in the basement playing in the tunnels Carson built for them."

The snowy Christmas Eve made everything feel cozy. It could never be the same as home, but at least I was surrounded by good people and adorable animals. I stared at the flickering fireplace and couldn't help wondering where in the world Nathan was spending Christmas. And even though I didn't mean to, I caught myself hoping he wasn't sad or lonely.

FACING THE FEARLESS

NATHANIEL

I traversed into Marcus's hotel room, startling him and his wife. Marcus closed the book he was reading. "Nathan, what is it?"

"I'm sorry to interrupt you on Christmas Eve, but I found Dedrick."

Without hesitation, they both leapt from their bed. Audrey moved impressively fast for a woman in her seventies. They scrambled to change while I divulged all the information I could.

"As of now, he's a moving target. You'll need to meet me at Saint Katharine's dock, as fast as you can get there. He's hosting a party of some sort on a boat, the August Queen Anne, on the River Thames."

Audrey clutched Marcus's hand. She looked at me with wide, doe-like eyes.

Marcus urged her along. "Dear, we must hurry."

"That party." Audrey swallowed hard. "Marcus and I received an invitation."

"What?" I asked. "From whom?"

Audrey sank onto the edge of the bed, appearing too weak to stand. Marcus held onto her arm but stared at the floor.

"James and Lillian," he said. "Members of our kindrily. We hadn't seen or heard from them in several years."

Audrey clutched onto Marcus. "You don't think they've joined Dedrick, do you? They couldn't possibly—but they invited us to that party. Why would they do that?"

Marcus sat beside her. "Dedrick is building a team of Elements with the most useful abilities. Of course they would want you."

She pressed her hands to her cheeks. "Oh my word."

Audrey was a paralyzer— the only one I had ever met or heard of. She could make anyone immobile just by looking at them. That kind of ability would be of great use to Dedrick.

"This James, what is his gift?" I asked.

Marcus blinked several times before looking at me. "He's the same as your Anthony, a time stopper."

"And Lillian?"

"A decoder." Decoders had become more useful as technology became more prevalent, but James was a much bigger concern than Lillian.

"Can James stop other Elements when he freezes time?"

"Of course not," Marcus said.

I decided not to disclose the fact that Anthony had mastered that ability. Our kindrily had agreed to keep it a valuable secret.

Anthony would have been one of my top choices to have with me for a meeting with Dedrick, but he wouldn't be able to get here fast enough. Oddly, we might have access to someone with the same ability—inconveniently, he could be on the enemy's side, but we still might be able to use him.

"This could work in our favor," I said. "If we confront Dedrick in a public place, and James is with him, Dedrick will order him to freeze time so there are no witnesses."

Audrey shook her head. "No. James wouldn't be part of such evil. He wouldn't."

I wanted to explain my theory to her, that I believed some members of Dedrick's clan were working with him against their will, but there was no time. "I must go. Saint Katharine's Dock. As soon as you can. I'll see you there."

I visualized a small alcove in the Tower Bridge. I'd been there several times before, and no one would be present on Christmas Eve to see me mysteriously appear. As I finished reforming in the shadows of the dark hallway, I grew anxious. We had been tracking Dedrick for months, traveling all over Europe and India as we received one false lead after another. Now, he was within my grasp, but I'd have to confront him without the strength and skills of any members of my own kindrily.

I paced along the high walkway of the bridge, looking out of the towering glass windows and searching the River Thames below me. His boat wasn't in sight yet, but soon it would be passing under the very spot where I stood. I hadn't been this close to Dedrick in almost two decades. Last lifetime, he had the upper hand.

Mary had stood there, thrashing in his arms, fighting with all the life and vigor inside her until he pressed the sharp blade to her throat. He whispered something in her ear that even I couldn't hear. She closed her eyes momentarily, and when she opened them, tears dripped down her cheeks. She mouthed the words, *I love you eternally*, then grabbed Dedrick's hands and slit her own throat.

I had no idea it was our final goodbye.

If I had known that day on the beach would be our last day together, if I had known she planned to erase, I would have done more. I would have done *something*, anything, to stop it.

This time, when I faced Dedrick, I would have nothing to lose, and I needed to make sure he knew he had nothing to gain by coming after Maryah again.

∞

We planned on waiting until they were off the boat, and following them to a place where we'd be out of the public eye—until the boat stopped several yards from the dock. The world around us stilled. The waves no longer lapped, the wind stopped, even the trees became motionless.

"James." Audrey gasped. "It must be."

Most of the guests on board were frozen, but we saw movement inside the cabin and then a bald man stepped onto the deck carrying a limp girl with a bag over her head. He and another red-headed woman were binding her hands and feet together.

"What are they doing?" Marcus peered through binoculars, but I could see clearly.

Dedrick followed after the bald bloke. His mouth moved, but even my ears couldn't make out his words. However, his flailing arms revealed his anger, and when Baldy returned carrying an anchor, it became obvious.

"They intend to drown her," I said. "We need to go right now."

Audrey grabbed my jacket. "We don't know how many there are."

Marcus replied before I could argue. "We can't let an innocent girl be killed."

Audrey nodded and Marcus turned his back to her, squatting low with his arms reached behind him. She climbed aboard him like a five-year-old ready for a piggy back ride. The established routine made me envious that I couldn't take people with me when I used my gift.

Marcus nodded at me. "See you on board."

As if a solid road lay before him, he stepped off the dock, jogging on air. Audrey bobbed up and down on his back with each step. I had seen Marcus aether walk before, climbing through the air to reach something on a high shelf, gliding down the stairway in his home as if flying because he said the impact was rough on the knees. But seeing him running over the River Thames with nothing but air and energy beneath him evoked a new level of marvel within me.

They had almost reached the boat, and by the looks of it, the red-haired woman had spotted them. I focused on the space behind Dedrick and traversed to it.

Dedrick had his back to me, facing starboard, watching Marcus and Audrey glide onto the boat deck. "To what do we owe this pleasure?" Dedrick bellowed. "I do believe you two responded to my invitation that you were unable to attend."

"Behind you," the redhead hissed to Dedrick.

He turned, gave me a once over then stared into my eyes. I let him study them. No more sunglasses. For years we hid behind dark shields hoping to never be recognized by the Nefariouns, but now I wanted Dedrick to know it was me.

Slowly, a vile grin exposed his crooked, yellow teeth. "Nathaniel, how nice of you to join us."

Baldy was ignoring the rest of us and tying the motionless girl's feet to the anchor.

I glanced at her, then at Marcus, and he must have known what I was thinking. "Dedrick," Marcus asked. "What are your intentions with this girl?"

Audrey crept out from behind Marcus, navigating between immobile guests: some frozen in mid-sentence with their mouths open, many with drinks in their hands half raised to their lips. One woman stood pointing at something in the distance. Audrey ducked under the frozen woman's arm. She assessed the scene like a feral cat, ready to pounce if anyone moved too quickly.

I hadn't seen Audrey use her ability yet. I prayed it worked fast and efficiently and that she could handle disabling more than one person at a time: all good questions I should have asked *before* we were surrounded by Dedrick and his goons, goons who no doubt, all had powerful abilities of their own.

Dedrick's grin didn't falter. "My intentions were to lure Nathaniel aboard this vessel."

My stomach dropped. He wanted me aboard this boat, and I fell right into his trap. What evil reasons did he have for confronting me? "Here I am," I growled. "Speak your peace."

"*Stop* following me around like a stray dog. My affairs are none of your concern."

"Stay away from any and all members of my kindrily and we have a deal."

He rubbed his dark beard. "You still sound bitter about our last encounter. Your lass cut her own throat. Perhaps you're carrying around misplaced anger. She ended her last life, not me."

Rage boiled inside of me. I needed to stay calm, but his taunting comments also gave me reason to act as if I didn't have control of my emotions, to plant the seed of vital information that would hopefully keep Maryah safe. I changed the tone of my voice to sound shaken. "What did you say to her right before she did it?"

His gaze darted around, landing on nothing particular, like he was searching for the memory. "I'm an old soul, lad. You can't expect me to recall one minute in time from nearly twenty years ago."

"Whatever you said caused her to erase." I gritted my teeth. "She erased. She's no longer an Element. You took her away from me for eternity."

He let out a coarse laugh. "The most powerful astral gadabout of all time threw away all of her knowledge and power because of little ole me? Even you aren't daft enough to think I'll believe that. Try again."

"She has no idea who she used to be. She doesn't even know Elements exist. And she no longer has her ability. She's of no use to anyone. Not even herself."

I pictured her empty eyes. Grief flooded through me. Even after so many years, even after spending time with her and seeing no flicker of recognition, my heart ached at my own words as if I was realizing them for the first time.

"He's telling the truth," a familiar grainy voice said from behind me. His tall, wide form cast a shadow across the gleaming white deck. I stepped to the edge of the boat so no one else could sneak up behind me.

"Ah, well." Dedrick sighed. "I suppose that would make sense given the uselessness of our experiment."

"What experiment?" I asked.

The 6'5'' matador stepped between Dedrick and me. He pulled out a dagger and stared me down. The muscles of his left arm bulged as he gripped the knife and prepared to strike.

We had fought side by side a couple times in previous lives, but I was sure he didn't remember me. I stared into the windows of his soul, letting him really see me, hoping to study the depths of his eyes so I could figure out where he made such an evil wrong turn. But there was no history there. None. His eyes were golden with thin black slits, no timelines or identifying markers whatsoever. He looked exactly the same as he had decades ago: the same tan Peruvian skin and long black ponytail. He hadn't aged a day. Come to think of it, neither had Dedrick.

"What's your name, soldier?" I asked.

"Argos. And I'm no one's soldier."

"Nice to see you again, Argos."

He didn't blink, not one spark of recognition. The unnaturalness of it left me perturbed and full of questions—questions that would need to be answered later. The important thing was that I knew he was a mind reader, and his fighting style. Killing him would be impossible, but knowing him so well gave me an advantage.

Dedrick peeked around Argos and squinted at me. "You're certain you heard all of his thoughts? Not an inkling of a chance he could be lying about the girl?"

"I'm sure," Argos grunted.

"Well then," Dedrick said. "We got what we needed here." He strutted over to the restrained girl and took the bag off of her head.

"Lillian!" Audrey shouted.

Lillian wasn't frozen, but she also didn't react to Audrey. She only stared ahead at Baldy as if nothing was amiss.

Dedrick lifted Baldy's chin so their eyes met. "Untie our girl."

Baldy gave a nod and loosened the ropes around the girl's feet and hands. Dedrick clapped and waved to the deck above. Seconds later, a young boy of about fifteen joined us. Audrey lunged when she saw him, but Marcus shouted, "No, Audrey!" and she stopped.

Based on her reaction and her pooling tears, the boy was James.

Dedrick laughed again and put his arm around the boy's shoulder. "You both did splendid."

I studied James and Lillian, realizing their eyes looked exactly like Argos's—golden with black slits, and vapid. Audrey and Marcus noticed too, and Audrey wasn't shy about questioning the change.

"What have you done to them, you hellion?"

Dedrick clutched his chest. "Such cruel names hurt my feelings. Your loved ones chose to work for me. I haven't *done* anything to them."

"Liar!" Audrey shouted.

Marcus was by her side in an instant. "Calm down, my love."

James and Lillian hadn't uttered a word. They barely moved. Neither had Argos, Baldy, and the redhead. It's like they were drones who didn't think or act on their own. They appeared to be waiting for commands from Dedrick.

Audrey hadn't calmed down. "We're taking them with us!"

Dedrick stepped uncomfortably close to her. "I'd love to see you try."

She spit in his face.

All of Dedrick's goons sprung to life, advancing on Audrey and Marcus. With a quick curling and flexing of her fingers, Audrey had all of them paralyzed. She was focused, but the feat seemed effortless. She had disabled five people with a flick of her hand.

"It's a shame," Dedrick groused, wiping the spit off his face. Was he immune to paralysis or did Audrey intentionally not include him? "I had hoped you would consider joining us. Everyone who joins me is treated like royalty, but I don't tolerate such blatant disrespect."

Audrey was rigid, and her voice scathing. "I'd want a permanent death before I ever teamed up with you."

James and Lillian's arms and legs twitched as they struggled to move. Audrey must have been taking it easy on the two of them, that or she was losing control of keeping five people paralyzed at the same time.

Dedrick growled. "We'll see if you still feel that way when we become the gatekeepers of this world."

"You will never accomplish that," Marcus said sternly.

Gatekeepers? What did he mean? Marcus obviously knew something I didn't.

"We shall see about that." Dedrick's lips curled into a satanic grin. "We're closer than you think, and we've got eyes everywhere."

I struggled to keep myself from snarling. Regardless of the hatred I had for Dedrick and his evil undertakings, my mission was to get him to stop hunting Maryah. He knew she was no longer of use to him. I didn't want to provoke him to come after anyone else in my kindrily.

I steadied my voice. "Audrey, we can't decide the fate of anyone but ourselves. These people have chosen a path with Dedrick. We may not like it, but we must respect it."

Dedrick stalked over to me. "Very noble and unassuming of you, Nathaniel, but I hope your precious family is ready. We have the troops required to gain control of who comes into this world, and we'll dispose of those we no longer want here—including any uncooperative Elements."

His plan sounded more calamitous than any of our kindrily suspected. I had to alert the others as soon as possible. I waved at Marcus, motioning for him and Audrey to leave the boat. "We will consider our options thoroughly, but for now, we are leaving."

Marcus took his piggy-back stance and Audrey climbed onto his back while staying focused on the five people she kept paralyzed. Marcus took several steps backward so that he and Audrey were hovering in the air above the river beyond anyone's reach.

I mentally assessed the logistics of our situation. James was still keeping time and people frozen around us, yet Audrey had him paralyzed. Was her paralysis only physical and not mental?

Dedrick pulled out a cigar. He lit it, took a puff, and blew a cloud of smoke in my face. Quietly, so no one but me could hear him, he said, "If you and your kindrily join my cause, I'll tell you what I told your sweetheart right before she killed herself. Then you'll know why she erased."

My fist crashed into his jaw before I could think it through, but I observed every detail as if in slow motion. My knuckles meeting his jawbone sent his cigar flying through the air. He fell to the ground. His skull hit the boat deck with a loud thud. He was on his back, trying to roll to one side while clapping at his drones, but Audrey kept them paralyzed.

"That was for Mary." I pressed the heel of my boot against his throat and leaned into it with all my weight, crushing his windpipe. I bent down so he'd be sure to hear my threat. "We will kill you before we ever partner with you."

Audrey yelled my name, but at the same instant, my back felt like I'd been hit with a hot branding iron. I turned around to see Argos holding a bloody dagger.

"I'm sorry, Nathan!" Audrey cried out. "I couldn't hold him."

I staggered backward, but not before stomping Dedrick's ribs.

"Go!" I shouted to Marcus and Audrey, but they hovered close to the boat. The other four Nefariouns were struggling to move, twitching and jerking, but no one else broke free. "I'll be right behind you."

"No," Marcus argued. "Not until you traverse out of here."

"Finish him!" Dedrick shouted, pointing at me. "Don't let him off this boat alive!"

Argos stalked toward me, the muscles of his arms rippling, intent on striking again.

Fire raged through my back, but I forced a smile. "We *will* meet again, Argos." Knowing he could hear my thoughts, I silently told him, *Next time I'll have an old friend of yours with me. The one person in this world who will do whatever it takes to bring you down.*

He braced himself, preparing to slash me again, but by the time he swung his arm at my chest, I had vanished.

DREAMING OF A WHITE CHRISTMAS

Maryah

Dream-version Nathan looked tired, or worried, or stressed, or an overdose of all three. He sat on Dylan and Amber's couch staring at the Christmas tree. Molokai and Baby Hilo were in the dream too, and snow fell outside, just like before I went to bed. Molokai was on the couch beside Nathan. He petted her and kissed her on the nose.

"Ha." I grunted. As if Nathan would be that sweet.

Molokai's focus locked on me and she whimpered. At first Nathan didn't react, but then she jumped down and sat in front of me. She barked once, wagging her tail as she looked back at Nathan. He watched her, but didn't say anything. She raised her front paws like she wanted to put them in my lap and Nathan's green eyes grew wider.

He slowly rose to his feet, glancing around the room then walked over to the Christmas tree. He looked in my direction and curled his fingers like he wanted me to come closer. "Merry Christmas, Maryah."

Why did my dreams feel so real?

He reached forward, removed a crystal peacock feather from the tree, and held it between us. He glanced up at the star tree topper and sighed. "I don't know what I miss more, you or my sanity."

I waved my hand in front of his face to see if he responded, but his eyes were shut tightly.

"All I want to do is protect you," he said. "No, that's a lie. I want you back, the old you, the you who knew everything."

An urge to touch him overwhelmed me. I moved closer, close enough to feel the body heat radiating from him.

He opened his eyes but stared at the ornament in his hand. "You'd be able to figure out what Dedrick is planning. I feel like war has been declared, and I'm helpless to stop it. I can't do this without you."

As usual in my ridiculous dreams, I had no idea who Dedrick was or why I'd be imagining Nathan talking about war, but he looked so vulnerable. I raised my hand, reaching for his face, but he turned and walked away. A huge brown circle covered the back of his ripped shirt. Panicking, I looked at Nathan's jacket, still draped over the arm of the couch. Sure enough, it had dried blood all over the inside.

Mikey, I told myself. *I'm dreaming about blood on his shirt because my mind is still traumatized from seeing Mikey get stabbed.* The real Nathan wasn't bleeding, and he certainly hadn't been standing in Amber's living room saying he missed me.

Molokai trotted along behind me as I checked the next room and glanced up the stairway, but Nathan was nowhere to be found. He had vanished into thin air.

"Stupid dream," I mumbled. Molokai barked at me.

I woke up and let my eyes adjust to the dark room. Molokai was barking downstairs, so that explained why I dreamed about her. I hated that I felt so drawn to Nathan in my dreams.

A beam of moonlight danced across my ring. I took it off and set it on the nightstand. My brain *really* needed to find something to dream about besides peacock feathers and Nathan.

Amber apologizing for Nathan earlier didn't mean much. It's not like *he* was apologizing. How could I forgive him if he never made any attempt to tell me he was sorry? Maybe his bloody back was a warning not to get close to him or he'd hurt me again, or stab me in the back. I wondered what April's dream dictionary would say.

I flipped onto my side, fluffed my pillow, and tried to forget the whole stupid thing.

∞

Waking up to the sound of a metal shovel grinding against concrete was comforting. It reminded me of snow days in Maryland when my father would clear the driveway and sidewalk before Mikey and I went sledding.

Then I remembered it was Christmas morning, and my heart sank. I stared at the ceiling, trying to convince myself I could survive Christmas without my family. I wanted to run into Mikey's room and bounce on his bed while shouting for him to wake up so we could open presents, but that would never happen again.

I sat up to look out the window and see how much snow accumulated overnight, but I froze with shock. There, hanging from the lock of Nathan's bedroom window, was the glass peacock ornament from my dream.

I pinched the skin on my wrist as hard as I could, but nothing happened.

I was awake and the ornament was real.

After rushing downstairs and searching the couch and living room for a bloody jacket, and finding nothing, I realized I had a better chance of finding Santa and his reindeer. As if any part of my dream could have been real.

Louise—or someone—would be awake and freaking out if Nathan had been injured so severely, and he wouldn't be sneaking into my room to hang an ornament in my window. The feather must have been hanging there since I arrived—I just failed to notice it.

I'd never been the most observant person in the world.

NAME CALLING

Maryah

We arrived home from Colorado late on New Year's Day. All the madness needed to stop. New year, new rules.

No more obsessing about crazy dreams. No more self-indulgent Nathan naps. Creating some fictitious alter ego for him just because he was hot was not healthy—or normal. My dreams were bordering on stalkerish.

The next morning at school, River stood outside our English class chatting with two screaming-for-attention brunettes. His faux-hawk looked more defined than usual.

"How were the Rockies?" he asked, turning his back on the devastated groupie duo.

"Nice. We had a white Christmas."

"Cool."

I scanned the classroom and hallway. "Where's April?"

"I'm guessing she's not coming today. We broke up."

"What? When?"

"New Year's Eve."

I gasped. "Why?"

"I wasn't feeling it anymore."

"Why didn't anyone call or text me?"

He shrugged. "Didn't want to bother you while you were on vacation. So did you see Nathan while you were there?"

"What?" I glanced at April's empty seat. She was probably crushed.

"Nathan. You know, the loner reject you don't get along with."

"Oh. No. He wasn't there. So tell me what happened. Was April upset?"

He turned to go inside. "I don't want to talk about it."

And he meant it. I passed him several notes during class, but River wouldn't say another word about it.

April wasn't in history class either. I thought about calling her after lunch, but I didn't need to. She was standing outside the cafeteria doors, so I made my way through the crowd to make sure she was okay.

"How could you do this to me?" she shouted.

I looked around. She couldn't be yelling at me.

"What?" I asked baffled.

"You pretend to be my friend then you steal my boyfriend!" A few people glanced in our direction.

"What are you talking about?"

"You know exactly what I'm talking about. Don't play all sweet and innocent!"

"April, I—"

"There I was feeling all sorry for you about your parents and your brother, spilling my guts to you about my mom, listening while you rambled about all your stupid psychotic dreams, and the whole time you were being two-faced and trying to dig your claws into River."

"April, I don't—"

"Save it, Maryah! I'm not falling for any more of your lies."

A large circle of students formed around us. I'd never experienced so many people staring at me. My heart raced. Why was April screaming at *me* about River? I had nothing to do with their breakup.

She ripped Mikey's hat from my head then put her face close to mine, practically spitting on me as she talked. "Tell me," she hissed, "do your precious dead parents know what a lying, backstabbing whore they raised?"

I honestly don't remember what happened next. It was a blur of rage.

The next thing I knew, Faith had me tight in her grasp, and Harmony held April. We were both flailing and swinging our arms at each other.

Faith's voice rang out through the chaos. "Maryah, control yourself! It's over!"

My eyes frantically scanned the area. The sleeve of my gray thermal shirt had been torn halfway off. The vice principal walked toward us, and Mikey's hat was nowhere to be found. The audience around us scattered.

"What in the world is going on here?" Vice Principal Shupe asked.

"She attacked me!" April shouted.

I couldn't think straight. My body was trembling. My breaths came too fast.

"Is this true, Miss Woodsen?" he asked.

I didn't know what to say. I couldn't remember attacking April, but I couldn't remember anything. April's lip was bleeding, and her hair was a mess. Did I really fight my friend? I'd never been in a fight!

"In my office—now," Shupe said.

An hour later, Louise arrived at the office to meet with the vice principal. I'd been suspended for two days.

We walked to the car in silence. I held an icepack against my face where a black eye was forming, but mainly I wanted to hide the disgrace I felt.

"I'm sorry," I murmured, two minutes into our car ride.

"What are you sorry about?" Louise asked calmly.

"That I got suspended."

She stayed silent.

"Aren't you going to say anything?" My guilt grew thicker by the second.

"What would you like me to say?"

"I don't know. Yell at me. Punish me."

Louise sighed. "Would that help you find peace?"

"Huh?"

"If I punished you, would that help you be at peace with your actions?"

"No, probably not."

"I didn't think so, but if you thought it would help, I would try my best to appease you."

This wasn't going anything like I'd expected. I'd been bracing myself for a long lecture. "My parents would kill me if they were here."

"I highly doubt that." Louise chuckled.

"Trust me, my mother would crucify me for fighting."

"Your mother understood no one is perfect."

"Ha. My mother must have changed a lot since you knew her. She wanted me and Mikey to be flawless. Not that I blame her, considering how perfect she was."

"Would you like to hear a story about your mother?"

I adjusted my icepack and pain bolted down my cheek. "Sure."

"When we were kids, your mother made up some dramatic stories." Louise shot me a reluctant glance.

"What do you mean?"

"Your mother had a vivid imagination, and she thrived on attention. She wanted life to be exciting. When it became too dull, she created her own drama. At times, not realizing that her stories or elaborations could hurt people she cared about."

"My mother was a liar?"

"Quite often, yes." Louise laughed. "But eventually she grew out of it, and I'm pretty sure everyone lies a few times in their life."

"I guess that's true." I studied my bruise in the visor mirror. April packed one hell of a punch. The whole left side of my face was swollen. "Still, a few lies when you're a kid doesn't compare to getting in a fight and being suspended."

"Well then, how about another story?"

"I don't know. Are you going to tell me more bad stuff about my mom?"

"Good and bad is a matter of perception."

I took a deep breath. "Okay, go ahead."

"Many years before you and Mikey were born—before she met your father—your mother was a dancer."

"Yeah, she and my father loved to dance."

"Not the kind you're thinking of." She looked at me over her hippie shades. "Exotic."

"WHAT?" I gasped. "No way. My mother would never do that kind of thing."

Louise swerved her head to one side. "Maybe not now, or for the past twenty years, but I assure you, she did that kind of thing many years ago."

"Oh. My. God," I stammered.

"In her defense, she never danced nude, and she didn't give into the temptation of drugs or obsessive drinking. It was simply a job to her, a means to an end. She didn't let it corrupt her or define her as a person."

I couldn't believe Louise just used nude and drugs in a statement about my mom. "She should have told me."

"She wasn't proud of it, and it's certainly not the kind of thing you want your children to know about you."

"Yeah, but she preached to me about self-respect and preserving my innocence. She said I should wait to have sex until I'm married. What a hypocrite!"

"That's what parents do. We think if our kids know how imperfect we were, or how many bad decisions we've made, they'll think it's okay to do the same. We don't want our children to learn the hard way."

"Just because she made stupid choices doesn't mean I will!"

Louise turned the radio off. "Before any of us are parents, we are first and foremost humans. All humans make mistakes and bad decisions. As we get older, we hope to make fewer, but when we're younger, we live in the moment without worrying about the consequences."

"Still, an exotic dancer! What was she thinking?"

"She needed to pay for college. The job paid well, and left her time to study."

"She didn't even graduate college!"

"Yes well, sometimes life happens, and we end up traveling a different path than we planned. It may not have been the most virtuous time in her life, but if she hadn't made the choices she did—including the supposedly bad ones—she may have never met your father."

I paused, not making the connection between my mother's undignified career choice and her meeting my charming father. "What do you mean?"

"That's how they met. Your father was here on a business trip, and he and some co-workers visited your mother's bar outside of town. It was love at first sight."

"My parents met while my mother was stripping!" All these years I'd been hoodwinked into thinking my parents had exceptional morals and manners. Now it made total sense that my mother was a liar.

"Oh, she disliked the term stripping."

"Well if the stripper shoe fits." I was shocked by my own catty, River-like comment, but I should've suspected something like this. I mean, how many mothers own a lingerie store? "So my father, what's his real story? Was he in prison or something?"

"No, nothing like that. His only issue was smoking pot."

My eyes bulged. "My father was a drug addict?"

"I wouldn't label him an addict. He simply strayed down a meaningless path for a short time." Louise smiled. "See, this suspension thing doesn't seem so bad now, does it?"

"I don't want to hear anymore."

"Do you think less of them now that you have this knowledge?"

I thought about it. My parents' past shocked me, but I didn't think less of them. They were the same loving people who gave me a good life.

"I just think they had a lot of nerve," I huffed. "Acting like they were so perfect."

"All parents want to give their children the best life possible. Right now you don't understand how tough it is to be a parent, but maybe someday you will. Let me ask you, do you live each day for your future children? Before every decision or action, do you stop and ask yourself, 'how will this affect my son or daughter?'"

"I don't even know if I'll have children."

"Exactly, because you're living your life for *you* right now. You aren't worrying that what you do today will be judged by your children. A time of consequence for every action we take is inevitable, yet we don't give it much thought because it seems so far away in the present moment. No one is perfect. I'm not sure how the theory came to fruition that parents should be an exception to that rule. All souls have some light and dark in them. Think of how freeing it would be if you could turn to the people you love and say, 'I'm not perfect. I never will be. I've made mistakes and some of them I'm very sorry for, but every choice, every experience, is a lesson. It makes me who I am. I'm a work in progress and I'm doing the best I can.'"

Louise was right. My parents had been teenagers. They had peer pressure and lessons to learn just like I did. I took a deep breath—somehow feeling lighter. "I'm glad you told me. It's nice to know they weren't perfect."

Louise squeezed my hand. "That's what stories are for—to learn something."

"I guess every story can't be rainbows and happy endings."

"Definitely not all rainbows, but happy endings are a matter of perception." She looked at me over her glasses again. "Who knows if there is ever an end to our story?"

∞

Being stuck at home on suspension meant I had plenty of time to do my schoolwork. Ms. Barby gave us an assignment on the meaning and history behind our name. My non-existent access to my family tree left me with limited information.

I was in the kitchen, searching the Internet when Louise came home with groceries.

"Louise, by any chance, do you know anything about my name?"

"Sure I do. What would you like to know?"

I helped her unpack bags. "Well, most websites say it means 'star of the sea', but that doesn't fit me, so I was wondering if it had personal meaning behind it."

"Actually, I played a part in the selection of your name. Your mother came to me when she found out she was pregnant. She suspected she was having a boy." Louise had a faraway grin on her face like she was picturing that moment in time. "She decided on Michael, but a few weeks later, the doctors informed her she was having twins." She winked at me. "And one was a girl."

I was thrilled Louise knew this stuff. In some small way I felt reconnected to my family.

"I asked if I could choose your name. We already had Dylan and Nathaniel by then, and Anthony and I weren't planning on having more children. Your mother knew I had always wanted a girl, so she agreed to let me name you."

"You didn't plan on having Carson?"

"No. Carson was an unexpected surprise. But a pleasant one," she added. "I chose the name Mary for you, and your mother liked it. However, on the day of your birth, she looked at you for the first time, and said you didn't look like a Mary. She didn't think it fit who you were. So she called you Maryah, but spelled it so my selection of Mary was within your name."

"Wow. I was almost a Mary. Why did you choose that name?"

"Mary means beloved or wished for child, and that's exactly what you were."

I held up a can of tuna before putting it in the pantry. "And now I'm a star of the sea. I sound like a brand of tuna fish."

Louise patted my back as she passed by me. "I think you have the best of both worlds. You are a beloved and wished for star of the sea."

"I am a Pisces. At least the water reference works."

Her faraway look returned. "Indeed, you are a water sign."

"Do you know what your name means?"

She imitated a manly voice. "Louise means famous warrior or renowned fighter."

I giggled. "Boy, your parents sure got that one wrong, huh?"

"What do you mean by that?"

"I didn't mean it in a bad way. It's just you're so sweet and loving. I couldn't imagine you fighting with anyone."

She raised an eyebrow and tossed me a pack of paper towels. "I fought for you, didn't I?"

I tried to hide my sappy grin. She did fight for me, and I was glad she did.

"Well, I have to call some clients," she said. "I'll leave you to your homework."

"Thank you for telling me that story."

"I have plenty more. All in due time."

I took my laptop to my room and relaxed in bed while I researched the rest of my family's names. Michael meant the same thing on every website I looked at: He who resembles God. It worked. Mikey had it all, and many girls referred to him as a god over the past few years.

My mother's name, Sarah, meant "beautiful princess" on the first site I searched. My mother was exactly that. Though, for a second I wondered if she ever had a stripper name.

I moved onto my father. Steven meant "crowned one." The genius of it made me smile. A crowned prince and his beautiful princess just like a fairytale. I thought about my parent's fairytale love continuing in another time and place. I smiled even bigger, realizing I still considered it a fairytale, even with the dark patches Louise revealed. They were imperfectly human, and I loved them even more because of it.

I thought about calling Krista and telling her about my name, but with the time difference she'd already be asleep. Finding the meaning of her name wasn't so easy. Some websites said it was derived from Christine, meaning "variant of Christ" but another definition said "anointed." I'd heard the word before, but had no idea what it meant, so I looked up the definition:

Anoint:
1.To apply oil, ointment, or a similar substance to.
2.To put oil on during a religious ceremony as a sign of sanctification or consecration.
3.To choose by or as if by divine intervention.

The first two definitions didn't fit, but I liked the third option. I texted Krista, knowing she'd read it in the morning. *Did u know u were chosen by divine intervention? Luv u.*

I drifted off to sleep, and it was no surprise that I dreamt about her, but Nathan was in the dream too.

Krista sat on her bed with a shirtless Nathan in front of her. His lean muscles and broad shoulders were enough to make any girl drool, but Krista just sat behind him with her hands pressed against his back, talking casually.

She had on old sweats that she refused to throw away even though they had holes in them. Her hair was a mess, but she didn't seem to care that a half-naked hot guy was in her room. And she didn't seem nervous, or even excited that she was rubbing his back. But that's the thing about dreams. They rarely make sense.

"You could do much better than him," I said to her. "In real life he's crazy." Lately, I'd resorted to talking in my dreams. Not that anyone ever heard me, but it made me feel less like an invisible spectator.

I stood, or hovered, or floated—or whatever it's called in Dreamland—in front of Nathan. His eyes were closed but his face was relaxed. Krista's eyes were closed too.

"You're all good," she said. "Even the ligaments are healed."

Nathan put his shirt back on. "As always, thank you, Krista."

"No problem. I'm happy to help."

Of course. First, the bloody back dream and now Krista helps him feel better. That made sense considering she wanted to be a nurse so badly.

"No pain in your hand at all?" she asked.

He stood up and leaned against her dresser. "No. You did a splendid job as usual."

Kris reclined into her pillows and swung her knees from side to side. "I still can't believe you punched him. Heck, I can't believe Maryah got in a fight. What's the world coming to?"

Nathan's lips curled upward and his shoulders bounced with an almost-laugh. "She's always been a fighter."

Once again, we'd wandered into dream territory that made no sense. Me, a fighter? Ha.

Nathan opened and closed his hand into a fist several times. "You're sure there's nothing romantic between her and River Malone?"

She blew her nose and sniffled like she had a cold. "I'm one-hundred percent sure."

He nodded and let out a whoosh of breath. "There are several matters I need to take care of. I won't be around much, but if you need me, or if she confides in you about…anything I should know, please call me."

"Will do." Krista stood up and they hugged each other so lovingly that I almost felt uncomfortable watching. "She sent me a text tonight saying my name meant I was chosen by divine intervention."

He pulled back and smiled. "Sometimes she has no idea how close to the truth she is."

"I know. It's freaky."

Freaky was right. I'd become a master of blending real life with my freakishly weird dreams. Krista and Nathan said they loved each other. That was the last straw. I couldn't handle anymore. One hard pinch of my wrist and I was out of there.

RIVER DANCING

Maryah

River made his way through the groups of gawking girls and greeted me with a haughty smile. "Let's ditch today."

"No way. I don't need another suspension."

"Fine, Miss Goody-two-shoes." Once we were in class, he put his arm around the back of my chair. "You weren't here when we discussed our name assignment, but I researched yours."

"So you know I'm destined to start my own tuna company?"

River snickered. "You're a star of the sea, and my name has no hidden meaning. It makes sense."

"You lost me."

More of our classmates filtered in and took their seats. River leaned so close to me his lips brushed against my ear. "Every river finds its way to the sea. Maybe you're the sea I was meant to find."

I threw my pen at him. "This is no time for jokes. In case you forgot, April challenged me to a boxing match. The last thing I need is people overhearing crap like that and thinking you're serious."

I had spent both days of my suspension leaving April voicemails, sending her apology emails, and texting her. She didn't reply to me at all. Not one word.

Faith poked her head between us. "Guess what I discovered about your name, River?"

He sat back and grinned. "What?"

"Sometimes a river flows directly into the ground and dries up before it reaches a larger body of water." Faith sounded all cheery like it wasn't mean, but I shot her a dirty look.

My evil eye must've looked like the work of an amateur compared to River's. The bell rang and Faith danced to her seat.

∞

I didn't give up on April.

Weeks passed but she didn't come back to school at all. I still sent texts and emails, I'd even asked her other friends if she was okay, but they told me nothing.

My biggest fear was that her mom may have gotten worse. Every morning I'd look through the obituaries, holding my breath until I confirmed her mom's name wasn't printed there. April did call River, but he didn't answer, or call her back, and I wanted to strangle him for it.

"You could at least find out if she's okay, if her mom's okay. Don't you have a heart?"

He kept bopping his head to the song on the radio as he cut off an SUV. Another reason I wanted to strangle him, he was a careless driver. "No good will come from us talking. She wants me to say I miss her, but I don't. She'll just get more depressed."

I sighed. His logic kind of made sense, but I was so worried about her and no one would tell me anything. Silence was the worst punishment in the world. It was even more torturous because I didn't do anything wrong. I'd rather April just punch me in the face a few more times, and get out all of her misplaced anger so we could go back to being friends.

River pulled into the lot of Barking Frog restaurant, and I climbed out of the Jag. For the first time since he picked me up, I noticed River's outfit. Black slacks had replaced his usual dark jeans, and he wore a button down shirt instead of one of his rocker shirts.

"Am I underdressed?" I glanced down at my jeans and sweatshirt.

He held open the front door. "Nah, you're fine."

The hostess asked for our name, and River told her we had reservations in front of the fireplace. Unlike our usual hangouts, the scene gave off a creepy romantic vibe.

"What's going on?" I asked, after the hostess seated us. "This seems a little much."

He grinned. "Happy Valentine's Day."

"Valentine's Day is tomorrow." And what did a holiday about love have to do with River and me?

"I know, but it's Saturday night, so I figured we'd kick it off now and spend all day together tomorrow." He set a black velvet box on the table.

I laughed, thinking he was kidding, but he insisted I open it so I did. It was the diamond heart necklace from our shopping trip.

"River, you bought this for April."

"No, I bought it for you. You *assumed* it was for April. I wanted to give it to you for Christmas, but figured I'd wait until I gave April the ax."

I stared at him in shock.

He rocked back on two legs of his chair. "You said you liked it. It's black and white, so it matches the haunted look you've got going on."

The room was too warm. I felt dizzy. "I don't understand."

"Sometimes you are so oblivious. Wait right here."

He left the dining room and came back a few minutes later carrying a black vase filled with white roses, and his guitar. I just sat there, paralyzed with denial. No way River did all of this for me.

He strummed his guitar while singing about two dark strangers joined by destiny, and how tragic roads led them to each other. It was slow, melodious, and haunting. People sitting at tables all around us stared with big grins, and a group of servers gathered across the room to watch. I was flabbergasted when he sang the last words "please be mine."

The whole place erupted into applause while River stared at me, waiting for a response. River wanted *me* to be *his*? The heat from the fireplace raised my body temperature a hundred degrees.

"Are you on drugs?" I whispered. It seemed the only rational explanation.

His face flushed and he glanced around the room, but thankfully, most people had returned to their meals or conversations. "Maryah, I like you. I know you feel the same way, so let's squash this best buddy charade."

Sweat dripped down my back. Had he lost his mind? Guys didn't like me that way. No guy had ever liked me that way. We were just friends. He was April's boyfriend, or had been anyway. I could never do something so cruel to her. "I—I don't know what to say. I need to go home."

"Are you kidding me? We haven't even ordered yet."

I struggled to swallow. "I just—I need time to—it—I had no idea you felt this way."

"Seriously?" He looked astonished, genuinely astonished.

"I swear."

"Wow, you're more clueless than I thought. I guess it would be overwhelming. It's not every day a rock star sings a ballad to you."

I pushed my chair away from the table, away from the seven-hundred-dollar necklace, the song, the roses, and River. All I could do was nod in agreement and bolt for the door. If I opened my mouth I was sure I'd throw up.

HEART RACING

Maryah

Even after taking all night and most of the next day to process what happened, I was still in disbelief. River asked *me* to be his girlfriend. Most girls would be walking on clouds and showing off the necklace to anyone who'd look at it, but I couldn't even try it on.

My mother's jewelry box sat on my dresser in front of me. Opening the lid and placing the necklace inside should've been easy, but as I reached for the wooden box, my skin prickled. I was scared to open it. Like it contained a dangerous secret, and if I unleashed it, my whole world would change. *Don't be stupid, Maryah. It's just a jewelry box.*

My fear disappeared after I forced myself to lift the lid. Some necklaces, bracelets, a few pairs of earrings, and several rings, were neatly arranged on the red velour lining. I took out each item, imagining my mother wearing them.

Tears ran down my cheeks. "Mom, I miss you so much."

I placed River's necklace in the box. He told me to take all the time I needed, and I needed more time.

Anthony and Louise were on a weekend getaway, and Faith and Shiloh were spending their Valentine's Day doing couple stuff, but Carson and Dakota appeared in my doorway.

"We're about to go four-wheeling," Carson said. "Want to come?"

Normally, I would've declined out of fear I'd embarrass or hurt myself, but I needed a distraction from the River drama. "Sure, but I've never ridden a dirt bike before."

Dakota tossed me a racing jersey. "There's nothing to it. You'll have a blast."

"Meet us in the garage," Carson said.

I debated leaving my ring on, but didn't want to get it dirty, so I placed it in my jewelry box then headed outside.

Carson loaned me riding pants that were way too big, but I made do. I hopped on the back of his four-wheeler and the three of us rode out to a huge opening of paths and red-dirt hills.

Carson popped a few wheelies and peeled around in circles several times, stirring up tornado clouds of dust, but I loved it. After a Riding 101 lesson from Carson, Dakota offered to let me ride his bike on my own.

"You sure?" I asked.

He bent down to tie the laces of his boots. "Yeah, jump a couple hills or whatever."

"Just be careful," Carson added. "That bike is powerful."

"Not compared to yours," Dakota grunted.

"It's not my fault you're mechanically challenged."

"When are you going to make mine faster? I told you I'd pay for the parts."

Carson ignored him and knocked on my helmet. "I'd offer to race you, but it wouldn't be much of a competition."

"No, let's do it." I clapped my gloves together, sending up a puff of dirt. "I might be faster than you think."

Carson and Dakota both laughed.

"Okay," Carson climbed on his bike and pointed west. "See that rock formation that looks like a camel? We race to there and back. I'll even give you a head start."

The cliffs up ahead did look like a camel—with three humps. I nodded, climbed on Dakota's bike and kick-started the engine to life. I was pretty sure I'd lose the race, but I didn't care.

We lined up our bikes side by side. Dakota stood to the right of us with his arm above his head. With his fingers, he counted from five then dropped his arm. I hit the thumb throttle and took off.

The bike roared and I smiled at the initial lurch forward. I concentrated on Carson's instructions, making sure I pulled the clutch and kicked the shift peg through each gear. The exhilaration of the increasing speed made my heart race. Even through my gloves, my hands had the pins and needles feeling from the strong vibration of the handlebars. I glanced back but Carson hadn't moved yet.

By the time I reached fourth gear, I felt like I was flying. I made a wide left turn right before Camel rock. When I straightened out again, I stood up and kicked it into fifth. Driving in the opposite direction, Carson zoomed by me, waving like he was on a leisure bicycle ride, but he had given me such a huge head start. I could beat him. I just had to keep up my speed.

Dakota stood seconds away, swinging his arms over his head. The closer he got, the more confident I was that I could win.

I blew past him, and he jumped up and down. My laughter echoed inside my helmet. I did it. I beat Carson.

I downshifted, but nothing happened.

I tried again. Nothing.

I pulled my handbrake then remembered Dakota saying only the footbrake worked on his bike. I tried stomping on the brake, but my foot overshot the pedal. Something caught the bottom of my pants and yanked me to the right. I was stuck. I kept trying to free my foot, but I couldn't. My hands were death-gripped on the handlebars as the force still tugged at my pants leg.

I kept kicking at the shift pedal, trying to get it into neutral, or to slow down, or anything.

I was gasping for breath. My helmet had become a sauna.

The bike felt like it increased speed. My heart beat a hundred times faster. I tried looking back at Dakota or Carson to signal them for help, but so much dirt had covered my helmet shield that I could barely see out of it. I was scared I'd get pulled off if I let go to wave my arms.

When I looked forward again, I had to blink and force my eyes to focus. Up ahead, it looked like the earth dropped off into nothing. The edge of the cliffs were nearby, but I couldn't be that close.

Rocks and pebbles flew up all around me. I turned hard and the bike skidded sideways.

I was that close. I was heading directly for the huge drop-off.

This was it. Death came to take me again. Not Nathan, not an angel—death.

As much I had begged for it, I couldn't stop pleading, "Don't let me die. Don't let me die," which sounded like a whisper inside the seclusion of my helmet.

For a fraction of a second, the wheels stopped rolling against the ground and spun against nothing but air. I braced myself for the long fall. The bike fell out from under me. My feet momentarily dangled in mid-air as my stomach flew into my throat.

I was flying. Falling.

Then, what felt like a steel claw, clenched onto my forearm.

My arm jerked upward so hard it should've come out of its socket. My hip and shoulder slammed into a wall of solid rock and I cried out in pain. Someone yanked me up again, and my feet hit flat ground right before they collapsed under me.

I opened my eyes to see a cloud of red dirt.

My helmet was tugged off my head, and through the hair hanging in my eyes I saw Carson. He took off his helmet. "Good gods, Sparky. How many lives do you think you have?"

I glanced behind me just in time to see Dakota's bike explode against the rocks a hundred feet or more below us. Carson's bike was beside us. I threw my arms around his neck, clinging to him for dear life.

"The bike," I gasped. "It got stuck in gear."

I wanted to explain the rest, but I couldn't. I started bawling.

"Aw, man," Carson groaned. But he didn't push me away. He awkwardly hugged me back then lifted me like I was a weightless doll and carried me to his bike. I was trembling, and couldn't stop crying no matter how hard I tried.

He climbed onto his seat, keeping me held against him with one hand and steering with the other. "You're okay," he shouted over the roar of his engine. "Trust me, I'd never let anything happen to you."

I nodded against his chest, wanting so badly to be off his bike and back in the safety of the Luna house. The engine was too loud for me to hear what he mumbled after that, but I thought he said something about Nathan.

We got back to the house after sunset, covered from head to toe in red mud.

Dakota helped pull my riding gear off while Carson made a couple icepacks. I shoved one inside the waistband of my shorts and gasped at the freezing cold against my hip. I gingerly placed the other pack against my shoulder. "Thanks again, Carson."

"Stop. You already thanked me a million times. It's not your fault Dakota's bike was a P.O.S."

As many times as I had thanked Carson for saving my life, Dakota had apologized to me a dozen more for his faulty bike. I felt horrible that I sent it flying off a cliff and exploding, but he didn't seem to care it was destroyed.

"I still don't understand how you caught up to me and snagged me off the bike in time."

Carson shrugged. "Lucky for you, I think and move fast."

"Car, seriously," Dakota said. "That was the most impressive thing I've ever seen."

I eyed Carson's biceps as he downed a Vitamin Water. He didn't look strong enough to pull off a feat like that, but I'd once heard adrenaline made a mother lift a car off of her trapped baby. People become superheroes in life-or-death situations.

"And by the way, I let you win." Carson slid a Vitamin Water and two Ibuprofens across the counter to me.

I graciously accepted.

The front door squeaking open caused all of us to shut up. Carson and Dakota turned to look at me as *he* came around the corner—the one person who could single-handedly make my day even worse.

"Hello," Nut Job hailed.

I sat frozen next to Carson, my drink bottle still lingering at my mouth.

"Hi, Maryah," Nathan said softly.

If looks could kill I would've been locked up for murder. I set down my drink, dropped my icepack, got up, and limped off to my bedroom.

Why did Nathan have to show up right after I stared death in the face yet again? And why was he here on a Sunday night? Didn't he have to be at school in the morning? I shook off my angst and grabbed a change of clothes so I could shower, but I gasped when I opened my door.

Nathan stood on the other side. "Carson said you were hurt."

"I'm fine."

He raised a brow then rubbed the back of his neck. "I'd like to apologize for what happened in Albuquerque, if you'd extend me that honor."

Why did he speak with such good manners? It made me feel like I had to respond with good manners of my own—not that he deserved any.

"There isn't much to say," I grumbled.

"I assure you, I have much to say."

I took a deep breath. My father always said people deserve a chance to say they're sorry. I didn't give my father that chance before he died. Listening to Nathan didn't mean I had to forgive him, but slamming the door in his face might cause another maniacal mood swing. Plus, as much as I hated admitting it, he looked so unbelievably gorgeous that I didn't mind looking at him a little longer.

"Fine." I stepped aside and let him in.

GIVING BACK

NATHANIEL

Carson wouldn't tell me much, but he did say Maryah injured her shoulder while dirt bike riding. I gestured at the chair beside her bed. "Would you prefer to sit?"

"Nope, I'm good." She crossed her arms over her chest, still holding her change of clothes.

My chest tightened when I saw she wasn't wearing her ring, but then my attention lingered on the polka dot underwear clenched in her hand. She glanced down and shoved them between her shirt and shorts so they were out of view. Her cheeks blushed so strong that they almost matched the red dirt in her hair.

I contained my smile to keep from embarrassing her further. "I know you have no desire to see me, but I couldn't bear the thought of you being angry with me for one more day." She didn't blink. "I have felt awful every minute of every day since the balloon fiasco."

Still nothing. I'd always been horrible at apologies, and I was failing miserably at this one as well. "Maryah, I am more sorry than you can imagine."

Her words were flat. "You tried to kill me."

"That wasn't my intention. I only meant to scare you, to make you realize you didn't truly want to die." My excuse was horrible and pathetic. "But it was wrong and inexcusable."

"You insulted my family."

"I am deeply sorry for that. Please forgive me for being such a monster."

She flinched at the word monster. I hated that she thought of me in such a way, but Carson said she had used that title and her guilty eyes confirmed it.

"I'm an inconsiderate imbecile and I wish I could take it all back, but there is no undoing what's been done. However, I'd like to make a peace offering as a sign of my regret, and to extend my respect to your parents and your brother."

"What?"

I bowed my head. "I have a gift for you."

"A gift?"

"Technically, it belongs to you by birthright, so you should think of it as an inheritance."

She gaped at me with confusion. "Why can't you just speak like a normal teenager?"

Because I'm not, nor do I want to be. I extended my hand. "Will you join me?"

"Join you in what?"

"I don't deserve it, but please, I am asking you to trust me." My hand was suspended inches away from hers. I craved her touch, but she threw her clothes on the bed and shoved her hands in her pockets.

"Well, lead the way," she said.

I ushered her out of the room and down the hallway. When we passed by the kitchen, Carson gave me an approving nod. Dakota pumped his fist in the air. I held the front door open, and Maryah and I walked to the driveway in darkness.

I pushed the gate open and her knees buckled, but I caught her by the arm. In the driveway, I had lit dozens of red and white candles and arranged them in a large circle. Parked in the middle of the heavenly glow was a white '57 Desoto with a red bow on top.

She shakily walked toward the car and touched the back fin. "It's just like my parents'."

"It is…theirs."

"What?"

"It's the car your parents owned. The fellow who bought it from your uncle agreed to sell it to me."

"Are you kidding me?" She looked at the car again, and a huge smile spread across her face, but when I stepped closer, I saw tears streaming down her cheeks.

"Are you all right?"

"Do you have any idea how much this means to me?"

"Then those are tears of joy?"

She nodded and wrapped her arms around my waist. Every cell in my body tingled with joy.

"How did you know?" she asked, pulling away. Her embrace was too short—much too short. I wanted to hold her forever.

"Anthony. He sensed how upset you were that the car had been sold."

She smiled and nodded. "But wasn't it expensive?"

"You'd be surprised how generous people can be when you share a story with them." Truth was that Dylan had to persuade the stubborn, coldhearted antique dealer to sell me the car. I disliked the man so much I told Dylan we should have made him give it to us for free, but Dylan remained levelheaded and negotiated a more-than-fair deal.

Maryah glanced between me and the Desoto at least five times. "Thank you so much, Nathaniel."

Hearing her speak my name so fondly made me feel like a new man. She no longer looked at me with resentment. "My pleasure."

An engine roared behind us and I turned to see a Jaguar pulling into the driveway. River Malone parked and stepped out of his car holding white roses.

"You forgot your flowers last night," he said to Maryah before glaring at me.

A bomb began ticking in my chest. I knew they were friends, but what sort of friends give and accept roses from the other? If she was dating him—dating anyone—it would cause an explosion that would annihilate my heart and soul.

"Oh, thanks." Maryah took the vase from him. "Nathan, do you know River?"

"He knows me," River said. "What's all this?" I assumed he gestured at the car and glowing candles, but I couldn't be certain because I couldn't take my focus away from Maryah. The ticking in my chest grew stronger. She couldn't be with someone of River's caliber. She couldn't be with anyone aside from me. We were destined to be together. *You and me for eternity.* Or had that also changed when she erased?

She stepped between me and River. "Nathan found my parent's car, and convinced the owner to give it back to me!"

"Is it a Valentine's gift?" River asked.

"No. It's a...a..." Maryah looked at me, lost for words.

Parts of me had gone numb, but I managed to force out, "peace offering."

"Where's the diamond necklace I bought you?" River snarled.

Diamond necklace? He had bought her jewelry? And she accepted it? Was that why she stopped wearing her ring? I held my breath as the final beeps of my internal bomb rang through my ears. Her answer would determine a false alarm or a detonation. Beep, beep...

"Umm." She shuffled her feet and brushed dirt from her shirt. "I went four-wheeling and didn't want to get it dirty."

KABLAM! Fragments of rage and devastation shot through me, ricocheting off of every memory I had of us together, shredding me into useless rubble. Visions of her kissing him made my stomach lurch. I had to walk away.

"Whatever," River said. "Let's take the peace offering for a spin."

I clenched my fists at my sides. The veins in my arms and neck throbbed.

How dare he lay a finger on the precious car that used to be ours. I wanted to grab him by his throat and shove him back in his pretentious Jaguar.

"Oh. Well, I guess we..." Maryah practically skipped over to me. She had a bounce in her step that I hadn't seen in decades. River made her *that* happy?

"Keys are in the ignition. Let's roll!" River strutted toward us. He handed me the vase of roses. "You don't mind taking those inside, do you, pal?"

I contemplated knocking his teeth out of his head, but instead I gritted my own.

Another man—an arrogant boy—had caused a spark in my soul mate that I hadn't seen since our last lifetime. Maryah looked up at me with gleaming eyes. "Is it okay if I take it for a drive?"

Behind her, River blew out the candles I had lit and kicked them to the side of the driveway to clear a path. I was squeezing the vase so hard it should have shattered. The scent of the roses turned my stomach. I'd never be able to smell the flower again without cringing.

"You're free to do as you wish," I told Maryah, turning and walking toward the gate, but she grabbed my arm.

"Wait! Do you want to come with us?"

I stared at her, silently questioning her. *How could you do this? How could you be with someone else?* Her smile didn't wane. We stood facing each other as complete opposites: joy and misery. I wanted to traverse out of the nightmare. I needed to get away from them. "Perhaps some other time."

She let go of me when River wrapped his grubby arm around her waist.

"Come on, babe."

Babe: that one word put the final nail in my coffin. Like a true pompous ass, he winked at me before dragging her to the car.

"Thank you again, Nathan!" She shouted. "I absolutely love it."

The Desoto's engine cranked to life. With each step toward the house, more and more of my soul withered away. I pushed the front door open and threw the vase across the foyer. A frenzy of white and green fell to the ground as black ceramic shattered all over the floor. I stared at the water dripping down the wall like the tears I wanted to shed.

Carson came around the corner, followed by Dakota. "Nate, what's wrong?"

"Everything."

HOME SICKENING

Maryah

Nathan had restored a sense of home to me. I felt nostalgic driving around Sedona. The white leather seats sticking to the back of my legs didn't even bother me like they used to. Even my hip and shoulder felt better. However, River was a killjoy.

"You don't think it's odd that he gave you a *car* on Valentine's Day?"

I shrugged. "It's not like he bought me a car. He got it back from the guy who bought it from my uncle." A heartfelt apology probably would have done the job, but Nathan blew me away with his thoughtfulness.

"He so wants in your pants."

"It's not like that! We have really bad history. He wanted to make up for being a jerk. If you keep harping on it, I'll kick you out at the next red light!"

"You wouldn't."

"Try me."

I was so annoyed by how River acted in front of Nathan. Asking me about the necklace I didn't even want, and flinging those roses around like he was some kind of Romeo. "And what's with the babe thing? I don't like being called babe."

He rolled his eyes.

What made me even madder was that before River showed up, I had been questioning if Nathan Luna, hottest guy on the planet—and maybe not as insane as I originally thought—could be interested in someone like me. The candles definitely seemed...romantic. He even held onto me a little longer than normal when I hugged him. It might've been wishful thinking, but he kept looking at me a certain way, like rays from an emerald sun were struggling to shine through his eyes. I prayed—as impossible as it seemed—that maybe I played some part in replacing his sad darkness with the happy sunrise I saw inside of him.

River slid closer to me. "So what about us? Are we officially an item or what?"

"This is my night to be reconnected to my family. We can discuss you and me tomorrow."

He gave one last angry huff before shutting up.

When we got back to the house, River got in his car and left, and I ran inside to thank Nathan again. Carson sat alone on the couch looking pissed off.

"Hey, where's your brother?"

"Gone."

"Gone where?"

"Back to Colorado."

"But he just got here." He must have driven the Desoto here, so how would he get back to Colorado? "Was he flying back?"

"No, he caught a ride on a meteor."

My heart sank. Not because of Carson's stupid star obsession, but because Nathan didn't mention he'd be leaving right away, and he didn't care enough to say goodbye to me, which meant, of course, I had imagined his interest in me. No big shocker there. The car thing was truly about keeping peace with the family. "I wish I could've said goodbye."

Carson avoided eye contact.

"Are you mad at me?" I asked.

"Nope."

"Are you upset about something?"

"Nope."

"Thank you again for saving my life today. I'd say I owe you one, but I'm not sure I'd ever be able to pay you back for something like that."

He grunted.

Back to cold shoulder status. Great. "Okay, well...guess I'll go to bed.

Not a word. I thought we'd had a real bonding moment out on the cliffs, but now he seemed to hate me all over again. I'd never figure him out.

I went to my room and called Krista to tell her about the Desoto. I left out the River situation because I still wasn't sure how I felt. I used to tell Krista everything, but since the Christmas incident I didn't know where I stood with her—or with anyone.

I showered all the dirt off me and went to bed.

Carson's arctic attitude and the River soap opera were stressing me out, but it all paled in comparison to the thrill of having my parents' car back. I got excited when Nathan appeared in my dreams.

At first, it was an incredible dream. We were flying through a star-filled sky. Snow-covered mountains whizzed by us at what felt like a hundred miles per hour, but exhilaration turned to worry when we landed.

Nathan disappeared just before he hit the ground. Then he reappeared, standing a few inches away from me and fell to his knees. He held his face in his hands like he was in pain. I bent over him and ran my hands over his head, wanting to make sure he was okay. But I didn't feel hair; I only felt tingling warmth against my invisible fingers.

"This can't be happening," he moaned. He shook his head over and over again, pressing his hands over his eyes. "I can't take anymore."

He sounded so defeated. My non-existent hands traveled down his wide shoulders. When he looked up, he let out a gut-wrenching scream that sent me jumping backward. He ripped the headphones from his ears and threw his iPod.

It went right through the place where my heart was supposed to be.

∞

In the morning, I walked into the kitchen and discovered Faith doing laps around the island.

"You're early," I said dryly.

"Are you and River an item, and I somehow don't know about it?"

I frowned, searching for a way to explain. "Not exactly."

"What does that mean?"

"It means I don't think I like him like that."

Faith's expression softened. "You deserve better than him." She grabbed a package from her bag then slid it across the counter to me. "Here, the other part of your gift from Nathan."

"What?" I unwrapped a black Gatsby style hat. Green, blue, and white crystals formed a peacock feather along the brim, a silver peacock charm dangled off the green satin banding. "What's with the peacock fascination?"

Faith shrugged then stuffed a nectarine into her messenger bag. "He heard you lost Mikey's hat in your heavyweight match with April, so he got you a new one. At least this one is pretty."

"How did you get it?"

"Um." Her gaze shot to the ceiling. "I drove him to the airport. He said you ran off with the wretched wannabe before he could give it to you." She grabbed a bottle of juice from the fridge. "You ready?"

Speaking of wretched. "Where's Harmony?"

"She's taking a day off. She didn't get much sleep last night."

I asked to be polite, but I honestly didn't care. Her ominous disposition and permanent pissed-offness unnerved me. Knowing I had to have "the talk" with River made this day awkward enough already. My new hat would come in handy. I could hide under it.

∞

I managed to put off the inevitable until school ended, but dragonflies buzzed in my stomach as River and I walked to his car. He was in his seat and looking at me before I even closed my door. I'd run out of excuses.

"Nice hat," he said.

"Thanks."

He drummed on the steering wheel. "Kind of messed up that you're not wearing the necklace I gave you."

"Flashy bling isn't my style."

He slammed his palm against the center console, startling me. "Nothing I do makes you happy, does it?"

"That's not true it's just—"

"Because it's not a car like Numbnuts gave you, it's not good enough?"

"What? No. I never said that." Suddenly River's car felt like the desert. I put my window down to let in some air. "I don't want to ruin our friendship, and April is my friend. I can't hurt her like that."

"She kicked your ass!"

"Hey, I held my own!" I unconsciously touched my cheek where a bruise remained for a week after our fight. "The thing is, I didn't have a lot of friends in Maryland, and this dating thing is new to me, but I've seen it end badly. Look at you and April. You won't even say "hi" to her. And she won't talk to me. I don't want to lose both of you."

River leaned closer. His leather seat squeaked under his weight. "Maryah, I want you. Now tell me, what do you want?"

I should've felt a surge of excitement because the most popular guy at school just said he wanted me—again—but instead, all I felt was my nose burning from the lemon-scented air freshener.

River sighed and tugged at his wristband. "What if I promise that no matter what happens, you and I stay friends? Until death do us part or whatever. We take it slow and see if we're meant to be. Because we are, and I want to spoil you rotten." He leaned across the seat, cocking his head to the side.

No one had ever tried to kiss me before, but I assumed that's what he was doing. I moved so far away from him that my hair hung out the window. I needed to say something to get him back to his side of the car. "You said you'd give me time to think about it."

He brushed a finger along my arm then kissed my hand. "Fine, but wear the necklace. You deserve nice things."

I breathed a sigh of relief when he moved away from me. He revved his engine and pulled out of the parking lot. "I know you'll make the right decision."

I pulled down the brim of my hat over my eyes and stared out the window. For the entire ride home, all I could think about was Nathan.

THE POWER OF EIGHTEEN

Maryah

I kept up the need-time-to-think charade for a few days. Even though I didn't feel *that way* about River, I didn't want to lose his friendship. Part of me hoped he would just give up on the dating thing. Another huge part of me wished he and April would get back together and solve all of our problems.

Amongst the drama, my eighteenth birthday snuck up on me. Faith and Louise were all hyped up about my "big day." For the first time ever, I kind of wished I could just skip the whole birthday thing, but no such luck.

Faith rented out the Black Cow Café and decorated the place with streamers and balloons. She made me wear a pink sash that said "Birthday Princess" and a jeweled tiara.

We were eating Helen's handmade pizza when Faith lowered the lights and announced the start of a slideshow. The song, "A Pieceful Life" played and a giant lump formed in my throat. I knew the lyrics by heart: *Pieces of me waiting to be put back together again, a soul so broken I don't know if I can live again.*

The first slide read, "We love you, Maryah!" Then a series of photos flashed on the screen, scenes from the time I arrived in Sedona up until a couple days ago. I had no idea anyone had taken most of them. There were photos of me arriving at the airport, gazing out the window at Cathedral Rock, the first day of school, holidays, and one of Nathan and me with hot air balloons in the background. It was a collage of at least thirty photos. They couldn't have chosen a more perfect birthday song considering the tumultuous year I had.

I looked like I was on the verge of death in the first few pictures then gradually my coloring, weight, and clothes changed. How did these people put up with me during my zombie stage? The next to last slide read, "Our gift to you..." The final photo showed Krista holding a sign that said "See you Saturday! XO"

I squealed and looked around at everyone. "Krista's coming to visit?"

"Yes!" Faith clapped excitedly. "Are you so excited, Ma-Ma?"

Louise smiled at me. She must've invited Krista to come back. Being that our birthdays were only one day apart we'd always celebrated them together, and because of Louise that tradition would continue. I hugged her. "Louise, thank you so much."

Harmony disappeared out the back door. I should've known she didn't want to be here, but I didn't care. Krista was coming to visit! Hands down, my best birthday gift ever.

Anthony carried a two-tier chocolate birthday cake to the table while everyone sang. Unlike the usual messy version of the birthday song, this version sounded like it was being performed by an angelic choir. Nathan crossed my mind. I wanted him to be here with us, but whenever I asked about him everyone said he was busy with school.

I excused myself so I could use the restroom, but when I got to the back of the store I overheard Harmony talking outside.

"Maryah won't believe that. Remember how you reacted?"

I was tired of being scared. What better time than my birthday to grow up and face my fear of Harmony. I pushed the door open. "I won't believe what?"

Harmony spun around with her phone to her ear. Her black-as-tar eyes stared at me over her sunglasses. "Nothing."

I wished for a rewind button. What was I thinking? Harmony and I alone in an alley—not my smartest move. But if I backed down now, she'd be bitchy to me forever. "I heard you say my name. Who are you talking to?"

She shoved her phone in her back pocket and crossed her arms over her chest. "Nobody."

The sour smell of old ice cream in the dumpster made my stomach turn. Or maybe fear had prompted the sudden desire to heave. "You said my name. If you're going to talk about me, at least have the guts to say it to my face." My brother used that line on a bully when we were kids, so I knew I *sounded* strong, but I felt like a terrified seven-year-old.

"It has nothing to do with guts. My conversation was private."

"Why do you hate me so much? I've never done anything to you."

"Never say never." She laughed. Harmony—whom I'd hardly ever seen crack a smile—actually laughed. Then she took off her sunglasses. "But I don't hate you, so spare me the theatrics."

Faith appeared in the doorway. "You two are missing cake and ice cream."

Harmony and I continued glaring at each other. If I looked away first, I'd lose. My heart hammered between my ears. I had no idea why this confrontation felt so important, but I'd stand my ground no matter how much she intimidated me.

"What's going on?" Faith asked.

Harmony looked away. I let out the breath I'd been holding.

"Maryah's newly attained adulthood has made her brave and delusional."

I stepped forward, clueless as to how my nerve got so strong. "You were talking to someone about me." I looked at Faith. "She said I wouldn't believe something."

"Harmony?" Faith questioned, but she glanced around like she expected to see someone else. I looked around too. Who were we looking for?

"This is pointless. I'm going inside." Harmony pushed past Faith and left us standing in the alley.

"What did I ever do to her?" I asked Faith with frustration.

"Let me talk to her. I might know what this is about, and if I'm right, she's only trying to protect you."

"Protect me? I don't need her protection."

"Maybe not, but you have it anyway. Come back inside. Literally, there is cake with your name on it."

Harmony left before I had even a bite of cake. It's nearly impossible to ruin my appetite for chocolate, but she managed to do it. When the party ended, Faith insisted that I go home. She promised to come over after she and Shiloh cleaned up, and I made her swear to give me answers about the Harmony weirdness.

∞

Luckily, I had the house to myself. Faith and Harmony were on their way over. At least there wouldn't be an audience like there was at my last fight. I was scared, but confident that Faith would make sure Harmony didn't hurt me too badly. It couldn't hurt any worse than my fight with April. Could it?

They found me in the backyard feeding the fish. I wanted to stand up and act tough, but instead I continued to sit there, skimming my fingers in the icy water and watching the bright red and orange bodies swim around.

Faith squeezed my shoulder. "Let's go inside. It's cold out here."

I glanced at Harmony, imagining the damage she could do. Not wanting my blood splattered all over Louise's house, I said, "No, I'd rather do it outside."

Harmony looked different. No glasses. No scowl. She almost looked concerned—an emotion I didn't know she possessed. "Maryah, are you sure you want to do this?"

No. I didn't want to fight Stinkerbell, but I didn't want to be treated like a doormat anymore either. "Do what?"

Harmony grunted. "Demand the truth."

Truth? Right. The whole point of this was to find out who she was talking to about me. Maybe the truth wouldn't involve fists. "I'm sure."

Faith sat down Indian style. Harmony plopped down next to her.

"Ma-Ma, you're going to think we're crazy when we tell you this," Faith began, "but you have to hear us out until the end."

I nodded.

She giggled and leaned in close to me then whispered, "Harmony sees dead people."

"Very *Sixth Sense*-ish of you," Harmony said.

I watched them both with confusion. "What?"

Faith wriggled up onto her knees. "Harmony has a gift. She can communicate with souls who have died, but haven't crossed to the Higher Realm. Some ask her for favors or to relay messages." She sounded so chipper about it. This had to be a joke.

"Really?" I asked with amusement.

"Yes, really," Harmony said.

Then it occurred to me, Harmony wasn't the joking type. "You swear?"

"On my life, and the lives of everyone I love."

I wasn't sure how much that really meant, but if she was serious..."Doesn't that freak you out?"

She bent one leg up and picked at the sole her boot. "Rarely."

After Faith's *Sixth Sense* comment, all I could picture were half-mangled bodies groaning and clawing at Harmony for help. The images in my head weren't pretty, and for a moment I thought I had some insight to her dismalness. I'd be the same way if dead people followed me around. "Are they scary looking?"

"I don't see their bodies. Only clouds of light, or dark. It all depends."

"Tell her Harmony," Faith urged.

"Tell me what?"

Harmony raked her fingers through her hair. Some purple pieces stuck straight up. "Remember, you have to hear everything then you'll have proof."

I nodded again.

"In the alley, I wasn't on the phone. That's something I do in case people see me talking to what appears to be no one." She took a quick breath. "I was talking to your parents."

The hair on my arms stood up. My mouth opened, but no words came out. If she was lying, this was the cruelest thing Harmony could ever do to me.

"They love you and miss you and all that jazz. Your dad says he's sorry, blah blah blah."

"Harmony," Faith whined.

"Ay dios mio, Faith! You know I'm not good at emotional translations. Just let me do this my own way!"

I wasn't sure if I believed in ghosts, and even if they were real, I'd sense if my own parents were hanging around. "I don't believe you."

Harmony's head snapped up to look at me. "I told you wait until—"

"If it's true, ask them what Mikey called me."

"Seriously, I'm getting to the part where…" Harmony's eyes jumped to the empty space beside me. "Okay! Okay. Ry. Your mother is *screaming* that Mikey called you Ry."

Goosebumps spread over my entire body. I hadn't told anyone he called me that.

My parents were actually here? Contacting Harmony? Some hopeful yet really scared part of me wished it were true.

A thousand questions ran through my mind. "Where have they been? Why didn't they say anything sooner?"

Harmony cracked her neck and said to Faith, "Told you this would be complicated."

"Come on," Faith insisted. "She'd do it for you."

Harmony sighed. "Don't be mad at me, but they've been hanging around since you arrived here. They won't cross over like most souls do by now."

"Why didn't you tell me?" I shrieked.

"You have to understand, Maryah. Once souls find out I can hear them, they don't shut up. They follow me everywhere and won't leave me alone until I find all the people they want to contact. It's exhausting. It was next to impossible to be around you when you first arrived. Your parents constantly talked to each other about you, and what they thought of our kin—family. So many times I wanted to give them a piece of my mind, but I knew if I did, they'd never leave me alone. Most of the things they said were meaningless, typical parental stuff, but today at your party, they were discussing something I couldn't ignore, so I spoke up."

I was stunned to hear Harmony say so much.

"Your mom says you have her jewelry box. There's a gift for you hidden inside of it." My mind raced, picturing every piece of jewelry in the box. Was she mad that I put River's necklace in there? "She says you have to pry the bottom of the box open. You'll understand when you find it."

"I don't understand," I mumbled.

Harmony threw her hands up and looked at the empty air beside me. "Sarah, did you drop this kid on her head?" A warm shiver ran through me as Harmony focused on me again. "I told you, once you find it, you'll understand."

Faith sprang to her feet. "Let's go find it!"

Harmony got up and they both looked down at me.

"Ma-Ma, come on!" Faith urged.

"No...I can't." I stared at the pond. My mind flashed back to the peculiar fear I had. I thought something awful would happen if I opened the jewelry box. That feeling was back stronger than ever.

"What are you talking about?" Faith asked. "It's a gift from your mother. Don't you want to see what it is?"

I shook my head. "I have a bad feeling about it."

Harmony stared into space for a few seconds then said, "Sarah understands. She wasn't sure if she should give it to you. She wants you to follow your instincts and if they tell you not to open it, then don't."

"For crying out loud," Faith whined. "How anticlimactic is this?"

I fought back tears. "Harmony, can you tell them I love them and miss them?"

"Trust me," she said. "They know."

"Is Mikey with them?"

"Mikey crossed to the Higher Realm a couple weeks after you came out of your coma."

"Oh," I uttered, disappointed but also relieved. "That means he's okay, right? Is the Higher Realm like Heaven?"

"They're basically the same place," Faith assured me.

How the heck did she know anything about Heaven?

"Maryah," Harmony said, "your dad is asking if there's anything else you want to say before they…leave me alone. We made an agreement that if I helped them communicate with you this once, they wouldn't bother me again." Harmony sounded guilty and rightly so. This was my last and only chance to talk to them?

"Why won't they cross over?"

The thought of them lingering in some in-between world didn't seem right. They should be with Mikey in Heaven, or whatever it was called.

"They want to make sure you're okay before they do."

A tear streamed down my cheek. "But I want *them* to be okay. They should be with Mikey." My voice cracked. "I can't stand the thought of them in some kind of purgatory."

"Aw, it's nothing like that," Faith said. "They aren't suffering by hanging around."

"How do you know?" I snapped. "Do you have a psychic power too?"

She bit her lip. "Um, well—"

Harmony interrupted. "They're proud of how far you've come since that night. They'll cross over soon. Your dad says until then, they'll give you space."

My ears began buzzing and a headache tugged at my temples. I wasn't sure if I could handle any more talk about ghosts. It felt strange to have Harmony—who up until a few minutes ago I thought hated me—acting as a mediator between my parents and me.

"I want to be alone," I announced, standing up.

No one argued. Faith and Harmony stayed quiet as I walked into the house.

I wondered if my parents followed.

TURNING THE PAGE

Maryah

I felt eerily haunted, like my parents were watching my every move. I kept saying things out loud like "I love you, but if you're here, can you leave me alone for a minute?" This new theory that my parents could be lingering at all times left me thinking through every move I made.

Dinner with River was out of the question, so I called and cancelled. Instead, I sat on my bed staring across the room at my mother's jewelry box—unable to bring myself to go near it. What could my mother have hidden inside? I looked at the clock. 8:18pm.

I crept toward my dresser where the box sat. My fingers traced the ridges in the wood before I opened the lid. Slowly, I removed each piece of jewelry then flipped it over to examine the bottom. It didn't look like it had been altered, or that anything would fit in the tiny space between the outside and the inner lining. I carried it into the kitchen and set it on the counter.

Was I really going to do this? Damage my mother's jewelry box just because Harmony claimed she could talk to dead people?

I scanned the room expecting to see a camera crew jump out and tell me it was all a joke. But there were no cameras. I was alone and the house was so quiet I could hear the wind outside. I pulled out a knife and tampered with the bottom of the box. I tried a few different knives, stabbing at the glued seam, but the seal couldn't be broken. The more frustrated I got, the more determined I became. My fear disappeared. I'd open the bottom of the box even if I had to take a hammer to it. *A hammer.*

I grabbed the box and headed out to the garage.

After digging out a flathead screwdriver and a rubber mallet from Anthony's toolbox, I placed the screwdriver along the seam and pounded away. Another failed attempt. I threw the screwdriver across the garage in frustration and looked at the heavy steel hammer hanging on Anthony's wall of tools. I shuddered as I pictured myself destroying the box. What if the object hidden inside was fragile and I broke it? What if there was nothing hidden inside at all?

Two seconds later my destructive vision became a reality. One powerful swing and the bottom of the box splintered. After another hit, the rest caved in. Using the claw side of the hammer, I pried away the remaining wood.

There, taped firmly to the next layer of the box, was an envelope with my name written in my mother's handwriting. My hands trembled. Two things terrified me: what the envelope might contain and that this meant Harmony wasn't lying—she could talk to ghosts.

I shook my head, trying to gain control of my thoughts, and whispered into the stillness, "Okay Mom, no turning back now."

I climbed into the Desoto, carefully opening the envelope, and removed several sheets of paper.

My Precious Maryah,

If you are reading this letter it means you are not eighteen yet and something tragic has happened to me. Tell your father and Michael that I love them both dearly, and thank your father for keeping his promise and giving you this letter. If you choose to tell him what you learn, please tell him I'm sorry for keeping it a secret.

As I sit here writing this, you are three years old—so sweet, innocent, and new to the world. It breaks my heart to think of ever having to leave you. However, if one day, I'm forced to go against my will, then there are things you should know.

I plan to tell you this in person, but not until your eighteenth birthday. Logic tells me you should enjoy your childhood. I should let you develop your own beliefs and theories on love and how the world works. Yet a stronger intuition, some unknown force within me, KNOWS I can't keep this from you. If it's true...I get chills as I write the words...then it's your divine right to know the truth.

My childhood best friend, Louise, just revealed something that has caused me to question life and wonder if things aren't always as they seem. (Louise has an imagination that runs deeper than any ocean on this planet.) She swears there is a never-ending cycle to this world. That we return again and again in different bodies, but we remain the same souls. There have been many times when I felt like I'd been somewhere before or experienced something I knew I hadn't (in this lifetime). Déjà vu is what many call it. Louise said it is memories from my past that haven't been entirely erased. Part of me believes that theory.

It's her erase-or-retain theory that I'm not sure I believe. She swears every soul is given a choice between lives. They can retain their memories and knowledge, or they can erase and start with a clean slate. Apparently there are a chosen few who get to decide the details of their return, so it makes it easier for them to retain. She swears YOU are one of those gifted souls. She called you an Element and said you are a part of her kindrily...an eternal family. She lost count of which number lifetime this is for you, but swears she's been a part of every one.

She said almost every normal human chooses erasure because they have no guarantees their new life will be better or worse than their former. The memories and emotional baggage are too much for most souls to endure. In their new life, they might never see anyone they previously knew or loved, but would still carry a torch for them. Furthermore, if they did return quickly enough to live in the same time span of the people they left behind, odds are those people wouldn't believe in a reincarnated version of their lost loved one. The rejection would cause so much heartache that the retainer would never make that choice again.

The whole thing sounds ridiculous, but as long as I
have known Louise (over twenty years) she has never lied
to me. So how can I doubt her now when she comes to me
so passionately to discuss one of the most precious topics
in the world to me? My daughter...her goddaughter.
Louise claims you chose your father and me as your
parents so that you could be close to her and her family.
She also claims her son, Nathaniel, is your soul mate.

When she first told me this information yesterday,
Nathaniel stared at me with wide, green, curious eyes.
He's a toddler! I'm supposed to believe that he loves you
and has loved you for centuries?

I thought Louise had lost her mind. I'm still worried
about her as I write this. I can't bring myself to tell your
father in fear that he'll make me reassign your
guardianship. Even as I sit here, worrying Louise has
gone insane, my intuition tells me that she IS the right
choice as your godmother.

~~If it is true,~~
I'm rambling. I'm not even sure what the purpose of
this letter is or how to finish it. I pray the day will never
come when you have to read this. I pray I'll live to see
your seventieth birthday. Yet somehow I feel better that I
wrote it all down even if no one ever reads it or knows of
Louise's bizarre theory, I feel better knowing it has been
written.

If by some awful twist of fate, you do someday read this, keep this thought in your heart...I love you more than words can express. I will always love you and I will do whatever is within my power to protect you. I might make mistakes along the way, but I will always follow my heart. And if by some divine miracle, you did choose me as your mother, I want to thank you for the honor and privilege. I have truly been blessed to give birth to such an angelic soul.

With every fiber of my being, I love you,
Mom

I curled up in the backseat of my car, clutched the letter to my chest, and cried like a baby.

∞

It was almost ten o'clock and I was more awake than I'd ever been.

That kindrily word, the one I'd heard Anthony say in a dream, stared back at me in my mother's handwriting. Why couldn't she have told me all of this at any age prior to eighteen? Then I would've known Louise had issues and I would've stayed in Maryland. But Louise never acted crazy—not once in seven months of knowing her. The longer I thought about it, the more I wondered if Louise really told my mother this stuff, or if it was one of my mother's lies.

The whiteboard next to the fridge caught my attention. For months I'd barely given the list of names and numbers a second glance, but now *Nathaniel* stood out like it was illuminated in flashing casino lights. I stared at his phone number and considered calling him, but what would I say? *Hello, Nathan. It's Maryah. I found this letter from my dead mother and she said Louise thinks we're soul mates. What do you think? Was my mom a chronic liar, or do we need to call the men with strappy white coats to take your mother away?*

Yet, crazy as it was, I clenched the phone in my hand, wanting to call Nathan so badly my head hurt. I took a deep breath and dialed his number.

After four long rings it went to voicemail. I listened to his greeting and his voice sent a warm tickle through me. I closed my eyes, remembering the same surge when I hugged him the night he gave me my car. All too quickly there was a beep announcing my chance to leave a message. I hung up without saying a word.

Louise came home seconds later. I shoved my mother's letter in my pocket.

"How has your birthday evening been?" she asked.

Act normal. "Fine."

"Are you excited about Krista arriving on Saturday?"

"I wish she were here now." More than ever.

Louise smiled.

I sat on a stool and folded my clasped fingers in my lap. I didn't want to look nervous, but my hands were shaking. "Have you ever heard of a kindrily?"

Her eyes met mine and it felt like a year passed before she blinked. "Yes. A kindrily is similar to the concept of a family. Kindred spirits that remain connected through many lifetimes."

Okay, so it was a known theory, but did Louise believe in it? My fingers were numb from the cut-off circulation. I tried to swallow and think of something to say, but I couldn't.

"What brought that up?" Louise asked.

I played it cool. "I heard it on some television show and didn't know what it meant."

She looked shocked. "Really? What show?"

"Oh, um, I can't remember." My fingertips were turning purple, so I released my death grip before looking up again. "Do you believe in that stuff?"

She rubbed the back of her neck, her bracelets jingling almost as loud as my heartbeat. "Anything is possible."

A non-judgmental, impartial answer. Louise stood strongly behind her beliefs. If she thought she and I were part of an eternal family, she would've said yes—plain and simple. But why would my mother want me to read her letter if she lied?

Faith! I could talk to her about this without looking mental. She believed in past lives. Her sister talks to the dead. What's more unbelievable than that? I hopped down off my stool. "I forgot to call Faith back. Better call her before she goes to bed."

"Okay."

I bee-lined it to my bedroom.

Faith answered on the first ring. "Hello, Birthday Princess!"

"Hey. Is it too late for a sleepover at your place?"

"Don't be silly! That's a fabulous idea. Should we rent a movie? Do you want to order pizza or Thai? We could—"

"Whatever. I'll be over in a few. See you soon."

I packed a bag and returned to the kitchen, but Louise was gone. I scribbled a note telling her I'd be spending the night at Faith's.

I stared at Nathaniel's name for eight heartbeats before leaving.

CLINGING TO THE OLD

NATHANIEL

I stood on the balcony of the cottage, staring out at the rocky shoreline. The moonlight reflected off the whitecaps of the crashing waves, making them appear iridescent. Regardless of how many hundreds of years I had roamed this planet, and how much I thought I understood about life, the beauty of our world still astounded me.

But so did the ugliness.

From inside the house, Sheila called out to me. "Nathaniel, your mobile was ringing."

"No need to answer," I shouted back.

The balcony door squeaked open and Sheila handed me my phone. "You should answer. The screen said 'Home.'"

I cleared the missed call and shoved it in my pocket. "I'm sure Louise just wanted to tell me she arrived home safely."

Louise and Anthony had spent days with me in Ireland and England, helping me find information about Dedrick's disturbing plan. We would need all the help we could get, but I had no updates for them, and so far no one else had agreed to get involved.

"There must be someone powerful enough to counteract Dedrick. Perhaps someone can put a binding spell on him?" I spun around and faced Sheila. She was nearing one-hundred years old, but even with sagging skin, deep wrinkles, and most of her hair whitened, she looked radiant. I had never wished for a soul to be an Element so badly. It was unfair that someone as wretched as Dedrick had found a way to never age, yet an exquisite soul like Sheila grew more fragile with each passing day.

Her Irish accent wasn't as strong as it used to be, but her tenderness remained constant. "Word is spreading far and wide. Every coven, old and new, is being notified, but Dedrick is practicing very dark magic. It would take a foolish witch or warlock to stand against him."

"Even with the support of two kindrilies?"

"Elements are still human, Nathaniel. Alchemy is the manipulation and control of the powers of nature. Whether white or black magic, the witches who practice it will never believe that anything, or anyone, is stronger. Not even all the kindrilies united together."

"But we are stronger. We could convince them if someone would step forward."

"Yes. If only." Using her cane, she lowered herself into a patio chair, still impressively nimble for her age and mentally sharp as well. I couldn't imagine the day her mortal clock would stop ticking. Losing her would obliterate me and everyone else in our kindrily.

"Someone will come forward. I have to believe that. The alternative is…" I couldn't think of a word severe enough to convey how tragic Dedrick's plan would be if he succeeded.

A gust of salty sea air blew Sheila's long hair into a tornado of white and gold. "How is our favorite girl? You don't mention her much. Did you pay her a birthday visit?"

Stabbing pains rippled through my chest. I would never understand how a heart as broken as mine continued to beat.

"No."

Sheila let out a disappointed tsk. "You've visited her every year since you were wee babes."

I'd visited Maryah on her birthday and Christmas every year like clockwork, but it had been for nothing. I pushed away the memory of River with his arm around her. I could only imagine the frivolous birthday gifts he gave her. Perhaps more jewelry, or something worse. "Not this year. Things are different. All trace of the soul we knew is gone forever."

Sheila took each of my hands into hers. "If it were anyone but Mary, I wouldn't have this unwavering faith in what seems like the impossible. But it is her. She proved there are exceptions to the system if you *will* it to be so. If anyone can recover from erasure, it's her."

Throughout all of my existence I could count the number of times I cried on one hand. I refused to let Sheila see me break down.

"How?" I pleaded through burning eyes. I wanted to feel the confidence Sheila possessed. But why were we fighting so hard to reverse the result of Maryah's free will to choose? My voice cracked as I finally asked the most painful question out loud. "How could she erase *me?*"

"I don't know," Sheila whimpered. Her tears welled for both of us. "But there had to be a reason, a reason more important than any of us understands."

We sat in silence, watching the waves crash below us. Sheila's eyes drifted closed, and I thought she was sleeping until she asked, "Ye gave her the ring?"

"Louise did. Maryah hardly glances at it. She doesn't see its power anymore."

"Bah. I still say she and I should have a sit down. My kind isn't a big secret like yours. She might believe a batty old psychic like me." Sheila shook her cane. "I'll show her my tarot cards, inject some history into that fresh mind of hers, and tug some memories loose. She needs a good shaking up, she does. That's all."

I smiled, seeing glimpses of the rambunctious child she had been ninety some years ago. She hadn't lost the fiery spirit she inherited from her mother. "Right now, you're needed here."

"I'll be visiting Amber once her babe arrives. That seems good a time as any."

I nodded, appeasing her until then. Several weeks remained until Amber's due date.

"So." Sheila rested her chin in her hand. It was hours past her bedtime. "I suppose you'll be on your way then, traveling around and sticking your nose where it doesn't belong rather than spending time with me here on the island."

I sat beside her and held her hand. Her skin felt like soft paper, another reminder of how fragile she had become. "I wish I could stay longer. Truly, I do. But Edgar found a new lead."

She squeezed my hand, shaking it gently. "I'll ring you if I hear anything from the covens or other psychics."

"I may not be reachable by phone at times, but as soon as I'm finished I'll come back here and spend time with you. We'll go letterboxing and find you some new treasures."

"That'd be lovely."

"Come, Sheila. Time for bed. You look tired."

She pinched my cheek. "Not as tired as you look, ye old handsome thing."

I assisted her to her bedroom and tucked her in. "Sleep well, love. The stars are waiting for you."

DIGGING TOO DEEP

Maryah

My hands were cramping from clenching Faith's fuzzy pink pillow too tight. I tossed it on her bed and cracked my knuckles. She needed to hurry up. I didn't want food or a movie. I wanted to pick her brain about reincarnation.

My reflection in Faith's full-length mirror caught my attention. The mirror hung on a door that joined Faith and Harmony's rooms. Should I walk in there and ask her to help me talk to my mother? See if she could explain more? If I did, Harmony would know everything. She'd think my mother and I were insane. Or she'd think Louise was insane. Either way, communicating with spirits about being part of some eternal family did not sound anywhere remotely close to normal.

I flopped down on Faith's bed and threw my arms over my head. My ring flew off and bounced onto the floor. I slid off the bed to search for it and saw a pair of scissors and the corner of a plastic storage bin peeking out from the bed skirt. Through the white plastic of the bin, I could see a glue stick, markers, and other craft supplies. I pulled out the box to toss the scissors inside, but sparkly pens rolled over a picture of me at my birthday party.

Scrapbooking. Another hobby Faith attempted to get me into but failed.

I leaned down and looked under her bed, still searching for my ring. It was sitting against a bunch of photo albums, so I grabbed it, slid it back onto my thumb then reached for the nearest two books among the piles. I made myself comfortable in Faith's beanbag chair. At least I'd have a distraction while I waited for her to get back.

Faith's artistic flare adorned every colorful page of dance recitals, holidays, and Colbert family history. She and Shiloh must have known each other forever. In a few pictures they looked like they were only four or five years old. I opened the second massively thick book, handling it delicately.

The pages looked old; faded to a color between white and brown. There were no stickers, sparkly quotes, or descriptions. The first few pages were hand-drawn sketches of people. Further into the book, little corner tabs held black and white photos in place. I studied each one, smiling at the old clothes and hairstyles—until one photo made me lift the book to examine it closer.

An old couple stood in front of a '57 Desoto. They looked old enough to be grandparents. Behind them was the gated archway to the Luna house. I carefully removed the picture from its tabs and stared at...*my* car. I turned over the picture and there, written in my handwriting, were the words *Nathaniel and Me—Sedona—new house*.

I read it over and over, expecting the words to say something else, but every time it said the same impossible thing.

I kept flipping through pages. Familiar eyes stared back at me from every page, but they were on faces of people I didn't recognize, until one photograph caught my attention. Three faces I *did* recognize stared back at me. The colors weren't as vivid or bright as today's digital photography, but Mary's green eyes looked just as bright as they did on Nathan's nightstand. She wore a wedding dress—and next to her, stood twenty-something versions of Louise and Anthony.

No. Freaking. Way. My ears buzzed so loud they hurt. I pressed my palm against one of them, but kept studying the photo.

The elderly Asian couple didn't look familiar at first. Then it hit me. It seemed genetically impossible, but the short woman in her silky kimono stared back at me through Faith's blue eyes. Add some height, braids, and youth to the old guy and the resemblance to Shiloh was uncanny. I turned it over. Again, my handwriting: *Our wedding (19).*

A dried white flower and a peacock feather were pressed into a piece of folded wax paper on the same page. What did nineteen mean? What did any of this mean?

Faith's voice coming down the hallway jolted me out of my disbelief. I snapped the book shut and shoved it behind the beanbag chair then jumped to my feet just as the bedroom door opened.

"Sorry, I thought I'd be back by the time you..." Faith paused and set the bags of take-out on her dresser. "Are you all right? You look pale—paler than usual."

My ears still hummed and my mouth felt like it'd been stuffed with cotton balls, but I forced myself to speak. "Getting a headache."

"No headaches allowed on your birthday. I'll get aspirin and make us party drinks!"

As soon as she left the room I grabbed the books and slid them back under the bed. I felt like I'd wandered onto another planet; a planet where lack of oxygen made it hard for me to think or breathe. How could my handwriting be on those pictures? Mary-Maryah. It couldn't be. I couldn't be her.

Faith came back holding two pink Shirley Temples in her hand. She set one on her nightstand and reached out with a closed fist. I opened my palm and watched two white pills drop into my hand. Every move I made felt alien to me, like I was disconnected from my body.

Faith took a sip of her pink drink then did a double take and focused on my thigh. I looked down. One black photo tab was stuck to my sweatpants.

When our eyes met, her face tensed. She grabbed my hand and the aspirin dropped to the floor. She squeezed my fingers tight. "Maryah, don't be scared."

"I'm not scared," I lied.

"You're terrified, and you're nauseous too."

My eyes widened. The room spun. I pulled my hand away from her. "I have to go."

"Please don't leave. We need to talk about this."

I kept walking, praying she wouldn't try to stop me. My mind was still stuck on the photos and drawings, but my feet kept moving. I passed Harmony in the hallway but couldn't look at her. I waved goodbye to their dad, and left the house without another word.

When I was a safe distance away, I parked in an empty lot, unclenching the steering wheel. My thoughts corkscrewed around each other. Why was the Desoto in that photo? My parents had the car before I was born, but had they ever mentioned who or where they got it from? Those old people couldn't be Nathan and me. That bride couldn't be me. All of it was insane. I hadn't moved to Sedona, I'd moved to the Twilight Zone.

I dialed Krista. *Please be awake. Please be awake.* Voicemail.

"Kris, it's me. Call me as soon as you get this." My voice cracked on my last words. "I want—no, I *need* to come home."

Next I tried River.

"What's up?" he shouted. Loud music and a rumble of incoherent noise blasted through the receiver.

"Where are you? I need to talk to you."

"What?"

I yelled louder. "Where are you?"

"I told you, my uncle's in town. You bailed on me so I'm out with him and his friends."

A girl laughed. She sounded so close she must've been on his lap. "Is April with you?"

"What?" More loud noise.

"Can I meet up with you?"

Another girly laugh was followed by rustling on the phone. I strained to hear if I could make out any of the conversation going on in the background. "I can't hear you," River yelled. "And my phone's about to die. I'll call you later."

He hung up. My head fell back against the headrest. I had no one left to turn to.

I cranked up my Beatles CD and waited for Krista to call back. I didn't care how long I had to wait. I wasn't going back to the Luna house.

HITTING WHERE IT HURTS

Maryah

Knuckles knocking against my window startled me out of my sleep. I lifted my head from my steering wheel and squinted through the frost at the back-lit outline of Anthony. I rolled down my window and tried to fake a smile. "Sorry, I got tired on my way home."

Anthony's sunglasses blocked any evidence of whether he believed me. "You all right?"

I nodded. Another lie.

"You should come home."

I glanced at my phone. No missed calls. "I think I'll go into town and get breakfast."

A smug smile spread across his lips. "And leave Krista waiting at the house?"

"WHAT? She isn't coming until tomorrow."

"She caught an earlier flight."

Oh, thank god! I needed her more than ever. I tried to start my car but nothing happened, not one cough or chug of the engine. Anthony shook his head. "Did you fall asleep with the headlights on, or the radio?"

"Radio," I admitted, biting my lip.

"You can ride with me. Carson and I will come back and jumpstart her."

Anthony and I didn't talk on the drive home, but I couldn't stop thinking about the photo of him and Louise at—*someone's* wedding. I felt my pocket. The bulge of paper from my mother's letter was still there. It wasn't a dream.

∞

I practically flew through the front door and into the living room. I squealed as soon as she sprang up from the couch.

"Happy Birthday, Pudding!" Krista exclaimed as I catapulted through the air and hugged her—candle smells wafted over me.

"You're here! You're really here."

"I heard your message and…caught a different flight."

"Happy Birthday, Kris." I lowered my voice. "I wanted to come to you, back to Baltimore." I hugged her for way too long, but eventually pulled away to look at her. "We need to talk."

She smiled and a sense of normalcy spread over me. Krista was here. Everything would be okay. I'd tell her about the eternal family insanity and she'd take me back to Maryland. Aunt Sandy and Uncle Dave didn't want me moving out here anyway.

Anthony never came into the house. He probably stayed outside to tinker in the garage. I didn't know where Louise and Carson were, but I didn't want to take any chances. "Let's go to my room."

I shut my door and pulled the letter out of my pocket. "These people are nuts. I should've stayed in Maryland. Read this."

Krista eyeballed the letter, but didn't take it. "Your mom told Harmony what it said, and Faith told me you found the photo album."

~ 285 ~

"Faith and Harmony? You talked to them?" I sat in my rattan chair, feeling weak and confused. "Wait. You know about Harmony talking to ghosts?"

"It's time I told you some things, things you should've known a long time ago."

She reached for my hands, but I stuck them under my legs. She raised her fingers to her lips in a prayer position. Since we were little she'd always done that same motion right before she announced something important—and true. Part of me was terrified.

"You *are* part of a kindrily. So am I."

"You're joking. Why are you playing along with this?"

"We're Elements," Krista said in the most serious tone I'd ever heard her use. "We all have supernatural gifts. I'm a healer."

My head shook. Not Krista too. No way.

"Think about the attack," she continued. "The doctors said it would take you months to heal, that you'd have scars. People don't heal that fast without supernatural help."

"But." I stared at her, thinking of a dozen incidents when Krista took away a pain or illness. I couldn't recall a time she was injured. The only times she got sick were right after I felt better. Sweat beaded on my forehead, but I couldn't pull my hands out from under me.

"When we were kids, I tried to tell you stories, hoping it would trigger your memory, but you always thought I was playing make-believe."

The speed of her words increased as she grew more emotional. "Like Pudding. I call you that because it's what you used to call me. And telling you the stars are waiting for you before you went to sleep, you used to tell me that every night." She paced the floor as she rambled. "One time I tried to tell you directly, at your tenth birthday party at Skateland. Nathan was there and we agreed I should tell you, but when I did, you got sick. It was your worst migraine ever. I was scared to mention it again."

I stared at her dumbfounded. "You know Nathan?"

"You two are kind of a big deal," she teased.

"He was at my birthday party?"

She sighed. "He always had to stay incognito, but yes, he visited every year on your birthday and Christmas."

My eyes widened. "Since when?"

"Since you were five."

"How is that possible? He was a little kid! I lived across the country."

"It's complicated, but we had plans worked out so he'd never pop in at a bad time. Remember, we all have gifts, Nathan's is traversing."

"Traversing?"

Krista smiled. "Remember that movie we watched, *Jumper?* That's what Nathan does. He can travel almost instantaneously."

I pictured the main character teleporting across continents. Krista wouldn't lie to me. She'd never take the side of a bunch of strangers, or non-strangers.

"Seriously?"

She nodded.

Nathan, the flesh and blood guy I had crushed on, hated, received a car from, and dreamed about, had some super power? I stared at the white comforter on my bed like it was a movie screen. My past several months of dreams played out in front of me: Nathan snowboarding, visiting foreign countries, and flying off mountains. "Wait. Can he fly?"

Krista laughed. "Not that I know of."

I nervously laughed too. As if *that* was a silly question, yet teleporting should be an acceptable concept. I thought back to my other strange dreams. "He didn't hang out in your bedroom while you healed some wound on his back, right?"

Krista's chin darted forward. "How'd you know that?"

My answer lingered on my tongue. Like I knew as soon as I said it out loud, everything would change. "I…saw you two…in a dream."

She braced her arms on the sides of my chair. "What else have you dreamt about?"

I leaned back. "Kris, you're suffocating me."

She released her death grip and kneeled in front of me. "Spill it."

I looked down at her and months of secrets spewed out of me: seeing Nathan the night of the attack, the hospital, every dream I had, even the Christmas ornament. I must have ranted for half an hour, but she never said a word.

When I finished, she rubbed her hands over her face and rested in her trademark prayer position. "Take a deep breath, because what I'm about to tell you is going to require an excessive amount of oxygen."

I inhaled as deep as I could.

"None of those were dreams," she told me. "Your gift is astral traveling. You can leave your physical body and watch over anyone at any time without being seen."

I laughed, but it got stuck in my throat when I realized she wasn't kidding. "My dreams were real?"

"Yes." She played with the ends of her dark hair. "Why didn't you tell me about any of this?"

She was right. I couldn't find enough air to breathe properly. "I thought you'd think I was nuts!"

Krista shook her head. "And we assumed you'd think we were crazy if we asked you."

I slid off my chair and sat on the floor in front of her. "You remember your..." I couldn't wrap my head around all of it. "Past lives? You remember living a life before this one?"

She rested her hands on my knees. "This is my third lifetime with everyone. I'm the thirteenth member. I was the newest member until Carson came along. In every life you and I have been family...kind of."

"Were we cousins in our last life too?" It felt ridiculous to say something so bizarre out loud.

"We can get into that later. I don't want your brain to explode."

I ran my hand over my head like it might be a real possibility. "There was a wedding photo of Nathaniel and Mary," I still couldn't bring myself to say me, "and the number nineteen next to it in my handwriting. What does nineteen mean?"

She looked up for a moment, fiddling with her hair again. "Probably means yours and Nathan's nineteenth wedding. Sounds about right."

I sat up so fast that the corner of the chair jammed into my back. "What? That's impossible. That's—how could—no way."

Krista's bottom lip folded into a pout. "You two were an item for longer than you can imagine. That ring you're wearing," she held my thumb. "That's been your engagement ring several times."

I gasped, staring at my ring like it was a UFO. I couldn't imagine anyone ever proposing to me, much less someone like Nathan. "This doesn't mean we're engaged, does it?"

Krista laughed. "No. He has to actually pop the question for that to apply. But there is more to that ring than meets the eye."

"Like what?"

"Nathan or Louise will have to explain that one. I still don't fully understand it."

"I can't ask Nathan about any of this!"

"Why? You do love him, right?"

My jaw went slack. "Love him? I don't—we never—I mean he's—he could have any girl on this planet. Why would he want me?"

"Oh, Maryah. Oblivious, feeble-minded angel." Her eyes glistened and she sighed. "You are his world. He has loved you for centuries. He's been broken without you."

Broken. No, I'd been the broken one. How could I be so important to him? He barely knew me. "It's not that I don't want to believe you. I do. I think, but, I…what do you call it? Erased, right?"

She nodded.

"Then think about it. I hardly know Nathan. I'm not sure I even know what being in love means. And if I don't remember being with him then…" I shrugged, lost for what else to say.

Krista went stone-faced. "I don't believe this. You're soul mates. You're supposed to be magnetically drawn to each other. Knowing all of this I figured…so wait, you don't feel anything for him?"

I didn't want to lie. I'd been attracted to him since my first dream, or what I thought was a dream. Even when I wanted to hate him, I thought about him constantly, but everything about the situation scared me. None of this was normal. Not even close to normal. "Can we take a break from talking about this for a minute? I'm getting a headache."

Krista glanced at my bedroom door. "They're waiting for us. They called a meeting."

I looked at the door too. "A meeting? Who called a meeting?"

"The kindrily. This is where you hear the rest of the story. They want to make sure you're okay with everything."

"But I don't know if I am."

"That's why they called a meeting. Come on."

CIRCLE OF LOVE

Maryah

E veryone had gathered around the huge dining room table.
Outside, rain fell, but inside, the chandelier burned
brightly. I'd never seen its candles lit before. The flames
glistened in the rainbow glass of the star skylight. The room and
all the people in it seemed to glow, including Dylan and Amber,
who I was shocked to see. Krista guided me to three empty seats
and pulled out the middle chair. I sat down, expecting her to sit
beside me, but she took the seat between Carson and Faith.

All of the couples sat beside each other holding hands: Edgar
and Helen, Anthony and Louise, Dylan and Amber, and Faith and
Shiloh. The seat on my left was obviously for Nathan. I glanced to
my right at Harmony one seat down from me. The empty chair
between us must be for Dakota, but, no, wait. Her brother couldn't
be her soul mate. Things couldn't be *that* twisted.

Helen spoke first. "Maryah, your mother shared part of our
secret with you; however, there is more to your story, and it's time
you are aware of it. We will try our best to explain as much as we
can without overwhelming you, but stop us if you have a question.
This will be a lot of information to comprehend in one sitting."

Carson laughed from across the table. "That's an understatement."

"I have a question." Every pair of eyes focused on me. I took a deep breath to calm my nerves. I looked pointedly at Dylan and Amber. "How did everyone get here so fast?"

"We flew," Amber replied.

"Both of you can fly?"

"No, we flew in the family plane," Dylan answered.

"The family plane?"

Carson tucked his hair behind his ears. "Come on, Sparky. Did you think a supernal bunch like us wouldn't have some cool toys?"

"If you have your own plane, why haven't I seen it, and why didn't we use it to go to Colorado?"

"It's a *special* kind of plane." Carson smirked. "You weren't ready for that kind of exposure to our way of life."

I looked at Krista. "Is that how you got here?" She grinned. A plane was the least of my worries. "Everyone is part of this kindrily thing? And you *all* remember past lives *and* have superpowers?"

Helen answered. "Everyone at this table is an Element. We are called Elements because of our divine consistency. We're all considered Aether because it's fundamental and the most powerful of the elements. However, we also take on a role as Earth, Fire, Air, or Water. Each lifetime, when we return, we are born under the same sign. Edgar and I are Earth. Anthony and Louise are Fire, and so on and so on. We were all gifted with unique abilities and yes, we all choose to perpetually retain our memories from all our lives."

"I'm so confused," I mumbled.

"You think you're confused now?" Carson laughed. "Just wait."

Louise spoke patiently. "The concept is nearly impossible for most human minds to comprehend. We don't expect you to understand it all right away."

Edgar put on his glasses. "Let me elaborate. Elements are exceptional souls who are created and gifted to the world in pairs."

"Edgar," Helen said sternly.

"My apologies, I haven't fully adjusted to the recent permutations. I meant neither ill will nor harm." He nodded at Krista and Carson before continuing. "*Originally*, the system dictated that Elements were born in pairs—soul mates or twin flames. Nathaniel is yours. He has been since your first birth, as Helen is mine, and so on throughout the family." He nodded at each couple. "However, recent developments have proven there are exceptions. Krista and Carson are our latest additions and it seems the twin flame theory does not apply to them."

Louise leaned forward. "You and Nathaniel have always been Air signs, however this time *you* were born as Water. It's the first time in any Element's existence that one of us changed roles. Only time will tell if there is a consequence or meaning behind it."

Helen smiled at Louise then looked at me. "Maryah, after reading your mother's letter, do you understand the concept of retaining or erasing?"

"I think I get it." I didn't get it at all, but I didn't want to admit how clueless I was.

"So you understand that we continuously choose to retain our memories after each life, and that many of us remember, and have been connected for centuries?"

I thought about the book series I recently read. "Are we like vampires or something, immortal? Do we live forever?"

Dylan chuckled. "No, we're far from immortal. We live and breathe. We get hurt and sick, and eventually our bodies die, but not our souls. The body is simply a vessel to allow us human experiences."

"But if you look at it that way then everyone is immortal. No soul ever dies?"

Amber pulled her hair into a ponytail. "In a sense that's true, however there's more to it. It's difficult to explain because you chose to erase. You have no memory of what we've been through, or the lessons we've learned throughout our lives, and our experiences in the Higher Realm."

That Higher Realm place again. I had so many questions about that too, but there was a bigger issue at hand. "Why would I erase?"

"We don't know." Several people answered in unison. I could see the pain in their eyes. I'd never intentionally hurt any of them, but what could I say? I didn't remember having a choice, much less why I erased. Faith looked the saddest, but Amber came in close second. Dylan watched me like he was expecting me to say something.

"What's your gift?" I asked him.

Louise placed her hand on Dylan's shoulder. "Dylan exhibits more self-control than any of us. At any time he could use his gift for personal gain, yet he continually lives an exceedingly virtuous life."

"Sometimes he uses it for personal gain," Anthony said.

Dylan looked offended. "All of you get to enjoy your gifts; I should too."

Anthony fought back a smile as he shook his head.

Dylan continued. "I have the power of persuasion. I can persuade anyone to do almost anything."

My mind raced at the unlimited possibilities. I thought back to how easily he convinced me to drive his new car. How did I miss so many telltale signs that this family wasn't ordinary? I looked at Carson. "The fire in my room. You put it out way too fast. Can you control fire?"

Carson smirked. "No. Anthony and I tag teamed that crisis."

"Carson is multi-gifted," Faith said.

His tan cheeks blushed. "I'm fast physically and mentally too. I can figure things out, like solve problems or see how to make things work, and I'm pretty strong."

"Pretty strong?" Faith sang, reaching around Krista and grabbing his bicep. "Those muscles stopped a hot air balloon from crash landing!"

"*You* stopped us from crashing?"

Carson brushed the hair from his eyes so fast that I barely saw his hands. "Basket, fabric, and two people: not much of a challenge."

I nodded, realizing that was also how he grabbed me off the dirt bike and saved me from falling off the cliffs. I knew something like that wasn't possible under normal circumstances.

Anthony hadn't said a word. "And Anthony—you fix stuff?"

He cleared his throat. "I acquired that talent through *a lot* of experience. My gift is something different."

"He freezes time," Carson announced excitedly.

I gasped. "I saw you do that in my dream!"

Anthony's eyes narrowed and every head at the table whipped around to look at me. Krista shifted in her seat. "Yeah, sorry, probably should've mentioned this earlier. Turns out Maryah still has her gift. She thought her travels were dreams."

Murmurs broke out around the table.

Faith knelt in her chair and leaned forward. "Jeez Louise! Nathan was right!"

They all had questions, but I had way more than them. Glancing around, I realized this was one of the few times I could see everyone's eyes. "Sunglasses. Why is everyone obsessed with sunglasses?"

Dylan spoke. "The eyes are the window to the soul. As Elements, we recognize people by the detailed light and coloring in their eyes. We have history with some evil souls we've been protecting ourselves from. They have no idea what most of us look like this time around, and if they see our eyes, they might recognize us."

"They have powers like we do?"

"We assume they still do," Dylan continued. "Edgar can only see the leader's plans up until about thirty years ago. Then he disappears as if he no longer exists, but we know differently. He was behind the attack on you and your family."

Snake Eyes and the other monster flashed before me. "Oh my god," I whispered. They *were* looking for me. I'm the girl they wanted to kill? "What if they find me again?"

Shiloh looked extremely serious. "Your eyes no longer reveal who you used to be. They wouldn't have tried to kill you if they knew it was you. You have the eyes of a stranger because you erased."

It was too much information. My head felt so heavy it actually fell forward until my forehead thudded against the table. When Snake Eyes looked at me, he said I wasn't her. Technically, I wasn't her anymore. Was I? I craned my head up and looked at Edgar. "Dylan said you could see his plans. So you read minds?"

"No, dear, I can only read the Akashic Records."

My eyebrows ached from rising so much.

Edgar elaborated. "The Akashic Records are a collection of human thoughts and intentions. Everything that ever happens, or any human thought, is recorded in the cosmos. It is the book of life, a detailed reference that is constantly evolving."

I looked at Faith. "That book you gave me about Edgar Cayce, it mentioned the Akashic records."

Faith giggled and pointed at Edgar.

"Holy crap." My head fell into my hands. I recalled my thoughts about suicide and how I hated Nathan. I thought of all the lies I'd ever told and the bad things I'd done. I mumbled into my palms. "Have you read my thoughts?"

Edgar waited for me to look up. "Maryah, my dear, I do not play judge or juror. I only wield my power with fellow members when it is critical to our wellbeing. Besides, I assure you, even if I had knowledge of every bad thought you had, it would pale in comparison to the iniquitous actions I have witnessed throughout my lives."

I nodded, relieved that Edgar didn't think I was an awful person, but made a mental note to be more conscious of my intentions and actions. *He* wasn't a judge, but if a permanent record existed, I wanted to keep mine as clean as possible. A thought came to me. "Can you read your book and find out why I erased?"

He peered at me over his bifocals. "It doesn't work that way. When you made that decision, you were in the Higher Realm. The Akashic Records document thoughts and intentions of the *human* mind. The Higher Realm and astral journeys are beyond my jurisdiction. It is believed by an elder of another kindrily that a collection referred to as the Sacred Scrolls records what transpires in the Higher Realm. However, we don't know if the collection truly exists. No soul has been known to access it."

"There are other kindrilies like us?"

Helen responded. "Yes, dear. Over six billion souls live on this planet. Many have abilities that would astound you."

"Why is it such a secret?"

Much to my surprise Krista answered.

"The theory isn't believed by the majority of the world. In the past, people have been killed or tortured for telling the truth about who they are. Many humans can't comprehend ideas or theories that are bigger than them. If they can't see it or understand it right away, they dismiss it. Some take it to an extreme and label it as evil or claim it's demonic. It's safer for us to stay quiet, at least until the world evolves enough to accept the possibility."

Centuries-old souls and superpowers? Of course the majority of the world didn't believe it. I sure as heck had trouble believing it.

I turned to Edgar. "Krista said Carson is the newest member. We arrived at different times?"

Edgar laid his hand on top of Helen's. "Helen and I were born into the world during the first century. Four centuries later, fate allowed us to cross paths with Anthony and Louise. Another four centuries passed before Dylan and Amber joined." My eyes progressed from couple to couple as Edgar explained. They were sitting in order of the timeline. "You and Nathaniel made the original eight in the twelfth century."

I looked at Nathan's chair beside me then at the other empty seat and five members to my right. "The original eight?"

"Six centuries passed before another synchronistic meeting occurred. For a short time we assumed it would be only the eight of us. However, the pattern picked up again in the eighteenth century with Harmony and her soul mate, Gregory. That same century Faith and Shiloh entered, then Krista—well, perhaps she should explain her own history."

Krista started in a wispy voice. "Three lifetimes ago, I was born in Egypt to psychically gifted parents, but they were killed when I was fourteen. My little sister and I were shipped off to an orphanage in England where you worked as a nurse. My sister got hurt, and you saw me heal her. After that, you and Nathan adopted us."

I couldn't blink. "What?"

Krista stretched her hands in front of her like she wanted to reach across the table. "You taught my sister and me about the system, and about Elements. Everyone thought you were crazy, but you believed in us. You loved us wholeheartedly, and you said you *knew* we were meant to be in your kindrily."

"And I was right? You chose how to come back?"

"No." Krista looked at her twiddling thumbs. "I lived to be thirty-nine. When I crossed over, I wasn't an Element—but you had made me a promise. In my first life, you told me when I died, if I wasn't an Element, but I chose to retain, you would find me. So I retained. I was born to awful, abusive parents, but you kept your promise." She raised her eyes to meet mine and tears were forming. "You came for me. You found me, just like you said you would, and you took me away from them." She sniffled quietly. "That was my previous life. I was forty-nine when I died at Dylan and Amber's wedding, but when I arrived at the Higher Realm again, things were different. I was an Element. I got to choose when and where I'd return just like you suspected."

Faith rose and sat in the empty seat next to me, taking my hand. "You beat the system," she said softly. "You believed it was possible when all of us told you it wasn't. You believed so deeply that you made it real. This time Krista is one of us by divine right. You're a superhero in our eyes."

"But—I'm not," I retorted through a choked voice. "I'm—plain and average."

"Maryah, you are our eighth member," Amber said. "Eight is a symbol for infinity. Your position represents the infinite source more than any of us. We think we've only begun to see what powers you possess."

I couldn't have done the things they were talking about. Adopting Krista? That made no sense at all. Not to mention it creeped me out. She was my cousin and best friend!

A tornado blew through my brain. One strong gust of wind blew Krista's earlier words back at me.

"Kris, you mentioned you had a sister. What happened to her?"

Krista lit up. "She's still alive. She's ninety-nine and lives on an island between Ireland and England—Isle of Man. Her name is Sheila."

I let go of Faith's hand and gripped the sides of my chair. If what they were telling me was true, then I had an adopted daughter from a previous life who was still alive. It was impossible.

"She's coming here for a visit soon," Edgar said.

I felt like someone was holding my head underwater. Breathing became impossible. Did they expect me to accept that we lived like secret comic book characters? To act like it was no big deal?

"I have to go," I mumbled, pushing back my chair.

"Go where?" Faith asked.

Good question. Where could I go? April wouldn't speak to me. River was the only one who wasn't a part of this. He was my only remaining connection to the normal world. "I have plans with River."

The front door seemed a million miles away. My legs felt like wet noodles. Edgar called my name, but I kept walking, hoping that Time Freezer and Speed Demon had brought my car back to the house.

As I passed through the gate, I saw the Desoto. I ran to it and climbed inside, but there were no keys.

"No," I moaned. "Get me away from here."

"Maryah," Carson shouted, blurring past my window. The passenger door opened and he was beside me before I could blink. "We won't try to stop you. We understand how overwhelming this is. But please don't tell anyone about us. You're one of us and look how you're reacting. Imagine if you told this stuff to a normal person."

A head nod was my only reply.

He placed my key in the ignition, and the engine roared to life. "Call us if you need anything. We're here for you no matter what. Forever."

SURPRISE SURPRISE

Maryah

Eightball barked and howled while I rang River's doorbell for the second time. I didn't call to tell him I was coming, so the look of surprise on his face when he answered the door seemed normal.

"Maryah, I didn't know you were stopping by."

Eightball waddled out onto the porch. His nubby tail wagged as I picked him up and hugged him for warmth.

"I needed to get out of the house." I eyed the tattoos all over River's bare chest and arms. I'd never seen him with his shirt off before.

"Give me a second." He shut the door and I stood on the porch feeling stupid. I forgot my coat and I was shivering. Why didn't he invite me in?

A few minutes later, the door opened and a girl with auburn hair shouldered past me without even glancing in my direction. She had to be in her mid-twenties and dressed like someone in a porno version of *The Matrix*. She climbed into a black Mercedes and drove away.

"Did I interrupt something?" I asked.

River stood in the doorway pulling a shirt over his head. His lips lifted in a cockeyed smile, and he wrapped his arms around my waist. "Friend of my uncle's. She got wasted last night and had to crash here."

"Eww, you smell like you bathed in beer!" I wriggled out of his arms. The scent of Jasmine and sweat lingered on him.

"You coming in?"

Against my better judgment, I nodded and went inside. I had nowhere else to go, and no one else to turn to—at least no one normal.

"You're still drunk, aren't you?" I set Eightball down on the floor. Beer bottles and shot glasses covered the coffee table.

River didn't answer me. "So what's up? You never show up here without calling."

"Sorry to ruin your party with Little Red Riding Whore."

"Hey, watch it." River pointed the neck of a beer bottle at me. "She's like family."

"Then why do you smell like her?" I mumbled under my breath.

"What?"

"Nothing."

Apparently the keeper of my secrets was keeping secrets of his own. I collapsed into the leather easy chair and ran my hands over my face. I came here to escape weirdness, but instead I stumbled into a scene from a sleazy soap opera. Part of me wanted to ask him if he slept with her, but another part didn't care. April was better off without him. Eightball jumped into my lap and snorted while I rubbed his ears.

"Where's your uncle?"

"Out." River hovered above me. "You look like you pulled an all-nighter too. What's wrong?"

Oh, let's see. Everyone swears Nathan is my soul mate, that we've known each other for a bunch of lifetimes, that we all have superpowers, and that some old lady is my adopted daughter. That's what ran through my mind. What came out of my mouth was, "I haven't slept much."

River sat on the couch across from me. He didn't take his gaze away from the collage of TV shows as he flipped through channels.

I didn't know what to do with my hands. I kept squeezing my fingers and picking at my nails until I finally shoved them between my legs and half-whispered, "I'm freaked out."

His eyes drifted sideways to meet mine. "What?"

"Some strange stuff has happened in the last day or two."

He pressed mute and set the remote down. "Do tell."

I took a deep breath, thinking about Carson's warning not to tell anyone. "You have to *promise* you won't say anything to anyone. I'm serious. The Lunas could be sent to an asylum if this got out."

He raised his hand. "Swear."

I leaned forward. Forget dragonflies, my stomach was filled with fire breathing dragons. I wouldn't tell him everything, just enough to make me feel a little better. "They said we were family in previous lives, like, reincarnated." I sat up straight, debating how much to tell him. "They said they remember their past lives."

His face didn't flinch. "Do you believe in that stuff? Past lives, or whatever."

"I don't know."

"I don't see the big deal. Lots of people in this town believe in some wacky stuff."

"They want me to remember my past lives too."

He grabbed a half empty beer from the table. "If you're so freaked out, move in here with me. You're eighteen now. You're free to do what you want."

The thought of deserting them never occurred to me. I needed a break from the flood of new revelations, but leaving them wasn't an option. I didn't know why, but just the idea of it felt wrong in so many ways. "I still love them. I mean, family doesn't have to believe in all the same things."

River squatted down in front of me. Eightball jumped off my lap. "They aren't your family. You don't share one drop of blood with any of them. You don't have to live with them. There's plenty of room of here, and I'll take care of you. You'll be spoiled rotten."

He pulled me so close our faces almost touched. His lips pressed against mine.

"What are you doing?" I pushed him backward and he fell against the coffee table. Empty beer bottles and glasses crashed and rolled around us. Wiping the taste of beer from my lips, I gagged on the bile burning my throat. "I need a friend, and instead, you're trying to kiss me! I'm not some skank like the girl who just left."

He stood up, kicking bottles away from him. "What the hell? I plan a big night for your birthday and you cancel on me. Then you come running to me because those people you live with are mental patients. Now you're shoving me around and accusing me of cheating on you? I don't get you."

Cheating on me? How could he cheat on me if I never agreed to be his girlfriend? "River, I'm sorry I pushed you, but I told you a dozen times, I don't want to mess up our friendship."

He shook his head then turned his back to me. What else could I say to make it clear to him? Were all guys so stubborn? I really did care about him, just not in the way he wanted. After a minute of uncomfortable silence he sat beside me and let out a deep breath. "You look exhausted. Want to lie down for a while?"

I nodded, wanting nothing more than to sleep and hopefully not dream—or astral travel.

We went to River's room, but when he climbed into his bed, I just stood at his door.

"Let me guess," he said. "We're not allowed to sleep in the same bed."

"It's fine. I can sleep on the sofa."

He sighed and rolled off the bed. "No. You sleep here. I'll crash on the couch."

"Sorry, but thank you." He slipped his hand under the bottom of my shirt, but I pressed my forearm against my stomach to block him. "River, forget it. It's never going to happen."

"I'm just trying to make you feel better, to be here for you and help take your mind off things."

"All I'll ever need from you is friendship."

Shadows swept over his eyes. I'd never seen him look so hurt. I felt awful, but he needed to know the truth. I'd put off telling him my decision for too long.

"Right," he mumbled. "Get some sleep."

He left and I crawled into bed. I closed my eyes and kept picturing Nathan. I couldn't imagine him acting like River. It occurred to me that if all this was true, if Nathan and I had been together in other lives and he remembered it; it meant we had kissed—lots of times. My cheeks warmed thinking about what other things we must've done when we were—it was hard to even think the word—married. Oh my god, did he think about stuff like that when he looked at me? How embarrassing.

How could I ever face Nathan again?

∞

I dreamed about Nathan non-stop: replays from the hospital, the balloon ride, him giving me my car. Every time he disappeared, I screamed for him to come back. The last time I called out his name, I woke myself up.

River was standing over me. The room was dark, but I could see his silhouette. I prayed I hadn't been yelling out Nathan's name for real.

River sat on the edge of the bed. "You've been tossing and turning for hours."

I rolled over and glanced at the window. Not a trace of sunlight. Eightball snored away beside me. "What time is it?"

"Almost ten."

"Wow," I groaned. "I slept all day?"

My eyes were adjusting to the lack of light, but I could see River fiddling with his wristband. "You needed it, and so did I. It gave me time to think."

"About what?" I heard footsteps in the hallway and worried his uncle might be home. I didn't want to look like a hussy coming out of River's bedroom at ten o'clock at night.

"I've been acting like a tool. Even if we can only be friends—" he paused, glanced at his bedroom door, and lowered his voice. "Are you still set on the nothing but friends thing?"

Why did being honest make me feel so guilty? "Yes."

"I figured."

The footsteps started up again then faded. Someone had definitely been in the hallway, but it could've been the maid putting linens in the closet or something.

"Anyway," River continued. "We never went out for your birthday, so I want to make it up to you. I planned a surprise."

He was back. The fun friend I didn't want to lose wanted to take me out for my birthday. I playfully nudged his knee. "Okay, but take it easy on me. I don't know how many more surprises I can handle."

STUMBLING THROUGH THE DARK

Maryah

"Where are we going?" I climbed into River's truck. He rarely took his 4x4 anywhere.

"You really don't get the concept of a *surprise*, do you?" He turned up his stereo and his voice flooded through the speakers. They were songs I'd never heard him sing before—hard, angry rock.

We headed south and drove through the town of Oak Creek. We made a right onto an unlit dirt road, passing a sign that showed the way to Montezuma Well and Castle.

"Montezuma Castle?" I asked. Faith mentioned something about the ruins, but she said it was a tourist attraction and only open during the day.

"Maryah!" he howled.

"Right, it's a surprise. Sorry."

We bumped along the dirt road for a few miles. I couldn't see anything except the few feet ahead of us illuminated by the headlights. After a sharp left, we off-roaded down a narrower path. I held on to the door handle and bounced in my seat until the truck stopped.

I stared out into the darkness. "Where are we?"

"Montezuma Well."

"The sink hole?"

"It's not a sink hole. It's like a lake at the bottom of a canyon. It's a sacred Indian site. An underground spring mysteriously fills it with warm water. Lots of magical things happen out here."

I laughed. "You don't believe in that stuff."

"Usually no, but this place is different."

"It's pitch black out here. It would be nice if I could *see* the lake. Can't we come back in the morning?"

"Tourists will be here during the day. If you come here at night and follow the Indian rituals, you can communicate with the other side."

"You mean talk to ghosts?" I never believed it was possible, but lately people were talking about it as casually as the weather.

"Yup. With all this adopted family drama going on, I thought you might want to talk to your parents or brother. That's my birthday gift to you."

This was my chance to talk to my mother about her letter and ask her questions without Harmony being involved. "You really think it'll work?"

"If so, this is your best shot." River sounded confident. Maybe he had communicated with his parents.

"All right. I'm in!" We got out and he grabbed a duffel bag from the truck bed.

"Supplies we'll need," he explained, turning on a flashlight then reaching for my hand. River had loaned me a jacket, but after five minutes of walking my teeth were chattering. I stayed close to his side, only able to see a small amount of ground from the flashlight. I paused at the top of an outdoor staircase made from rocks. "Where do these steps go?"

"Down to the ruins—close to the water."

"I've heard Indian sites are sacred. Maybe we shouldn't be here."

"It's fine. I silently requested permission from the spirits when we parked."

"Really?" I asked in astonishment. River wasn't the spiritual or respectful type.

"They said it's cool with them," he snickered.

I laughed and it eased some of my fear. "Can you shine that flashlight around so I can see where we are? It's kind of scary out here."

"Fine, you big sissy." The light spanned out into an enormous hole that ended in darkness. Cliffs of jagged rocks surrounded the sides, but railings and tourist signs were nearby. There was even a cement sidewalk, so how off limits or dangerous could it be?

We made our way down the twists and turns of the rocky stairs. For being such a magical place, it sure was spooky at night.

River dropped his duffel bag at a clearing near the water's edge. "This is the place."

He handed me the flashlight and I scanned the area around us. We were at the bottom of the massive well. The murky water was only a couple feet in front of us. A slimy film floated on its surface.

"Keep the light over here!"

"Sorry." I aimed the light on him and the bag.

"I brought tea to keep us warm. It has herbs in it to help us relax and make a connection with the other side."

I doubted herbs would connect me to spirits, but a hot drink sounded like heaven. I thought about the time Nathan brought me hot chocolate. I would have preferred that, but I was so cold my hands were going numb. River pulled out two thermoses and handed me one.

"Thanks." I took a sip and struggled not to spit it out. Gross or not, it eased the cold so I choked down another sip. "It tastes like dirt."

"Don't be so dramatic. It's not that bad." He sipped his tea, and through the dim lighting I saw him smile.

"So, what do we do now?" I took a few more swallows, growing more worried by the second. What if an animal attacked us? There was no one around for miles if something went wrong. I felt my back pocket, confirming I had my cell phone.

"We relax and try to open our minds." He spread out a blanket and sat down.

The cold had almost completely numbed my hands and feet. I dropped the flashlight and almost fell down, but I played off my swaying and settled onto the blanket. I leaned back against a tree and took another sip of dirt tea. River hummed a song I'd heard him sing before, but I couldn't remember the words, which was strange because I never forgot lyrics.

He fiddled for something in his pocket. "Are you stoked to talk to your family?"

"It would mean the world to me." My lips felt fuzzy and when I rubbed them together they became numb.

River clicked on a black-light keychain. "This is a scorpion finder. See, this place has a unique ecosystem. The lake has no fish because of the high carbon dioxide in the water, but scorpions and leeches live here. They come out at night to feed."

"Gross," I murmured. My lips were stuck together. I couldn't move my tongue. A wave of panic ran through me as I made a muffled sound in my throat.

River leaned closer, illuminating his face with the black light. His pupils were huge. "Looks like the tea is working."

I tried to make another noise, but nothing happened.

"As I was saying," River went on, "scorpions even hang out in the trees." He shined the black light right above me. "Careful, some are crawling on the tree you're leaning against."

I tried to leap up off the ground, but I couldn't. It wasn't just my voice or face. My whole body was numb. My neck muscles went limp, and my head bobbed forward. What the hell was going on?

River pushed my head back up. "The tea has some not-so-natural stuff in it, drugs that paralyze your muscles, but still let your mind work—kind of." He caressed my face. "Don't worry. You won't need to move for what I have planned."

Dread sank in. River drugged me? I knew about date rape drugs and to never accept a drink from a stranger, but this was my friend! Panic rushed through me with such intensity that my body should've been shaking.

"My uncle has been trying to rid this world of people like the Luna Lunatics for years. They're part of some power-hungry cult. He warned me about your makeshift family and their delusions about having magic powers or whatever. At first you were just an assignment. I had to keep an eye on you and report anything suspicious. If I did my job well, he'd keep providing me with money, cars, and whatever I needed." He stood up and paced above me. "But then I really fell for you. I told my uncle you were different from the Lunas, that if you knew about their reincarnation cult you'd never stay with them."

His steps grew quicker. "Why couldn't you just agree to be with me? I don't know what else I could've done to win you over. I drive the best cars, I'm rich and good looking, I'm going to be a rock star for god's sake!"

He leaned down, looking into my eyes. "My uncle gave me no choice. The house is bugged. He knows you know about everything. He knows you defended them. He heard you say we'd never be anything but friends. If I don't do this, then I lose everything. I'll have nowhere to live, no car, no money, no future whatsoever."

Do what? What did River have to do to keep his snooty lifestyle? And why did his uncle care so much about any of this? He lived overseas!

"That family doesn't deserve you. I know you'd rather be with your parents anyway." He fumbled through his bag. "I didn't want it to end like this, but at least you'll get to be with your real family again."

I'd never known true terror until that second. I wanted to cry, scream, to plead for mercy, but I couldn't do anything. I couldn't even shut my eyes.

"You won't feel any pain. That's why I made the tea. Between the leeches and scorpions, all evidence of your body will be erased. Those Luna freaks will think you ran away from their deranged little world." He bent down in front of me again. "I'll take good care of you."

I wanted to spit on him and claw his eyes out.

"I know your brain is working. I've tried this tea a few times, so I know what you're going through. I wanted to be able to tell you why I had to do this. You deserved an explanation." He reached into his bag and pulled out a roll of duct tape. "This stuff is so strong it doesn't lose its hold, even in water. We just need a big rock so you'll sink to the bottom."

How could he do this? How could he give a step by step play of his plans to murder me? Did he have no heart or conscience? He disappeared from view for a minute, but returned rolling a boulder half his size. He dragged me to it and spun me around. I couldn't feel it, but my back was against the rock.

"Experts aren't sure how deep the water is." He struggled to catch his breath. "They tried to explore it with scuba equipment, but when they reached fifty feet, the divers couldn't see through the wall of leeches."

I didn't know if he could see the horror in my eyes, but I was petrified. Why couldn't my brain shut down like the rest of my body?

He lifted my hand into his. "You don't think I'd throw you in there while you're conscious do you? I'd never do something so evil." He drew a heart on my palm with his finger. It was the only time during this nightmare that I was glad I couldn't feel anything. "It's the shooting you part I'm not looking forward to."

Oh god! Why wasn't my heart pounding? Was I already dying? River pulled out a gun and placed it next to the bag. The dense sound of duct tape being reeled off its roll echoed to the side of me.

"I'm sorry my uncle is forcing me to do this, but you'll be on the other side in seconds."

He circled me, wrapping the tape around me and the rock. I kept waiting to feel the tight binding against my chest, but physically I was numb. My mental hell, however, got worse with each passing second.

Months ago, I wouldn't have cared about the gruesome way my life was ending. I would've been thrilled to be reunited with my family, no matter how I got there. But now, I didn't want to die. I wanted to fight for my life. I wanted to fight harder than I'd ever fought for anything.

Faces flashed before my eyes. Krista, Aunt Sandy and Uncle Dave, Louise and Anthony, what would they think if they heard I went missing? Faith had warned me. Carson warned me. They knew River was bad, but I didn't listen.

"I left something in the truck. Be right back." River's footsteps trampled away.

My cell phone rang underneath me. Probably Faith or Krista calling to check on me. I started sobbing inside. My soul ached as I thought of one last person, the one person I wanted to see more than anyone, more than any god or angel who might save me from River. I wanted to see Nathan.

My intuition whispered the same words it did on the night of the attack.

Concentrate on the eyes.

Except, it wasn't intuition. It was my own voice. Four words from another time or place that I promised myself I'd remember. *Concentrate on his eyes.*

The truth hit me like a Mack truck. Nathan had been there the night I was attacked. At first, I saw him like in a dream, but then he was really there. Krista said my "dreams" were real. Somehow I must have communicated with him. He knew I was in danger so he traversed to me.

He was the only one who could get here in time. I needed to dream or travel or do whatever I did before. But how could I? My eyes wouldn't shut.

I stared at the dark water in front of me, watching one fallen branch bob repeatedly, up and down, but my mind wouldn't relax. At the very bottom of my scope of vision I could see my ring resting against my thigh.

Eye. Concentrate on the eye. I could do this. I had to.

I focused on the eye of the peacock feather, remembering how it swirled and shimmered in my dreams—in my astral travels. A glimmering wave danced under the glass.

Yes, I mentally begged. *Please work.*

A beam of light formed a tunnel between me and the ring. The dark, horrific nightmare disappeared behind me. The tunnel grew brighter and I kept being pulled forward until I saw Nathan's eyes. Green and gorgeous. Beams from an emerald sun. Enough love to fill eternity.

Nathan. Nathan. Nathaniel...

He stood on the balcony of a hotel room, staring at a sky full of stars.

"Nathan!" I shouted.

He blinked then shook his head and leaned against the railing, staring into the drink he was holding.

I waved my hands in front of him. "I'm here! Please hear me. I need your help!"

He took a deep breath and stood up straight, lifting his face to the sky. "And the stars will weep for those who have fallen, haunted by the light that once shone beside them."

"I'm here! It's me!" I tried to shove him. "Feel me!"

He raised his glass to his lips.

Frustrated, I swung at him. My hand went through him, but his glass slipped and shattered at his feet. He stepped away from it and looked around the balcony.

I stayed close, hovering in front of his face. "Yes. It was me!"

He moaned, clasping his hands over his ears.

My body, or whatever I was, kept passing through his. "No. Don't block me out! I need your help!"

He dropped his hands. "Stop haunting me."

I tried grabbing his face, but it was impossible with no hands. I wanted to cry and scream all at once.

Rays of light and swirls of colors formed all around Nathan. It looked just like one of Louise's paintings, the one I'd seen hanging in Nathan's room. I imagined myself as a shimmering cloud of color and pressed myself against him, hugging him with all the desperation and fear inside me. "Please, Nathaniel, help me. River is going to murder me."

He stared right at me. He looked where my eyes would've been if I really was in front of him.

"Please," I begged.

He vanished.

I looked at the glass balcony doors in front of me. There was no reflection of me, no colors, no signs of life, just shattered glass glistening on the ground.

River's sinister shouting jolted me back to Montezuma Well. "Where the hell did you come from?"

"What have you done to her?" Nathan asked with fierce rage. He appeared in front of me, studying me with fury in his eyes.

"Maryah's about to be reunited with her real family."

River barely finished his sentence before Nathan punched him, knocking him off his feet. River let out a guttural groan when Nathan crouched over him and hit him again.

A vapor trail of color followed every move they made. *Tracers.* I'd heard kids talk about hallucinations when they tripped on acid or mushrooms. They said you imagined things that weren't real. I prayed I wasn't imagining this. I begged for Nathan to be real.

River grabbed Nathan by the neck and the two of them rolled into the shadows. I couldn't see them, but I could hear them. Branches snapped. Their shoes raked and skidded though dirt and gravel. They grappled in the darkness. They sounded like rabid animals fighting to the death.

Then, silence.

Please don't let Nathan be hurt. What if River killed him?

After what felt like an eternity of eerie quietness, Nathan stepped into the pool of gold created by the flashlight. *Oh, thank god!*

He rushed over and cupped my face in his hands. He still looked flawless. Definitely a hallucination. Nobody fights like that and comes away without a scratch.

"Maryah, can you hear me?" He ripped through the tape, trying to quickly peel it off me.

He looked so real. Seeing him should've sent my heart racing, but it thumped slow and steady while I sat motionless. The loud tearing of duct tape continued while I tried to scream to warn Nathan that River, all bloody and mangled, was creeping out of the dark behind him. He leaned over the duffel bag. *The gun!* Nathan had no idea there was a gun.

"Nathaaan!" River sounded as psychotic as he looked.

Nathan turned to face him and took several steps to the left of me. In a calm voice he said, "You'll have to kill me to get to her."

River coughed up blood and swayed on his feet. "How noble. Total ladies man, huh?"

"More of a man than you will ever be."

"Don't push it. I'm the one holding the gun!"

"Then shoot me."

The gun fired but Nathan instantly disappeared. He reappeared just as fast in front of River. Then another gun shot rang through the air.

I thought my heart might explode. I waited for Nathan to fall. Instead, River groaned and slumped to the ground. The switch happened so fast I didn't realize Nathan had the gun.

He emptied the remaining bullets, shoved it in the back of his pants and walked over to me then gently pressed my eyelids shut. "I'm sorry you had to see that."

Nathan's ragged breathing and the remaining tape being peeled away from my jacket almost drowned out River cussing and pleading for help. Nathan lifted me into his arms and carried me a few steps before placing me down again. He delicately opened my eyelids. "Can you hear me? You're a fighter, Maryah. Fight to stay with me."

This was real. I wasn't going to die. Nathan put a cell phone to his ear, but never took his eyes off mine.

"Harmony, I'm at Montezuma—" I heard the murmur of Harmony's voice on the other end. "How did you know?" Nathan asked. There was more murmuring. "Who's with you?" More murmuring. "We'll be in the parking lot. Hurry. I can't call 911 until you get here with a vehicle."

He whispered as he caressed my face. "I'll only be gone for two seconds."

Nathan returned with the blanket and wrapped it around me. He carried me up the stairway to the top of the well. I wanted to hug him but my arms wouldn't work, so I just listened to him breathe. A few minutes later he set me down on the sidewalk by the parking lot. He sat, facing me, his knees on either side of mine. My ears buzzed, but they didn't hurt.

"I have to keep you warm." He rubbed his hands up and down my back and arms.

I thought a tear was forming in his eye, but then it glimmered with gold and silver. I concentrated on it, trying to figure out where the sparkle came from.

That's when my world spiraled out of control.

At first there were only intense colors, like looking at his irises through a magical microscope. Every line, speck, and difference of color became life-sized. Incredible shades of blue, green, silver, and gold three-dimensional shapes danced around us. I didn't want to look away, but he pulled me toward him and kissed my forehead.

I felt it. His warm lips against my skin. I could feel it!

A symphony of music sang through my veins. My body gave one involuntary jerk as rapture rushed through me. He hugged me and a beautiful song that slowly grew more familiar pulsed throughout my whole being.

Flashes of scenes played in my head: Nathan's voice, his laugh, his love. Different places, different bodies, even different faces, but eyes that never changed—bottomless pools of detailed light that could never be mistaken for anyone else's. They were memories, *my* memories of Nathan, of us. Louise had told my mother the truth.

The buzzing in my ears diminished to a faint ringing. My visions were choppy, but they were real. More joy than I ever thought possible coursed through me. I loved Nathan more than anything in this world. I had loved him for ages. The excitement made me convulse.

Nathan held me tighter until my body calmed. "I know it's cold. It won't be long."

He pulled out his phone and after four beeps said, "My name is Nathaniel Luna. I'm in the parking lot of Montezuma Wells. A kid has been shot and another friend appears to be drugged and in shock. Please send help right away."

Minutes later, the lights of Carson's Mustang and Shiloh's truck lit up the darkness. Chaos erupted all around us, but Nathan didn't let go of me. Carson whooshed by us at sonic speed. Faith wrapped her arms around me. I was so happy to see everyone.

"Extreme happiness," she said all perplexed. "I think she's okay." She let go and looked at me. "Oh sweetie, we were crazy worried. Your parents told Harmony you were here and that River was...ugh, I can't even say it!"

My parents. They must've been horrified watching all of this.

Faith turned to Nathan. "We've been trying to reach you for days. Maryah knows everything. She's not taking it well, but she knows."

Nathan squinted and moved his face closer to mine. His jaw went slack and a cloud from his warm breath formed between us. I wanted to part my lips, to breathe him in.

"Does she remember anything?" he asked.

"No, nothing," Faith whispered from behind me.

No! I wanted to shout. *I do remember!*

"How did you know she was here?" Faith asked.

Harmony yelled for Nathan from somewhere in the distance. "Long story." He squeezed my hands then disappeared. The traversing thing still shocked me.

I was trembling again. I wasn't sure if it was from being overwhelmed, or shivering, but Faith had her arms around me in an instant. She yelled for Shiloh and he wrapped his arms around both of us.

"We love you too," Faith said. "I know it's cold, but hang in there."

Nathan and Harmony came back and joined the group. Nathan explained they all needed to have the same story. He recited the details as sirens wailed in the distance.

"Maryah informed everyone that she was going out with River," Nathan said. "The four of us were out late and witnessed River's truck swerving on the road. We noticed Maryah in the passenger seat, followed them out here, and lost them on the unpaved trail. Upon arriving at the lot, I ran down to the well. You four remained at the top. You heard two gun shots—several seconds apart."

Shiloh put his arm on Nathan's shoulder. "I'll say I went with you and witnessed it."

"No," Nathan said. "No one lies more than is critically necessary."

"But, Nate," Carson started, "River will tell the police about you appearing out of nowhere."

Harmony waved her hand. "I forced tea down the bastard's throat. They'll assume he hallucinated. Remind me again why can't we kill him?"

"We should call Dylan," Faith said.

Nathan shook his head. "He'll be too late. He can handle the repercussions later as needed."

I couldn't keep track of their conversation anymore. My thoughts whirled. My vision blurred. My eyes felt heavy, so heavy I couldn't hold them open.

Next thing I knew, paramedics were shining lights into my eyes and asking me questions. Officers were talking to Nathan. Bright flashlights and the headlights of emergency vehicles lit up the parking lot. One cop carried the bagged thermoses we had drunk from and River's gun. They rolled me away on a stretcher while an officer told Nathan to come to the station for questioning. Harmony volunteered to go too.

Faith insisted on riding in the ambulance with me and argued with the medics. "I've known her all my lives! She needs a friend right now."

To anyone else it may have sounded like a mispronunciation if they noticed it at all. But I caught it. Not life—*lives*. I was anxious, wanting so badly to tell her what I'd seen, what I knew, how much I loved Nathan.

Faith hopped into the ambulance and held my hand. "It's okay, Ma-Ma. Try to relax."

Nathan's voice echoed near my feet. "I'll be at the station awhile. Look after her."

My love for him overwhelmed me. I had slight sensation in my fingers, so I tried to squeeze Faith's hand.

"Nathan," Faith gasped. Her eyes danced between the two of us. "Love. She's feeling an unbelievable amount of love."

Nathan climbed in and leaned over me. I swallowed and it burned like hell, but at least feeling was returning to my muscles. I tried to get my lips and tongue to work so I could say three simple words to him. Three words were all I needed and I'd be satisfied, but I only managed a pathetic whimper.

"We have to get her to the hospital. Let's go, kids." The paramedic ordered.

Nathan brushed the side of my face with his thumb and my insides danced, ecstatic by his touch and that I could feel it. "See you soon."

He disappeared from my view. I wanted to beg him not to leave me again, not to ever leave me. The ambulance doors shut and the medic hooked me up to a monitor.

Faith squeezed my hand, "What is it? What are you trying to say?"

Finally, I summoned enough strength to murmur two important words.

"I remember."

SOMETHING TO REMEMBER

Maryah

Faith never left my side at the hospital. A couple nurses and a doctor came and went, but my motor function and speech were returning. I waited until the police officer finished taking my statement, and when he left the room, I turned to Faith.

"Nathan's eyes, I could see for miles into his eyes. It's true—I love him!"

Faith's face was practically glowing. "I can't believe it. I kept undying faith it would happen, but now it seems so surreal."

"How did we know each other?" I asked.

Her smile dropped away. "You don't remember *me*?"

I shook my head.

"Aw crap!" She slapped her hand against her forehead.

Just then, Louise and Krista hurried into the room.

Louise saw me and her hands flew to her mouth. "Dear celestial creation and all that is magical."

Faith whipped her head around to look at Louise before grinning at me. "I know! What a ripsnorter, huh? I can imagine how incredible she must look."

"Oh, thank heavens!" Krista hugged me. "I was so worried." She sat on my bed and squeezed my leg. "Dylan will convince my parents to let me stay here for as long as you need me."

Louise came closer, reaching forward, but didn't touch me. "Some of your light has returned."

I stared at all of them like they had ten heads. "What are you talking about?"

Faith giggled. "Your soul. The light has come back into your soul. Krista and I can only see it in your eyes, but Louise sees it everywhere."

"Huh?"

Louise folded her hands in front of her. "My gift is that I see a soul's essence in great detail. I experience their energy as an intricate cloud of light and color surrounding them. No two souls look the same."

"Wow," I said. "Just like your paintings."

Faith giggled. "The paintings at the house are portraits of all of us."

All the colorful canvases that sparkled and shined in every room were Louise's family photos. No wonder I caught myself staring at them so much.

"Faith." Krista sighed. "You said she remembered."

"She remembers Nathan. Like *remembers* him." Faith threw her arms above her head like she scored a touchdown. "And she loves him!"

"Is that all you remember?" Louise asked.

I didn't want to tell them that my small portfolio of memories was getting weaker as the drugs wore off. "What else should I remember?"

They all smiled at each other.

"More. An endless amount more," Louise said. "But we're off to a promising start."

∞

My legs felt like jelly, so Anthony carried me from the car into the house. Edgar, Helen, Dylan, Amber, Shiloh, and Carson were already gathered in the living room. They all watched me like I was an infant who needed constant supervision, but to them I guess I was.

Louise told Anthony, "Put her on the couch, please."

He gently set me down and spread a blanket over my legs. "Can we get you anything?"

"No, thanks. I'd just like to rest." I shut my eyes, but couldn't fall asleep. All I could think about was Nathan. Krista swore he still loved me, but did he really? Eighteen years was a long time to be apart, and my knowledge of who I used to be was pathetically weak, but I was pretty sure I'd been way more interesting in my other lives.

My heart almost danced out of my chest at the sound of the front door opening and closing. I looked over the back of the couch to see Nathan and Harmony standing side by side. They looked dangerous. Harmony—straight-faced and covered from head to toe in black, and Nathan—wearing dark jeans with his black and red leather jacket. Devilish in appearance, but they were angels in actuality.

Harmony stepped away and stood next to Faith, holding her hand. Carson moved to Harmony's side, and she wrapped her arm around him.

At first, Nathan didn't budge. He just stared at me. Louise took a breath to say something, but Nathan walked around the couch and stood over me. "Are you able to walk?"

"Maybe?" I answered quietly, worried my legs wouldn't hold up.

He scooped me up and carried me across the living room.

"Nathan," Helen called out. He pressed me closer to him. Through his open jacket, I felt his heart beating strong and fast in his chest. "I'm not sure if it's a good idea to be moving her yet."

"We need to keep an eye on her," Edgar added.

Nathan's grip on me tightened. His nectar of the Gods smell intoxicated me. "Are my eyes not fit to watch over her?"

Dylan stepped toward us. "It's not that. We don't think—"

Nathan didn't let him finish. "I am forever grateful to all of you." He glanced around the room making deliberate eye contact with each person. "However, none of you have any comprehension of my emotions right now. It is my divine right to have time alone with her."

We headed for the hallway. My pulse quickened. I kept my chin lifted, hoping to see his beautiful eyes, but he never looked down. He carried me into my room and sat me in the chair beside my bed then turned his back to me. A pain burned in my chest. Why wouldn't he look at me? "Nathan?"

"Please, shh," he said, taking off his jacket and pulling back the covers.

He gathered me in his arms again, placed me on the bed, pulled the comforter over me, and knelt on the floor. He bowed his head and rested his forehead on his closed fists.

He stayed that way for what seemed like forever. It felt like the world wouldn't continue to turn until he looked up again. I couldn't stand it anymore. I brushed my fingers across his. His head flipped up and our eyes met.

Time stood still. At that moment nothing existed except Nathan's eyes—his soul—shining brightly through two beautiful green scepters and radiating into mine.

His eyes widened, and the sides of his lips almost curved into a smile, but seconds later his brows furrowed together. "What do you remember?"

"Everything."

His left brow lifted and he cocked his head to the side. "Everything is a grand concept."

"I remember pieces of our other lives together."

"Right. Pieces."

"My mother wrote me a letter, then the others explained everything and I didn't know if I believed it, but at Montezuma Well your eyes lit up and...I remember us."

He put his hand over mine, running his thumb over the face of my ring, then he lowered his head again.

"The photo on your nightstand, it was me. I was Mary."

He squeezed my hand so hard it hurt, but then released his grip. His jaw remained stiff. "Yes, you were."

"I remember being Mary. I'm still the same soul."

He smoothed my hair away from my face. "The same, but very different."

It hit me. No, it bulldozed me. I had been beautiful in my former life—stunningly beautiful. Tears welled up and a damn of anger broke open inside me. I was angry at God, or whoever created me to be so ordinary. Nathan couldn't love this version of me. That's why he was so sad.

"Oh," was all I could say.

"What do you mean by 'oh'?"

"I used to be pretty." I turned away, hiding my face in my pillow. "How could you love someone who looks like me?"

"Maryah!" he shouted, suddenly appearing next to me on the other side of the bed. I glanced back to where he'd been kneeling. The teleporting thing wasn't easy to get used to. He lifted my chin. "You are the most beautiful creation I have ever seen throughout all of my time on this planet or beyond it. You don't understand a fraction of the love I feel for you. There is so much more to our story than you remember. You can't fathom what we've been through together." He pressed his lips to the top of my head and breathed in. "I've missed your heavenly smell."

His touch triggered more memory flashes. I remembered Nathan as the guy I'd seen in the photo album. He was lying on a beach laughing, pointing at oddly-shaped clouds in a sunny sky. Ukulele music played in the background.

Another memory flipped through my mind like I was watching an old filmstrip: us with our limbs wrapped around each other, floating in a sea of turquoise water. Some part of me knew it was Hawaii, and I ached to go back.

I forced myself to look at him, but choked on the words. "Do you still love me?"

He caressed my cheek. "I was put on this earth to love you. I know no other kind of existence but to live and breathe for your wellbeing. It's who I am, and who I will always be."

Goosebumps covered every inch of my skin. "I thought this would feel weird to say, but it doesn't. I love you, Nathaniel."

He smiled, but not like I had hoped he would. His smile never reached his eyes. "I know. That's the beauty of our relationship. I can *see* how deeply you love me."

"You can?"

"Yes." He almost looked sad, but then he traced a figure eight around my eyes. "The eyes do not lie."

My brain melted at his touch. "I have so many questions," I murmured, "but I can't think of them right now."

"We have all the time in the world. You should rest. You've endured more than enough."

"Stay with me?"

A real smile surfaced. His eyes shined brighter than ever. "There is no place in this entire universe I would rather be."

He wrapped his muscular arms around me and I rested my head on his chest. It fit perfectly, like I was designed to fit the contours of his body. Nathan's heartbeat was the sweetest lullaby I'd ever heard.

I was home. *He* was my home.

"Thank you for saving me," I whispered.

His deep voice was the last thing I heard as I drifted to sleep. "Thank you for saving *me*."

THE UGLY TRUTH

NATHANIEL

The sound of rain pattering against the roof and windows nudged me from sleep. For a moment I thought I was dreaming. I had dreamt of her being in my arms so many times only to be disappointed when I awoke. But no, my soul mate was really, finally, with me again.

I laid there, breathing in her comforting scent, and running my fingers through her hair. Would all of her memories ever return? Would we ever be able to discuss our first life together, or our eighth, or eighteenth, with her actually recalling details? It didn't matter. She remembered pieces. She said she loved me, and I believed her. That's all I needed.

I kissed the top of her head and whispered, "I'm sorry I ever doubted you."

She bolted up in bed. As did I.

"Maryah? What is it?"

She stared ahead at our reflection in the mirror, trying to catch her breath. "River. His eyes were crazy and peering out of a tree in the dark and I was all alone and tried to scream but I couldn't."

I wrapped my arms around her. "It's all right. It was just a nightmare. He's in jail and will be for a very long time. He will never set foot near you again."

"There's something I have to tell you. River said his uncle made him kill me. He thinks our family is some sort of cult."

"Shh," I reclined back and tucked her head against my chest. "I already know. River confessed everything while we were at the police station."

"What if his uncle comes looking for me? Or hurts someone else?"

"Don't worry yourself with that. Eric Malone is a wanted criminal. He left town and he wouldn't be foolish enough to return anytime soon. Besides, I'm here, and so is the rest of our kindrily. No one is ever going to hurt you again."

Her muscles softened as some of her tension eased. She snuggled up against my neck while thunder rumbled outside. I couldn't get close enough to her. I squeezed her tighter and relished her breath against my skin, but I had to adjust myself when my body ached to do more than just hold her.

"I'm not getting out of this bed until tomorrow," she cooed. "And neither are you."

"While I do love that idea, the others won't allow it. I'm surprised they haven't besieged us yet. I'm certain they're out there waiting for an update." I was also certain we needed to get out of bed so I could take a cold shower.

Maryah looked at the closed bedroom door and sighed. "I guess we do owe them some details, considering all they've been through."

I chuckled. "That's the understatement of the millennium."

∞

My first instinct was to wait for her outside of the bathroom, but that was much too overbearing. No one would harm her while she was showering. I made it a few steps down the hallway, but that felt too far away, so I straightened the paintings lining the walls.

I was straightening them for the fifth time when Maryah walked out of the bathroom. "Are you peckish?"

"Not really, but I am thirsty." She smiled. "My father always used British words like peckish."

While in bed, she felt familiar. The contours of our bodies fit together perfectly just like in every other life. However, now it felt like we were on an awkward first date. "Do you remember anything about our lives in England?"

"Lives? With an s? We lived there for more than one…cycle, or whatever?"

Louise appeared at the end of the hallway. "You two missed breakfast, but would you care for some lunch?"

I spoke so that only Maryah could hear me. "You don't have to eat, but we should join them."

"Fine, but later we are discussing England. And everywhere else we've lived."

"Happily." I ushered her down the hallway.

Krista, Faith, Louise, and Helen were scattered around the kitchen, but all of them were focused on Maryah and me. Helen kissed each of us on the cheek and ladled hot cocoa into a mug. She handed it to Maryah, who only looked at it skeptically.

"I assumed you'd want to avoid tea for a while," Helen said. "It's cocoa with ginseng, ginko, and gotu kola. It helps the memory."

Maryah took a sip. "Your gift has something to do with herbs and stuff, doesn't it?"

"I have a way with nature." Helen untied her apron and hung it in the pantry. "Herbs, plants, flowers: if it's borne from the earth, I can make it flourish. Many plants and flowers have medicinal properties."

The doorbell rang and Faith sprang up to answer it.

From the foyer, Faith squealed.

Maryah clenched onto me, and I wrapped my arm around her. "You're safe. Don't worry."

She let go when she realized Faith was talking—friendly talking—to whomever was at the door. A dog barked, then a bulldog came charging in just as Faith and April came around the corner.

"April?" Maryah gasped.

Louise had told me about their fight. April had been in one of my classes last year, but she looked much skinnier and sadder than I remembered, maybe even sick. Her arms cradled her torso like she needed to hold herself up.

Louise and Helen said a quick hello then excused themselves to do chores at Helen's.

"How have you been? How's," Maryah hesitated, "your mom?"

"She's hanging in there." April's voice quivered. "I'm so sorry, Maryah. I've been such a horrible friend. River called me from jail, so I went to see him and he wouldn't tell me much, but he told me you wouldn't date him, how you said you'd never do that to me. And then I found out he tried to…I can't even say it. Forget about me, are *you* okay?"

Faith, Krista, and I glanced at each other, silently debating whether or not we should leave the girls alone to talk.

"I'm fine," Maryah said, but I heard the fear in her voice. "It's good to see you. This is Nathan and my cousin, Krista."

"Yeah, I know Nathan. Nice to meet you, Krista." April's eyes were glassy. She fanned herself with her hand like she was trying not to cry. "I'm sorry I never returned your calls or emails. I'm sorry for so many things."

"It's fine." Maryah hugged her, causing Faith and Krista to smile. All the estrogen in the room was a bit overwhelming. I wanted to traverse to somewhere with fresh air and open space, but Maryah shot me a loving glance and suddenly there was no place else I wanted to be.

"I'm so glad he didn't...you know." April wiped away her tears. "Gosh, you think you know someone."

The bulldog pawed Maryah's feet.

"Oh, I almost forgot." April let go of Maryah and looked down at him. "River asked me to take care of Eightball, but I'm hardly ever home and I can't take him to the hospital with me, so I know it's a lot to ask, but you've always been so good with him. I was hoping maybe you'd take him?"

Maryah's face lit up, blossoming into an uncontrollable smile. Faith clapped with approval and dropped to the floor to pet him.

"Um." Maryah looked at me. "I'd have to make sure Louise doesn't mind."

I laughed and leaned on the counter. "This is your home. If you love him, he's welcome here."

"Thank goodness," April said. "I didn't know what I'd do if you said no."

We all stood there in awkward silence watching Faith scratch Eightball's head and back. Memories flashed through my mind of other pets we had adopted in the past. I smirked at how perfect the name Eightball was as a pet for our eighth member who used to have premonitions about the future.

"Well," April wrapped her arms around herself again. "I've got to get back to my mom, but I'd love to get together soon. That is, if you forgive me."

"Yes," Maryah said. "I'd like that. A fresh start."

"Great." April's spirits seemed to lift. "I'll text you."

Maryah and I walked April to her car, but I lingered in the garden so they could say goodbye without an audience. I was happy to see Maryah make amends with her friend. Having someone to talk to outside of our kindrily would be good for her—*if* she had learned her lesson about keeping our way of life a secret.

Maryah was glowing as she came toward me. The flowers lining the path she walked along were put to shame by her beauty. "That was unexpected."

"I suspect it's one of many happy surprises you'll encounter."

"What do you mean? Do you know something I don't?"

I held her hand and tried not to let my smile be too smug. "I know a lot of things that you don't."

We went back inside and Amber was standing in the kitchen pulling chicken off a bone. Eightball grunted at her feet. "Faith told me you adopted this dog."

"His name's Eightball," Maryah said. "Cute, isn't he?"

Amber looked annoyed. "The poor guy is starving. Here," she handed Maryah a bowl filled with chicken. "Give him this."

Maryah set the chicken on the floor and he gulped it down, snorting with every bite. "I almost forgot you can communicate with animals. Did he tell you he was hungry?"

"Tell me? He was sending up smoke flares."

"So," I sensed the need to lighten the mood. "We have a new four-legged son. He takes after me in the face a little, don't you think?"

Maryah and Krista giggled, but Amber didn't crack a smile.

"Where is everyone else?" Amber asked. "I've got interesting news."

"Louise went to Helen's," I said.

Krista and Faith barely glanced up from watching Eightball devour his food, but Faith explained that the guys were working in the garage, and Harmony was busy at home.

Amber rested her hands on her big belly. "This can't wait. We'll update them later. Maryah, you should sit down."

Faith and Krista's heads both snapped to attention.

"I'm okay," Maryah assured everyone, but I pulled out a stool for her. If Amber said someone should sit down, she meant it.

Amber set a bowl of water on the floor. "Eightball was abused. He's happy to be here because he senses he won't be hurt anymore."

Eightball lapped up his water while keeping an eye on Maryah. Their connection was already strong. "No one will ever hurt him again," Maryah said. "I'll make sure of it."

"The guy that used to beat him," Amber continued, "was River's uncle."

"No surprise there," Faith huffed. "I mean, he ordered River to kill Maryah. Evil bastard. Only a heartless soul could ever abuse such a sweet and innocent animal."

Amber fixed her eyes on me. "Eightball confirmed what Louise expected."

"Of course." My fists tightened. "We should have figured that out a long time ago."

"Huh?" Maryah asked. "Figure what out?"

Amber sat in the stool at the end of the island, took off her glasses, and rubbed the bridge of her nose. "River's uncle. Eric is his alias, his real name is—"

"Dedrick." I snarled.

Maryah swallowed hard. "The head of the Nefariouns?"

Amber nodded somberly. "And one of the men who attacked you and your family."

Good thing I had the stool positioned behind Maryah, because she collapsed into it. "Does he know who the other guy was?" Maryah asked. "The one who almost killed me."

"No," Amber said. "Communication with animals works differently than with humans. It's not like I can just ask him questions. Most animals think a loop of one-sided thoughts. They think about whatever affects them most on a primal level."

Amber's ability had always fascinated me, but given the current situation, and the secret I was hiding that affected me at a primal level, I was thankful that Amber could only read animal minds. Because I knew the answer to Maryah's question. And I had to keep it a secret.

KEEP BREATHING

Maryah

After everyone—mainly me— calmed down, and the rest of the kindrily had been updated, Nathan suggested we take Eightball for a walk. I eagerly agreed. I was in desperate need of fresh air.

The rain had stopped and it felt much warmer than the night before. We strolled along the cliffs talking endlessly until the sun slowly descended from the sky. Guilt had been suffocating me all day. I couldn't keep it bottled up anymore. Nervously, I apologized about River. I rambled through excuses and details, and when I got to the part about almost puking when River kissed me, a grin spread across Nathan's face.

"You felt nauseous when he kissed you?"

"Yes, I mean, I'd never kissed anyone before so maybe I—"

He put two fingers over my lips. "It's *who* you kiss that bodes what you feel."

"I don't know," I argued. "What if I'm just bad at it?"

He wrapped his arms around my waist, pulling me close to him, and tucked my hair behind my ear. My heart soared. I started trembling.

"Breathe," he ordered gently.

I took a deep breath and shakily let it out.

"Again," he whispered. His lips were less than an inch from mine.

My next breath was more calm and fluid.

"Keep breathing."

I closed my eyes. Slowly, his breath synchronized with mine. Every time I inhaled, he exhaled, and every time I breathed out he would silently draw in my air. By the fourth or fifth cycle every cell in my body tingled. We were only breathing each other in, over and over, but I felt euphoric.

"Maryah." His voice sounded like harp music.

I opened my eyes and met his gaze. His lips cut through the invisible cloud of energy floating between us as he smugly—but sweetly— smiled. Before I could return the smile, his warm lips closed over mine.

It felt like the Earth fell out from under us, like we were floating into the sky. With each caress of his lips I floated higher, a whirlwind of electricity swirling around us. He gently pulled back, and I let out a moan of pleasure. He kissed each of my eyelids so softly it felt like silk brushing against them.

"Are you nauseous?" he asked.

I opened my eyes. "No, but my whole body is weak and tingly."

"Yes, I know. Your knees gave out sometime ago. I've been holding you up."

I blushed and regained my footing. "That was incredible."

"*That* is how a kiss is meant to be, and I assure you, you did exceedingly well."

"Mmm," I felt drunk. I craved more of his kisses. I glanced around to make sure Eightball hadn't run off, but he was stalking a lizard nearby.

Nathan looked at the sky. "Bollocks."

"What?" I asked, confused by his frustration.

"The irrational part of me hoped our first kiss would return your star to the sky." He laughed. "Brainwashed by fairytales, I suppose."

"The stars aren't even out yet."

"The stars are always shining. You can't see them, but I do."

His take on the world seemed so magical compared to mine. "All Elements have a star that represents them?"

"Yes, the older the soul, the brighter the star. If you could get close enough, you'd see every detail of a soul's history in the light and energy of their star. It's similar to how we see history and details in each other's eyes. A star contains everything: every thought, feeling, action, and desire. It's intense."

"Wow." I craned my neck and scanned the shades of pink and purple weaving between the clouds. "Every soul is a story shelved away in an infinite library in the sky."

He raised my hand to his lips and kissed it. "You used to say things like that all the time."

My hand tingled from his kiss. I couldn't get enough of him, but I also had so many questions. "You said my star fell from the sky before I was born, and I still can't see yours. Is that because I erased?"

He sighed. "You reset your soul. You're operating on basic senses, unable to see the energy around you."

"When we were in the other realm or wherever, before we came back here, wouldn't I have told you I planned to erase?"

"It's different there. Talking is a human function. Souls communicate in the Higher Realm, but through energy, not words. Plus, linear time is an Earthly concept. In the Higher Realm, decisions are made in what would feel like the blink of an eye here. You wouldn't have been able to tell anyone."

Tears formed as the new me—the ordinary, furthest thing from a superhero, oblivious person I was—despised the old me for what I had done. "How could I have done that to you? It's so selfish."

Nathan held my face in his hands. "You must have had a paramount reason. Although we don't know what that reason is, I'm certain it was *selfless*, not selfish. That's who you were, and who you still are. We need you to believe in yourself and have faith in the magic of this world."

A rainbow had formed a bridge between Cathedral Rock and Bell Rock. I pointed to it. "Anything magical or mystical I should know about rainbows?"

"Yes." His grin made me shiver with excitement. "Whomever you kiss beneath a rainbow will be yours, then, now, and eternally."

Nathaniel, my soul mate, leaned down and kissed me for the second time—well, second kiss of *this* lifetime—and made me believe anything was possible.

CIRCLE OF LIFE

Maryah

Louise, Anthony, and Carson celebrated the first day of spring by taking an overseas trip. The house felt odd without the three of them, but Krista staying indefinitely made up for it. With a couple easy phone calls, Dylan persuaded my aunt and uncle to let her stay with us, and he persuaded her school to let her finish the year remotely.

The more time I spent with Nathan, and the more I heard about our past, the deeper my love grew. But no matter how hard I tried and wished for my memories to return, I made no progress.

The night after the Spring Fling festival, I shot up in bed and glanced around the darkness. I could hardly breathe.

"Maryah, what is it?" Nathan wrapped his arms around me and instantly my panic dissolved.

"Peacocks," I mumbled, turning to see his reaction.

He smiled and kissed my shoulder. "So, it was a good dream."

"I remember a peacock in my dream. A huge, beautiful, iridescent one." I looked up at my dream catcher, then at the blue and green mirror, and pressed my ring to my chest. "I meant to ask you about your obsession with peacocks."

He laughed. "My obsession? No. *Your* obsession."

"Mine?"

"The peacock represents everything you believed in: psychic duality, all-seeing watchfulness, renewal, resurrection, spiritual evolution. The list continues depending on which teachings you research. You used to stare at your ring for hours. You said the feather's eye showed you stories."

"Really? What kind of stories."

"All kinds. Can we please talk about this in the morning?" He laid his head in my lap and rubbed his sleepy eyes. Even in the dark, the jewel-like shade of green glimmered with love when he looked up at me. How did I get so lucky to have someone like him as my soul mate?

I tried to fall sleep, but several minutes later I shot back up. "Something's wrong!"

"What do you mean?" Concern filled Nathan's voice. "What's wrong?" He turned on the light.

"I don't know. I feel a presence lurking, like something is coming. I've never felt like this before. I feel sick to my stomach."

Nathan stared at me, looking worried, but then turned his focus to our bedroom door. Someone ran down the hallway. Nathan vanished. For a few seconds I was terrified that he left me alone, but he reappeared at the side of the bed with a smile on his face.

"Some *thing* isn't coming, but *some one* is. The baby is arriving early."

I jumped out of bed.

"I'm going to inform the others." He kissed me before traversing.

I ran down the hallway to Dylan and Amber's room.

∞

I assumed Amber would've given birth in a hospital, but Helen delivered the baby at home. She explained that she delivered dozens of babies throughout her lifetimes, and in earlier centuries they didn't have the drugs and technology that hospitals offered. And as Nathan pointed out, we had Krista in case anything went wrong.

Nathan helped Helen. He'd been a physician in a previous life, and he retained his medical knowledge. He kept his position at Amber's side so she wasn't exposed to anyone but Helen. He said it was out of respect for Dylan and Amber's privacy, and it made me love him even more.

A few times I thought Amber would break my hand from squeezing so hard, but Dylan coached her through breathing, and she relaxed. Krista made her sip tea that Helen had made.

After hours of wiping sweat from Amber's face with a washcloth and keeping her wet hair pulled back, I was relieved when Helen announced she could see the baby's head. Several pushes later, a tiny, slimy boy arrived into the world. Dylan wrapped him in a blanket and laid him in Amber's arms. I was sure they'd been through this baby thing plenty of times in other lives, but based on how proud Dylan looked, I would have assumed it was their first time.

Nathan and I congratulated them then left to update the others. Edgar, Faith, Shiloh, Harmony, and Dakota were waiting in the living room.

"It's a healthy baby boy," Nathan announced.

Everyone erupted into celebration, but then Louise burst through the front door and rushed past us to the bedroom. Anthony and Carson were talking to someone in the foyer. That someone had an Irish accent.

When she appeared in the archway, I forgot to breathe or blink. How could she be ninety-nine? She walked with a cane, and slightly hunched over, but she was luminous. Her long curly white hair had strands of gold mixed through it. Her ivory and gold flowing dress matched her hair perfectly. When she saw me, her brown eyes lit up.

Her voice sounded like harp music. "Hello, Maryah."

"Hello, Sheila." As much as I wanted to, I couldn't recall one memory of her. But I *knew* I loved her. My heart felt full—fuller than it ever had.

Krista rushed forward and hugged her so tight I thought she'd break her.

"Look at you," Sheila laughed at Krista. "No more than a young school girl. What I wouldn't give to be so young."

The joy on Krista's face when she looked at Sheila was priceless.

Sheila walked over to me and studied me in silence. She took my hand in her soft fingers, and examined my palm. "Yer lines have changed."

"What? Since when?"

The wrinkles around her eyes deepened as she smiled at me. "We have much to catch up on, but it must wait. There is a wee babe I must visit first."

Krista and I helped her down the hallway to the guest room. It was a lot of bodies crammed into one bedroom, but they all cleared a path when Sheila entered.

"Thank you for coming." Amber sighed. She looked happy but exhausted.

"My pleasure, lassie." Sheila stared at the baby, almost in a trance. "He's the most beautiful soul I've ever laid eyes on."

"Thank you," Amber replied graciously.

I discreetly backed out of the room and made my way down the hallway. When I got to our room, Nathan emerged from thin air. He opened his arms and I practically collapsed into them.

"It's a lot to take in," I confessed.

"No explanation necessary, my love. You're doing brilliantly given the circumstances."

"Louise and Anthony sure got home quick. How fast is this family plane of ours?"

I sat on our bed listening to Nathan explain the one-of-a-kind plane Anthony designed, but a flicker of light in my ring distracted me.

Nathan continued talking, but I wasn't listening. All I could focus on was the swirling colors in my ring. His words became fuzzy and distant. The tunnel of light I'd seen at Montezuma Well started forming again.

The peacock feather's eye and the iridescent sheens of blue and green divided, growing into a sapphire and emerald figure-eight. Specks of gold and silver darkened inside each half, deepening and forming more lines and layers.

Eyes. The feather had formed into two larger-than-life human eyes.

I stared. Mesmerized. Watching. Learning.

They were telling an almost unbelievable story. Except there were no words, only energy, emotions, and shimmering colored lines connecting infinite paths of people and places throughout history.

The eyes do not lie, echoed through my mind.

The intricate tale they told was true. I knew it with every fiber of my being. Wind blew all around me, surrounding me in a funnel of swirling, glowing feathers until I could no longer see the huge eyes. I reached forward and the radiant feathers burst into millions of tiny pieces that looked like stardust. I took a deep breath and inhaled every speck until nothing was left.

The bedroom came back into focus as my glowing ring faded back to normal. Nathan was still rambling about who-knows-what.

I slammed my hand against my pounding heart and jumped up. "Where's Sheila?"

"With Amber, where we just left her."

It felt like I had been staring at the ring for hours. I understood so much more. So much needed to be done. Weeks ago, suspecting I had some kind of psychic power freaked me out, but this was different. My ring showed me the truth. I didn't need confirmation, that's how deeply I knew, but I wanted to see for myself.

"I need to see Sheila and the baby." The sternness in my voice shocked me.

Nathan took my hand and led me back down the hallway to Amber's room. Sheila still sat on the bed at Amber's side. Edgar, Helen, Louise, Anthony, Dylan, Harmony, Faith, Shiloh, Dakota, Carson, and Krista all stared at me. I stood in front of Sheila with new confidence.

She held the baby, asleep in her arms, and a wide grin spread across her face. "You know."

I nodded.

"Know what?" Faith asked.

Sheila lifted the baby like she was presenting him to the world for the first time. "He's an Aries, *another* fire sign."

Dylan's voice rang through the quiet room. "Sheila, do you mean...?"

"Yes, you have a fifteenth member."

Cheers erupted. Krista hugged me, but my focus was crazy-glued on the baby.

Sheila waved her hand and the room fell silent. She handed him to me. "He was connected to this kindrily before this life."

How did she know? How did *I* know? It didn't matter. His tiny eyelids opened just enough for me to see the familiar sky blue.

"Hi, Mikey," I whispered, "I missed you so much."

"*Our* Mikey?" Krista gasped.

I let out something between a giggle and grunt. "Kind of weird, huh?"

Dylan sat beside Amber and held her hand. "Wow. Never saw that one coming."

"I just *love* happy reunions!" Faith sang, twirling around. Shiloh and Carson both wore the biggest cheese grins I'd ever seen.

"How'd you know?" I asked Sheila.

"I come from a long line of psychics. I tune into a babe's essence and see who they were in past lives. I read their souls."

"We always have her present when a baby arrives," Helen explained.

Nathan stroked my hair. "How did *you* know?"

I glanced at my thumb. "I saw it in my ring. Just like you said. It told me an incredible story."

His gorgeous green eyes gazed into mine. His were the eyes that led me home, watched over me, saved me, and showed me more love than I ever knew was possible.

"Did you see or remember anything else?" he whispered.

"Not about us, but I will. I *know* I will. Look around, Nathaniel." Our kindrily, young and elderly, big and small, new souls, and old ones surrounded us with an infinite amount of love.

And Mikey was back. The term "circle of life" never had a more hopeful and beautiful meaning. "We share an unbreakable and powerful bond. We've already come so far."

"I'm sorry I didn't believe it was possible," Nathan said.

"Believe what was possible?"

"You. Your gift." He leaned down and kissed my forehead. "I should've known you were too powerful, and stubborn, to be erased."

"We tried to tell him." Louise walked up beside us and shook Mikey's tiny hand with her fingers. In high-pitched baby talk she said, "It looks like we're going to need a bigger table."

NOT THE END

ACKNOWLEDGEMENTS

I'm fortunate enough to have my own kindrily, and while they may not remember their past lives, I'm almost certain they have supernatural powers. This book wouldn't be a reality without the following beautiful souls:

Mom, my very first reader and biggest supporter. Thank you for loving my Kindrily characters almost as much as I do, and for reading (and loving) every version I wrote.

Dad, for gifting me with a magical upbringing, and gifting Maryah with her Desoto.

John, for believing in me, and going above and beyond to support me and my dreams.

Krista, look how far we've come since you read that first draft on the plane ride to Sedona. It's finally real!

Marie, you've helped this story through endless revisions, and taught me so much along the way.

Natalie, thank you for being honest enough to tell me you originally hated Nathan. He is a much better man because of you.

Megan, I can't begin to count all the ways you made this story (and me as a writer) so much stronger.

Alexandra, for critiquing, encouraging me, and creating my breathtaking cover.

Andrea, thank you for rolling around in rose petals and feathers until I snapped the perfect photo of you.

Sara, your critiques, advice, and support are treasured and priceless to me.

Sarah, your purple sweatshirt is magical and I'm convinced it's the reason this story was so easy to write. Sorry, but I'm never giving it back.

Steve, thank you for your everlasting faith in this story, and for creating the Kindrily website.

Ron, for helping with all my technological and author website needs.

The Indelibles, for giving me the knowledge and courage to share this series with readers.

Louise Geczy, for teaching me so much about writing, and assuring me that someday I would write a book. You were right, as always.

Ella Fitzgerald, for singing the song that inspired this story.

Sedona, (because I swear that town has a soul) thank you for being so mystical, inspiring, and the perfect home for my characters.

And to my growing family of readers. You mean the world to me. I am eternally grateful for each and every one of you.

ABOUT THE AUTHOR

Karen was born and bred in Baltimore, frolicked and froze in Colorado for a couple of years, and is currently sunning and splashing around Florida with her two beloved dogs. She's addicted to coffee, chocolate, and complicated happily-ever-afters. She is a co-founder of the teen focused blog, YA Confidential, and a proud member of The Indelibles.

Other novels by Karen include:

Taking Back Forever (coming soon)
and *Tangled Tides*.

Find Karen and her books online at:
http://www.KarenAmandaHooper.com

MESSAGE FROM THE AUTHOR

Dear Reader,

Thank you for reading *Grasping at Eternity*. I realize you have an almost-endless number of books to choose from, and I'm extremely grateful mine was among your selections.

Writing novels is a dream come true for me, and I can't imagine doing anything else. Storytelling is a very subjective art. For me, it's a passion. I'm a constant work in progress. (I believe every artist should be.) My craft will never be perfect, all of my books will probably bend some rules, and I'm sure I will make mistakes along the way, but I'll always try my best to create imaginative and magical worlds for you to explore.

Feel free to email me, visit my blog, chat with me on Twitter, or find me on Facebook. I love interacting with other readers, writers, and dream-chasers.

The biggest compliment you can give any author is to help spread the word about their work. Tell a friend, suggest the book to your local library, or post a review on book websites where readers seek honest reviews and recommendations. Authors appreciate the support and encouragement more than you can imagine.

I sincerely hope you enjoyed Maryah and Nathan's story. They still have a very long way to go. I hope you'll follow their journey in *Taking Back Forever*, Book 2 in The Kindrily Series.

My eternal thanks,
Karen

BOOK 2 OF THE KINDRILY SERIES

Taking Back Forever follows Maryah as she fights to restore her memories, strengthen her ability to astral travel, and discover why she erased. Harmony's search for her soul mate Gregory puts the kindrily in danger, but they'll stop at nothing to save their missing member before they lose him forever.

SNEAK PEEK

Maryah

"The heart is a muscle," Harmony explained. "Muscles have memory. Scientists have proven that the heart retains memory function even when removed."

"I don't understand what that has to do with Gregory."

She pulled a chair in front of me and straddled it, sitting so close to me that our knees almost touched. "Imagine someone ripped your heart out of your chest and threw it in a cage. Outside the cage, vultures, rats, and coyotes circle, waiting to rip your heart apart and devour it. Worse yet, as they circle, their wicked energy surrounds the cage, tainting the pure and good soul inside. Over time your heart starts to change; it becomes evil too. Smothered by negativity, it slowly stops beating until it ceases to exist."

"So you're saying you feel like you're trapped in a cage?"

"No." She sighed. "Gregory is trapped in that cage. I have no idea where the cage is or who holds the key to unlock it, but I will find him, and I will fight to the death against any vulture, rat, or coyote who comes between us."

Nathan stood behind Harmony and gripped her shoulder. "Give us a bit more time. Maryah will be able to help you find him. I'm certain of it."

I nodded, even though I wasn't as confident as Nathan. Plus, I was terrified of what we might find if and when I did locate Gregory.

Harmony stood and walked toward the door. "Each day that passes I know I'm one day closer to losing him forever. I can't wait any longer, I have to find him. And when I do, even if he is corrupted, even if he is no longer pure and good, I will love him and bring him back. Because as science has proven, *the heart remembers*." She slid her sunglasses on and smiled at me. "And *you* proved that the soul never forgets."

TAKING BACK FOREVER
Book 2 of The Kindrily Series